# WRAPPED *in* MERCY

*by Sharla Hallett*

*To my husband, Ted. I praise God for His plan
that brought us together. Thank you for being my
cheerleader, my rock, and sometimes the voice
of the Holy Spirit - Go write the book!*

*To my parents, Thank you for always championing
me. I am beyond blessed to have you as parents.*

*To Olivia and Hunter, I am delighted God
picked you out at birth, could see the future,
and selected me to be your mom.*

*To my friends and the people at UHP, thank you
for reading pages, letting me pick your brains,
asking me challenging questions, and helping me
see this story birthed. You are all a blessing!*

*To God, thank you for sharing your heart
with me and trusting me with this story.*

# *Melissa*

Melissa sat upright in bed, trying to regulate her breathing.

Did that really happen, or was it a dream? she asked herself.

She looked over at her sleeping husband as she touched her cheek. She felt fresh tears on her face.

Again, she asked herself, Did that really happen, or was it a dream?

Melissa looked again at her husband to assure herself he was still sleeping. She quietly got out of bed and tiptoed to the bathroom. She always felt the need to be super quiet around Blake when he was asleep, even though she frequently joked that a freight train could go through their room and he would not wake up.

Melissa closed the door soundlessly behind her and flipped on the light. Squinting at herself in the mirror, she did indeed see the evidence of tears on her face. Melissa smiled and pictured the little face she had held moments ago.

The little girl was so beautiful. Her face glowed, and her hair was a lovely dark brown. Her beaming smile was radiant. She and her husband had decided to name her Joy. And even though they had never officially met her, she could now confidently tell her husband they picked a perfect name. Their little girl was, in fact, the picture of Joy.

Once again, Melissa smiled at herself in the mirror and wiped away the last tears. She was still unsure about her experience, but she would think about that later.

Melissa flipped the light off in the bathroom and padded her way back to bed. She slipped under the covers and closed her eyes. She smiled again as she pictured that beautiful face and fell into a deep and peaceful sleep, hoping she might see Joy again.

# *Amy*

Amy looked down at her phone and smiled. She loved it when Melissa posted pictures of her kids on social media. All three were so precious, and each carried a part of Melissa and Blake. Amy moved to Chicago shortly after graduating from college and took a job at a commercial real estate firm. Melissa and her husband had remained in Texas, close to where Melissa and Amy had gone to college. The girls did not get to see each other in person very much anymore, but they still kept in touch via social media, texts, and phone calls.

Amy was happy Melissa seemed to be living the life she had wanted. Still, Amy also enjoyed her own life of making money and being an independent woman in a fun, what she considered, adventuresome city. She liked meeting clients at a bar after work without checking in with someone else. Amy also relished that she did not have to share her apartment with anyone unless she asked them to spend the night. Amy knew Melissa could have made a very successful career woman, but she also knew that was not what Melissa wanted. Amy was proud that they had remained friends even after understanding they wanted vastly different things in life.

Amy thought back to the last time she had seen Melissa. It had been a while, she realized. A pang of guilt hit her. Oh well. Melissa, of all people, should understand the challenges Amy faced with her family and why she had not been back to Texas in quite a while. Amy made a mental note to call Melissa and catch up. She really appreciated how much Melissa had been there for her in college.

Amy heard her phone chime and looked at the screen to see it was her sister. Another pang of guilt hit her. Amy loved her sister, but as long as Annalise lived close to her dad, Amy's visits to her sister and her family would be limited. After she left home, Amy decided she was an adult and no longer had to put up with her dad's antics. He had ruined her childhood, and she honestly had no interest in a relationship with him. Amy was not interested in her dad negatively impacting any more of her life.

Annalise had insisted that their father had changed and constantly sang his praises until Amy begged her to stop.

"Annalise, you just don't understand what it was like. You were too little to have memories of what was actually happening." Amy had replayed the conversation she and her sister had had multiple times. Accustomed to protecting her younger sister, Amy was still uncertain if she should tell Annalise everything that happened. The only person who came close to knowing everything about Amy's crazy childhood was Melissa.

"Amy, I know. You've told me, and I'm so sorry you were put through that. But . . ." Annalise began.

"You should not be the one saying this to me!" Amy had interrupted. "He should be the one apologizing."

"But how can he do that when you won't be in the same

room with him!" Annalise sputtered, clearly frustrated.

Amy knew Annalise's heart was in the right place. She wanted everyone in her family to get along and have lovely holidays together. But Annalise just did not understand what she was asking of Amy.

"Let's drop it," Amy said, defeated.

Amy always ended up frustrated and disappointed that Annalise did not understand where she was coming from. However, in fairness to Annalise, Amy had protected her from the truly scary things that occurred during their childhood.

Amy looked down at the papers on her desk and the laptop before her, breaking the memory and sending it, like clouds, to the back of her mind.

"Okay," Amy said sternly. "This isn't helping." She made a mental note to call Annalise soon and refocused on the work in front of her.

# 3

# Amy - College

Amy sat on the floor of her bathroom, shoulders slumped against the wall, knees drawn up to her chest, and stared at the white stick in front of her. This can't be true. She was not pregnant. Amy was always so careful. She did not want to end up pregnant or diseased. "How did this happen?" she whispered.

A knock at her bathroom door startled her.

"Amy! Amy, are you okay? Do you want me to get you some crackers and ginger ale? I was going to make a run to the store anyway." Melissa's voice came through the door.

Amy knew Melissa was assuming Amy's lengthy stay in the bathroom just meant she was hungover, again. Amy briefly debated whether to let Melissa in on this moment, then decided she would. Melissa was the only person she could trust with this information.

"Come in, Mel," Amy called through the door, not moving from her spot.

Melissa opened the door, saw Amy holding the pregnancy test stick, and joined Amy on the floor.

"Oh no, Amy. Are you sure?" Melissa said quietly. Amy nodded, trying to keep the tears at bay. The shock of her situation was still clinging to her.

"Let me go buy you another test, Amy. Let's be absolutely sure," Melissa said comfortingly.

"There were two pregnancy tests in the box. I'm pretty certain."

"Well, let me go get a different brand. We can make sure."

Amy nodded. "Okay," she said quietly. However, Amy was fairly certain another brand of pregnancy test would say the same thing. But maybe . . . She let the thought trail off.

Melissa breathed a sigh of relief. Amy couldn't tell whether it was because Melissa could leave their apartment for a minute to process what was going on or because Amy was willing to make doubly sure she was indeed pregnant.

"I will not be gone long. I promise." Melissa put her arms around Amy. "We'll figure this out." Quickly, Melissa left to finish her errand.

When Amy heard Melissa shut the door to their apartment, the tears began to fall. What was she going to do? She was not at all ready to be a mom. She had come to college to escape the responsibilities of her childhood. Once Amy had arrived on campus, she had given herself full permission to celebrate her freedom from her dad and his alcoholism. And celebrate, she had.

Amy felt lucky to be assigned such an amazing roommate during her freshman year. She had been nervous about rooming with a stranger. *What type of person would she be?* Also, with everything Amy had been through as a child, she did not find making friends particularly easy. Amy hated discussing her childhood and the impact her mom's death and father's alcoholism had on her. She knew she had difficulty letting people in, but was not interested in changing that right now.

However, there was something different about Mel from the beginning. She was motherly in all the right ways, and Amy had found comfort in their friendship. Melissa had a way about her that made Amy trust her. She and Melissa had bonded and became like sisters. They rushed the same sorority and became inseparable.

The girls agreed to watch each other's backs regarding guys, but Amy rolled through guys like she was on some sort of mission. Melissa focused on one guy at a time, looking for a possible serious relationship, whereas Amy worked hard to let guys know she was just in it for a good time. She had no interest in any sort of relationship. Relationships meant you had to give and take and share life, and Amy wanted no part of that right now. She somehow knew, way back in the back of her mind, that she was numbing the pain of her childhood. But she didn't care. She was having fun.

Or she was having fun, until now. What was she going to do if she was indeed pregnant? She couldn't tie herself down with responsibilities like she had experienced in childhood. She just couldn't. She wasn't ready. And whose baby was this anyway? Momentary shame filled Amy as she realized she wasn't sure who the father might be.

Father. Did providing sperm make you a father? She didn't think so. Amy's father said he loved her and was actually a good father, right up until Amy's mother died. Then, her father ceased being a parent. He would rather spend time with alcohol than with his children. Didn't her dad understand that was the very moment she and Annalise needed him the most? Why had alcohol become more important to him than his own daughters?

Amy shook herself out of thoughts of her dad. In her mind, this well-traveled road was rarely helpful and never solved any problems. Amy refocused her thoughts on the problem at hand: *What would she do if she were pregnant?*

Just then, Amy heard Melissa come back to the apartment. Amy quickly wiped the evidence of tears from her face. She heard Melissa drop her keys and a bag on the kitchen counter, then footsteps as Melissa headed toward the bathroom.

"Hey," said Melissa softly. "I bought you two different brands just in case."

"Thanks," said Amy.

"I'll be right out here when you're done."

"Thanks," she repeated.

Amy stood from her spot on the floor and opened both boxes of tests. She knew this was futile and what the tests would say, but she might as well do it to satisfy her or Melissa's lingering doubts.

Amy once again followed the directions on the box to complete the tests, washed her hands, and set the timers. Then, she opened the bathroom door and found Melissa standing just outside. Melissa's eyes were filled with concern. That is what Amy loved about Melissa. Melissa might not have made all of Amy's wild choices, but she also didn't judge Amy for her choices.

Melissa wrapped Amy in her arms and said, "No matter what those tests say, we'll figure this out. I will help you figure this out."

"Thanks, Mel," Amy managed to say around the lump in her throat. A fresh batch of tears formed behind her eyes, threatening to spill. Amy took a step back, not wanting to cry.

Just then, the timer went off. Amy stepped to the counter, and the tests confirmed what she already knew. Amy was pregnant.

**4**

# Amy - College

Until college, Amy had never taken a stance on abortion either way. She shrugged her shoulders and adopted a live-and-let-live attitude. Amy knew religious people claimed women were killing their babies if they chose to have an abortion. However, other women said they were defending women's rights. They said it was healthcare and a woman's right to choose if they wanted to go through with a pregnancy. In Amy's first year in college, she took a class on women's history, and the professor explained how important a woman's right to choose was. The professor would say no man should have the right to decide what a woman should or should not do with her body. Amy found herself agreeing with the professor. How could anyone else argue that a woman shouldn't have the right to choose? I mean, this is America. People have the right to choose in this country.

Still in the back of her mind, something niggled at her. Do people getting abortions really kill a baby, as religious people claim? Was it a baby already or a fetus? She wasn't sure. And if it were a baby, was it right to choose life or death for that baby? But all of these were hypothetical questions anyway.

Until Amy found herself pregnant.

Amy looked at Melissa, tears streaming down her face. "I can't have this baby, Mel. I will have to give up everything I've worked towards, including my scholarships, and possibly move back in with my dad. I just can not have this baby."

Melissa listened quietly and thoughtfully. She passed Amy the tissue box. Amy took another handful of tissues, mopped her face, and blew her nose.

Amy composed herself a bit more and met Melissa's gaze. "What options do I have?"

Melissa took a deep, steadying breath. "There is always adoption."

Amy looked up at Melissa. "That still means I have to be pregnant and go to school."

"Yes," Melissa acknowledged. "But other than your social life, your life wouldn't really change. You can carry the baby, continue your schooling, and then give the baby up for adoption. I hear plenty of people in this country are waiting to adopt."

Amy chewed on her lip and thought about adoption. Could she carry a baby to full term and then hand it over to strangers? Could she be brave enough to do that? Amy wasn't sure. Did she want to put herself and her body through something like that? She was young and supposed to be carefree. She had cared for her sister and her dad well before that responsibility should have been placed on her. Hadn't she done enough good deeds in her life without adding another one? Besides, isn't that why abortion and abortion clinics existed anyway? It didn't seem right to bring a baby into the world who would never know its biological father and mother. Also, there was no guarantee this baby would have a good life, no matter how carefully she chose the family to place the baby with.

Amy focused on Melissa once again. "I don't know if adoption is the right choice. I mean, even if I get to pick out the family, there is no guarantee this baby wouldn't end up in a bad situation anyway. Maybe the best thing to do is just to end the pregnancy before it gets started."

"Okay," Melissa whispered. "Is there a guy you want to tell about this first?"

"No, I don't think so," said Amy. Even though Melissa was her best friend, Amy didn't want to admit to her that she wasn't entirely sure which guy it was.

"Do you want a few days to think about this, or is your mind made up?" Melissa asked.

"I think . . . I think my mind is made up," Amy admitted, and a fresh batch of tears streamed down her face.

"Okay," Melissa nodded. "Oh, Amy." Melissa moved to hug Amy once again. "It's okay. You are going to be okay," Melissa comforted Amy.

Amy wasn't sure she would be okay, but she had made her decision.

Although Amy felt firm in her choice and the justifications and rationales made sense to her, there still seemed to be something in the back of her mind that said: Don't do it. Don't go through with the abortion. She decided to turn off the voice.

And so, just a few days later, Amy found herself at an abortion clinic. Melissa agreed to go with Amy to the clinic for support and to drive her home. Melissa was just that kind of friend—a real treasure. Amy sat in the clinic waiting room. Even though the clinic should represent freedom of choice, it felt more like desperation. Other women in the waiting room seemed uncertain or weighed down by the decision they were about to make. Melissa sat with Amy, but when the time came, Amy had to venture to the room alone. She tried to push all thoughts from her head and told herself *it would be over soon.* It wasn't that big of a deal. Women did this all the time. This was part of living in progressive America. This was a good decision for her and the baby.

Amy, not big on doctors or medical treatments, tried not to overthink what was happening and focused on other things. Thankfully, the pain medicine they gave her helped her numb out a bit, and she was drowsy in the recovery room. Once the nurses said it was okay for her to leave, Amy found Melissa in the waiting room. Melissa gave Amy a reassuring smile.

"Are you okay?" Melissa asked.

"Yes. I am very glad that is behind me. Let's get out of here," Amy said.

Melissa agreed.

The drive home was quiet, and Amy was glad Melissa didn't insist on talking. Amy leaned against the car seat and focused on the white, puffy clouds drifting by in the brilliant blue sky. Sometimes, Amy would focus on the clouds and wonder about her mom. Was she in heaven, if there was a heaven? If she is, what is she doing? These thoughts comforted her as a kid, but today, they just made her sad. She wasn't sure she would want her mom to know what she just did. Today, she hoped her mom was not looking down on her, watching from heaven.

Amy didn't want to talk about the abortion after that. She had decided, and there was no going back, so why discuss it? Melissa respected her space and did not try to bring it up. Amy put the abortion out of her mind, determined to live her life the way she wanted. The crazy part was that there were times when thoughts of her baby came unbidden. Amy thought about when it would have been born. Sometimes, she would catch herself adding up how old the baby might be. She would wonder if it would have been a boy or a girl. She never discussed these thoughts with anyone, including Melissa. She didn't want any-one else to know she thought about these things. Amy truly believed women had a right to choose what was best for them. And sometimes, the best choice was not the easy choice. But Amy firmly believed she had done the right thing for everyone involved.

# 5

# *Melissa - College*

"Hey!" shouted Melissa to be heard above the pulsating music.

"What?" Amy shouted back, momentarily pausing the conversation with a random guy from the fraternity her sorority had invited to this party. The guy was mildly amusing but handsome, and Melissa could tell Amy wasn't drunk enough yet to decide if she would sleep with him.

"Who's that?" Melissa nodded towards a guy, slowly making his way across the room, stopping to talk with people as he went.

"I don't know," Amy yelled back. "You should go talk to him." Amy nudged Melissa for emphasis.

"Maybe." Melissa was noncommittal as she took a sip of her beer.

For Melissa, these college parties were old. Like Amy, she had a blast when the girls first landed on campus. Both girls had gone potluck in the roommate draw and ended up paired together. They instantly bonded over feeling like a fish out of water and decided they wanted to be roommates after their freshman year.

The parties were fun at first. Melissa had never been much of a rebel in high school, so she relished that there wasn't anyone to answer to. She could stay out as late as she wanted, she could drink as much as she wanted, and she could talk to as many guys as she wanted. Melissa guessed she had too great a time at the beginning of her college career as her parents sat her down and told her they would no longer pay for college if she did not take her studies seriously. So, she tried to go to fewer parties and study more. She majored in marketing because why not? Melissa thought she would be very hirable with a marketing degree. However, Melissa didn't want to admit she wasn't very passionate about her degree. What she wanted was a husband and a family. She deeply longed to be a wife and mother, caring for her family. Those desires weren't very progressive of her, so she kept them to herself.

The girls were almost at the close of senior year. Whatever path they choose after college, Melissa was pretty sure their carefree partying days were ending. Amy was actively looking for jobs as far away from Texas and her family as possible. Amy would tell Melissa it was because she wanted to explore while still young. But Melissa wasn't fooled. She knew Amy was running.

Melissa trained her eyes on the guy who snagged her attention as he walked across the room. She caught him looking at her a few times with curiosity, but Melissa was unconvinced he would talk to her. She was trying to decide whether, if he wouldn't come to speak to her, she would be willing to make the first move. He was cute but not the most handsome man she had run across or slept with, for that matter. However, something about him was different. Maybe it was the way he carried himself with confidence, but not arrogance. Melissa wasn't sure what it was about him, but she was interested in having a conversation with him.

Melissa looked at Amy, who was still talking with the random guy. Jake, Melissa thought his name was. Jake had a reputation as a player, but that wouldn't deter Amy. Amy always joked that guys couldn't play a player. She had no interest in getting to know these guys, but she had fun with them—or so she said.

Melissa watched with mild amusement as this guy reacted to Amy's charm.

"Oh my God. You did NOT!" Amy giggled at whatever story Jake had chosen to share with her and leaned over, purposely touching his arm. She doubted Amy could repeat the details of the story he told her if her life depended on it. "Ohhh . . ." Amy cooed, stroking his arm. "I love a guy who hits the gym. Funny and strong. Nice!" Her hand worked its way up to his bicep and squeezed.

Jake smiled, clearly pleased that he was impressing Amy even in his increasingly drunken state. "Maybe we could go to the gym sometime. It would be fun to work out together."

"That would be SO fun! Yes, we should definitely do that," Amy said, nodding her head, her hair bouncing around her shoulders.

Melissa rolled her eyes and chuckled to herself. She knew there was no way Amy would ever step foot into a gym with this guy. Why were some of these guys such easy targets? Really? Giggle at a few of their "jokes" and then comment on their physique, and they are hooked. So predictable.

At first, Melissa admired Amy's inhibitions, but she later

realized that most of Amy's actions were meant to cover up the childhood pain she had experienced. Melissa was no expert, but she had taken a psychology class. Melissa could see that Amy was trying to find the love she felt she didn't get from her father, and to be in control of the relationship.

Melissa knew some of what Amy was trying to forget. When Amy got drunk, she became honest about her life, her past, and her dad. But Melissa remained increasingly worried about Amy's destructive behavior. She knew they were doing nothing to fix her grief with her mom and her disappointment and anger towards her dad. In fact, she got the distinct feeling that the more Amy slept with these guys, the less it was helping fill that hole.

For the most part, Melissa kept her opinions to herself. She knew Amy didn't want to hear it right now, and Melissa didn't know what to tell her to do differently. She didn't have answers for Amy. So, she would listen when Amy opened up and try to comfort her as best she could. Melissa only spoke up when she felt Amy wasn't safe. She would make Amy promise to call her if things went sideways with a guy, and Melissa would come pick her up.

Melissa once again glanced at Jake. He seemed harmless enough, but he was getting drunk faster than Amy. He could pass out before he and Amy could even accomplish anything other than talking.

Melissa turned to search for the cute stranger once again and was surprised to see him suddenly beside her. "Hi!" He grinned at her, revealing straight teeth and a dimple set prominently in just one cheek. His cuteness factor went up a bit.

"Hi!" She echoed with a smile that was her most charming.

Suddenly, an entire colony of butterflies took up residence in Melissa's stomach. *Well, that is new,* she thought to herself.

"I'm Blake." His smile was electric, but his eyes were what caught Melissa's attention. They were a beautiful shade of green, but the genuinely unusual part was the peace and kindness Melissa saw reflected there.

Most guys she met in college had eyes full of arrogance or lust. At first, it was flattering, but it grew tiresome. Melissa quickly learned the hard way that most guys had wanted THAT right off the bat. She could tell. The more gentlemanly guys would pretend they didn't want sex so soon. They would say seemingly romantic things like, "I want you to feel safe with me," or "I want the time we both decide to do it to be special," and other forms of nonsense. The problem was that after Melissa had been duped into believing it a couple of times, she realized they were only after one thing. Once they got that thing, they were often gone. Sometimes, they were gone the next day, and sometimes, they were gone in a few months. They all seemed to have the same attitude: girls were for conquering, and once the conquering was done, they were ready to move on. Were these the sort of men who cheated on their wives once they were married? After a few of these guys, Melissa began to feel ashamed and cheap.

However, Blake, this cute boy standing before her, already seemed different.

"Melissa." Melissa smiled and asked, "So, out of all the ragers this evening, what brought you to our humble sorority party?" Genuinely curious, she leaned closer to be heard above the music and noted that he smelled of sandalwood. She narrowly avoided sniffing him again before she caught herself.

"My sister."

"Honestly?" Melissa chuckled in surprise.

"Yes." Blake returned her smile and leaned closer to her to be heard. "This really isn't my scene, but I just returned from India, and she begged me to meet some of her friends."

"You just got back from India?" Melissa echoed.

Blake nodded.

"Why?"

"I lived there for a year," said Blake.

Melissa hadn't traveled much and couldn't imagine someone living in a foreign country like India without a real purpose. "What for?" Melissa asked with intrigue.

"I was there as part of a mission organization. We were there to build churches and stuff like that."

"For real?" Melissa didn't know what to do with this information.

Blake chuckled and nodded. "For real."

"Wow!" Melissa said. "Are you like a Mother Theresa type?"

"Well, I don't look great in a habit, so probably not," Blake answered good-naturedly.

Melissa chuckled. "Duly noted."

"I bet that was an adventure." Melissa was impressed. Was this guy the real deal, or would she later find out he was like the rest?

"Yeah, it was. In a lot of different ways." Blake continued, "I'm glad I went, but I'm also happy to be home. It was an eye-opening experience for sure."

"So, which one is your sister?" Melissa asked, eyeing the group of freshman and sophomore girls congregating near the house's entrance.

Blake pointed out a petite girl with long blonde hair, chatting with a few other sorority sisters off to the side. Melissa could see the family resemblance. They both had a smile that drew you to them.

"Oh yeah," said Melissa. "Alex, right?" Blake nodded in affirmation. "Oh, I know her." Melissa continued, "We've had a couple of classes together. She's sweet." Alex was not the partier she and Amy were known to be. Melissa found Alex to be genuinely friendly to the people around her. In a sorority that attracted its fair share of fake girls, Melissa liked that about her.

"Yes, she is," Blake agreed with evident pride for his sister. "Until she steals your clothes and claims them as her own."

Melissa chuckled. "Isn't that the job of siblings? To annoy us and keep us humble?"

Blake grinned and rolled his eyes, "I guess. I mean, no one told me when she was born that I would spend my life guarding my belongings, and all she would have to do is grin her mischievous grin, and my mom and dad would think she hung the moon."

"Clearly, we have some unresolved childhood trauma," Melissa said with a wink. "Do you need some professional help to work through this?"

"Nah, I'll be alright." Blake grinned in his sister's direction and then glanced back at Melissa. Melissa liked that he was proud of his sister.

Usually a fairly good conversationalist, Melissa searched her mind for something else to discuss with Blake. She liked this guy and didn't want him to lose interest and wander off.

She found herself uncharacteristically nervous around him. It suddenly mattered what he thought about her.

As if Blake could read her thoughts, he turned to her and said, "Hey! Would you consider going to lunch with me sometime?"

Melissa was taken aback that he had asked her out so quickly. Most of the guys she'd met poured on the charm and then left you guessing at their intentions. She kind of liked that Blake was being direct. "Sure," she said, hoping for nonchalance instead of the eagerness she felt.

*Play it cool, Melissa*, she inwardly chided herself.

"How about tomorrow?" Blake asked.

Melissa chuckled. "Sure," she said again.

"Well, we can meet after I get out of church. Or," he paused for effect, "you could go with me to church, and then we could go to lunch."

Melissa was uncertain of this invitation. Lunch, she was ready for, but church? Melissa went to church as a child, but as she grew older, she lost interest in church, God, and everything that came with them. The church did not seem relatable to her life. It was okay if others wanted to go and experience religion. Melissa's motto was to each their own. It gave people some sort of comfort, and who was she to stand in the way of that? But Melissa wasn't sure church was for her.

However, a guy who was different from the other guys she had met stood in front of her. She wasn't really interested in church, but if going with him would score her some points, maybe it was worth her time. She could just say "yes" to lunch and not church, but something about him made Melissa not want to disappoint him. Melissa turned to Blake and, before she could change her mind, said, "Sure. I would love to."

"Great," Blake said again. "Give me your number, and I'll text you."

They quickly exchanged information and agreed on when Blake could pick Melissa up. Blake flashed his fantastic smile, clearly pleased with himself that Melissa had accepted his invitation to church.

Melissa hoped she was not some missionary project, but quickly shoved that thought aside. So, what if she were? He seemed worth getting to know better, and she would get lunch out of it. A girl needed to eat, right?

Blake voiced his goodbye, saying he needed to find his sister.

Melissa couldn't help smiling, more excited than she thought she would be. She took a sip of her beer. It was warm now, and she had lost interest in finishing it. She should find Amy and see if she could convince her to go home. Melissa had to decide what to wear. What was appropriate for church but would get her noticed? She inwardly squealed with anticipation as she set out to find Amy, trying not to analyze why an invitation to church was more exciting to her than most of the dates she had been on recently.

# 6

# *Melissa - College*

Melissa inspected herself in the mirror. She woke up early this morning, showered, carefully applied her makeup, and styled her long, dark hair with her blow dryer and flat iron. She had changed her outfit four times. What did people wear to church these days? She had heard of more contemporary churches where the dress code was pretty relaxed and more traditional churches where people still dressed up on Sundays. The problem was that Melissa had no idea which type of church she was about to enter. She decided to wear a dress and hoped to fit in with whatever this church might be.

Melissa didn't care about impressing the people at church. However, she wanted to impress Blake. She was excited about this date—surprisingly so. Could she call it a date? Melissa wasn't sure, but she thought she could. Some guys invited her to the movies. This guy just happened to ask her to lunch with a church appetizer.

Melissa applied her subtle lipstick and gave herself one last critical look in the mirror. Satisfied with what she saw, she found her purse and phone. She looked at the screen and realized Blake had texted her a few minutes ago, letting her know he was on his way. She tried to tamp down her nervousness and smoothed her dress.

"Hey!" Amy said, entering the kitchen.

"Hi!" Melissa said. "I was just leaving you a note. I didn't think you would be up this early."

"Wedding or funeral?" Amy asked, still half asleep.

Melissa chuckled. "What?"

"Well, with how you are dressed, it has to be one or the other," Amy said as she poured some coffee, dumped sugar, and a ton of flavored cream into her cup. Melissa frequently gave Amy a hard time, telling her she could just drink the sugar and cream and leave out the coffee.

"I am going to church," Melissa said.

"So a funeral, then," Amy deadpanned.

Melissa ignored her. "Do you remember the guy I was talking to last night?"

"Mel, I barely remember the guy I was talking to last night," Amy said flatly.

Melissa smiled. Amy meant that to be funny, and at one time, it was, but Melissa did worry about Amy at times.

"I was talking with Blake, Alex's sister."

"That's right," Amy said, remembering. "How is the old-goody-two-shoes brother doing? Hey!" Amy added, suddenly remembering. "He is actually kind of cute! Are you going to church with him?"

"Yes!" Melissa said. "He invited me to his church."

"Wow!" Amy said. "When you said you were tired of the party scene, you meant it. Well, I hope he's worth it. At least he's nice to look at."

"Yeah," Melissa said dreamily. "He is."

"Oh, does someone already have a crush? Well, at least make him take you to lunch," Amy said good-naturedly. "If you have to sit through church, you should get something out of it, too."

Just then, there was a knock at the door. Melissa's eyes widened. "That's probably him," Melissa whispered.

"Then you should probably open the door," Amy whispered back. "And make him pay for lunch!"

Melissa chuckled. "You got it."

Amy disappeared into her room, and Melissa went to open the door. Blake stood in front of her, looking more handsome than yesterday. He wore jeans and a casual polo shirt that brought out his beautiful green eyes. His smile made her heart flutter. *Was Amy right? Was she already crushing?*

"Hi," said Melissa with what she hoped was her most charming smile.

"Hi," said Blake. "I hope you don't mind me saying this, but you look beautiful."

"Thank you," Melissa said, blushing. "Honestly, it has been a while since I attended church. Am I dressed appropriately?"

"Yes!" Blake said, putting her at ease. "There are people who dress up, and there are people who go pretty casual. What you have on is perfect."

Melissa blushed again. "Thank you."

Melissa and Blake made their way to his car and climbed in. Blake was a gentleman and opened her car door for her. Melissa tried to hide how much the simple gesture impressed her. For the first time in a long time, she felt like a treasured lady.

The conversation on the way to church was easy. Melissa noticed Blake spoke about God as if He were a person or a friend. Melissa had never heard anyone talk about God like that. The impression Melissa felt from others who described God was that he was an old, often angry man who hung out in the sky and judged the people below. Don't get too far out of line; He would zap you back into place. Clearly, Blake knew a different God than her other friends. The God he spoke of was kind, forgiving, slow to anger, and wanted a relationship with all the people on Earth. This glimpse into Blake's relationship with God fascinated Melissa.

Blake's church was unlike any Melissa had ever attended. The people didn't seem stuffy or uptight, fulfilling a sort of religious duty by coming to church. They seemed genuinely happy to spend their Sunday morning together and at church.

The service began with upbeat music, and a full band was on stage. The people sang songs to God as if they loved Him and wanted more of Him. They sang to Him as if He were in the room, not far away. It also struck her that they sang praise to Him rather than about Him. Some people raised their hands to heaven; some knelt in their seats. She even noticed some people wiping tears from their eyes.

Melissa began to wonder what it would feel like to be so connected to God that she would experience the kind of emotion she saw in the people around her. He had to be a more approachable God than she thought if people had these reactions. Just as Melissa began to relax and feel comfortable, the music was over, and everyone took their seats. Melissa was a little disappointed that part of the service was over.

The pastor took his place behind the pulpit and began to speak. He shared about God's loving kindness and the power of the cross to free people from sin. Melissa was captivated.

The other people in the room, including Blake, began to fade into the background, and she leaned forward in her chair, not wanting to miss a word the pastor said. She had never experienced a God like the one Blake—and now this pastor—spoke of. Was this the real God and not the version she had come to believe?

At the end of the sermon, the pastor asked if anyone wanted to receive Jesus as their personal savior. Melissa had a weird feeling in the pit of her stomach and knew she did, in fact, want Jesus as her personal savior, even if she wasn't entirely sure what that meant. She just knew she wanted Jesus in her life. Melissa had been looking for more. She wasn't just tired of the party scene; she knew it was no longer fulfilling. She felt this was maybe the missing piece she had been searching for in her life.

The minister asked everyone to bow their heads and close their eyes. He instructed anyone who wanted to ask Jesus into their hearts to lift their hands so only he could see them. Melissa raised her hand, a little self-conscious but hoping Blake's eyes were closed as the minister had asked them to be. The minister instructed everyone to repeat a prayer after him. He called it the sinner's prayer. Melissa wasn't entirely sure what a sinner was, but she knew she had made mistakes in her life. Appealing to a higher power for forgiveness seemed like a logical first step. The minister then prayed over the ones who had raised their hands, and Melissa felt a peace flow through her that she had never experienced before. It was truly amazing. The pastor then said if you committed your life to the Lord today, please tell someone before you leave, and let's talk about baptizing you as soon as possible.

Melissa wasn't sure she was brave enough for all that. She had taken a crucial step today, and she could feel it. However, she had been baptized as a baby. She had the pictures to prove it. Did she need to be baptized again? Also, all these people were strangers to her. Why did she need to tell a stranger she had just prayed a prayer? She placed it in the back of her mind and refocused on Blake.

Once the minister dismissed the congregation, Blake turned to Melissa with a bright smile and asked, "How about lunch?"

Melissa smiled, with what she hoped was not a too-eager smile, and said, "Sure! I am hungry."

As if on cue, Melissa's stomach growled loudly. Melissa felt a deep blush creep up her neck and onto her face. Blake laughed. "Well, it sounds like we need to get you to lunch ASAP!"

Blake turned to make his way toward the exit. He must attend this church often because many people stopped him to say hello. Blake was friendly and personable, introducing her to many people who stopped him. She felt hopeless trying to remember any of their names.

After a quick discussion about where to eat, they settled on Mexican food. Once the waitress brought them their drinks and took their order, Melissa turned to Blake.

"Soooo, tell me how you ended up in India for a year?"

Blake smiled and took a deep breath. Melissa did not feel it was too personal a question, but Blake seemed to be weighing his words.

"Well, it's kind of a long story. Are you up for it?"

"Absolutely." Melissa wanted to seem neutral, but her curiosity was rising by the minute.

Blake took another deep breath. "Well, I graduated from college and was applying for jobs. A few companies were interested in interviewing me. I was dating someone pretty seriously then, and I felt my future was set. I would marry her, get a high-paying job, and live the American dream. You know, nice house, nice car, 2.5 kids, and a dog. Then, my girlfriend showed up at my house and told me she no longer loved me. In fact, she wasn't sure she had ever loved me, and even worse, she and my best friend had begun seeing each other behind my back."

Melissa's heart melted. "I am so sorry," she whispered.

Blake smiled at her and continued. "Honestly, it rocked my world. Everything I was working toward seemed to vanish into thin air. The girl I thought I loved and would spend the rest of my life with and my best friend, who I considered a brother, betrayed me, and I was devastated. I lost my way for a bit. I was angry at God for doing this to me. I felt I'd committed my life to Him, and here I was, crushed. I began to go to a lot more parties and tried to find solace in the party life and drinking. However, I felt emptier and emptier. It was definitely a low point."

Melissa could relate to that part. She nodded and hoped he would continue.

"The former best friend and the ex-girlfriend decided to get married. I was very bitter. I'm sure my parents, out of concern for me, brought up this opportunity to go to India. They have missionary friends there, and they're always looking for people to come and help them. I agreed to go. Looking back, I'm surprised I agreed. But I think the appeal was that I could get far away from my pain."

Blake chuckled ruefully, "However, instead of escaping my pain, I took it with me. I arrived in India very bitter towards God, which made me very unpleasant to be around. The man who ran the missionary organization, Bob, became like a second father to me. He was very patient and showed me that, although I was wronged, every story always has two sides. He forced me to look at my relationship with my girlfriend and see where I had been in the wrong. It was a painful but freeing experience. Learning to walk in forgiveness is difficult, but it will free you."

"Also, you can't leave India without realizing that if your only goal is to live the American dream, you are living far below what God wants for you. There is so much more to this life than accumulating earthly wealth. The real wealth is what we receive in heaven."

Melissa appreciated his story and heart, but was having trouble fully grasping what he meant. So much of this was new to her. She had never been around people who spoke of God like this. This was more than religion to Blake. She could tell.

Blake must have sensed he had shared enough and changed the subject.

"So, what did you think about church today?"

She blurted out before she could stop herself, "I prayed the prayer at the end. Do I really have to get baptized now?"

Blake laughed but was pleased with her admission. "No, you don't have to. But do you know what baptism is or why it is important?"

Melissa slowly shook her head. "No, but I do know I was baptized as a baby. How is that different?"

Blake smiled at her, not at all put off by her questions. "The main difference is that when you were baptized as a baby, your parents made that decision for you. Now, you get to make the choice. Do you want to leave your old life behind and become a brand new creation in Christ? Are you ready for that? If you are, baptism is a way to publicly make that statement. Even Jesus was baptized."

"He was?" Melissa asked.

"Uh-huh." Blake continued as he popped a chip with salsa in his mouth. He chewed and swallowed his chip and said, "John the Baptist, Jesus' cousin, baptized Jesus before Jesus officially began His ministry on Earth."

"Oh," Melissa said thoughtfully. She wasn't sure about all Blake was saying. When she went to Sunday school as a small child, she learned about Noah and the Ark, Jonah and the whale, and Joseph and his mean brothers. But her knowledge of the Bible kind of stopped there. She didn't remember the last time she had opened a Bible. She knew she owned one but wasn't sure where it was. Melissa thought for a few more minutes, then said, before she lost her courage. "I didn't know all that about Jesus. I guess if Jesus was baptized, I should be too?"

Blake nodded approvingly. "That's great! Let me know when you think you're ready, and I can help you schedule it."

Melissa nodded. She felt she should do this sooner rather than later, or she might talk herself out of it.

Melissa continued to go to church with Blake. She was always amazed at how peaceful she felt after leaving the services. She bought a new Bible and began reading. Blake recommended that she start in the New Testament. There were still parts she found difficult to understand, but there were also stories of healing that made Melissa cry. When she got to the part about Jesus's crucifixion, she wept. She thanked God for sending Jesus to die for her sins.

She was sure this was the missing piece she had been searching for in her life. She was eager to learn all she could. She also knew Amy was disappointed that Melissa didn't want to go to parties with her anymore.

"Are you sure this isn't some kind of cult you have gotten mixed up in?" Amy would ask her. "Why do you suddenly feel the need to abstain from everything?"

"Well, no snakes have been released during services or any suspicious-looking Kool-Aid, so I think I'm okay." Melissa would try to deal with Amy with humor. She wanted to share with Amy what she was finding in church and God, but Melissa quickly learned Amy was also mad at God for her childhood. Amy was not a person with whom she could share this experience. She hoped this would not divide them. She wanted to maintain her relationship with Amy.

When she talked with Blake about Amy, he encouraged her to be patient.

"The fact is, you are the one who chose to change. She is going to need a minute to adapt to the new Melissa. Pray for her, Melissa. Don't give up on her."

Melissa knew Blake was right. It wasn't fair to expect Amy to support all her decisions, especially the ones she didn't understand. Melissa did her best to maintain the relationship with Amy without compromising her new convictions. Melissa also tried to balance her time between Blake and Amy. She didn't want to lose her relationship with Amy.

A few weeks later, Blake mentioned that there was a particular Sunday for baptisms. "The pastor will meet with you as a class and explain the significance of what you are about to do. I can help you get signed up if you feel you are ready."

Melissa decided it was time. She found herself excited about her upcoming baptism. She still wasn't entirely sure why she needed to be baptized. She couldn't explain it, but knew she needed to do it. Melissa did admit, if only to herself, that she was a little nervous. She was anxious about being in front of so many people. Blake assured her they were only there to support her. They would celebrate with her.

Melissa decided to tell her parents about her scheduled baptism at the last minute. They were supportive, but Melissa could tell they didn't completely understand why she wanted to do this. Melissa did feel her parents thought this might be a positive step for her.

Two days shy of her 22nd birthday, Melissa was baptized. When Melissa came up out of the water, she could feel a difference. Melissa stood in the water with her head bowed, watching drops from her dark hair drip back into the water as the pastor who baptized her prayed over her. She smiled to herself. She felt hopeless in describing this experience to anyone. She just knew everything had changed.

# 7

# Melissa - College

Melissa sat on the couch with her journal and Bible on one side and a textbook on the other. Amy appeared in the room, her perfume announcing her presence. Melissa looked up at her with a smile. "You look nice."

Amy ignored the compliment. "Are you sure you don't want to go? Ya know, this is at the epic frat house where we always have so much fun?"

Melissa braced herself for the conversation she and Amy had been having on repeat since her baptism. She knew Amy did not understand her changes, and Melissa wanted to be sensitive to that. However, she wished Amy could be a little more supportive.

Amy liked Blake and seemed happy that he and Melissa were dating, but her chief complaint was that she had lost her wingwoman and partner in crime. Melissa wished Amy would cut her some slack.

Melissa smiled patiently at Amy. "Not tonight. Blake's coming over in a bit, and we're going to watch a movie."

Amy sighed, clearly trying to keep her annoyance at bay. "You know, you only get the college experience once. After this, it's all responsibilities and bills to pay. I think you are wasting precious time you won't get back."

"Okay, I will make you a deal. I know there is another fun party next weekend. I promise to be there, and I will stick to you like glue and annoy the heck out of you. You will get so much wing-woman time you'll regret asking."

Amy nodded. "Deal."

Melissa was relieved that Amy was satisfied. "So, you got an eye on a certain prize tonight, or are you gonna wing it?"

"Wellllll, there is this one guy. He's pretty cute, but he's a sophomore." Amy wrinkled her nose. "If he can hold a conversation, there might be a possibility with him."

Melissa inwardly groaned. She knew none of these guy-conquering missions Amy seemed to be on were helping her in any way. It made her sad how willingly Amy was giving herself to these guys. Melissa knew Amy did it because she felt in control of the relationship, but she knew better. There were consequences to handing yourself out so freely to guys. Amy was more valuable than that. Melissa just wished Amy could see it.

Not wanting to sound preachy or judgmental, Melissa chose to keep quiet for now and do what Blake constantly encouraged her to do: pray for Amy.

"Well, as always, if you need me, call me. I can still be your wing-woman from afar."

"You got it. And I am holding you to next weekend." With that, Amy breezed through the door, leaving Melissa in her wake.

Melissa chuckled and opened her Bible. She had finished studying for the night and wanted to catch up on her reading for a women's Bible study she had joined at church. She had a little time before Blake was supposed to be here. Blake was the person she most wanted to spend time with these days. She was trying not to be one of those girls who went all in in a relationship and dumped all of her other friends. But it was hard. They were getting close, and Melissa grew increasingly drawn to him.

Blake was different from most of the other guys she had dated. He wanted to spend time with her. He had kissed her, but didn't want things to go any further. At first, Melissa didn't know what to think of Blake's actions. In her experience, how could she tell if a guy was romantically interested if he didn't want to do more than hand-holding and kissing? It took Melissa a bit to realize how backward she had been thinking.

Melissa guessed Amy was probably a little frustrated because Melissa was making new friends at church as well. For the first time, these were not friends with whom Amy interacted, like in their sorority. Melissa knew Amy probably felt a little sidelined. She was trying her best not to make Amy feel that way, but she also wanted to explore these new friendships with the women at church.

When Melissa joined a women's Bible Study at church, she met women who were very earnest in their faith. They spoke about Jesus the same way Blake did. These women spoke of God as if He were God *and* a friend. Melissa was fascinated. One of the women in the group took some time to get to know Melissa. Her name was Megan, and she was a young mom of three. Megan invited Melissa to lunch at her house. Melissa accepted.

Melissa allowed her mind to drift to her lunch with Megan. Megan was organized and kept a spotless house, but her home was more functional than fancy.

Megan had caught Melissa looking at her patched couch. "Yes, we need a new one, but it is currently low on the priority list. My husband and I think it is important for me to stay home with the kids. That means no extras for now."

Megan said this with a warm smile, but Melissa, embarrassed she had been caught, tried to cover. "Oh, I think it is charming!" Melissa gushed.

Megan laughed and said, "Charming . . . that's a nice way of putting it. You know, I was very much like you at one time."

Melissa tilted her head and said, "What do you mean?"

"I had my pick of guys, was in a fun sorority in college, and had my whole future ahead of me. But I was miserable. I met Jesus, and then my husband and my life turned around, including what I thought was important. Before being a stay-at-home mom, I made good money at a well-known advertising firm. But when I had kids, my priorities changed." Megan shrugged. "I guess I began to realize that things like new couches were not nearly as important as well-cared-for children."

Melissa found herself curious. "What do you mean you were miserable?" she asked.

"I mean, although I was doing everything the culture told me would fulfill me, I felt empty. With every new guy I slept with, I felt emptier. I contemplated suicide before a friend took me to church. I will never forget the church service when I literally felt God stand beside me. With tears streaming down my face, I walked to the front and asked Jesus to come into my heart. I am not saying my life is perfect, but it is much more fulfilling with God."

Megan was right, Melissa thought. *She was me!* Unexpected tears began to spill down Melissa's cheeks, surprising herself and Megan. Megan pressed a tissue into Melissa's hand and started apologizing. "Ohhh . . . I didn't mean to upset you, Melissa," Megan said sympathetically.

Once Melissa had somewhat of control over herself, she asked Megan, "How did you deal with the shame? How do I get rid of the shame I have from giving myself to so many guys?"

"Oh, girl! The second you asked Jesus to come into your heart, He took that shame from you. If you are still experiencing it, you've taken it back from Him." Megan paused and let her words sink in with Melissa for a minute.

"Can I pray with you?" Megan asked quietly. Melissa nodded.

Megan began, "Lord, we come to you right now and thank you for Melissa. We thank you for your faithfulness in bringing Melissa back to you. We also thank you for dying on the cross and taking all our sins and shame from us. So, we come to you now and ask for a divine exchange." Megan instructed Melissa to hold out her hands. Melissa obeyed. "Now, picture all the shame in your hand. Now, picture Jesus taking the shame; in its place, He is giving you forgiveness, peace, hope, and joy. You never have to experience any shame again. God has taken complete care of it. If you feel it coming back, remember it's not yours and think about what God gave you in exchange."

Melissa already felt ten times lighter. No one had ever prayed for her like that. "Thank you, Megan."

"Of course. Anytime," Megan said with a comforting smile. "God will always take what you are not intended to carry, if you let Him."

Melissa smiled. "I feel a ton lighter."

"Now," Megan said, shifting the mood and the conversation. "Can we talk about Blake?"

Melissa responded with a wide smile.

"Ohhhhhh," Megan exclaimed. "This is more serious than I thought!"

Melissa giggled. "He's so different from the other guys. He is kind and sensitive and wants to make sure that I'm okay."

Megan nodded. "That is because Jesus is first in His life, and you want a guy like that! So, you see a future with him?"

Melissa nodded slowly. "I do. I think he does, too, but I am just trying to be patient and enjoy the process."

Megan smiled, "Smart!"

Just then, Megan heard one of the babies crying. Melissa stayed much of the afternoon and enjoyed cuddling and playing with Megan's three children. They were precious, but Melissa could see motherhood as a full-time job. Megan must be exhausted by the end of the day.

Melissa's mom was also a stay-at-home mom. Growing up, Melissa did not fully appreciate her mom being home when she got home from school. Many of her friends had both parents at work when they arrived home from school. There were times growing up when Melissa envied her friends. What would it be like to get home from school and get to do whatever you wanted until your parents came home from work? However, reflecting on her childhood, Melissa realized how blessed she was to have a mom home ready to give her a snack, talk about her day, and help her with homework.

Melissa refocused on the Bible in her lap, returning to the present and realizing her mind had wandered. She checked her watch. She still had a little time to figure out how to focus. She finally gave up and shut her Bible. *I will catch up in the morning,* she told herself. She just couldn't seem to settle her mind at the moment.

She was almost done with her senior year of college, and graduation was approaching quickly. While some of her friends were excited about finally leaving school and beginning their lives, Melissa felt she was at a precipice. For the first time, the next steps of her life were not planned. She had decisions to make, and she had to begin making them.

Where would she live? What city did she want to live in? Where should she apply for jobs?

These are all things she did not think about when she entered college. It all seemed overwhelming. And did Blake fit into her future? Was Blake thinking about any of this at all? She had already sent out some resumes for jobs that fit her marketing degree, but none of the positions she had applied for seemed to fit with what she wanted. Of course, Melissa admitted to herself that she was not entirely sure what she wanted.

A knock at the door startled Melissa out of her thoughts. She stacked her books on the coffee table before her and went to get the door. After looking through the peephole, she opened the door to Blake.

"Hi! We didn't decide on food tonight, so I thought I would bring food from our favorite Italian place."

"My hero," Melissa jokingly swooned.

Blake put the food on the table and turned to Melissa. "I asked for extra garlic knots as well. Does that earn me more hero points?"

"Always." Melissa knew she had a silly grin on her face,

and she felt more butterflies in her stomach. There hadn't been another guy who had made Melissa feel this way. *Is this what love felt like?*

Before she could follow that thought trail, Blake began unpacking the food, and Melissa went to grab plates and forks. As she laid the table for them, she could feel Blake watching her.

"What?" she said with a giggle.

"Do you know how beautiful you are?" Blake leaned in and kissed Melissa until her toes curled, and they both needed air.

Blake set Melissa a little away from him. "Okay, no more of that for now."

Melissa giggled again. She was still getting used to dating a guy who wanted boundaries, but she felt treasured every time he put the brakes on. Melissa finished getting napkins and drinks for them and joined Blake at the table.

Blake said a quick prayer, and they each opened their side salads. Melissa reached for a warm, gooey garlic knot and tore it in half. She handed one of the halves to Blake. He chuckled at her.

"What?" Melissa said.

"I love how you eat this bread one half at a time."

With a playful smile teasing her lips, Melissa said, "You caught on to my trick, did ya?"

Blake smiled his broad smile. Melissa liked it so much; that smile made anyone who came into contact with Blake feel important. "Yes," he said. "As long as you eat halves, you don't have to feel guilty about how many halves you've eaten."

Melissa giggled, pleased he had noticed things about her.

Blake continued, "That is one of the many things I love about you."

Melissa froze and slowly met Blake's eyes. He was still smiling. Either he didn't realize what he had just said, or he said it intentionally. Melissa just didn't quite know which at the moment. In the next sentence, Blake cleared it up.

"Melissa, I am totally, one hundred percent, head over heels in love with you." Melissa gulped, trying not to choke on the tiny bits of bread still in her mouth. He continued. "If I had already spoken with your father, I would ask you to marry me. But I'm old-fashioned and will not officially do that until I meet him and ask him."

Melissa took a drink of water and swallowed hard. She finally opened her mouth to speak, hoping her silence was not too long. Her cheeks burned with both happiness and embarrassment. Melissa finally met Blake's eyes and blurted, "Blake, I love you too! But why would you ever want to marry me?"

Blake chuckled again and said, "Why would you say that?"

Melissa knew her insecurities were getting the best of her, but she also knew she needed to get this out. Melissa sighed and dove in. "My life was a mess before I met you. I partied. I did not go to church. I was with other guys."

Blake looked at Melissa with more kindness than Melissa had ever experienced. "Melissa, sweetheart, I know all this. You have been honest about your past, and I appreciate that, but why would that disqualify you from a future with me? That was your past. I have a past, too. We all have a past. Mine may not look like yours, but there were times I struggled with my relationship with God. There were times I wanted to walk away from Him completely."

Melissa remembered what he told her about his time leading up to and in India. She nodded slowly. Blake continued,

"I want to be your future with God in our story. I feel like He brought us together. I'm just hoping you want that as well."

Melissa didn't know what to say. She had disqualified herself all this time, but God had not. Apparently, Blake had not disqualified her either. She briefly wondered what else she was disqualifying herself from. If she believed Jesus had died for all her sins, why was it so hard for her to realize God had good things for her?

Blake continued, "Look, Melissa. I may not have done some of the things you have done, but I am not perfect either. As I see it, if we love God and pursue Him, He will give us the grace we need to make a life with each other."

Melissa smiled at Blake. "I do want a future with you. I want it very much. I would love to build a life with you. I love you so much, Blake."

Blake reached for Melissa's hand. When Melissa met Blake's gaze again, tears were in his eyes. Blake said, "Okay! Then, I guess it is time for me to talk with your dad."

# 8

# Amy - College

"Amy!" Melissa squealed. "Amy, are you here?"

Amy thought there had to be some sort of emergency. Melissa was a fairly quiet person who rarely yelled.

Amy rushed out of her room. "I'm here! What's going on?"

Melissa thrust her left hand at Amy. On Melissa's ring finger rested a beautiful diamond engagement ring. The ring sparkled and winked at Amy.

"Are you serious?" Amy covered her mouth with her hand, grabbed Melissa, and hugged her tight.

"Oh, Mel! I am so excited for you! Here, sit down and tell me everything!"

They sat on the couch, face to face, and Melissa, smiling and shedding happy tears, told Amy that Blake had suggested they go for a walk in the park. Partway through their walk, Blake stopped and knelt in front of her and asked her to marry him.

"Oh my goodness! I am so excited for you," Amy repeated. "This is so great! I know you love him, and I think y'all will be very happy together."

"Amy, I want you to be my maid of honor," Melissa said,

tearing up again. "You're like a sister to me and my best friend, and I can't imagine someone else being my maid of honor."

"Your sister won't be mad?" Amy asked, partly out of genuine concern of stepping on Melissa's sister's toes and partly out of amusement, already knowing that Melissa's little sister would be mad.

"She'll get over it." Melissa waved off her concern.

"I would be honored to be your maid of honor," Amy said, and meant it.

Melissa was the best thing that happened to Amy in college. She was Amy's confidant, her shoulder to cry on, and her ever-present encouragement. Amy was glad college was ending, and unlike Melissa, she had a definite plan for her life after college. She was already speaking with a commercial real estate firm in Chicago, and things were looking promising for her to land there once she graduated.

Amy would admit to no one, including Melissa, that she wanted to create as much distance from Texas as possible. She could have applied to many firms in Houston, Dallas, or Austin, but she needed to get far away from her dad. She did not, on any level, want to be sucked back into life with her dad and sister. The only guilt Amy felt when she left for college was leaving her sister in her dad's care. However, her dad had been doing better by the time Amy was a senior in high school, and Amy decided she had to get out of her house.

Melissa was the only one who knew the accurate and mostly complete story of Amy's family. Amy had gotten drunk one night and told Melissa things about her childhood she hadn't been willing to discuss with anyone else. Even Annalise, Amy's sister, didn't know everything that happened. Melissa always encouraged Amy to share as much as she wanted, knowing it would be good to get it out. And Amy trusted Melissa wouldn't tell anyone her secrets.

Melissa changed a lot after meeting Blake. The changes weren't bad. In fact, Amy recognized Melissa was much, much happier. At first, Melissa tried to share what was happening with her with Amy. Melissa would come home from church or Bible study, and Amy would politely ask how it was.

"It was so great!" Melissa would say. "I'm constantly overwhelmed by the goodness of God. Today, the pastor shared how we can never wander too far from God."

Amy found herself tuning Melissa out, and unfortunately, Melissa caught on, so she began to answer with, "It was good."

Amy felt a tinge of guilt because she knew Melissa always listened to her. However, Amy did not feel there was room for God in her life. Why would she want to submit herself to a God who wanted people to follow all of His rules but then still let them down? After all, when Amy was only ten years old, she prayed all the prayers she was supposed to pray, but her mom died of cancer anyway. No girl should have to watch their mom get sick and die in such a cruel manner. If God had loved her like he claimed he did, and He was such a good God, He would not have let her mom get sick.

If Melissa found God and it made her happy, then good for her. But Amy wasn't ready to hear about a supposedly good God when He had not been good to her. Amy's dad was a wreck after Amy's mom died. He wasn't sure how to handle Amy and her sister on his own. So, Amy was forced to grow up quickly. She learned to take care of herself and her sister while her dad tried to make it through each day, crippled by grief and unaware that his two children were grieving as well.

More and more, Amy's dad had turned to alcohol to numb the pain. Thankfully, he was not a mean drunk, but he did spend his time passed out more than anything. Amy had to remind him to pay the bills and eat his dinner. Amy saw college as her ticket out. She was smart, made good grades, and could easily obtain a couple of scholarships, so she would not be in enormous debt upon graduating. As the years went by and Amy was not in her dad's house surviving, the bitterness toward her dad began to mount.

"Have you set a date?" Amy asked, bringing herself back to the present.

"We want to get married this summer. " My mom will probably want more time to plan the wedding," Melissa said, rolling her eyes. "But we would rather be married and then decide where we want to live and work." Blake is checking with the church to see their availability, but we are looking at July."

"That is quick! But you can get this done. Your mom is nothing but organized!" Amy said, chuckling. "And I think it is perfect timing."

"Be honest . . ." Amy continued teasingly. "How many bridal magazines are stacked up in your room?"

Melissa blushed. "I may or may not have a couple. A girl needs to be prepared."

"Absolutely!" Amy giggled. "Just promise me one thing."
"Okay."
"Please don't make me wear something pink and fluffy."
Melissa laughed, "You got it! No puff pastries on stage."
Amy hugged Melissa again. "You have a lot of decisions to make between now and July. What does this do to your job

hunt?"

"Well, now that I know Blake is for sure in the picture, we have been talking about moving to Austin. Blake thinks there is more opportunity for his career there, and I don't think it would be hard for me to find a job there either."

"And let's be honest. You don't care what kind of job you get as long as you can begin a family," Amy said with a smile.

Melissa opened her mouth, beginning to protest, but then she thought better. "How did you know?"

"Mel, you were born to be a mom. There isn't anything wrong with that. You should embrace it rather than pretend you want a career."

Melissa stared at Amy for a minute. "When did you get so wise?"

"Oh, I think you have rubbed off on me. You have an uncanny way of seeing through my stuff. Turnabout is fair play occasionally if you ask me," said Amy, clearly pleased with herself.

"Okay, so the sorority sisters are definitely going to want to give you a shower," Amy said, clicking into planning mode, "and who else are you planning to have in the wedding besides me and your sister? Alex? I guess it is my job to help you wrangle these girls."

Melissa laughed. "Oh my goodness. There is so much to think about. Let me get some paper and start making a list."

Amy watched as Melissa headed to her room, searching for paper and pen. Although this was the opposite path Amy had chosen for herself, she was honestly happy for Melissa.

The next few weeks were a blur for Amy, and she knew they were also for Melissa. While Melissa picked out a wedding dress, went to fittings, and registered for china and tableware,

Amy was busy finishing her classes, finalizing things for the job in Chicago, and finding a place to live. The firm had agreed she could start at the end of July. Amy planned to move there as soon as Melissa was married. Amy wanted to spend as little time at home with her dad after graduation as possible.

Amy finally found the courage to tell her sister, Annalise, about her plans.

"But why Chicago?" Annalise asked. "There wasn't any other job closer to Dallas or in Dallas, for that matter?"

"Not ones I was interested in." That was mostly true. She wasn't at all interested in living anywhere near Dallas. She was offered an excellent opportunity in Chicago and was not about to turn it down.

"But seriously, so far away. What if I need you?" Annalise continued.

"Annalise, you are starting college right after I leave. You will love college, and you will not need me checking in on you. You will make so many new friends and have so many fun adventures. You won't even know I'm gone. Besides, I am always a phone call away." Amy understood Annalise's nerves about leaving home for the first time. Amy also felt that way despite focusing on getting away from her dad. Annalise was the only reason Amy had chosen to go to college so close to home. But now, it was time for both girls to spread their wings and fly. Annalise was going to be just fine.

"Look, I promise to visit often. And we will make arrangements for you to come see me. You will love Chicago. There are so many fun things to do there." Amy didn't intend to visit too often but knew she needed to make Annalise feel better. And the part about Annalise visiting her was true. In fact, if she got to Chicago and liked it as much as she thought she would, maybe she could convince Annalise to move there as well.

At the end of May, Melissa and Amy received their university diplomas. It was a fantastic accomplishment that they were both proud of. Melissa's entire family, including grandparents and cousins, attended the ceremony. Amy's dad and sister came. Upon seeing her dad, Amy thought he seemed somewhat better. He didn't appear to be between two drunken binges. He acted coherently and was quite pleasant to be around.

"Your mom would be so proud of you," Amy's dad said as he awkwardly put an arm around her in an attempt at a hug. "I'm very proud of you as well. I know you are going to do great things in Chicago."

Before Amy was tempted to let the ice around her heart melt towards her dad, she quickly drew her familiar bitterness towards him back to her like a comforting blanket. Her dad left her to grieve for her mom on her own when she needed him the most. She was not ready to let him off the hook for any of that yet.

# 9

# Melissa - College

With classes and graduation finally behind her, Melissa felt free to devote all her time to the wedding. On the one hand, she was thankful her wedding was in July rather than at the end of May, as she and Blake had initially discussed. But on the other hand, she was ready to marry Blake today. It was difficult not to completely zone out on her studies and go full force on the wedding, but her mom, sensing this in Melissa, kept encouraging her to cross the finish line well. Melissa knew her parents were proud that she earned her diploma and finished with a good GPA.

Amy had been tremendously helpful with the wedding planning. "You know, if this job in Chicago doesn't work out, you could have a career in event planning."

"Oh no, friend. This is just for you. I am not cut out to handle a typical bride's emotions. I would probably get fired for slapping some nonsense out of them," Amy quipped.

Melissa giggled, knowing Amy was probably right. Amy had no patience for some people's emotional roller coasters.

"But my bridal shower was beautiful, and you even worked your magic on my sister. She's not terribly mad at me for picking you as the maid of honor."

"Well, that is just because I told her that if she were the maid of honor, she would have to be in constant contact with all your sorority sisters," Amy teased.

Melissa laughed. Melissa's sister was the opposite of Melissa. She was sort of a tomboy, into sports, and not a girly girl. As her sister often told Melissa, she would rather die than have to be anywhere near a sorority. Melissa caught her rolling her eyes more than once at the bridal shower.

"I bet that did work. She probably saw you as her savior at that point."

"You're welcome," Amy deadpanned.

Melissa's mom had turned out to be a big help as well. She had a way of narrowing down the decisions, so Melissa did not stay overwhelmed with the details. The only place they butted heads was over the wedding location. Melissa always dreamed of an outdoor wedding, and the church had a beautiful garden they could use.

"Melissa, I know the garden is beautiful, but you are getting married at 2:00 in the afternoon—in the middle of July—in Texas," Melissa's mom reasoned. "Your guests will melt. You will melt. We will have to provide fans and water. The church is beautiful, and we can decorate it to look the way you want." Melissa did not want to relent on this point.

But Amy was the one who convinced her. "Your mom's right," she said. "Think of how your grandma will handle this heat. Also, there are other variables out of your control. What if it rains and we have to move everything inside frantically? This is unneeded stress, especially with the number of guests you have coming. If it were thirty, then fine. But your wedding is a little bigger than that."

Melissa knew they were right, and in the end, the sanctuary was decorated beautifully.

When it came time to pick out her dress, she only wanted her mom and Amy there. They were the two opinions she trusted most. She fell in love with the fourth dress she tried on, and when she walked out of the dressing room, she knew her mom and Amy agreed.

"Oh, Melissa, you look beautiful." Her mom whispered, wiping at her eyes.

"I think this is it!" Amy agreed. "You look absolutely gorgeous."

Melissa looked at herself in the mirror. She felt like she needed to pinch herself. Picking out a wedding dress was a very surreal moment for her.

"And now, what kind of veil do you want?" Amy asked.

Melissa's mom smiled at her. "Do you want to wear mine?"

"Really? I would love to!"

Melissa looked over at Amy just in time to see a look of longing cross her face before Amy covered it up. Melissa knew it was hard for Amy to face monumental events in her life without having her mom. But she knew Amy would be offended if Melissa shifted any attention Amy's way. So, Melissa tucked that away as a point of prayer for her.

Melissa breathed a massive sigh of relief once the dress was purchased and the fittings were scheduled. They had the venue and the dress; the other things should fall into place. Blake assured Melissa he was taking care of everything for the honeymoon. All Melissa knew was she needed to bring plenty of beachwear and her passport. Sitting on a beach staring at the ocean sounded heavenly to Melissa.

The night before her wedding, Amy sat cross-legged on Melissa's bed at her parents' home. Melissa was packing her clothes for the honeymoon as Amy went over the schedule for the next day one last time.

"How many divas can we pack into the church nursery to get ready?" Amy asked.

"I hope I am not one of the divas included in this," Melissa chuckled.

"You, friend, are far from a diva. I am not sure I have ever seen such a level-headed bride. Bravo."

"Oh, well. Thank you, but you don't see everything going on inside. I'm like a duck—smooth sailing above the water. Feet kicking furiously below the water," Melissa laughed at herself.

"I don't know what I would have done without you the last few months," Melissa said, her voice wobbly. "I am going to miss you so much."

"Nu-uh. You promised me no emotional speeches," Amy said, only half joking.

"I did? I don't remember that."

"Yes, it was item fourteen in the friendship contract."

"You mean the pretend friendship contract you whip out when convenient?" Melissa retorted good-naturedly.

"Exactly!" Amy stated.

"Well, I think the contract needs to be updated."

"I'll have my lawyers be in touch."

Melissa rolled her eyes. "Well, until then, I guess I will be in breach of contract." Turning serious again, Melissa continued, "Please don't be a stranger. I know we will be far apart, but I want you to always be in my life. I can't imagine these last four years without you."

Amy, allowing herself a rare moment of emotion, responded, "Of course. Just because I am moving to Chicago doesn't mean we won't ever talk again. I love you, Mel. You have no idea how much you mean to me. I fully plan for us always to be friends."

Melissa allowed tears to slide down her cheeks. "That's good. Because I always want you in my life. You will come back to visit even after you have your fancy job, right?"

"Yes," Amy assured her. "And you have a standing invitation to Chicago as well. I would love for you to come visit me."

Melissa nodded, satisfied with Amy's answers, and turned to put some more clothes in her suitcase. She hoped Amy would come to visit. She knew Amy was running and maybe needed to distance herself between her new career and childhood. But Melissa couldn't shake the feeling that her visits would be few and far between once Amy left Texas. Melissa hoped she was wrong.

The next day dawned brilliant and bright. The Texas sun beamed on Melissa as she made her way into the church and to the room set aside for her to get ready. Melissa had to admit that even though it would be a beautiful day, her mom had been right, of course. The day would be a scorcher. She was secretly relieved to be talked into an indoor wedding.

The day flew by in a cloud of hairspray, makeup, and perfume. Melissa was determined not to let the day's details stress her out, no matter what they were. She wanted to enjoy this day, so she would let the wedding coordinator worry for her.

In what seemed like the blink of an eye, Melissa was

dressed, and the room cleared of her bridesmaids. Only Amy and her mom were left, helping her with the finishing touches. Melissa had this weird feeling that this was all happening to someone else, and she was watching.

"You look beautiful," Amy said, squeezing her arm. "I'll see you out there."

Amy slipped from the room, and Melissa's dad came in. "You look beautiful, sugar. It's still not too late to change your mind."

Melissa rolled her eyes. She knew her dad adored Blake, but she was still his little girl. "Thanks, Dad. I think I'm good."

Her Dad leaned over and kissed her cheek. "Alright. If you say so."

"Okay, you two. I have to go now. Can I trust you together?"

"We're fine, Mom."

"Okay, the wedding coordinator will return in a second to get you."

Melissa took a deep breath. She was ready to get this show on the road. She was so excited to marry Blake, but hated being the center of attention. She was ready to walk down the aisle.

As if the wedding coordinator could read her thoughts, she appeared and told them she was ready for them.

The ceremony and reception were everything Melissa had hoped. And before Melissa was ready, the whole thing was over. She hugged her mom and dad and thanked them. She hugged Amy, making her promise one last time to call once she got settled in Chicago.

Melissa took Blake's hand, and with cheers from their guests, they headed into their life together as a married couple.

# Amy

Amy looked at the computer screen in front of her, not really seeing what was on the screen. Amy enjoyed her job, but lately she felt the pull of it not being enough for her. She went home most nights to a beautiful, yet empty apartment. She had met plenty of handsome men, but none who seemed to capture her attention beyond one or two dates. Truthfully, when Amy first moved to Chicago, she didn't mind that men were a revolving door in her life. She wasn't sure she was cut out to be with one person. But lately, she had a longing for someone to know her honestly and be there for her consistently. Her life was beginning to feel a little empty.

Amy stared at the papers in front of her, trying to focus. There was a light knock on the open door of her office. Amy looked up and was pleasantly surprised to see Tyler standing there. Tyler's classic charm and dark hair, paired with ocean-blue eyes, made him everyone's favorite office crush. Amy got the impression from his overly friendly smirks that he knew the impact he had on women.

Amy smiled warmly at Tyler and put her pen down on the papers she was desperately trying to focus on. "What's up?"

she asked casually. Amy didn't want to admit it, but Tyler affected her, too.

Tyler returned the smile and said, "Oh, I just had a quick question about our project and the numbers we were discussing at our weekly meeting. Have you finished your projected numbers yet?"

Amy groaned internally, wishing she were finished. She looked at Tyler with her practiced professional smile and said a little too brightly, "I am just about done with those. May I bring them to you in about an hour?"

"Sure!" said Tyler as he turned to leave. He hesitated a moment and then turned back. "Hey! Would you be interested in getting a bite to eat after work today?"

Amy raised her eyebrows in surprise. "Are you missing a companion for this evening? How did I wind up in the rotation?" Instantly regretting her words, Amy bit her lip. "I'm sorry. That was uncalled for." Amy had tried for dry humor, and it had come out mean.

Tyler chuckled, "Don't hold back on how you really feel." He continued with that charming smile of his, "It would take a lot more than that to hurt my feelings. And you can't believe everything you hear around the office. I am just inviting you to a casual dinner. I think we are going to get to know each other a lot better with this project, and I thought it might be fun actually to get to know each other. I'm sorry if I made you uncomfortable."

Amy jumped from her seat and hurried around her desk. "I am so sorry. You're right, and yes, I would love to grab dinner with you."

Tyler's demeanor instantly changed. His face softened, and

his eyes lit up with excitement. "Great! I know a little place just around the corner. Why don't you bring those numbers to me when you are ready to leave for the day, and we will go together."

Amy smiled, "Okay, sounds good."

After Tyler left, Amy found herself rehearsing the conversation. She got the distinct feeling that Tyler was playing this off as a casual dinner, but to him, it might be more. The truth was, Amy noticed Tyler around the office. He was smart, handsome, and charming, and he shared Amy's ambition to climb the career ladder. Although Amy knew she would date Tyler if he didn't work at the same company, she tried to keep her professional and personal lives separate. Dating someone at work could get messy real quick, and Amy hated messy. Oh well. It was just dinner, she thought to herself.

When it was time to leave work, Amy was relieved. She had tried to put Tyler and dinner out of her mind and focus completely on work, but she was struggling. She didn't know why. She was asked out all the time. Some she accepted, some she didn't. Dating was not a foreign thing to her. Sometimes she accepted only because she didn't have anything in her fridge and would rather go out on a date than go to the grocery store.

Tyler piqued her interest for some reason. Aside from being pleasant to look at, he seemed motivated to make a name for himself in commercial real estate, as was Amy. She enjoyed his quick wit and even temperament at work. She was curious if he was the same outside of work. Amy didn't want to admit it, but Tyler was pretty much the type of guy she pictured herself with long-term. But was she ready for that? Amy was beginning to think she may never be ready for marriage, and for some odd reason, that kind of bothered her.

Amy tidied her desk, checked her planner to remind herself what was in store for tomorrow, snapped off her desk lamp, and made her way to her door. Amy shouldered her computer bag, took a deep breath, and opened her office door. To her surprise, Tyler stood in front of her smiling. "Hi!" Amy said with a bright smile, her stomach doing some strange fluttering. "I was just headed your way."

"I thought I would come to you," Tyler explained. "I realized the elevator is closer to your office."

"Oh," Amy said. "I have the information you need." She shoved the papers at him and tried to ignore her uncharacteristic nervousness. Seriously, what was wrong with her? Was she actually nervous? Amy couldn't remember the last time a guy had truly made her anxious. She needed to move past this—and quickly.

How cliche would it be to fall for a guy at work who didn't like you back? And Amy had always had the upper hand in a relationship. She enjoyed being the one in control, and she wasn't about to change now, no matter how adorable that grin Tyler kept flashing at her was.

Tyler smiled and thanked her. He shoved the papers into his backpack and motioned toward the elevator without looking at them. "Shall we go?"

"Sure," Amy said, smiling. Relax, she told herself. This is just dinner, and it will probably be fun.

Tyler and Amy made their way to the elevator. Once outside, Amy noted the air was humid and the day had been unusually warm, even for a mid-summer day in Chicago. Chicagoans loved days like this, so they could soak up as much sunshine as possible before fall and winter hit. Even though Amy had lived here for over ten years, she still marveled at the Chicago weather. Unlike Texas, there were four seasons. Texas was much hotter, with a brief period of chilly to cold weather in winter. Amy sometimes missed the weather in Texas, but experiencing each season was wonderful.

As they walked to the restaurant, Tyler pleasantly chatted about a conversation he'd had with a coworker they both knew. Amy smiled at Tyler's laid-back demeanor. As her nerves calmed, she realized Tyler was comfortable to be around and also very easy to talk with. The restaurant Tyler took her to was one she had passed multiple times on her way to work, but for whatever reason, Amy had never eaten there. Since the weather was nice, they chose to sit on the little patio outside the restaurant. The hostess handed them their menus and assured them their waitress would be around shortly. When the waitress arrived, Tyler ordered a glass of water and a glass of red wine. Amy ordered the same. The waitress turned to fetch their drinks, promising to be right back to take their food orders.

Tyler and Amy perused the menu and settled on their choices. Closing his menu, Tyler reached for a piece of bread the waitress had placed on their table. He glanced at Amy, smiled, and said, "So, Amy, tell me about yourself." Amy hated that question. What did it mean? Was she supposed to begin at birth or give a condensed version? Besides, Amy was a fairly private person. Until she had built some trust with a person, she wasn't sure how much that person should know about her.

Amy sucked in a breath and said, "Well, I was born and raised in Texas. After college, I was looking for something different, so I decided to take a chance at a job in a different state.

I worked at that job for a couple of years, then took another job at a different commercial real estate firm. I liked that firm, but the growth potential wasn't as great as this firm's, so three years ago I took the job at this firm. Turns out, I like Chicago. It is a beautiful city with a lot to offer, so for now, I am content here."

Before Tyler could ask any follow-up questions, she turned the tables on him. "What about you?" Amy asked. This trick usually worked for Amy. She had discovered very few people really wanted to know that much about you. They were more interested in talking about themselves.

However, Tyler seemed to ignore her question. "No family?"

Amy did not want to talk about this yet, so she attempted to lighten the mood. "Well, I don't tell many people this," she said with a conspiratorial whisper, "but my parents are rodeo clowns and keep busy riding the circuit. I didn't want to follow in their footsteps, so I decided to leave Texas behind."

Tyler studied Amy for a full minute before breaking into his charming grin, which made Amy's stomach flutter. "You're lying. You almost had me, though. I am going to have to watch out for you. Okay, for real. Tell me about your family."

Amy smiled, what she hoped was an easy smile, even though the mere mention of her family made her clench inside. "I do have a family. My mom died when I was young, but my dad and his new wife live in the Dallas area. My sister is married with two kids and lives fairly close to my dad."

"Are you close with your family?" Tyler asked.

Why does he keep pressing this issue? Amy thought. Usually, guys were satisfied with her vague answers and moved on. Even if she wanted to get to know Tyler better, Amy was not comfortable revealing how much of a mess her childhood was so soon. She tried to think of how to word things without revealing all the family skeletons.

Amy finally said, "My sister and I are close. We talk often. My dad and I mainly see each other at holiday gatherings." Amy smiled, what she hoped to be a light-hearted smile, and crossed her fingers that she could successfully change the subject.

"So what about you? Have you always lived in Chicago, or are you a transplant like me?" Tyler didn't look like he was ready to change the subject just yet, but thankfully, he decided to let her.

"No. I am from the Midwest, though. I grew up in Minnesota and went to college in Missouri. I thought I would go back to Minnesota after college, but like you, I landed a job here in Chicago and haven't wanted to leave. I actually have an accounting degree and began my career in an accounting firm. But I quickly learned I don't have the personality to be a good accountant. Those people take their numbers VERY seriously. I landed a job at another commercial real estate firm in Chicago and learned all I could. When I found out there was an opening at this firm, I jumped on it."

Amy nodded and smiled. "And family?" she asked, feeling it only fair that she ask in return.

"Oh, I have a big family. Four brothers and a sister." Amy's eyes widened. Tyler laughed at her response. "Yes, we were a handful for my mother. She was always busy with us. She also had to run us to all of our various sports practices. Even my sister played three different sports."

Amy could not imagine this. His life was so different from

her own, and she was genuinely curious. "Where are you in the lineup?"

"I am the youngest brother," Tyler said, "But my sister is the youngest sibling. I think that is why she and I are so close. I always got picked on because I was the youngest of five boys, but she got picked on because she was the youngest sibling. She and I decided early on we needed to band together to have a shot at survival."

"Wow!" Amy said. "I bet your house was loud."

"Yes, it was," Tyler laughed, his eyes softening. "We had a great time growing up together, though."

"Do your parents still live in Minnesota?" Amy asked.

"Yes, and my sister still lives close to them. I think they like having her nearby," Tyler answered. Then he abruptly changed the subject, catching Amy off guard. "You said your mom died when you were young. How old were you?"

Amy truly hated talking about this, but she knew she would eventually have to answer Tyler's questions if they were to move forward. She tried to keep the details to a minimum. "She died of cancer when I was ten," Amy said matter-of-factly. She hoped that not expounding on her answers would prompt Tyler to move on from this topic.

"Oh, wow. How old was your sister?"

"Six," said Amy. "She doesn't remember as much as I do."

"I am so sorry," Tyler said. "I bet you miss her."

*You have no idea*, Amy thought to herself. To Tyler, she only nodded.

The waitress came by, put their meals in front of them, and refilled their water glasses. "Can I get you another glass of wine?" Tyler and Amy both said yes. They dug into their meals.

Amy did not know whether Tyler sensed the subject needed to change or just ran out of things to say on the topic. However, she was relieved when they moved to another topic. The rest of the conversation was pretty easy-going.

Amy wasn't sure whether it was the wine or the fact that they had finally changed the subject, but she began to relax. They spoke about their favorite things to do in Chicago, what their goals were at the company, and some of their favorite travel spots. Tyler had traveled more than Amy, and she enjoyed listening to his stories. He had a way of pulling Amy in and making her feel like she was living the experience with him.

The waitress came by again, offering dessert. "Let's do dessert!" Tyler said.

Amy opened her mouth to protest, but before she could say anything, Tyler said, "Come on. We can't pass up dessert. We can even share one if you would like."

Tyler reminded Amy of a kid begging for candy. She chuckled despite herself and said, "Okay, as long as it is chocolate. Because if not, it may be a waste of calories."

Tyler grinned at her, "You've got a deal!"

Turning to the waitress, he ordered the triple chocolate layer cake. Amy's mouth watered in response. She wasn't sure the last time she allowed herself dessert at a restaurant. The waitress returned quickly with the cake, two forks, and another glass of wine for each of them.

Amy picked up her fork and sliced it into the cake to make sure she got plenty of chocolate icing. She slid her fork into her mouth and, before she could stop herself, groaned in delight.

Tyler, who had been watching her the whole time, chuckled. "You do like chocolate. Duly noted."

For some reason, that comment sent a weird sensation through Amy. As much as she wanted to keep Tyler at arm's length when it came to her family, it pleased her that he noticed something that she liked and wanted to remember.

Amy took another couple of bites, put her fork down, and sipped on her wine.

"You can't be done yet." Tyler grinned at her.

"I think I've had plenty. Everything was so good. I can't believe I haven't tried this place before now."

"Stick with me, kid. I know all the good restaurants in Chicago. My mom said I missed my calling as a food critic."

"Really?"

"Yeah, I think she thought I might go to culinary school."

"Wow, how DID you end up going into accounting?"

"I don't know. I think I didn't really know what I wanted to do, and I knew most accountants made money. So . . ." He shrugged. "But it worked out. I do like working in real estate. It is still a lot of numbers like in accounting, but I enjoy the property side of it as well."

The conversation continued to flow naturally as they finished their wine. Again, Amy wasn't sure if it was the wine or Tyler, but she found herself very much enjoying his company. He was so easy to talk with, and Amy didn't feel like she was having to pretend to be interested in what he was talking about. He also seemed to be genuinely interested in Amy.

When the check came, Amy offered to pay her share, but Tyler insisted on paying, saying he had asked her to dinner. Amy thanked him. Score another point for Tyler.

Tyler offered to walk her to her car since it was getting late.

Amy agreed. As they strolled to the car, Amy noticed she felt safe with Tyler. Amy had always felt she only had herself to depend on. There were very few guys with whom she felt safe. When Tyler reached for her hand, she let him take it, feeling a quick jolt of electricity go through her body.

When they got to her car, Amy knew Tyler was going to try to kiss her, and she had to decide quickly whether she was okay with it. Her body decided for her. Tyler looked at her, and Amy involuntarily leaned towards him. That was all the invitation Tyler needed. He leaned down and gently pressed his lips to hers. Sparks flew in Amy's body that she had not experienced in a long time. Tyler must have felt it too, because his arms went around her, and he gently pressed her to him as he deepened the kiss. Finally, he pulled away, and Amy peeled her eyes open and tried to look him in the eye.

Tyler smiled at her and whispered, "Wow!"

Amy blushed. She hurriedly said, "Well, thanks for a fun evening!" She turned awkwardly to get in her car, hoping Tyler wouldn't notice just how awkward she felt.

On the drive home, Amy blushed again, thinking about what had just happened. She was no stranger to kissing guys, and well, more. But there was something different about Tyler, and it had snuck up on her. What did he think of her? Would he think of her at all, or was this so common to him that he would quickly forget it? Amy hated feeling vulnerable. This was the reason she kept most relationships casual. Her relationships got physical, but she refused to invest her emotions fully in any of them. She had been hurt before, deeply. She did not want to feel that again.

Amy cursed under her breath and tried to control her emotions. It wasn't that big of a deal—it was a kiss. They would both probably forget about it by morning. Amy replayed the kiss in her mind again, knowing she was lying to herself. There was no way she was going to forget that kiss anytime soon.

# 11

# *Melissa*

Melissa awoke to the smell of fresh coffee. She slowly opened her eyes and peeked at the clock. 6:10. Time to get moving. All at once, Melissa's dream rushed back to her like a wave in the ocean. She smiled to herself slowly as she once again pictured that beautiful face fully alive and glowing, framed with the most stunning dark hair. She longed to tell her husband the story, but something held her back. Melissa wasn't sure she was ready to share such a personal experience with anyone just yet.

Melissa began to revisit the what-ifs as she showered and changed. Melissa knew this was a fruitless exercise, but sometimes she couldn't resist going down this path. What if she had four kids on Earth instead of three? How would that make her family different? What if the oldest child was not Lily but Joy instead? How would Lily have done as a middle child sandwiched between other siblings? Lily definitely had leadership skills, which her siblings translated as bossy. Melissa was not sure how Lily would have done being the secondborn. She smiled to herself, imagining Lily having someone else older than her trying to tell her what to do.

Then there were the what-ifs that were absolutely not help-ful. What if Melissa had determined she was pregnant sooner and had been more careful with what she was eating and drink-ing? The doctor assured her she had done nothing wrong, and miscarriage happened to many women. But if she were truly a good mom, wouldn't she have known she was carrying a life inside her and done a better job of protecting it? She knew deep down the miscarriage wasn't her fault, but on the other hand, it was hard not to blame someone or something for what happened. This what-if path could be dangerous, and Melissa had to guard her thoughts not to let Satan lead her directly down this spiral.

However, Melissa mused, isn't that what we often do as humans? We identify the person we believe is responsible for what we are experiencing and resolve to hold them account-able. Melissa had been here before in her thoughts, looping around endlessly like a hamster on a wheel. She tried hard not to stop at another who was easy to blame. God. The miscar-riage happened pretty early in Melissa's walk with the Lord, and she found herself in an intense struggle with God. It was hard to be mad at God and need His healing at the same time.

Melissa spent many days wrestling with herself and God over the death of their baby. She had finally realized, after much prayer and many, many tears, as well as conversations with Blake, that God did not cause the death of their precious baby. Their baby was a gift from the Lord. Melissa began to realize that bad things happened in this fallen world and trying to find someone to blame for her baby's death was not produc-tive. God had gifted them with three more children, and now, He was gifting her with this vision of her beautiful daughter, happy and healthy in heaven. One day, she would get to join her daughter, Joy, in heaven, but for now, she would cherish each day she had on this earth with the rest of her family.

Unbidden memories of sitting in the clinic waiting for Amy to have an abortion came back to Melissa. Melissa felt so much regret from that day. She wished she had done more to stop Amy. Amy had been in a desperate situation, and at the time, neither of the girls felt abortion was killing a baby. Once Melissa became a Christian, she began to grow in her faith and develop a relationship with the Lord. Her eyes were opened to the lie of abortion. Melissa knew the procedure had some emotional aftereffects on Amy, some of which she was not sure Amy was even aware of. Amy seemed to be depressed after it was all over and was more determined in her bitterness towards her father. It was not lost on Melissa that as soon as Amy could, she left Texas. And despite her promises to the contrary, Amy had not been back to visit often.

Melissa understood that as the girls got older, their relationship would change as they became caught up in their own lives. However, Melissa tried to check in with Amy as much as possible so the relationship wouldn't be lost entirely. Melissa knew God was not done with Amy. He wanted Amy to have a relationship with Him and to be completely whole, not living her life in unforgiveness and bitterness. However, Amy was the only one who would get to decide when she was done holding on to the past. She would have to be the one to decide she wanted more in her life.

Now that Melissa was older, she could look back on her life and see how God had pursued her. At the time she met Blake, she was tired of her life and knew there was a missing piece she had yet to find. It still kind of surprised Melissa that it took one trip to church with, admittedly, a very cute boy, to change her life. But now, looking back, she could see how God had been preparing her for that fateful Sunday morning. She knew if God did that for her, He could do it for Amy.

For now, she felt her job was to keep the lines of communication open with Amy and to continue praying for her. Although Melissa wasn't seeing any change yet, she knew her prayers were not in vain.

The next thought took Melissa's breath away. What if Amy's aborted child was being raised in heaven with Joy? Tears formed in Melissa's eyes and slid down her cheeks. Wouldn't that just be like the redeeming power of God? Melissa prayed constantly for Amy's salvation, but this only added another layer. Amy needed the promise of heaven, her opportunity to be with Jesus for eternity. She also needed the hope of seeing her precious baby once again.

**12**

# *Amy*

Amy ran into Tyler in the breakroom, getting coffee. She pushed the memory of kissing him out of her mind. Amy smiled at him and said a cheerful and what she hoped was not an awkward, "Good Morning."

Tyler smiled his easy smile in return. He motioned towards his cup and said, "Third cup already today. You?"

Amy said, "My second, but I am sure I will catch up to you."

Tyler nodded and said, "Well, good luck." He then turned to head back to his office. Amy stared at his back as another woman, known to date many men in the office, joined Tyler in the hall. They stopped to talk, and the woman repeatedly touched Tyler's arm. Tyler continued the conversation with his easy charm. Amy wondered if Tyler was asking her out to dinner tonight. The rumors about Tyler had to come from somewhere, right?

*Interesting*, Amy thought. Amy was not usually prone to jealousy, but that was precisely why she didn't date co-workers. She had work to do, and she didn't want to spend the day analyzing that interaction.

Amy turned to get her coffee and chatted pleasantly with another co-worker who came into the break room, determined to forget about Tyler. She returned to her office and stepped behind her desk. Before sitting, she stretched her arms to the ceiling, trying to ease the tension in her back. She had not had time to go for a run last night. She began to bend to one side when she heard Tyler's quiet voice say, "Hey!"

Amy jumped. "Hey!" she said, hoping he didn't notice that he startled her.

"I wanted to know if you had any plans for the weekend. I have tickets for the theater on Saturday and wondered if you would like to go with me. We could eat dinner before, if you are up for it."

Amy very much wanted to go but paused for a brief moment to assess if this was a good idea. She finally decided she didn't care. She wanted to go. She looked at Tyler and smiled, "I would love to."

"Great," said Tyler, clearly pleased she had accepted his invitation. "I will pick you up at 7:00, if that works for you. Will you text me your address?"

Amy nodded. Tyler responded again, "Great! This will be fun!" He stared at her for a moment, leaving Amy to wonder if he wanted to say something else. But when he spoke, he said, "Well, I'd better get back to work. See you later."

After Tyler left, Amy stared at the office doorway that Tyler had been standing in only a moment before. She was excited about spending time with him, but she also reminded herself to be cautious. She did not want to get caught up in her feelings, especially with a guy from work. It was best to follow her casual dating rule and not let things get out of hand.

At that moment, Brooke appeared in the doorway. "Hey, Amy! I feel like I haven't seen you at all today. I think the meeting room is holding me captive today." Brooke looked as beautiful today as she did every day. She was dressed in professional attire, with her dark hair styled loosely around her shoulders. Her bright blue eyes were a startling and lovely contrast to her dark hair. Amy knew many guys would like to date Brooke, but Brooke's standards were very high. Too high, if you asked Amy.

Brooke reminded Amy of Melissa, which might explain why they connected so quickly. Brooke was kind-hearted and easy to talk with. Even though Brooke made it clear she loved God and attended church regularly, Amy felt comfortable talking with Brooke about her life. Like Melissa, she didn't feel Brooke would judge her for her choices.

"Did I just see Tyler leave your office?" Brooke asked with open curiosity.

Amy waved Brooke into the office, and Brooke complied, coming closer to Amy's desk so they could keep their voices lower. "You did." Amy couldn't help herself. A grin spread across her face.

"Uh oh," Brooke said jokingly. "Do I need to ask him about his intentions? You know he's a bit of a player around the office, right?"

Amy chuckled. "I know. He kind of has a reputation. I try not to date guys at work. You know that. But he asked me to dinner the other night, and I just said yes."

"And you had fun?" Brooke asked.

Amy answered with another grin. "Uh oh," Brooke said again. "Looks like this might have potential."

"I don't know," said Amy, sobering. "We'll see. He is a guy from work, and I don't want anything serious right now. For now, it can just be fun."

"True," Brooke said. "But you may want to make this clear sooner rather than later. I don't think Tyler is the only heart-breaker in this scenario," Brooke said in a light-hearted tone, but Amy could sense her worry. Amy had shared enough about her family with Brooke that she knew Amy struggled with getting serious in any relationship.

"He invited me to dinner and a play at the theater this weekend, so I will keep you posted," Amy said, in what she hoped was also a light-hearted tone.

"Ooooo, can't wait to hear all about it," Brooke said, choosing to drop the subject of Amy's heart. "I'd better get back to the conference room. There may already be a search party forming."

Amy chuckled. She knew how much Brooke hated sitting in meetings all day. "Have fun," Amy said sarcastically.

The rest of the workday went by in a blur as Amy immersed herself in her current project. When she glanced at the clock, she was surprised to see it was already time to head home. Amy gathered her things to leave for the weekend. She tried not to take things home over the weekend, but she was working on a big project and knew the deadline was looming. She shouldered her computer bag and walked towards the elevator. Most of her colleagues had already finished for the day and left. She wondered if Tyler was still here. She glanced down the hall towards his office. It seemed pretty quiet and dark down that hallway. With a pang of disappointment, she stepped into the elevator and pushed the button for the parking garage.

Amy drove home, thinking about what she would wear for her date. She had a few options appropriate for the theater, but she wanted to look just right. It had been a while since she had been this excited about a date, but again she felt herself trying to insert caution.

The next day, Amy was ready promptly at 7:00 p.m. She decided on her go-to little black dress. It was the one she felt most confident and comfortable in. Thanks to a social media tutorial, she styled her long, silky blonde hair in a partial updo. After one last look in the mirror, she walked quickly to answer the knock on her apartment door. She swung the door open with a welcoming smile, and Tyler greeted her with his charming smile.

He took in her appearance and breathed, "You look beautiful."

Amy tried not to blush as she thanked him and returned the compliment. She grabbed her black clutch and asked, "Should we get going?"

Tyler agreed. They rode the elevator down and entered the lobby of her apartment building.

Tyler said, "I thought we could do a rideshare tonight. It will make everything easier."

"Perfect," Amy said.

They stood on the curb, making small talk as they awaited their driver. Once they made it into the car, they continued to make small talk and sometimes included their driver. They were deposited at the restaurant Tyler had chosen for the evening. Tyler strode to the hostess stand, announcing he had a reservation. They were quickly escorted to their table and given menus. The restaurant was beautiful, and Amy could tell from the menu prices that their dinner wouldn't be cheap. Upon perusing the menu, Amy verified this was indeed an upscale restaurant. Amy wondered, not for the first time, what Tyler's intentions were. But she told herself to relax and not read too much into anything.

Amy ordered a pasta dish whose menu description made her mouth water, and Tyler ordered a lobster dish. After the waitress took their orders and brought them each a glass of wine, they clinked their glasses and took a sip, each confirming that the wine did not disappoint.

Tyler turned to Amy, "Thank you for going out with me tonight. I had these theater tickets and wasn't sure I was going to use them."

"Do you go to the theater often?" Amy wasn't sure why, but this side of Tyler surprised her.

Tyler nodded, "I grew up going to the theater with my mom. She took all of us kids individually, but I was the one who fell in love with it. So from then on, I was her theater buddy. I may or may not have told my friends in high school that she forced me to go, but I enjoyed going with her." He chuckled, "Bless her, she kept my secret from my friends. I think part of her knew if she spilled the beans, I wouldn't be as willing to go with her. I still try to go with her at least once a year."

Amy wasn't sure why, but this tidbit of information made Tyler all the more likable. She imagined him as a March Madness type of guy who was lost to the world during the height of basketball season. Amy had nothing against sports and actually enjoyed going to games, but it was good to know Tyler had another layer to him.

Their conversation flowed easily as they discussed their

college days, and Tyler told Amy more stories from his chaotic childhood with multiple siblings. Amy was fascinated by these stories because his childhood was so different from her own. He seemed to have the perfect television sitcom family, while she had the perfect after-school special family.

The waitress brought their food, and they enjoyed the tastiness of their meals. The show started at 9:00 p.m. The theater was directly across the street, so Tyler and Amy took their time over dinner. Tyler used the excuse of them having plenty of time to order dessert. He clearly had a sweet tooth.

Amy put down the spoon she used to share the dessert with Tyler and declared, "I cannot eat another bite. I am going to explode and have a hard time staying awake in a darkened theater."

She giggled. "I think that would be an expensive nap."

Tyler smiled at her, his eyes softening. "You really are beautiful," he said.

"Thank you." Amy blushed, both embarrassed by the comment and by his effect on her.

Tyler laughed. "I love it when you blush."

Amy rolled her eyes and said, "I don't know if I can say the same. I don't like giving myself away."

Tyler said, "I can tell. Before we began talking, I could never have guessed what was in your head. You always seemed like a closed book. I think that is why it took me so long to ask you out."

Amy said in a rare moment of vulnerability, "Yeah, that is probably true. When an alcoholic father raises you, you tend to keep things to yourself, stuff your emotions, and have a poker face."

Tyler raised his eyebrows. "Alcoholic, huh?"

"Yeah, " Amy said, trying to decide if she had already over-shared. "I spent much time protecting my sister and putting up walls."

"Was he ever abusive?" Tyler asked cautiously.

"No, not physically," Amy continued hesitantly. "He was drowning his grief in the bottle. He would sometimes say some truly mean things, but he never got physical with either my sister or me. When I left for college, he wanted to get his life back together. He started attending AA meetings, and when my sister was in college, he met a woman who is now his wife."

"Do you like her?" Tyler asked.

"I like her for him," Amy said. "They are good companions if nothing else. I think she also made it clear to him that if he started drinking again, she was out. I honestly don't know her that well, but she doesn't make going to see my dad unpleasant. My sister and her family live near them, so she is much closer to them than I am. My sister was so young and barely remembers my mom, so I think it is easier for her to accept Stephanie."

Amy couldn't believe how much she was sharing. It must be the wine. Maybe it was acting as a truth serum. She decided to change the subject before she shared anything more. "So, how often do you go to the theater?"

Amy could tell Tyler wanted to ask more questions, but, to his credit, he took the hint and let her change the subject. "Oh, probably three to four times yearly, depending on what is showing. Speaking of which, are you ready to head on over?"

Amy looked at her watch in surprise. Time had passed quickly. Amy had dated quite a few men, but there was something about Tyler she enjoyed. He was fun, easy to talk to, and definitely easy on the eyes. He had a friend quality about him, but she also found herself extremely attracted to him. The intensity of the attraction, along with her liking being around him, was causing internal caution bells to ring in her head. She did not want to get hurt.

The show was terrific. It definitely lived up to its hype. Amy had not been to the theater often, and she found herself caught up in the story. At intermission, Tyler excused himself to get a drink for Amy and himself. Amy used the time to watch the people around her and reflect on the evening. She was having a very good time and hoped Tyler was, too.

Tyler returned with a glass of white wine for each of them. They cheered and then made small talk about the show until the lights dimmed. The show's second part went as fast as the first, and before Amy knew it, the cast was bowing. After much applause, the audience dispersed and began to make their way out of the few exits. Tyler reached for Amy's hand as they entered the lobby and the ride-share car Tyler had ordered. Amy began to get butterflies in her stomach, thinking about what would come next. Would he try to find a way into her apartment, or would he kiss her goodnight and leave? Amy wasn't sure which one she wanted to happen.

They pulled up to Amy's apartment building, and Tyler got out with Amy and wished the driver goodnight. He looked at Amy's face with a question in his eyes, and then he gently cupped her face. Butterflies unleashed in Amy's stomach at his touch. Tyler leaned down and kissed her lightly, but once their lips touched, Amy leaned into him, and the kiss grew in intensity. Tyler drew back, and Amy found herself wanting much more.

"Let me walk you to your apartment and make sure you get in alright. I won't be able to sleep unless I know you were able to unlock your apartment door successfully," he said with a teasing smile, but Amy wondered if he felt as light-hearted as he sounded.

Amy was sure his gentlemanly behavior was a ploy to make it into her apartment. She suddenly decided she didn't care. Amy wanted Tyler to come in, and she hoped he would stay.

The elevator ride to her apartment answered her question. As soon as the doors closed, Tyler's lips were back on hers, and then he left a trail of kisses down her neck. The elevator dinged, startling them both and indicating her floor. The doors swooshed open slowly. They walked down the hall towards her door, and Amy finally found herself whispering, "Would you like to come in for a bit?"

"Sure," Tyler said, keeping his tone casual.

Amy unlocked her door and pushed it open. Tyler followed her and shut the door behind him. Amy turned to ask Tyler if he wanted something to drink, but Tyler stepped forward and swallowed her question with another kiss. His hands pressed her to him. Finally, he lifted his head, and they were both breathless. "Is this okay?" He whispered. And she knew what he was asking. She slowly nodded, mentally grateful she had just changed the sheets on her bed. She briefly wondered if this would make things awkward at work, but Tyler's next kiss dismissed all those thoughts as Amy became swept away by the moment.

**13**

# Amy

Amy awakened and, at first, was startled at the sight of Tyler in her bed. A slow smile spread across her face as memories of the night before came back to her. Then, as uninvited ants to a picnic, the familiar doubts began to march into her thoughts. Would this be the last time she saw him outside of work? Did he get what he wanted, and now he will make excuses and leave? Would he only be intimate with her until he grew tired of her and moved on? Amy knew being intimate so soon in a relationship was pretty much the norm in dating these days, but why did she always feel so empty and anxious afterward? At the time, Amy thought Melissa was crazy to wait until after marriage to have sex with Blake, but each time Amy's insecurities got the better of her, she wondered if Melissa might be onto something.

Amy remembered asking Melissa about it once. "How do you know you are sexually compatible if you don't have sex before marriage? Once you are married, you are stuck with a partner and bad sex for the rest of your life." Amy remembered thinking it was a truly legitimate question.

Melissa's response stuck with her. "Well, I guess I trust the

Lord that if we are compatible in all other ways, sex will also work out. Also, what if there are problems in your sex life? Wouldn't you want to work those out in the security of a committed marriage rather than with someone who could walk out at any time?"

Amy remembered thinking Melissa might have a point, but didn't want to admit it. Amy thought she enjoyed the freedom of sleeping with anyone she wanted. She felt in control. But with the feelings of insecurity that often plagued her after being intimate with a guy, she wondered if she really was in control. She couldn't control Tyler walking out on her after getting what he desired. Then there were the insecurities about how she might measure up to the other women he had been with. She had often wondered if, in different relationships, she had stayed too long because she was so busy trying to figure out how he felt and hadn't truthfully sorted out her own feelings. She also wondered if she hadn't stayed long enough in some instances because the walls would eventually go up to protect herself. In her mind, it was easier to say goodbye than to deal with the intensity of her feelings.

Amy sighed and asked herself, Why was love so complicated? Love. When was the last time she used that word? When was the last time a guy had told her he loved her without sex being involved? Was there love outside of sex? If she didn't have sex with a man, could he entirely fall in love with her?

She remembered something her grandmother told her once. "Amy, guys will come and go. There will be good guys and some guys you will later wish you had never met. But never forget how valuable you are. You, your mind, heart, spirit, and body were never meant to be someone else's playthings.

If a guy is messing with your mind, he is playing games and is insecure. If a guy is messing with your heart, he is playing games and is insecure. And always remember this: No guy has the right to touch your body. Your body is a gift and should only be touched by those you have permitted to, preferably your husband."

Amy had listened intently to her grandmother but thought the last piece of advice was a little old-fashioned. Still, it had her thinking. Was her body a gift? Was she giving it away too easily? It was confusing. She really did believe in equal rights for women. And with that, she should have total control of her body and be able to have sex when and with whomever she wanted. But again, why did it always seem to produce these feelings of emptiness and uncertainty afterward? Oh sure, in the moment, the sex was fun. Her body craved it at times. But if she was really in control, why the doubts?

Tyler's voice startled her. "Are you okay?" he said.

Amy jumped and then giggled. She had no idea he was even awake. How long had he been watching her? "Yeah, I'm fine." She hoped she had kept the insecurities currently running rampant in her mind out of her voice.

"You looked lost in thought?" Now, he looked uncertain. Did guys have doubts about all this, too? Amy wasn't sure, but she didn't think so.

Amy chuckled. "I think I am still waking up. Coffee?" Before Tyler could answer, Amy jumped out of bed and pulled on her robe. "Actually, would you like some breakfast? I make a mean waffle."

Tyler smiled in return. "Well, a guy's gotta eat. I will take you up on those waffles. Do you mind if I jump in the shower real quick?"

"Not at all," Amy said, hoping her tone sounded normal and not nervous.

Amy made her way to the kitchen and began making waffles, sausage, and scrambled eggs. She had just finished placing the food on the table when Tyler appeared in the kitchen.

"Wow! This looks like a feast. I am definitely going to have to hit the gym later," Tyler exclaimed cheerily.

Amy smiled, secretly pleased. "I do like to cook, but it is often not worth the effort for one person. That is something few people know about me."

Tyler took a sip of his coffee. Amy noticed he liked it black, not Amy's heavily filled cream-and-sugar cup. Tyler took Amy's hand, his thumb rubbing circles on the top of her hand. Amy knew that her entire body was responding to this simple gesture. It had been a long time since there was this much attraction between her and a guy. She wondered if Tyler felt the same level of attraction she did.

When Tyler spoke, his voice sounded thick. "I very much enjoyed last night," he said just above a whisper.

Amy nodded and smiled, "Me too." Her response seemed to satisfy whatever questions he had. He picked up his fork and finished his plate. Then, in a much more light-hearted tone, he said, "Well, I hope I can experience your cooking again. This is delicious!"

The compliment pleased Amy, and for a very brief moment, she wondered what it would be like to wake up with Tyler every morning and enjoy breakfast together. Amy immediately flicked the thought away. She reminded herself sternly that she was not into serious relationships. This was fun, but she knew she needed to stay casual.

Tyler stayed to help with the breakfast cleanup. Amy noticed his good manners. Once the dishes were done and either loaded into the dishwasher or put away, Tyler turned to Amy. "Well, I guess I'd better be going. I have a few things I need to get done today." Tyler grinned. "I had fun."

Amy smiled back. "I did, too."

"Can I see you again?" Tyler asked.

"I will see you tomorrow!" Amy teased.

"Oh, you are going to play hard to get. Okay, challenge accepted," Tyler said confidently. Amy was thrilled and panicked at the same time. She didn't know what Tyler meant by that. Was she worth being chased? Amy decided he was just teasing her back to keep this safe in her complicated mind.

Amy laughed and said, "I would love to go out again. But I will see you tomorrow."

"Sounds good," Tyler said casually and leaned in for a kiss that spoke anything but casual. All too soon, Tyler lifted his head, effectively breaking off the kiss, and stared into Amy's eyes. She wasn't sure what to make of the emotions she saw playing across his face. Then, he quickly stepped back from Amy.

Tyler cleared his throat. "See you tomorrow."

Amy grinned. "Yeah, see ya."

Once Tyler was safely out of the apartment, Amy was alone with her emotions. They were truly all over the place. She couldn't help smiling to herself as parts of last night played in her head. He was so cute and so charming, and they had fun together. Then, the more practical thoughts began. What will work be like now? Would it be awkward? She hoped Tyler didn't tell anyone at work about them yet. Amy wanted to maintain her professional demeanor. Hopefully, things didn't turn weird.

Amy padded back to her bedroom. She wanted to take advantage of the nice day and go for a run. The exercise may help her sort out her thoughts. Or she could focus on something else altogether.

**14**

# Amy

Amy awoke to her alarm clock. As memories of the weekend returned to her, they were accompanied by a mixture of feelings. She wanted to see Tyler but cautioned herself to stay calm. He could indeed be one of those guys who got what he wanted and disappeared. She hoped he wasn't like that, but she had no guarantees. Amy dressed carefully for work, wanting to look her best, but she also did not want to appear as if she was trying too hard. Finally satisfied with what she saw in the mirror, Amy gathered her things and rushed for the elevator, not taking time for coffee or breakfast. She knew she would regret that later. Maybe there would be bagels in the break room again.

As Amy drove to work, she tried to focus on what she needed to do today. She was still working on a big project. A prime piece of commercial property was rumored to be up for sale soon in Chicago. Since Tyler worked more with the budgeting side of the firm, they had been asked to team up and analyze the income potential of this property if the firm chose to purchase, restore, and resell. This project had great potential for the company and could translate into significant career advancement if she got it right. Truthfully, Amy was ready to complete this particular project and move to the next one. However, she knew she needed to stay mentally engaged so the partners would be pleased with her work and consider her for a promotion.

Try as she might to push Tyler out of her mind, he kept creeping back in. She couldn't deny she liked him. Something about him was thrilling yet comfortable. She hadn't heard from him since he left her apartment, except for a quick text late in the evening that said, "Hope you had a great day. Good night!" She smiled at the thought that he was thinking about her. Again, she cautioned herself to manage her expectations.

Amy slid into a parking spot and walked quickly toward the elevator. She did not love that she began and ended her day in a parking garage. She probably watched too many movies about women in peril, but she stayed on high alert until she reached her floor safely. Once there, she exited the elevator and headed for her office. She dumped her things on her desk, turned, and headed for the break room, hoping someone had already made coffee. She was in luck. The coffee was fresh and almost a full pot. Bless them. She put cream and sugar in her coffee and looked around the break room, hoping someone had brought some breakfast food with them this morning. That is, unfortunately, where her luck ended. *Oh well*, she thought. *It's my own fault. I think I might have a granola bar in my desk. If not, I'll hit the vending machine.*

Amy headed down the hallway toward her office and noticed Tyler hovering near her door, talking with another co-worker. Was he there to see her? Butterflies took flight in her stomach at the sight of Tyler. What was with her? It had been a long time since she had felt this way about a guy.

She smiled first at the coworker and then at Tyler. "Good morning!" she sang. "How are both of you?"

"Good!" Tom said. "Tyler and I were just discussing our weekend." Amy's eyes darted to Tyler to see if he had said anything about his plans, including her.

Tyler said, "Yeah. I was just telling Tom that I couldn't resist yesterday's beautiful day and ended up taking my dog, Bruno, to the park. Other than that, it was a pretty quiet weekend."

Amy let out a breath she hadn't been aware she was holding. She liked Tyler, but she didn't want other people to know they were spending time together outside of work. Amy was a private person, and very few co-workers knew about her personal life. She didn't want to start living under their scrutiny now.

Tyler smiled at her and said, "I came by to discuss the numbers in the report you sent me."

"Okay," Amy said in what she hoped was a casual tone, although the butterflies in her stomach confirmed that casualness was not at all how she felt. *How was she supposed to do this every day? What mess had she gotten herself into?* Tom took the hint and said his goodbyes, and Tyler followed Amy into her office.

Tyler smiled, sending her heart racing. "I actually have no numbers to discuss. I wanted to bring you this." He held up a plain brown paper bag, and in it was the most delicious-smelling breakfast taco. In the midst of their conversations, Amy admitted to Tyler that one of the things she most missed about Texas was the abundance of good Mexican food. Well, score a point for Tyler. He pays attention.

"Thank you," Amy said politely, not revealing how much

this simple act truly meant to her. "I skipped breakfast this morning, so this will taste really good."

"Don't mention it. It is the least I can do after the delicious breakfast you served me." Tyler's intimate tone made Amy blush immediately. As if he had successfully received the response he wanted, he said, "Well, I guess I should get back to work."

Amy smiled, "Me too. Thanks again," she said, lifting the bag slightly.

After Tyler left, his scent lingered in her office, reminding her of the intimacies they had shared. Amy pushed her traitorous thoughts out of her mind. She opened the bag and pulled out the taco wrapped in aluminum foil. She folded back the foil and took a bite. *Mmmmmm ... so good.* She made a mental note to ask Tyler where he purchased this. She had not been able to find tacos this tasty in Chicago. She quickly finished the taco, drank a gulp of her coffee, took a deep breath, and dove into her work.

After a couple of hours, Amy stood and stretched out her back. She looked down at her coffee cup and contemplated getting a refill. She finally decided that, yes, she wanted another cup. Another cup should get her through lunch. She took her cup and started the walk to the break room.

All of a sudden, Sheila was beside her. "Hey, Amy!"

"Hi, Sheila!" Sheila had always been friendly to Amy. However, Amy knew Sheila could be a bit of a gossip, so Amy found herself on guard around her.

"I saw Tyler hanging out by your door this morning. Rumor is he might have a crush on you." Sheila nudged Amy playfully.

Amy thought. *Oh no. You are getting nothing out of me.* This is precisely what Amy did not want to happen. She did not want to be a part of "water cooler" talk. Some people never grow out of high school gossip, and Sheila seemed to be one of those people.

Amy, keeping her voice light, said, "No more than any other girl in this office."

Sheila said, "Are you suggesting Tyler is a player?"

"Not at all," Amy said, chuckling. At least, she certainly hoped not. To Sheila, Amy continued, "He is friendly to everyone."

"Oh, okay. If you say so," Sheila nudged Amy again. Sheila seemed disappointed that she could not get any more dirt out of Amy. However, before Sheila could ask any more questions, Amy asked Sheila about her weekend. Sheila was happy to discuss all the details about the new guy she had met on a dating app and seemed to forget all about Amy and Tyler.

Amy listened politely and asked questions at appropriate times. She refilled her coffee cup, and when Sheila took a breath, Amy said, "Well, I'd better get back to work."

Sheila nodded but didn't protest Amy's departure. Tom had just walked into the break room, and Sheila had a new person to overshare her weekend with.

When Amy got back to her office, she thought about her conversation with Sheila. Again, she chastised herself for getting involved with someone she worked with. Well, she couldn't take it back now. She had to decide, though. If Tyler was interested, would she continue to pursue the relationship, or did she cut it off now? She knew the answer before the question was fully formulated in her mind. Tyler made her feel special. He seemed to care about her genuinely. If he were interested, she would continue to pursue it.

Amy had just resettled in her chair when the object of her thoughts appeared in her doorway. "Hey!" Tyler said.

"Hey!" she responded. The butterflies took flight once again in her stomach.

"Would you like to grab some dinner after work?"

"Sure," Amy said and smiled.

"Great!" Tyler said. "Start thinking about where you want to go."

"Okay," Amy said. "Oh, and thank you for the taco. It was delicious! You saved a girl from starvation this morning."

"You are very welcome," he said and was gone as quickly as he appeared.

So many thoughts inundated Amy's brain all at once. What was Tyler really thinking? Did he like her as much as she liked him? Maybe tonight's dinner was to tell her that he just wanted to be friends. No, he wouldn't take her to dinner for that. Maybe he did like her. Perhaps he did see this going somewhere. Suddenly, Amy pictured her life with Tyler, walking down the aisle in a white dress, buying a small home with beautiful trees on the property, and a child with the same dark hair as Tyler.

Amy stopped herself. What was she doing? She never did this with guys, but she made fun of girls who did. She wasn't even sure she wanted to get married, and children—that was definitely not in her plan right now. Where was this coming from? Amy shook her head as if to clear it. *Whatever*, Amy thought, and dove back into her work.

The rest of the day passed quickly, and Tyler was standing back at her office door before she knew it. "Hey!" he said, startling Amy, who was deep in thought. "Didn't you hear the bell? School is over. Put your pencils down, gather your belongings, and head to the nearest exit."

Amy laughed, "Okay, okay. I probably am at a good stopping point." Amy began to gather her things.

While Amy packed her bag, Tyler said, "You can totally say no, but I have an idea."

Amy looked up and smiled. "No, I am not ready for skydiving. It is a difficult activity to accomplish while eating."

"Okay," Tyler laughed. "That's fair. Maybe next time."

"I'm just kidding," Amy said, secretly pleased he would spar with her. Some guys were not sure what to do with her sense of humor. "What is your idea?" She continued to gather her things.

"It may not be as thrilling as skydiving, but there is a movie theater that serves food. They're showing *Casablanca* tonight. Interested?"

Amy had heard about that theater and was eager to try it. Apparently, you could lounge in comfortable chairs and eat good food.

"Sure! I think I can eat and watch a movie at the same time." What Amy did not reveal is that *Casablanca* was her mom's favorite, and Amy had practically memorized the movie. Instead, Amy said, "I think that would be fun. What time does the movie start?"

"8:00," Tyler said.

Amy nodded. "I think I will run home and change then. Can I meet you there?"

"I will run home and change as well, and then swing by and pick you up if that is okay? Unless you don't trust my driving.

I can print out my driving record for you."

"That won't be necessary," Amy deadpanned. "I have already run a background check on you. You seem clean."

"Oh, good. That guy I paid off to clear my record did his job," Tyler chuckled.

"Pick you up at 7:15?"

"Sounds good," said Amy. "See you in a little bit."

Amy mentally ran through the options in her closet as she drove home. She wanted to wear something cute but comfortable. Thankfully, she did laundry this weekend, so everything was clean. Once home, she ran toward her closet, knowing she didn't have much time. She pulled out her most comfortable jeans and a blue sweater she knew went with her eyes. She quickly pulled off her skirt and button-down blouse, then put on her jeans and sweater. She ran to the bathroom to see if her hair and makeup needed touching up. She ran her straightener back over her hair to smooth it out and put on a light coat of mascara. A little touch of powder and some lip gloss, and she was ready to go.

Her phone buzzed, telling her Tyler was waiting out front. She grabbed her keys and purse and headed for the door. Once settled into Tyler's car, she smiled at him. "You look amazing," he said. Amy blushed and said a quiet thank you. He smiled, and away they went.

The movie theater was different from any other she had experienced. They sat in comfortable reclining chairs. The chairs were grouped for privacy for couples on the sides of the theater and longer rows in the middle for larger parties. Tyler and Amy found their seats against the wall and perused the menu. A waiter came to their seats. They each ordered a glass of wine.

Amy chose pasta, and Tyler chose a burger. After their meals were done, they settled into their chairs to watch the movie. At some point, Tyler reached for Amy's hand, and she enjoyed the feel of her hand in his.

As Tyler drove Amy home, she had a hard time concentrating on what Tyler was saying. She was trying to decide whether to invite Tyler in. She didn't want to seem too eager, but the truth was, she was eager. She liked Tyler, which was new territory for her. When he pulled up to her building, she was still undecided.

"Thank you, Tyler! I had a wonderful time."

"You're welcome, Amy," he said with a smile. Then he reached over and cupped her neck in his hand. A tingle ran all the way down her spine, and she could feel her body leaning into him. Tyler touched his lips to hers gently at first. Then he pressed his lips firmly to her mouth. They both lost themselves in the passion of the kiss, awakening more desire.

When they finally came up for air, Amy whispered, "Do you want to come inside?" Her voice still sounded husky.

Tyler whispered, matching her tone, "I can't tonight. I'm sorry. I still have some work to do before I go to bed. Also, my roommates are gone tonight, so I need to go let my dog out."

Amy felt as if cold water had been thrown into her face. "Oh, no worries." She tried to cover her disappointment. "I will see you tomorrow then," she said a bit too cheerily.

Tyler either pretended not to notice the change in Amy or did not notice it.

"Yes, see you tomorrow," he said.

Amy tried to tamp down the disappointment all the way to her apartment. She told herself it didn't have to do with her, but that he really did have work to do. He really did have to take care of his dog. But isn't this the stage where he should always want her? Was his interest already waning? I mean, that kiss was unforgettable, and he just said no after that kiss. Amy reasoned with herself. Was she reading too much into things? She had always kept things casual before and honestly did not invest in relationships with feelings. She had to try to keep her feelings at bay. Yes, they had slept together, but maybe Tyler wanted to keep it casual as well. After all, they did work together.

These questions and more ran around Amy's head as she changed into her pajamas, brushed her teeth, and took off her makeup. By the time she was ready to settle into bed, she was mentally exhausted. She decided to put it all out of her head. She picked up her phone, looking for a distraction. She opened social media and began to scroll. Then, before she could stop herself, she found herself on Tyler's page. She began to scroll through his feed. Pictures of his family, his dog, sporting events, and then a picture of a beautiful blonde woman. This particular picture was taken over a year ago. As Amy continued her scroll, she realized this was an ex-girlfriend; as best as she could tell from social media, they had dated for almost two years. Two years! That seemed like a lifetime to Amy.

Now, Amy was more confused than ever. How had this relationship ended? Who broke up with whom? What was Tyler looking for? If he had come out of a two-year relationship, maybe he really was looking for something casual. However, maybe he was one of those guys who only dated girls seriously. Was he looking for his next serious girlfriend? Both of those answers scared Amy. She liked Tyler, but she still wanted to remain casual with him. Amy didn't think she was ready to date someone seriously. She wasn't sure she would ever be ready. And if Tyler was ready to date someone seriously, could she break her rule for him, or should she move on before anyone got hurt?

Amy sighed, plugged her phone in, switched off her lamp, and tried to go to sleep. The last time she looked at the clock, it read 3:47. "Ugh," she groaned to herself. She was going to be exhausted tomorrow. She tried counting sheep, redecorating her apartment in her mind, and recounting episodes of her favorite reality TV show. Nothing seemed to work. This was going to be a long day if she didn't get to sleep. She rolled over and tried her best to relax, letting sleep overtake her.

**15**

# *Melissa*

Melissa loved the sound of the chirping birds that filled the air this time of day. That, coupled with the beauty of her backyard, made this Melissa's favorite spot to read and pray. She clutched her cup of coffee in one hand and held her place in the Bible nestled in her lap with the other. Melissa treasured these times, first thing in the morning, before her kids were awake. The summer was in full swing. Melissa could tell this was going to be another scorcher. She made up her mind that it would be a day best spent at the pool. She knew her kids would agree.

Melissa loved having her kids home for the summer. She enjoyed being set free from the day-to-day demands of the school year and after-school activities. She also enjoyed the extra time with her kids that summer allowed. She was determined to soak it up before the flurry of back-to-school shopping and routines began again.

Melissa had been reading in Jeremiah about how God assured Jeremiah that He had formed him in the womb and knew him better than anyone else. Melissa loved this particular verse. It reminded her that God was a deeply personal God who knew all about her. She also took comfort in the fact that

God had formed and fashioned her children. They all held their own beautiful talents and giftings, and Melissa treasured the time to pray into those things for her children. She prayed over her kids and their future each morning, desiring that none of them would fall away from God as she had done. She hoped they would always walk closely with the Lord.

Once again this morning, she found herself thinking of her beautiful daughter in heaven, which led her to think of Amy. For various reasons, she found herself praying for Amy more than usual. She wasn't sure about the day-to-day details that went on in Amy's life anymore, but she felt, maybe more than ever, that God wanted to move in Amy's life. Melissa prayed Amy would have a tender heart and ears to hear God's love for her. Melissa knew most of Amy's problems stemmed from the bitterness she felt first towards God for not healing her mom and then towards her dad for the way he treated Amy and her sister after their mom's death.

Melissa knew Amy could not see how the bitterness she had become so intimate with was actually holding her back in life rather than moving her forward. Melissa knew a thing or two about bitterness as well. After her miscarriage, she had every opportunity to allow bitterness to take over.

Melissa allowed her mind to travel back to that time period. The backyard faded away as the memories came.

Blake had come home to a beautifully set table and scrumptious smells coming from the kitchen. He walked in and smiled at Melissa.

"What is all the fuss? I didn't miss an anniversary, did I?" Melissa smiled at his question.

"I did! I missed something. Okay, it is not our wedding anniversary. It is not your birthday. Is it the anniversary of our first date or something?" Melissa chuckled again, wanting to put an end to his distress but also enjoying teasing him a little.

Most women remember more than men do, but Melissa had an unusually clear memory. She could remember what she was wearing the day she first laid eyes on Blake. She could remember what Blake wore the first time he picked her up for church. Melissa's memory sometimes struck fear into Blake. He wanted to remember the things that were important to Melissa.

"Relax," Melissa finally said. "There are no anniversaries. Although this may turn into one, so remember it!" Melissa winked at Blake, and she could see him visibly relaxed. He shrugged off his jacket and tossed it on the chair.

Melissa checked the oven for the baked potatoes. They were just about perfect. She gave the salad one last toss and put it on the table.

Blake said, "What can I do to help?"

"I have this all under control for the moment. Why don't you go change, and then we can eat?"

Blake smiled and reached over to kiss Melissa lightly on the lips. He quickly changed and rejoined Melissa in the kitchen. Their small apartment did not have much space in the kitchen, but it worked for the two of them. They had begun discussing buying a house. They had the finances set aside for it, but they had yet to be in a hurry. They enjoyed apartment living. The location was close to any restaurant they could want, and they enjoyed the exercise room and pool. But Blake said he knew they needed to get serious about house hunting financially. Besides, they wanted to start a family in the next few years, and this apartment would definitely not be big enough.

Blake helped Melissa carry the rest of the dinner to the table. It looked and smelled so good. Blake's stomach growled.

Melissa smiled and said, "Well, I guess we should pray. Someone is hungry."

Blake laughed and grasped Melissa's hand. He prayed a blessing over the food and them as a couple. When he said amen, he quickly helped himself to a potato.

"So," Blake said, looking up from buttering his potato. "What is the special occasion? If I haven't missed an anniversary, what is going on?"

Melissa reached into her pocket and put something beside Blake's hand. He put a forkful of steak in his mouth, chewed, and then nearly choked as he fully grasped what was sitting next to his hand. It was a pregnancy test! And it was positive! He quickly grabbed his glass of water and took a healthy swig, trying to wash down what seemed to be stuck in his throat.

"I am going to be a dad?" he whispered. Melissa nodded, unsure of how Blake was feeling. "I am going to be a dad?" Blake said louder. Melissa nodded as tears sprang to her eyes. Blake stood up, shoving his chair back. "I'm going to be a dad!" he shouted joyfully. "And you are going to be a mom!" He grabbed Melissa and pulled her to her feet.

"That's usually how it works," she said, laughing. He crushed her to him, laughing and crying at the same time.

Then, he suddenly stepped back. "How far along?" he asked.

Melissa said, "I have no idea. I am as surprised as you are."

"Well," Blake said teasingly. "You can't be that surprised. You took a pregnancy test."

"True," Melissa conceded.

Blake asked, "What made you take one?"

Melissa smiled. "I just didn't feel like myself. I was tired and a little nauseous in the mornings, and suddenly I was like, what if? So I picked one up on the way home from work and here we are."

"Oh, my goodness. We have so much to do! We need to buy a house, tell our parents, buy diapers, and get something for it to sleep in . . ."

"Whoa, Blake." Melissa cut him off laughing. "One step at a time. We should have at least eight months and maybe more to prepare for the baby. I won't know until I go to the doctor."

"Well, when will you do that?" Blake asked.

Melissa chuckled again. "I don't know. I will need to call them tomorrow. So, let's enjoy this meal and talk about everything you want to do."

Blake and Melissa spent the evening dreaming and planning for the future. They talked about all the what-ifs. What if it were a girl? What if it were a boy? Did they have names? Where in the city did they want to buy a house? Would Melissa keep working? So many decisions, but mostly, they enjoyed dreaming about the future. It was funny how they were perfectly happy being the two of them, but now they were ecstatic that someone was on their way to join their family.

The next morning, Melissa called the doctor. The nurse said they would see her in three weeks to confirm the pregnancy and listen to the heartbeat. Three weeks! It seemed like a long time to wait, but Melissa made the appointment. She and Blake discussed waiting to tell their parents until after the first doctor's appointment. They went back and forth about it and decided to stay quiet.

The three weeks went by fairly quickly. Melissa was so excited about the appointment but only slightly nervous. She couldn't wait to hear their baby's heartbeat. She and Blake held hands while the doctor fired up the sonogram machine. The doctor placed the instrument on Melissa's belly while speaking to her. She told her she could definitely see something in Melissa's womb. But then, the doctor became eerily quiet as she moved the instrument around. She finally shut the machine off and looked at Melissa and Blake. "I am so sorry," she said. "You are pregnant, but unfortunately, the baby does not have a heartbeat."

Tears sprang to Melissa's eyes. "Are you saying my baby is dead?"

"Well," the doctor said, "that is one way to say it. We have no way of knowing if your baby ever had a heartbeat. It just isn't a viable pregnancy. I am so sorry. Let's discuss what we need to do now."

The doctor went over the options for helping Melissa's body expel the baby from her womb. All of which sounded awful. The doctor touched Melissa's shoulder. "Unfortunately, these things happen. However, it does not mean you and Blake should not try again. You should. Just give your body some time to heal." Melissa nodded. "I'm going to leave so you can get dressed. You and Blake take as long as you need, and then let's schedule a follow-up appointment to ensure your body is healing properly." Melissa nodded again.

The second the door closed behind the doctor, Melissa burst into tears. Blake held her as she cried and found some tissue for her to blow her nose. "Why did this happen?" Melissa cried. "Doesn't God want us to have a baby? Does He not trust us to be parents? Do you think He is displeased with me?"

Blake held Melissa as she cried. "Melissa, I don't have answers for you, but these are all the wrong questions."

Melissa tilted her head, and anger rose in her. What did he mean by saying these were all the wrong questions? If she had these questions, doesn't that mean her questions need to be answered? Before she lashed out at Blake, she remembered he had lost a baby, too. He was hurting, too. She climbed off the table and dressed. She suddenly wanted to leave the doctor's office as quickly as possible.

Dressed again, she and Blake walked out the door to face the doctor. The doctor smiled kindly and said again, "I am so sorry. Please check in at the front and schedule a follow-up appointment. I want to make sure you heal properly." She smiled reassuringly and headed down the hall, presumably to her next patient. Melissa suddenly wondered how many women walked into this office daily full of hope and joy and left with crushing disappointment.

Melissa and Blake obediently scheduled their next appointment and then headed out the door to the parking lot. The change in temperature from the air-conditioned office to the blazing August air shocked Melissa's body. She glared up at the sun and turned to find their car. Once in the car, Blake turned to Melissa. "Would you like to go eat, or would you rather go home?"

Melissa said, "I just want to go home." She didn't think she could bear to be in public right now. She was carrying a dead human being inside of her, and the shock had not worn off.

Blake nodded in agreement and started the car. On the drive home, Blake must have picked up on Melissa's need for silence. He sat quietly, navigating the car as Melissa stared out the window. Once they got home and Melissa was safe inside her apartment, she let the tears fall again. Blake sat on the couch with her and held her as she cried. He cried a little with her as well. When Melissa regained control, she turned to Blake and said, "Why did you say in the doctor's office that I was asking all the wrong questions?"

Blake took a deep breath. "Do you believe God loves you?"

"Yes, of course I do," she said a bit incredulously, wondering where this was going.

"Do you believe He only wants good things for you?" Blake continued.

"I think so," she said.

"Well, if He loves you and He gives good gifts like a loving Father does, why would He give us a child and then snatch that gift from us?"

Melissa shrugged. "I don't know, but if God is in control, why did He allow this to happen?"

"God is definitely on the throne, but we live in a fallen world. We are not going to have answers to the why in all that happens, but I do know God is not the author of death and destruction. Satan is. So my point about your questions is I think you are giving God credit for the things that sin and destruction do," Blake said gently.

Blake continued, "I know God loves us and He loves our baby. Our baby went back with Jesus before we could meet him or raise him."

"Or her," Melissa interjected.

"Or her," Blake smiled. "But I do know he or she is safe with Jesus, and Jesus will be faithful to walk us through our grief. I also know Jesus is not scared of our grief and will comfort us in this."

Melissa sighed and sat back. "How could I already love something so much without ever having met him or her?"

Blake said, "I don't know, but I do think that is how God designed it. I also know we will get to meet him or her in Heaven."

Melissa nodded. "I hadn't thought about that."


Melissa was not prepared to walk through the grieving process of a miscarriage. Part of her was relieved she hadn't told anyone she was pregnant because she didn't have to tell anyone she wasn't pregnant anymore. On the other hand, no one knowing she was pregnant meant no one knew she was grieving for a child she had never met. It was a weird line to walk. Melissa spent a lot of time reflecting on who God was to her and praying that she would not be fearful to get pregnant again. She prayed that once she became pregnant again, the fear of losing another child would not overtake the excitement of the pregnancy.

Once Melissa's body healed, she and Blake began trying again. Melissa was determined not to make their sex life about getting pregnant. She had seen women do that with their husbands, and while it would be tempting to lapse into that way of thinking, Melissa wanted to maintain her authentic intimacy with Blake as much as possible. Still, she couldn't help but feel what if this was it, after each time they were intimate.

Then, one day, she just knew. She knew her body felt different. So, once again, she stopped on the way home from work and picked up a pregnancy test. The test confirmed what she already knew. She was pregnant. Melissa was a mix of emotions. She was thrilled, overjoyed, excited, hopeful, and scared. Really, really scared. She debated briefly whether or not she should tell Blake yet, and then decided quickly she was thinking stupid. He was the dad and deserved to know as soon as she did. This time, she did not cook a fancy meal. She ordered pizza. Blake came home, and Melissa said she didn't feel like cooking that night. Blake was fine with that.

Then he looked at her, really looked at her. "I know you have been tired lately." He smiled at her with reassurance. "What's going on, honey? You seem apprehensive."

"Well, Blake . . . we are pregnant." Blake hugged Melissa.

"It's going to be okay," he said. "No matter what happens, it is going to be okay."

It turned out Blake was right. The doctor confirmed they were indeed pregnant, and eight months later, their first child was born! Lily! Lily was everything they named her. She was sweet and beautiful, and all who knew her admired her. She was truly a blessing.

A year later, Blake and Melissa found themselves pregnant once again. This time it was a boy! Ryan was born and quickly became their little firecracker. He was definitely all boy. Two years later, they welcomed little Jasmine. She was precious, and the other two kids loved her. Blake and Melissa decided their family was complete. And although she and Blake rarely discussed the miscarriage, Melissa knew their family would never be complete on this Earth. They had a child in heaven.

# 16

# *Amy*

The chirping from Amy's alarm eventually awakened her. She groaned and rolled over to shut off the intrusive sound. This was going to be a long day functioning on so little sleep. She stumbled to the kitchen, knowing she needed coffee to even think of getting ready for her day. She turned on her coffee maker, high-fiving herself mentally for setting up the machine last night. Amy yawned and waited until about a full cup brewed, and then poured her coffee into her favorite mug. She replaced the pot quickly so the coffee could continue brewing. She turned toward the bathroom. After her shower, she towel-dried the excess moisture from her hair, already feeling a bit more awake. Amy examined herself in the mirror. Her eyes were a little swollen from lack of sleep, but nothing a little concealer couldn't hide. She continued to down the coffee as she got ready for work and made herself a fresh cup of coffee to go.

When Amy arrived at work, the brain fog had receded, and she was mentally going through the day's checklist. Amy wasn't sure about facing Tyler, though. She was still thrown off by last night. They had had a great time at the movie, but his rejection of her invitation to come in still stung. She didn't want to stop and analyze why it stung.

She also revisited what she found on social media. Amy knew many people brought up past relationships when they were getting to know each other, as a way to gauge how people felt about relationships. Amy was generally not one of those people. She did not like discussing her past relationships, so she often avoided the conversation in hopes the guy would not bring it up. Most of the time, it worked. And so far, with Tyler, it had. They had not discussed past relationships at all. But now that she had done a deep dive into his social media, she was left with so many unanswered questions about where he stood. Maybe she should have left well enough alone and not gone down that particular rabbit hole. Maybe ignorance was bliss, as the saying went.

Amy arrived at the parking garage elevator to find Brooke scrolling through her email while waiting for the doors to open. "Good morning!"

Brooke returned Amy's smile, "Good morning!" Brooke echoed, snapping off her phone and giving Amy her full attention.

"I haven't seen you in the last couple of days. How's it going?"

"Oh, it's going," said Brooke with a half smile.

Amy chuckled. "Still in the meeting marathon?"

Brooke rolled her eyes. "Yes, but I think this is the last week, and then this phase of the project will be over. I am looking forward to quiet days in my office again."

The elevator doors swooshed open, and Amy and Brooke stepped in. Brooke pushed the number for their floor, and the doors swished closed.

Brooke was mainly a positive person. Even when she was annoyed, she could find the silver lining. Amy actually liked that about Brooke. She felt it balanced out her own cynical way of seeing the world.

"How are you this morning?" Brooke asked.

Amy smiled ruefully. "I'm great. It's normal to function on a couple of hours of sleep, right?"

Brooke groaned. "Oh, I hate nights like that. Too much caffeine?"

Amy agreed quickly, so she wouldn't have to explain to Brooke why she couldn't sleep.

"Oh, gosh!" Brooke suddenly exclaimed, "I am a terrible friend! I am so sorry. I have been meaning to text or call you and ask how your date with Tyler went the other night. I guess I really have been caught up feeling sorry for myself in these meeting marathons." Brooke chuckled at herself. "Soooo, how did it go?"

Amy smiled warmly at Brooke. She felt Brooke was being way too hard on herself. Amy didn't think Brooke could be a bad friend if she tried. "It went well," Amy said, not being able to help the grin that spread across her face.

"Yes, if that silly grin on your face is any indication, it went well!"

"Yeah," Amy continued, knowing a blush was creeping up her neck. "We went out to eat at a very nice restaurant and then went to the theater. It was a lovely evening."

Amy purposely left out the part about Tyler spending the night. While Brooke would not say anything judgmental, she also knew that she would disapprove. In conversations with Brooke, Amy had come to understand that she and Brooke had very different views on relationships and sex. Amy knew it was important to Brooke to save herself for marriage and wanted a man who shared her religious beliefs. Amy had, on occasion, joked with Brooke that she was missing out. Sex was fun, felt good, and was a natural part of being an adult. Brooke would just smile and say, "Yes, and all of that will be amazing with the person I decide to spend the rest of my life with." Amy would just shrug. To each their own, she decided.

The elevator dinged, and the doors swished open. The two women exited the elevator and walked together toward Amy's office.

"How has it been with Tyler since your date?" Brooke asked. "I know you were afraid it would get awkward at work."

"It's been good. We actually went and saw a movie last night."

"Oh, fun! It sounds like he's interested," Brooke said with a grin. "How do you feel?"

Amy entered her small but functional office, and Brooke followed her in. "I like him. He is definitely fun to hang out with and easy on the eyes." Amy chuckled. "I am trying not to overthink things at this stage. I just want something fun, and I think he does too. I guess I want to be extra cautious because we still have to work together."

"That makes sense," Brooke said, nodding. "Don't want to make things awkward at work."

"No," said Amy. "And I don't want to be the talk of the office. I already had to head Sheila off at the pass."

Brooke laughed and rolled her eyes. "Oh yes, Sheila. The self-appointed town crier."

Amy smiled and said, "I actually used the trick you taught

me."

Brooke raised her eyebrows in question. "Oh yeah, what trick is that?"

"I got her to talk about herself, and all thoughts of me flew out of her head," Amy said.

"I taught you that? I thought that was common knowledge," Brooke said, laughing.

"You are a woman of many talents," said Amy, bowing. "I am eager to learn more."

"Okay, before you have Yoda t-shirts printed, I am going to my office," Brooke said teasingly. "See ya later."

As Brooke took her leave, Amy chuckled as she took a quick glance at her calendar. She needed to get her thoughts organized for the day. She muttered an expletive under her breath as she realized she had forgotten she had a meeting first thing this morning. Her boss would expect an update on the project she was working on. She was actually over-prepared for the meeting, but frustrated when she realized Tyler would be there as well. Amy was still trying to process last night and had hoped to avoid him today—no such luck.

Oh well, Amy thought to herself. There was nothing she could do about it. She opened her laptop and mentally clicked into work mode. The charts and graphs she prepared for the meeting were precisely as she had left them. After refamiliarizing herself with the data, she was satisfied that she could confidently discuss and answer questions about her charts and graphs. Amy decided she should get one more cup of coffee before the meeting.

Amy walked into the break room and straight into Tyler.

"I'm sorry. Didn't mean to run into you like that," Amy

said, her voice sounding stilted in her own ears.

"No worries," Tyler said in his easy manner. "Great minds think alike," he said, tipping his already-filled coffee mug in her direction.

"Seems so," she said with a smile. She made her cup of coffee with her usual amounts of cream and sugar.

Tyler chuckled. "Do you even have any coffee in that cup, or is it just cream and sugar?"

Amy laughed good-naturedly, secretly pleased he noticed. "I love cream and sugar, and if you add a little coffee to it, you get the added benefit of caffeine."

"I see," Tyler said. "How can you go wrong with that type of logic?"

"Exactly," said Amy. "I am glad you understand."

"Well, now I know how you like your coffee so that I can bring you some in the future."

Color worked its way up Amy's cheeks. Future? So, he did think this relationship was going somewhere? *Chill, Amy*, she told herself. *He is just discussing coffee.*

Tyler stared at Amy for what seemed like an eternity, and then his signature slow grin made its way across his face. "Okay. Well, I am going to get my laptop for the meeting. See ya in there."

"Yeah, see ya in there," Amy said weakly.

Amy took a deep, steadying breath. Maybe it was good that she saw Tyler before the meeting. It would hopefully make the meeting less awkward. Amy strode to her office, gathered her laptop and notepad, and headed to the conference room. The room was already half full, and Tyler was already seated, engaged in a conversation with another coworker. Amy chose a seat far from Tyler and opened her laptop.

Amy's boss, Mr. Turner, entered the room in his typical take-charge manner. He seemed eager to get the meeting started right away. Everyone quieted instinctively, and Mr. Turner took control of the meeting. His secretary, a blonde bombshell of a woman who was rumored to be hired for more than her typing skills, sat dutifully in the corner, taking minutes of the meeting.

"Good Morning," Mr. Turner began. "I scheduled this meeting to see where we are on this project. As you know, this could be a big deal for our company, and I want to make sure we have all the information necessary before moving forward. With that being said, Amy, I would like for you to begin. Please share with us your findings thus far, and then we can discuss next steps."

Amy had already hooked her laptop to the projector. She rose with confidence and went to the front of the room, where she could be near the screen. Amy knew she was good at her job, and she enjoyed the times she could show Mr. Turner that she did know what she was doing. She looked around the room with a smile and forced herself to look at Tyler as long as she looked at everyone else. She did not want this to be weird, but she also did not want to lose her concentration and look like a fool in front of her boss. She went through her slides and graphs, and fielded questions from Mr. Turner. Amy felt pleased when she finished her portion of the presentation, and her boss seemed satisfied with what he had seen so far.

"Okay, Tyler, please show us what you have," Mr. Turner said.

Amy tried to focus on the screen where Tyler shared his

slides so she did not have to look directly at him. She concentrated on what he was saying and did not let her mind wander. After all, she needed to hear what he had to say to finish her part of the project. When Tyler finished, Mr. Turner said, "Nice work, Tyler. You and Amy have done a great job. Can you both have this completed by Friday?"

*Friday!* Amy thought. She thought they would have until at least Monday. Looks like some late nights were in her future. Amy smiled—what she hoped was a confident smile—at her boss and echoed Tyler's, "No problem." She could tell by the look on Tyler's face that he also thought this would take some late nights.

The meeting was adjourned after a few updates on smaller projects, and everyone gathered their belongings to return to their work areas. As Amy walked towards her office, she noticed Tyler already hovering near the door. She hoped her concealer was still covering her dark circles. She did not want to reveal that she had difficulty sleeping last night.

"Hey," Tyler greeted her.

"Hey!" Amy returned.

"So, Friday?" Tyler said.

"Yeah," Amy said with a sigh.

"Okay," Tyler said. "I think at this point, we need to work together to finish. That way, we are not waiting on the other to finish a piece to keep going."

He was right, Amy thought. But she was not sure how she felt about being in such close quarters with Tyler in a work environment. She felt trepidation but was thrilled at the same time. *Why did she decide to go out with a guy at work?* She asked herself for what seemed like the hundredth time. This was going to get complicated, and it was her fault. At this point, she would need to make the best of the situation. Her career was important to her.

Tyler noticed the multiple expressions that crossed Amy's face. "Will that be okay?" Tyler asked uncertainly. "I promise not to get in your way."

Amy did not realize she had been standing there so long, staring. "Oh yeah, I'm sorry. Yes, I think we should work together. It makes sense."

"Good!" Tyler said. "Let me go to my office and grab my laptop. I will be right back."

"Sounds good," Amy said in what she hoped was a professional voice.

Amy glanced at her watch. It was only 10:15. It might be a long day. She sighed again and entered her office. She put down her laptop and turned on her computer to bring up the necessary files. Tyler came in with some sparkling water and a big smile. He made himself comfortable at the small table in Amy's office. They both fell quiet as they began to pull up the things they would need on their computers.

The time passed surprisingly fast. At 1:00, Tyler asked Amy if she just wanted to get some lunch in the cafeteria.

"Sure," Amy said.

"Why don't you tell me what you want, and I will run down and get it. Unless you need a break," Tyler offered.

Amy smiled at his thoughtfulness and then said, "You know what? I will go with you. I have been in this chair probably way too long."

They walked to the cafeteria, discussing parts of their project. Stretching her legs felt good, and Amy hoped this would also help clear her head. The smells of the cafeteria assaulted Amy's senses before they made it there. She followed Tyler to the line and debated about what she wanted. A hamburger and French fries sounded great, but she knew they would also make her sleepy. She opted for the Cobb salad instead.

"Do you just want to get it and head back upstairs?" Tyler asked.

"That sounds good."

They each paid for their meals—a Cobb salad for Amy and a Philly cheesesteak for Tyler.

The conversation was light as they rode the elevator to their floor. Back in Amy's office, they settled in with their meals and both went back to staring at their computer screens. Amy quickly became engrossed in what she was doing and absently ate her salad while she worked. At one point, one of her bites fell off her fork onto her keyboard. Amy quickly reached for a napkin to clean up the mess. She glanced up to find Tyler staring at her. Her heart flipped.

"What?" Amy said. "Do I have something on my face?" Amy's cheeks began heating as a blush began working up her face. She reached into her desk for the small mirror she kept there. Nothing on her face or in her teeth. She put the mirror back in her drawer and looked back up at Tyler, who was now chuckling. "What?" Amy said, beginning to chuckle.

"You're adorable," Tyler said.

"Thank you?" Amy said.

"Yes, Amy, I meant it as a compliment. I have noticed you struggle with compliments," Tyler stated matter-of-factly.

Warning bells went off in Amy's head. Amy knew why she likely struggled with compliments and that it probably stemmed from her childhood. She definitely did not want to discuss her childhood in detail with Tyler at this stage in the relationship. Maybe not ever.

"Thank you," Amy tried again.

Tyler smiled, and Amy could see he had chosen to let it go for now.

"I need to go back to my office and grab a few more things. Can I bring you anything?"

"No, I think I am good," Amy said, "But thank you."

As Tyler walked away, Amy considered what he said. Did she have trouble with compliments? Probably. As a child, she often felt inadequate. She was not the mom her sister needed her to be, and apparently not the daughter her dad required either, since alcohol was his best friend. Amy shook herself out of her thoughts and told herself to refocus.

She bent over her computer and became so engrossed that she didn't realize Tyler had come back into her office until she finally heard him say her name. She glanced up, understanding dawning on her. He had said her name several times. A blush crept up her neck. Why did he have this effect on her? Would she ever stop blushing around him? Anyone else, she would have shrugged it off.

"I'm sorry," Amy said. "I didn't hear you come back in."

"Clearly," Tyler chuckled. "I know you said you didn't need anything, but I brought you some water."

"Thank you," Amy said. She was struck again by his thoughtfulness.

Around dinner time, Tyler asked Amy what she wanted to eat. Amy chuckled to herself. He obviously had a feeding schedule, which she guessed most guys did.

"Do you want to call it a day, or do you want to grab dinner and keep going?" he asked her.

Truthfully, Amy was exhausted. It had been a very long day, and despite her caffeine intake, Amy's short night was catching up to her. However, they had hit a good stride; she would rather finish earlier than later. Also, they would need to practice their presentation once the project was finally finished.

"Let's grab dinner," Amy said decisively. "But I am afraid to leave the office. My car will just find its way home. Do you want to order in?"

Tyler smiled. "Just what I was thinking. What sounds good? Chinese, pizza, chicken, burgers?"

They settled on Chinese since there was a great little place around the corner that would deliver. Once the food arrived, Amy sat back in her chair and sighed. The only thing keeping her from rubbing her eyes was her makeup. She closed them for a second and then yanked them open when she realized how easily she could fall asleep. She finished her food and downed a bottle of water.

Tyler looked her way. He stood and crossed the room. He went around behind her chair and put his hands on her shoulders. Electricity sparked through her body at the touch of his hands. Desire arched through her immediately, and she worked to tamp it down. They were at work, she scolded herself. Besides, even though they had been intimate, and boy did her body remember, she still did not know where she and Tyler stood after last night. And with what she found on social media, she did not know where Tyler's head was.

She looked up through her office window, confirming that the office had emptied. Tyler followed her gaze, "Don't worry," he said. "The only people still here are the janitors."

He began working her shoulders with his strong and sturdy hands. She closed her eyes and let out a sigh of relief. Tyler chuckled. "I will take that as a compliment."

Amy said, "Please do."

He continued to work his hands over her shoulders and down her upper back, gently moving her hair to one shoulder and starting on her neck. Amy's relief turned to awareness, which in turn became an electric pulse coursing through her.

Finally, Tyler stopped, and Amy didn't know if she was relieved or disappointed. She immediately missed the feel of his hands on her body. She smiled, what she hoped was a teasing smile, and said, "You are a man of many talents. Where did you learn to do that?"

"Oh, I actually considered massage therapy school for a while."

Amy studied him to see if he was joking. "Really? Culinary school, food critic, and now massage therapy. What drew you to accounting and now real estate?"

Tyler laughed. "My parents were not sure massage therapy could be a legitimate career. I think they thought I would end up running some sort of brothel, and I could not convince them that masseuses made really good money and also helped people. So, I decided on a different career path."

Amy tipped her head to one side. "So you didn't choose a career because you thought it would disappoint your parents?"

"Yes," Tyler admitted.

"Have you lived your whole life like that?"

Tyler looked at her thoughtfully. "Probably. I guess it is my religious upbringing. All kinds of guilt were baked in for me. I just did not want to disappoint them."

Amy understood only partially. She had lived her life trying not to disappoint her mom, even though her mom lived only in her mind. So, really, she was living not to disappoint a ghost or an image she held of her mom. Before she could examine the healthiness of that pathway, she looked at Tyler and said, "You must really love your parents."

"I do," Tyler said. "They aren't perfect, but I do love them. I know I haven't always made great decisions, but I think they approve of most of my life choices."

Amy sighed wistfully. She was not sure if her dad had approved of her life choices. She knew he was proud of her for going to college and landing this big job. Although Amy pretended she didn't care what he thought, she knew she did care. However, that did not negate what he did when she was a child. Therefore, as far as she was concerned, he had no right to an opinion on her life. He had emotionally abandoned her when she needed him the most. She was aware she still carried bitterness towards her dad, but until there were apologies and real evidence that he was genuinely sorry, she didn't see herself letting it go.

At a very young age, Amy was thrust into a world of grief for her mother. She also had to become her sister's mom and her dad's caretaker. It was too much for such a young girl. This is why she didn't like emotional attachments. They were messy and hurtful. Her sister, Melissa, and even Brooke had all tried to talk to her about it, but she shut them down. They had no idea what she had been through and didn't understand why she felt the way she felt. Why was everyone on her dad's side anyway? Shouldn't they be on her side? She was the victim of all of this. Even her sister had been shielded from so much because of Amy. Amy thought they should be applauding her for her strength rather than discussing forgiving her dad.

Amy pushed her thoughts away. They had work to do. "Ready to get back to work?" Amy asked, and Tyler nodded in agreement.

They worked late into the evening and finally called it quits around midnight. Amy was pleased with their progress and felt confident they could finish on time. She desperately wanted to go home and sleep. They shut down their computers and made their way to the elevator bank. Tyler offered to walk Amy to her car since it was so late. Amy was relieved but tried not to show it. The parking garage gave her the creeps even in the daylight. They walked to her car in relative silence. Amy was exhausted, but that did not dull the awareness she felt with him by her side. She wondered if he felt it, too. They reached her car, and Amy offered to drive Tyler to his car. He accepted and climbed into the passenger side. They drove the short distance to his car.

How did Tyler smell so nice after such a long day at work? she wondered. She knew she needed a shower and a chance to brush her teeth.

Tyler looked at Amy before he climbed out of the car. "You okay to drive home?" he asked. "You look spent."

"I'm okay." Amy nodded, not really sure herself.

"Okay," he said. "Drive carefully."

Tyler reached over and gave her a quick peck on the lips. Amy looked at him, surprised. Then, they gazed into each other's eyes, and the next thing Amy knew, they kissed deeply again. Amy drank him in. She wanted to press closer, but the car's console and her seat belt prevented it. All too soon, Tyler pulled away. She missed him already.

"I really like doing that with you," he whispered intimately.

Amy smiled dreamily.

"When we finish our project, let's go out for a celebratory dinner," Tyler said.

"Deal," Amy agreed.

Tyler hopped out of the car and closed the car door. Amy lowered the window, and he leaned down into the window. "Good night, Amy. Drive safe."

"You too, Tyler. See ya tomorrow."

Amy drove home, replaying the scene over and over. He was a great kisser; maybe that is why she felt things so strongly for him. Once Amy was home, she wasted no time washing her face, brushing her teeth, and putting on her pajamas. As her head hit the pillow, she fell asleep almost instantly.

# 17

# Amy

When Amy arrived at work the next day, she found Tyler already hard at work in her office. With some much-needed sleep, Amy felt like a new person.

"Good Morning!" Amy greeted him cheerily.

"Good morning!" Tyler returned.

"How did you sleep?" Amy asked cordially.

"So good! What about you?"

"Same," Amy said with a smile. "How long have you been here?"

"Oh, long enough to grab a cup of coffee, overhear some office gossip, and find where I left off yesterday."

Amy chuckled. "Anything good?"

"No, the coffee is terrible. Justin must have made it again. He either waters it down or makes it too strong. There is no happy medium 'Goldilocks' in him."

Amy chuckled again. "I meant the gossip."

"Oh," Tyler said. "No, not really, unless you think people being traumatized over a bad manicure is good gossip."

"That is actually very traumatic," Amy said seriously. "I mean, you take the time to drive over to the salon and not use your hands for an hour. You expect results."

"Oh," Tyler said. "I had no idea."

"You're welcome," Amy said sarcastically. "I'm going to grab a cup of coffee and be right back."

"Sure," Tyler said.

Amy returned with her coffee and quickly found where she had left off the day before. With her good night's sleep, she felt ready to tackle the project. Tyler and Amy discussed how to divide the remaining work, and then each shut out their surroundings to accomplish their goal. The day flew by. At 4:30, Amy stood and stretched, trying to relieve the tension in her shoulders and back. She looked over at Tyler. He was grinning at her.

"What?" Amy asked.

"Nothing," Tyler said. "You just have no idea how beautiful you are."

"You are delusional," Amy said, laughing.

Desperate to change the subject, Amy looked down at her computer screen. She gave Tyler a brief description of where she was with her part of the project.

Tyler looked at his computer screen. "Great!" he said. "I don't think we will have to stay so late tonight. I think we'll be able to finish tomorrow morning and then practice our presentation for the rest of the day. What do you think?"

"I agree," said Amy. "I think we are in a good spot."

Tyler and Amy worked in silence for another couple of hours. Then, Tyler shut down his computer, stood, and stretched. "Okay, I am going to head home. I may work a little more tonight, but I need to go home and let my dog out. My roommates are both out for the evening."

Amy smiled. "Sounds good." She was slightly disappointed there would be no goodnight kiss tonight. For the thousandth time, she wondered if dating a guy from work was a good idea.

"See you tomorrow," Tyler said, and Amy watched as he left her office and headed down the hall to the elevator.

"So, how is that going?" Brooke's voice startled Amy. Brooke was nodding toward Tyler's disappearing back.

"Good!" Amy said. "We've accomplished a lot. I think we are going to finish on time. I was a little worried yesterday."

"That's great!" Brooke smiled. "But that isn't what I meant, and you know it."

Amy laughed. That was another reason Brooke reminded Amy of Melissa. There wasn't a lot she could get past either of them. "It's going," Amy said in a lowered voice.

Brooke stepped further into Amy's office and gracefully lowered herself into the chair near Amy's desk. Amy was struck by how lovely Brooke appeared, even so close to the end of the workday.

"So, have you decided what this relationship is yet?" Brooke asked.

"No, the project has kind of taken over everything else. He wants to take me to dinner when we are done to celebrate the end of the project, so maybe I will get a read on it then," Amy said.

Brooke nodded, "Well, keep me posted."

Before Brooke could leave, Amy asked her about her project. "Still in meeting marathon mode?"

"No, thankfully, that part has ended, and it's back to me and my computer screen, making magic happen. I actually have a big presentation at the beginning of next week, so I'd better get back to it. It may be a late night for me. I can't wait to hear how dinner goes."

Amy watched Brooke go and turned thoughtfully back to her screen. Amy decided to pack up her laptop and call it a day. If she went home now, she could possibly squeeze in a run.

---

The next day flew by, just as fast as the two before. Amy and Tyler finished the project that morning, as planned, and spent the rest of their day building slides and practicing the presentation. Once they were satisfied they were completely prepared, they both breathed a sigh of relief.

"Okay," Tyler said. "I promised you dinner."

"You don't have to keep your promise. I know we've had some long days. You might be tired of me," Amy said, teasing.

"Not possible, and by the way, I always keep my promises," Tyler said with his signature charming smile.

They decided on one of Amy's favorite restaurants. As a bonus, it was close to work. This place served a little bit of everything, but they had the best fried pickles around. The waitress took their drink orders and then came back with their fried pickles. Amy dove in. At that moment, she realized she may have missed lunch. Tyler laughed at her and then dove in himself.

They briefly discussed work and the presentation until Tyler said, "Okay, enough work talk. Let's talk about something else." Amy nodded in agreement.

Tyler asked, "What is your favorite holiday?"

It was an innocent question, but Amy felt uncomfortable. The truth was, Amy avoided most holidays. They did not hold good memories for her. Amy thought momentarily and then said, teasingly, "St Patrick's Day. I look good in green."

"Hmmm," Tyler said. "Interesting choice."

Amy hoped he would let it go at that. "What's yours?" Amy asked.

"Global Handwashing Day," he said seriously. "It's a thing. I am intent on raising awareness. You know what they say. Cleanliness is next to godliness. By the way, did you wash your hands before eating these pickles?"

Amy laughed, ignoring his question. "Do you exchange gifts on this holiday?"

"Well, that really goes without saying, doesn't it? I mean, we do, but then we need to wash our hands instantly. You gotta be aware of those germs," he said, wriggling his fingers.

"Interesting. Did you grow up celebrating this holiday?" Amy asked, playing along.

"Of course. I already told you there were five boys and one girl. My mom had to keep us clean somehow."

"Fair enough," Amy conceded. "So, this is your favorite holiday?"

"Well, my true favorite holiday is Christmas. I just didn't want to be the only sap since yours is St. Patrick's Day."

Amy laughed as she dipped a pickle in ranch dressing and popped it into her mouth.

"Of course, Christmas is my favorite," Tyler continued. "I love the lights and decorations and traditions. It is all so fun to me."

Amy nodded. She did not reveal to him that the very things he loved about the holiday were what she dreaded. Her mom loved Christmas, but after she died, they did not celebrate. Her dad, in his drunken stupor, rarely knew what time of year it was, and although she tried to make things pleasant for her sister, she knew she could not come close to what her mom did.

Amy did not express any of these thoughts to Tyler. Instead, she listened intently to his description of how his family celebrated Christmas. It sounded just like something out of a Hallmark movie. All of a sudden, Amy was jealous and skeptical at the same time. Could his family really be that nice? Could they really all get along that well? Would her family have been similar if her mom had lived? Amy was suddenly shaken out of her thoughts when she heard Tyler say, "Maybe you could meet them sometime."

Everything around Amy slowed, and it felt like her head was suddenly stuffed with cotton. She struggled to focus. What did Tyler mean by that? She hoped they could stay in a casual relationship. It was safer that way.

"Um, sure. That would be great," she finally responded, sounding casual. Before Tyler could cover it up, she caught the disappointment across his face. It suddenly became important to Amy not to hurt his feelings, so she forced a smile and said, "No, really. I think it would be fun to meet the people responsible for you." She chuckled at her own joke, and Tyler looked relieved. Amy shoved down any panic she might feel and told herself that this would never get that far.

But was that what she wanted? She really liked Tyler more than any guy she had met recently, but she had not let anybody in close for a long time. There was too much risk involved. Too much of her heart could get hurt. She didn't think she would survive any more heartache.

The words Melissa had once spoken to her came back to

her. "Amy, you keep guys at an emotional distance to protect yourself," she had said. "But what you don't know is that your physical intimacy with these guys is still chipping away at your heart."

Amy mentally dismissed these thoughts and forced herself back to the present. She looked back up at Tyler. He was smiling at her. Her stomach did a flip-flop. Tyler leaned over and pecked her on the lips, lingering for a moment. Amy felt tingles all over her body.

Thankfully, the waitress chose that moment to appear at the table with their food. She set their plates before them and asked if they needed anything else. After getting drink refills, Tyler and Amy ate silently for a bit, enjoying their food. Tyler chose to move the topic of conversation back to the work presentation, and Amy let him, feeling that was a much safer topic for now. They both felt good about the presentation the next day and rehearsed. As they sat back from their plates, both satiated, Amy felt herself relax. That was the thing about Tyler. He definitely made her body tingle and her heart flip-flop, but Amy, at times, also felt very relaxed around him. That was a new experience for her. Most guys, most people, made her nervous. Even though she enjoyed people, they exhausted her. It took a lot of energy to keep a guard up.

Tyler paid the bill, and Amy thanked him for dinner. They began the walk back to their cars. Amy knew she wanted Tyler to come back to her place, but she decided she definitely was not going to initiate it. In the end, she didn't have to worry about it. When they arrived at Amy's car, Amy turned towards Tyler. He gently cupped her neck, winding his hand through her hair. Her pulse accelerated as she gazed into his eyes. Tyler, ever so slowly, leaned down and kissed her gently at first, but then urgency took over. He tilted his head, and their lips fit perfectly. Every part of her was on fire.

Tyler pulled away and looked into her eyes. "Want to go back to your place?" he whispered.

"Very much," Amy said, nodding.

Tyler walked quickly to his car and followed her back to her place. Once inside Amy's apartment, it did not take long to shed their clothes and make their way to Amy's bed. Amy remembered why the night with Tyler had been so memorable the first time. She fell asleep with a smile on her face. All warnings and thoughts of figuring out where this relationship was going were dismissed from her mind.

# 18

*Amy*

Amy awoke to find Tyler beside her. She smiled, remembering the night before. Then, she remembered they had a presentation today. She sat up quickly and looked at the clock. Okay, they still had plenty of time. She began to ease out of bed slowly when Tyler grabbed her and pulled her back into bed.

He nuzzled her neck, "Where do you think you are going?"

"I am off to plot your demise," Amy teased.

"That's fair," Tyler teased in return.

"I was actually headed to the bathroom," she laughed playfully. "We do have a presentation today, and I think it is a good idea to show up for it."

"Okay. I guess that is valid," Tyler said, letting go of Amy. "I probably need to run home and change."

Amy smiled. "Yes, probably. You don't want to give Sheila any more to talk about by showing up in yesterday's clothes."

"Oh, Sheila. She's fairly harmless," Tyler scoffed.

"Not when she smells new gossip!" Amy exclaimed. "Would you like coffee before you go?"

Tyler checked the time and said, "Yes, that would be great!"

Amy quickly went to the restroom and then to the kitchen to start the coffee. Eventually, Tyler joined her in the kitchen. He approached her with a mischievous grin and then backed her into the kitchen counter. He grasped the counter on either side of her and kissed her nose. She smiled, and he kissed her chin, forehead, and lips.

Amy laughed playfully, enjoying the attention. "You don't have time to start this again."

Tyler stepped back, laughing. "You're right. But after today . . ." His voice trailed off.

Amy suddenly felt both excited and anxious. She wanted to spend a lot of time with Tyler, but wouldn't that mean she could grow attached? Amy pushed the thoughts away. She liked Tyler. He was a nice guy. It didn't seem he was going anywhere, so maybe she should just enjoy this for what it was.

Thankfully, the coffee maker finished, and she turned to pour each of them a cup of coffee. They sat on her couch, enjoying their coffee, and briefly discussed their presentation. They both felt confident things would go well today. Tyler finished his cup and went to put it in the sink. He gathered the rest of his things, kissed Amy lightly on the lips, and with a 'see you at work,' he was gone.

Amy wasn't sure if she was relieved or sad. She didn't feel like analyzing her feelings right then, so she put on her favorite podcast and began getting ready for work. She took extra care with her outfit for the presentation, but if she was honest, she also wanted to look extra nice for Tyler.

Amy arrived at work with time to spare. She pulled into a parking spot next to Brooke just as Brooke was getting out of her car. Brooke waved and waited for Amy to get out of her car. Brooke smiled genuinely at Amy.

"Are you ready for your presentation today?" Brooke asked.

"I think so," Amy said. "I think I have all my i's dotted and t's crossed."

"I saw you leave with Tyler last night. Did you have a good dinner?"

"We did." Despite herself, Amy felt a deep blush climbing up her neck.

"Oh," Brooke said. "It looks like more than dinner happened last night."

Amy looked at Brooke. "Please don't say anything to anyone at work."

Brooke looked at Amy with concern. "You know I won't, Amy. Tyler is a very nice guy, and if this is what you want, I am happy for you. Just be careful with that heart of yours."

Amy knew Brooke wasn't lecturing her. Brooke really was always there for Amy, especially when Amy needed help picking up the pieces. Brooke had often been there when Amy felt she had let a guy get too close and had to break it off abruptly. She was also there as Amy's confidant when a guy Amy liked and slept with had not called back. Brooke believed in God and saving yourself for marriage and all that went with that. Amy had made it clear she did not, but Brooke did not reject her or treat her like a pet project. Amy felt Brooke genuinely cared for her. This was another reason Brooke and Melissa seemed so similar to Amy. Amy was unsure why she deserved to have both of them in her life. But she was grateful for them.

Amy smiled at Brooke, took a deep breath, and changed the subject. "Is your project still going well?" asked Amy cheerfully.

Brooke gave Amy one last look of concern and then let the subject change. She smiled at Amy and gave her a quick update. Amy listened to Brooke, both intimidated by and thankful for Brooke's kindness.

The women rode the elevator up to their floor and then parted ways with a "see you soon" and a "don't worry, you will do great."

Amy made her way to her office and put her things on her desk. She walked with purpose to the break room, hoping a pot of coffee was already made. They really needed to invest in a single-serve coffee maker. Thankfully, there was a freshly brewed pot, and Amy helped herself to a cup. As she made her way back to her office, her thoughts drifted to last night. She smiled to herself as she remembered the moments she shared with Tyler. Her stomach fluttered in response to the memory.

Get ahold of yourself, Amy, she chided. She should focus on her very important presentation. Her musings were interrupted by Tyler himself.

"Oh, good. You already got coffee," he said, smiling warmly at her.

Amy's stomach did that flutter thing again. Amy frowned.

Tyler said, "What's wrong? Something missing from the presentation?"

Amy didn't realize her emotions were on her face.

"Oh, nothing. I thought for a moment I had forgotten something at home, but I am good," she lied smoothly. Amy returned Tyler's warm smile, "Did you want to get a cup of coffee and go over our notes one last time?"

Tyler nodded and said, "Just what I was thinking. Be right back."

Amy organized her desk and found her notes. Tyler returned quickly, and they spent the next half hour reminding each other of the key points they needed to cover in their presentation.

Finally, Tyler looked at Amy and said, "I think we are good. We make a great team."

Amy was more pleased by this statement than she should have been. "Let's get our things and head over to the conference room. I want plenty of time to set up our computers and hook them to the projector."

Tyler agreed, and they gathered their things and walked to the conference room. They passed other offices where people were busily looking over paperwork and spreadsheets. They entered the conference room, and Amy was thankful to find it empty. Even though it was still twenty minutes before the meeting was scheduled, some people trickled in early with their laptops and waited for the meeting to begin. Amy had been guilty of this in the past as well. The conference room held a stunning view of the Chicago River. It was easy to hang out there with all the natural light and beauty of the view. One year, Amy was lucky enough to be invited to a company party held in this room on St. Patrick's Day. She witnessed the famous river being dyed green and the parade.

Amy and Tyler plugged their laptops in and connected them to the projectors so they could quickly and seamlessly tag-team each other. They adjusted the lighting and angles, ensuring everyone in the room could see the projection on the screen. As they were finishing, more people began to trickle into the room, discussing their plans for the following weekend or their next vacation.

Finally, Mr. Turner, their boss, bustled into the room, signaling it was time for the meeting to begin. Everyone hushed instinctively. "Well, Amy and Tyler," Mr. Turner boomed, "I am eager to see what you have for us today."

Amy took a deep breath and smiled at Mr Turner. "Good morning! We would like to begin with a series of charts showing the advantages of this purchase." Amy took the time to explain each chart thoroughly so everyone could clearly understand the information she compiled. She saw some co-workers taking notes, which she felt was an affirmation that she had pulled the key points to discuss. When she finished her section, Tyler stood and continued the presentation without wasting time. Once they were both done, they looked at Mr. Turner.

Mr. Turner nodded and asked several clarifying questions. Satisfied, he said, "Great work."

Amy blew out a breath she wasn't aware she had been holding. That was high praise coming from Mr. Turner.

"Please send all of this information to my assistant. I have a leadership meeting later today and will take your reports with me. I hope the information you have here will more effectively guide this purchase. Can you both be available for questions?"

"Yes, sir." Tyler and Amy nodded in unison.

Satisfied, Mr. Turner moved to the next order of business in the meeting. Amy sank into her chair with relief. She truly didn't mind the research. In fact, she enjoyed it. She actually didn't even mind putting together the presentations, but her least favorite part was giving them. She wasn't a big fan of knowing all eyes were on her. All of a sudden, her week caught up with her, and she felt exhausted. She tried desperately to focus on what others were saying and not zone out.

Finally, the meeting wrapped up, and they were free to leave the conference room. Tyler followed Amy out into the hallway.

"Well, that seemed to go well," Tyler said in a low voice.

"It did." Amy agreed with a smile. "But I am glad that is over for now."

"Same," said Tyler. "Well, I'd better head to my office and make some phone calls."

Amy felt oddly let down. She had become accustomed to him spending so much time in her office over the last couple of days. Before she spent too much time picking apart that particular feeling, Amy checked her watch and confirmed it was lunchtime. She thought she would head down to the cafeteria and get a salad. She needed to catch up on some other work that had been neglected, as she had spent all of her time on this project and presentation.

Amy grabbed her wallet and headed to the elevator. She made her way downstairs to the cafeteria, found a decent-looking salad, and walked over to the checkout line. Brooke appeared behind her.

"Hey, Amy! How did it go?" Brooke asked.

"Good! Really well, actually," Amy said. "But I must admit I am glad that part is behind me."

Brooke chuckled, "I bet."

"Do you want to find a table down here, or do you need to go back to your office?" Brooke asked.

Amy had planned to go back to her office, but suddenly, she wanted to sit and talk with Brooke. Brooke's peaceful demeanor usually put Amy at ease when she spoke with her.

"Let's find a table," Amy offered. "It doesn't look too crowded down here today."

Brooke nodded in agreement, and they made their way to

one of the open tables. They sat and opened their salads, each taking a couple of bites.

Amy looked at Brooke as she chewed her salad. "How's it going with Luke?" Amy realized she had been so focused on herself that she had failed to ask Brooke about her own life.

"Oh," Brooke said with a sad smile. "We broke up." Amy suddenly felt ashamed of herself. How had she not asked sooner? she chastised herself.

"I am so sorry," Amy said. "And I am sorry I didn't ask sooner. It's okay to tell me it is your turn to share."

"No," Brooke said. "It's okay. I needed some time to process and be able to talk about it without getting emotional. Work and you," she said with a grin, "has been a good distraction. I think I am struggling because I really thought this was going somewhere."

Amy looked at Brooke with a sympathetic smile and asked, "What happened?"

"You know," Brooke said. "I'm not entirely sure. I think that is why I have needed time to process. I thought things were going well. The more I think about it, though, the more I think things were getting too serious too fast for him. I'm not sure he could handle it."

"Really?" Amy asked.

"Yeah," Brooke continued. "His parents are divorced, and I think he is scared of that happening to him, too. However, divorce doesn't just happen. Marriage is a choice between two people, and you have to choose each other every day, not just on the days you feel like it. He doesn't have to repeat his parents' mistakes." Brooke chuckled, "At least that is what my mom says. I really liked him, though. And honestly, when I prayed about it, I did feel peace about our relationship. I guess now I get to choose if I am going to continue to trust God for the right man to come into my life." Brooke sighed and twirled her lettuce with her plastic fork.

Amy could tell Brooke was trying to be positive, but she was still hurting. Amy really had no idea what Brooke was talking about with trusting God. The last time she had prayed was for her mom to be healed of cancer, and look how that turned out. Amy had conflicting feelings about God.

Amy returned her attention to Brooke. "I am so sorry," she said again. "You are gorgeous and kind-hearted, Brooke. I know another guy will come along and snatch you up!"

Brooke smiled at Amy sadly and said, "Thank you. You are good for my ego. I know that when the time is right, God will bring the right guy into my life. I trust God with this. I am just hurting a little right now."

Again, Amy had no idea what Brooke was talking about. Amy wasn't sure she had ever had a faith like hers. Part of Amy wanted to call Brooke a fool for trusting God instead of just going out there and taking what she wanted, but truthfully, there was a part of Amy that admired Brooke for sticking to her faith.

"So, how's it going with Tyler, having to see him every day at work?" Brooke asked. Amy knew Brooke was trying to change the subject, but she also looked for signs of judgment on Brooke's face. Amy found none.

"Well, this week has definitely been interesting, having to work in such close quarters every day. But it has been okay. There has been a little weirdness, but for the most part, we have navigated it well."

Brooke studied Amy. "You seem like you really like him. Are you doing okay?"

Leave it to Brooke to get to the heart of the matter. Amy thought, How does she do that?

"I do like him, but you know my policy on keeping things casual."

Brooke laughed ruefully and said, "Yes, I know your policy well. That's part of the reason why I am asking."

Amy laughed with Brooke, but inside, she questioned once again whether her casual-only policy really protected her.

Brooke interrupted her thoughts with, "I have always liked Tyler. He seems like a good guy, and I think he does like you. Again, I would just caution you to be careful with your heart."

Amy knew Brooke well enough to know she was saying this because she genuinely cared about Amy and not because she was a religious zealot. Brooke had invited Amy to church a few times. Amy had always graciously turned her down, but Brooke still wanted to be her friend. Amy wasn't sure why, but she very much appreciated her friendship. Again, she drew parallels to her friendship with Melissa.

The women finished their lunches, threw away their trash, and headed back to their offices, chatting about their next steps on their projects. Amy was grateful for the time with Brooke and mentally made a note to call Melissa.

As they were leaving the cafeteria, Amy saw Tyler enter with another female co-worker. He was laughing and smiling and engrossed in what she was saying. The woman reached over and grabbed Tyler's arm as she continued her seemingly hilarious story.

Amy was not prone to jealousy. Or so she liked to believe.

But this was not easy to watch. How many people was Tyler talking to? Maybe the connection Amy thought Tyler had with her was the same one he had with multiple women. Amy wanted to keep things casual but did not want to look like a fool.

To make matters worse, Tyler was so engrossed in the conversation with this woman that he did not even see her. Amy began to doubt the last couple of weeks with Tyler. Maybe it had all been a sham. Maybe he decided to get close to her so he could advance his career. Maybe he was not at all what he seemed to be.

Amy glanced at Brooke, who was watching Amy's face. It was clear Brooke had seen the same thing Amy had.

"Don't read too much into it," Brooke cautioned. "Tyer is a nice guy but also a charmer and a flirt."

Amy nodded, but uncertainty filled her. She would not be made to look like an idiot at work. Amy may have to break her own rule on this one and actually see where Tyler stands in this relationship. She did not like feeling this way.

Then she stopped. What way did she feel?

Vulnerable. That is how she felt, and Amy hated feeling vulnerable. She inwardly checked to make sure all her walls were still there and secure. She did not need anyone, especially a guy, to find a crack in her protection. It was there for a reason, and she had no plans of taking it down anytime soon.

**19**

*Melissa*

Melissa stared at her phone. She didn't recognize the number calling and was about to ignore it. She was in the middle of cooking dinner, lost in her own thoughts, and really wasn't in the mood to talk on the phone. However, she felt an odd nudge in her spirit. One she was working on constantly, not to ignore. She fortified herself with a deep breath and picked up the phone. Not really convinced she heard the Holy Spirit correctly, she prepared herself for a salesperson.

"Hello?" Melissa said guardedly.

"Melissa?"

"Amy?"

"Yes!" Amy said. "Sorry, I probably should have texted first. I just realized you don't have my office number. My cell phone is charging, so I called you from my office phone."

"No worries," Melissa said. "It is so good to hear from you. I have been thinking a lot about you lately. How are you?"

"I'm good," Amy said. "I saw pictures of your kiddos on Facebook the other day. I can't believe how big they are getting."

Melissa laughed. "Yes, and getting close to the age where

they know absolutely everything."

Amy chuckled, "Oh, to be young again."

"Yes," Melissa said. "How are you, Amy? How is that big fancy job of yours?"

"I am good. I just did a big presentation at work, which has afforded me more job security and possibly a raise."

"That's exciting!" Melissa said.

After the girls chatted a bit, catching up on their lives, Melissa asked Amy, "Are you coming home for Thanksgiving this year? I would love to see you."

"I haven't decided yet," Amy answered honestly. "My sister really wants me to, but I don't know if I am up for it."

"How long has it been?" asked Melissa compassionately.

"Three years," Amy said, trying not to let the guilt that she had taken the path of least resistance creep into her voice.

"Hmmmm," Melissa said. "Maybe it is time then. Your sister shouldn't be punished for your dad's actions. And your dad may not have many years left on Earth. I don't want you to be in a position where you have to live with regrets."

"I know you are probably right, but it is easier said than done. I will keep thinking about it," Amy said honestly. "And if I do decide to come, I will definitely make time to see you and Blake and the kids."

"Deal," Melissa said. "I would absolutely love that! It has been too long."

The women finished their conversation and hung up, promising to keep in touch and call or text soon.

Melissa clicked off her phone and thought about her conversation with Amy as she finished dinner preparations. She was so glad she answered the phone. She had been thinking so much about Amy lately. Every time the Lord brought her to mind, Melissa prayed, but she had no idea what was going on with Amy. It sounded like she was doing well. Maybe it was the things with her family.

Blake came home in the midst of her musings. They greeted each other, and then Blake leaned over and kissed Melissa.

"Where are the kids?" Blake asked.

"Upstairs."

Blake laughed. "Taking advantage of their mom being busy, I see."

They both knew the kids were more than likely on their devices, which would be very limited after dinner. Melissa laughed.

"What's going on?" Blake said. "Are you alright? You seem a little distracted."

"Amy just called."

Blake's eyes widened in surprise. "Oh, really? What's going on with her?"

"I don't really know," Melissa said. "She seemed like everything with her was fine. If that's really true, I am so glad. However, she has been repeatedly on my heart and mind lately."

"I know you mentioned that," Blake said. "Maybe it is for something she is about to go through, rather than what she is currently going through."

"True." Melissa nodded in agreement. "She did say she is thinking of coming home for Thanksgiving. She hasn't been home in three years. I hate it for her sister and her sister's family. They love Amy so much, but I am afraid Amy sees her sister's reconciliation with her dad as a betrayal. I don't think

Amy would ever admit it, but I think it is hard for her knowing she practically raised her sister until her dad finally got a hold of himself when Amy left for college."

"Yeah, that's sad," Blake said. "None of it is her sister's fault, and it should be okay for her to have a relationship with her dad. But Amy did lose out on part of her childhood because she chose to be there for her sister. I'm not saying this to excuse Amy for not forgiving her dad, but you do see how she got there. I am afraid without allowing the Lord to heal those hurts and wounds, she is going to be stuck in this way of thinking."

Melissa nodded, knowing he was right. Maybe this is why Amy had been on her heart so much. Maybe there was some softening there Melissa didn't know about, and God was ready to move. Melissa loved her journey with the Lord so much. She was in constant wonder about how the Lord wanted to use His people to bring about his heart and purposes on the earth. It was a very humbling thought for Melissa.

Melissa purposed in her heart right then to pray for Amy every day. Clearly, the Lord was up to something in her life, and He wanted Melissa to partner with Him in bringing it about. Melissa found herself excited. She hoped this would finally be a breakthrough for Amy.

# 20

*Amy*

Amy clicked off the phone, glad she had called Melissa. She decided to gather her things and head home. She needed to go for a run and clear her head.

Once home, Amy quickly changed into her workout clothes and running shoes, grabbed her earbuds and phone, and headed out the door. Close to where she lived, there was a trail through a park that was both safe and relaxing. Although her apartment building had a nice workout room, she much preferred the outdoors when the weather was nice.

When Amy reached her favorite trail, she pocketed her earbuds and let her thoughts run with her. She revisited her conversation with Melissa.

There had always been something about Melissa that calmed Amy and made her less anxious. Even before Melissa quit partying and began going to church, Amy felt safe with her. After Melissa found Blake and God, Amy didn't want to admit it, but she felt even safer with Melissa.

Amy chuckled to herself at the times she had given Mel a hard time about not going with her to parties anymore and turning into a goody-two-shoes. Ahh, to be young again and think those parties were so important. The truth was, Amy had been a little jealous. Amy had never admitted this to anyone, but as the years passed and she periodically reflected on her last year of college, she began to be curious about what had appealed to Melissa so much that she gave up all the fun.

Amy thought about the fateful day when she decided to abort her baby. She rarely let these thoughts come to mind. When she did, she justified what she had done. She was too young. She didn't want to marry. She was a little embarrassed to admit she wasn't entirely sure she knew who the guy was. And if she took the time to figure it out, the guy was too young to be saddled with a child. Raising a child would mess up all her plans. She had already raised her sister. This was time for her.

Amy did not like this way of thinking. For some reason, there was weird guilt accompanying her decision. Although she believed women deserved all the rights and freedoms men had, including making decisions about her body, she was never able to shake the sense of guilt accompanying her decision. She knew she would choose the same path today if she faced the same circumstances, but it didn't sit right with her. Amy decided to think of something else.

Her dad.

It was true; her sister had been begging her to come home for Thanksgiving. Annalise had told her they were going to celebrate the holiday at her house this year, so Amy wouldn't even have to go to her dad's house. Amy knew she was being stubborn and not very fair to Annalise, but it was so hard to think of being across a dinner table from her dad. And worse, people would expect her to smile and make polite conversation with him. She just didn't know if she could do it.

Ah, well. Thanksgiving was still a few months away. She had plenty of time to make this decision, didn't she? She would look up ticket prices to Texas. Maybe she could make the excuse that it would cost too much to fly this year.

Amy finished her run and began slowing her pace as she turned towards her apartment. Her phone buzzed. She glanced down at it to see a text from Tyler. "Dinner?" it read. All thoughts of her family and past decisions flew out of her head.

Amy had not seen or interacted with Tyler since she had seen him in the cafeteria. In fact, she had purposely tried to avoid him. She reasoned if he was truly interested he would continue to pursue her.

Before Amy could change her mind, she texted back, "Sure." The truth was she enjoyed spending time with Tyler, and even though she had her doubts about him, she wasn't ready to end it.

Tyler sent another message. "Great! Can I pick you up in an hour?"

Amy evaluated. She needed to jump in the shower. However, she still thought she could make it in an hour.

"Sounds good," Amy messaged back and picked up her pace a little.

Amy quickly showered and applied a little makeup. She put some product in her hair and decided to let it be wavy tonight. She dressed casually in a pair of jeans and a loose-flowing top. She decided if this were a fancy dinner Tyler would have had to make reservations somewhere, so she would be fine dressed casually. Just as Amy was slipping on her sandals, she heard a knock on the door. Grabbing her purse from the dresser, she walked to the front door. She checked the peephole just in case it wasn't Tyler. She smiled and swung open the door.

"Wow!" said Tyler. "You look amazing."

Amy could feel herself blushing. Why did this guy have this effect on her? "Thank you," she said a little shyly.

Tyler, with his ever-present charming smile, said, "Well, it looks like you're ready to go."

"I am!" Amy said. She shut and locked her apartment door, and they headed downstairs to Tyler's car.

"I thought we would go over to Taylor Street and try some Italian food. How do you feel about that?"

Amy nodded. "Sounds great! I hear wonderful things about those restaurants, but I haven't tried many of them."

"Great!" said Tyler, and Amy could tell he was pleased with himself.

They drove in comfortable silence for a bit before Tyler said, "Well, all in all, I think the presentation went well."

"Oh, I do, too! I think Mr. Turner was pleased. Were you called in to answer any questions?"

"Yes," Tyler said. "Just one. It was something I guess I wasn't completely clear on in one of the graphs. But it seemed the meeting was going well, and they appreciated our presentation."

"That's great!" Amy said. "I am glad that is behind us." Tyler nodded in agreement.

"So, how has your day been?" Tyler asked, moving the subject from work.

"I actually spoke with my college roommate today," Amy said, smiling.

"Where was college for you again? In Texas?"

"Yes," Amy said, impressed he remembered. Amy chatted about Melissa for a few minutes and then turned the question on him. She had no desire to tell Tyler about wrestling with her Thanksgiving plans or anything of the sort. She did not want to open the door to discuss her family again. She listened to Tyler chat as he included a funny story about his dog chasing a squirrel across the park, interrupting a couple of picnics along the way, and marveled again at how easy their rapport was.

At the restaurant, the hostess told them there would be about a half-hour wait. Tyler and Amy ordered drinks from the bar and stepped out onto the patio to find a place to sit and sip their drinks while they waited for their table. They found a table near the end of the patio and sat. It was loud, with a lot of activity around them, but neither of them seemed to mind. Tyler kept looking at Amy while he sipped his drink.

"What?" Amy finally asked with a sheepish smile.

"I just can't get over how beautiful you look tonight."

Amy giggled despite herself. "Thank you. You don't look so bad yourself."

Tyler leaned over and gave Amy a slight kiss on her lips, but lingered a moment, sending Amy's pulse racing. At that moment, the pager the hostess handed Tyler lit up, signaling their table was ready. Amy let out the breath she seemed always to be holding around Tyler. She really did not want to examine her thoughts and feelings yet. She just wanted to enjoy dinner and maybe more.

The food did not disappoint. The restaurant lived up to its hype. By the time Tyler and Amy finished eating, they were both complaining that they were full. They collected their boxed leftover food and strolled to the car, enjoying the cool night air. It was much cooler since the sun had gone down, and Amy shivered. She knew she should have brought a sweater.

Tyler glanced over at her and said, "I think I have an extra jacket in the car."

Once at Tyler's car, he took her food box, put it in the trunk beside his, and pulled out a gray zip-up hoodie. "I know it doesn't go with your outfit, but it's clean," he offered.

"Thanks," Amy said, reaching for the hoodie. Instead, Tyler wrapped it around Amy, giving him an excuse to come in close. He looked at her for a long moment and then bent his head toward her. Amy responded by lifting her lips to his. Why did they fit so perfectly? Amy's hands gently embraced Tyler's face and then made their way into his hair. He groaned and deepened the kiss. Every part of her was responding to him with desire. He finally lifted his head, and she collapsed her head on his broad chest, feeling safe.

He said in a husky voice, "I better get you home." He opened the car door for her, and once he knew she was safely inside, he closed the door. He ran around to his side, got in, and started the car. Before he put the car in reverse, he looked over at her. He leaned over the console and cupped her chin in his hand. Gently, he kissed her again. This time she pulled away before she got completely caught up in the kiss. Making out in the car was what teenagers did. She had a perfectly comfortable apartment. She would admit this was very exciting. She tried to tamp down her feelings of doubt that she was getting too close to this guy by telling herself she was just very physically attracted to him.

Once at her apartment, they wasted no time getting upstairs and unlocking the door. Then, it was just a blur of hands, kisses, and clothes being shed. They made their way to Amy's bed, and then it was just succumbing to the moment.

---

When Amy woke up the next morning, she was relieved to remember it was Saturday. At least there would be no mad dash to get ready and get to work. She rolled over and cuddled up to Tyler.

"Good morning," he said.

"Good morning," she responded. They lay there, content for a few minutes, and then Amy said, "How about coffee?"

"Sounds awesome," Tyler said.

Amy padded into the kitchen to start the coffee maker.

Tyler followed her into the kitchen and said, "Do you have any plans today?"

"No, I don't, actually," Amy said.

"Would you like to spend the day together?"

"I would love that," Amy said. "What did you have in mind?"

"Well," Tyler said, "I would like to take my dog to the park since the weather seems to be nice, and then we could maybe go see a movie or something else you would like to do."

Amy smiled and said, "That actually sounds wonderful."

"Okay!" Tyler said, "Then why don't I come to pick you up in an hour? Dress comfortably, and we will just see where the day takes us."

"Sounds great!" Amy said.

True to his word, Tyler picked up Amy in an hour with his dog Bruno, in tow. Bruno was a hopeless mix of breeds, too complicated to sort out, but he was adorable. Amy loved dogs but didn't want the responsibility of one in an apartment. Tyler lived in a house with a couple of other guys, making his situation much more conducive to owning a dog. Tyler seemed pleasantly surprised at how well Bruno and Amy took to each other. Amy wasn't sure why Tyler had thought Amy wouldn't like his dog, but clearly, the thought had been hovering in the back of his mind. It seemed to please him that Amy and his dog got along so well.

When Amy recalled aspects of her relationship with Tyler, this day always stuck out as one of her favorites. They played in the park with Bruno, then found a farmer's market and wandered around, drinking lemonade thick with sugar and eating street corn dripping with butter. It was truly a spontaneous day where they just enjoyed being together. This day stuck out in Amy's memory because it also seemed to be the turning point in their relationship.

After this day, they fell into a routine of spending more and more time together. Most nights, Tyler spent the night at Amy's apartment. Sometimes, one or more of Tyler's roommates would be gone, and they would go to Tyler's house, where he wasn't sure if Amy was more excited to see him or Bruno.

The days turned into weeks, and soon, Amy realized they had been dating for a couple of months. One night, when Tyler's roommates were going to be out for the evening, Tyler offered to cook for her. Amy was pleased he wanted to cook her dinner. Tyler was her favorite person to spend time with, but she was also hoping he wasn't getting too serious too fast. As close as they had become, Amy still wrestled with her nagging fears that Tyler would want more than she could offer. She hoped this dinner was just because he wanted to show off his cooking skills.

When Amy showed up at Tyler's house that night, she took in the beautiful table he had prepared, complete with flowers and candles. She also realized he had made one of Amy's favorite dishes, lasagna with garlic bread. He poured some wine into the only two glasses he and his roommates kept around. "Wow!" Amy said. "This is beautiful. What's the occasion?" She thought quickly, hoping she hadn't missed some sort of anniversary and hoping even more Tyler wasn't the type of guy who kept track of those sorts of things.

"Nothing," Tyler said casually. "My roommates just happened to be gone, and I wanted to take full advantage of the situation. Besides, you cook amazing meals for me all the time."

Amy relaxed and told herself to enjoy someone doing something nice for her without strings attached. Tyler served them both the salad, and they ate and chatted about their day. Amy still marveled at how easily their conversations flowed. Tyler then served the lasagna.

"This is really good," Amy said. "Either you have been holding out on me, or you found a superb frozen lasagna."

Tyler chuckled, "I may still have some hidden talents. Oh, by the way, save room for dessert. I made cheesecake."

Amy put down her wine glass and looked at Tyler. "Seriously, did you commit a crime and are trying to figure out how to tell me?" She deadpanned.

"No," he assured her. I just wanted to do something nice for you and tell you something important."

Warning bells went off in Amy's mind. To deflect, she said, "Are you pregnant?"

Tyler rolled his eyes.

Amy tried not to think of all the things that could change their relationship. Was he moving? Did he get another job? Did he change his mind about her, and he was letting her down easy? Amy looked around at the beautiful table, real easy she amended. Why was he going to all this trouble?

She finally looked up at Tyler, who was carefully watching her. He took Amy's hand.

"Amy," he began, and Amy could tell he was nervous. What was he doing?

"These past few weeks with you have been incredible. You are an amazing woman full of surprises."

Oh God, Amy inwardly pleaded. Please don't say it. Please just stop there.

"You brighten my days, and I so enjoy spending time with you." Tyler continued. He paused briefly, took a deep breath, and blurted, "Amy, I love you!" He finished with a flourish and looked at her with expectation.

No! He said it! She tried not to choke on the wine she had just sipped. He looked at her hopefully. She knew he wanted to hear the same in return. But Amy knew she couldn't say it back. She just couldn't. Pretty soon, he would be talking of moving in together or marriage, and that, for sure, she knew she couldn't do. She wasn't entirely sure how she felt about Tyler. She actually might love him, but she couldn't allow herself to give in to such sentiments. These were dangerous. These led to heartbreak, and her heart could not survive another break.

She looked at Tyler, and she knew what she had to do. Once he had told her he loved her, there would always be an imbalance in the relationship. They could never go back to being casual. She should have been more clear that casual was what she wanted. Ugh. This sucked. Amy had to get out of here so she could think. She couldn't think with him looking at her like that.

"Thank you, Tyler," she began. Tyler, having watched the different emotions play out across Amy's face, was confused. This was clearly not the way he expected this evening to go. "I really like you, but I'm not sure I am ready to say that yet."

"That's okay," Tyler said quickly, disappointment edging his voice.

"No, it's not," Amy said. "You deserve better than me." And then she thought, *I'm not sure I will ever be able to say it back to you. You don't deserve my baggage.*

"No," Tyler said quickly, and she could tell he was trying to backtrack and fix whatever he had done wrong. "It's okay, Amy. I moved too quickly. Let's just forget it."

"Oh, Tyler. You made this whole dinner for me and put a lot of thought into this night. I don't think we can just forget it."

Amy could see from Tyler's facial expressions that he was moving from confusion to disappointment. Anger may soon follow. She had to get out of there. Amy moved to leave.

"Wait," Tyler said, desperation in his voice. "Where are you going? Please don't leave. Let's talk about this."

Amy seemed to ignore him. "Thank you so much for the delicious meal, Tyler. Let's just spend a little time apart, okay? I don't want to hurt you. I will see you soon."

Amy walked out of the house and into her car before she could change her mind. Tyler must have still been in shock from the whole thing because he let her go. The tears began about five minutes from his house. Why was she like this?

What was her problem? Tyler was a fantastic guy whom she might have more than just "like" feelings for. Why could she not let herself love him?

She knew why. She did not want to end up like her dad. For all of his faults, he loved her mom. He was absolutely lost without her and, therefore, almost drank himself to death after she died. Amy did not admit that to most people and did not like to think about it herself. She did not want to excuse her dad's behavior or let him off the hook. He was an adult. He was her parent. He should have picked himself up and been the father he knew he needed to be. Her mom would have been so mad at him for the way he acted after she died. Amy and her sister had desperately needed him, and he wasn't there for them. He couldn't deal with his own pain in a healthy manner, so he essentially abandoned his daughters in their time of need.

Amy held the anger in her thoughts. It was so familiar that it comforted her. She did not want to think about her relationship with Tyler, what had just happened, or what she had just lost. Instead, she wanted to focus on the person whose fault all of this was: her dad.

A subtle thought came into her head. *Amy, you are an adult now. You are the only one responsible for your own choices.* Amy pushed the thought away as soon as it came. *No way.* The only one to blame here was her dad. And since he had never taken responsibility for his actions, he was still to blame.

The anger made Amy feel better. Her tears slowed and stopped. She would miss Tyler, but she would not focus on that. She was doing him a favor. He did not want to be in love with someone like her.

She was broken.

# 21

# Amy

Amy awoke the next morning with a massive headache. She groaned as memories of the night before flooded her brain. She vowed not to cry anymore. Tyler had called her several times last night, and she finally shut her phone off, not feeling strong enough to speak with him yet. Amy made herself move. Coffee with lots of cream and sugar would help. If that didn't take care of her headache, then she would find some pain meds.

After her coffee was brewed and fixed how she liked it, she curled up on the couch. She was grateful that today was Saturday and she did not have to go to work. She was certain her eyes were swollen. She tried her best not to relive what had happened. She reasoned with herself that she had done what she needed to do. Some guilt niggled at the back of her brain that maybe she should have been more honest with Tyler from the jump and not let things get this far. She quickly shoved the thought aside. They had said upfront that this was a casual relationship.

But had they, though? Had she really made it clear this was casual, or had she assumed that because Tyler was so quick to jump into bed with her without a commitment, he viewed this relationship the way she did? Amy replayed the past few weeks in her head. She admitted that she and Tyler had started spending more and more time together. In fact, they had pretty much been inseparable. They shared most of their meals, slept in each other's beds, and spent most of their weekends together.

If Amy was being truthful with herself, a few warning bells had gone off in her head. She knew she was allowing herself to get comfortable in the relationship—probably too relaxed. Sometimes, she would drive to work, lecturing herself that she needed to distance herself from Tyler. But then she would see his smile, look into his eyes, and cave. She didn't want to put distance between them. She really liked Tyler and enjoyed having a companion in her life.

She knew Tyler wasn't seeing anyone else, and she wasn't either. Amy admitted she was deluding herself into thinking this was still casual. But still, Amy did not want a commitment. Commitments caused problems. Someone was always bound to get hurt.

Amy recalled a conversation she had with Brooke just last week.

"This looks like it is getting a little serious," Brooke said.

"Oh, no. We are just enjoying spending time together and having fun."

"Does Tyler know that? I see the way he looks at you. I think he may think it is more than that."

Amy dismissed Brooke's comment and changed the subject. Brooke meant well, but she didn't know anything about these types of relationships. Amy knew Brooke was waiting for marriage to have sex, and she was fairly sure Brooke was still a virgin. Good for her if that is what she wanted, but she would not understand her and Tyler's relationship.

Amy sighed. She had not meant to hurt Tyler. She liked Tyler, but maybe she should have been more upfront about why she couldn't have anything serious. It would just never work. She hadn't thought things all the way through, but deep down, Amy was pretty sure she would never get married or have children. Now that she articulated the thought in her head, it made her sad. Would she really spend her life alone?

Amy pushed the thought aside. She had so many mixed-up feelings that she did not have the energy to sort them out. Her headache was subsiding, and Amy decided the best thing to do was go for a run to clear her head.

Amy quickly changed, pulled her hair into a ponytail, and grabbed her keys, phone, and earbuds. She put her earbuds in her ears and headed downstairs. She had a path around her apartment building, the perfect distance for the type of run she was interested in today.

Amy opened her phone. She did not want to look at any of the messages. She just wanted to find her music. She looked down at the screen. Five more messages from Tyler, a message from Melissa, and a message from her sister. Amy's curiosity piqued. Why was her sister calling so late last night? Eh. She was probably going to try to talk to Amy about Thanksgiving again. It was still a few weeks away, but Annalise was a planner. Annalise was pushing hard for her to come this year. Amy quickly clicked on the message. She would listen and then go for her run and call her sister back later, once her head had cleared.

However, as Amy listened to the message, she realized her

sister's voice sounded shaky. "Amy," she said. "It's Annalise. Something has happened with Dad. Please call me back as soon as you get this. Please."

Amy's sisterly instincts kicked into gear immediately. She clicked on the callback button without thinking. She was just reacting. This had nothing to do with her dad and everything to do with Annalise needing her.

Annalise answered right away. Amy could tell that she had been crying. "Amy?"

"Annalise? Are you alright?"

"I'm okay," Annalise answered. "Amy, Dad had a massive heart attack last night. Stephanie found him on the kitchen floor and called the ambulance. They were able to revive him on the way to the hospital, but the doctors decided to do emergency bypass surgery. He is in the ICU, and although the surgery went well, he is not out of the woods yet."

Amy took in the news. She was not sure how she felt. She never wanted to wish ill will on someone, but she had spent so many years being angry with her dad and hardening her heart toward him that she was not sure how she felt about any of this. She almost felt like this was happening to Annalise's friend, not her dad.

"Amy?" Annalise shook her out of her thoughts.

"I'm here," Amy said.

"Please come," Annalise said.

"Annalise . . ." Amy hedged.

"Please. I need you."

That was all Amy needed to hear. "I will get on the first flight I can," Amy said.

"Thank you," Annalise breathed. "I feel so much better

knowing you're coming."

Amy tried to tamp down the feelings of instant regret. She needed to grow up and do this for her sister. Her sister needed her, and she could not remember a time she had not been there for Annalise. Amy turned and headed back up to her apartment. "I will hop online right now and see what flights I can find. Then, I will text you my flight information once I have something."

"Thank you," Annalise said again. "Yes, let me know as soon as you have something. Either Graham or I will be there to pick you up."

"Nonsense," Amy objected. "I can get a ride-share."

"No," said Annalise. "You most definitely will not. One of us will pick you up."

Amy chuckled at this suddenly bossy side of her younger sister. Ride-sharing was almost a way of life in Chicago, but Annalise had become much more assertive and protective after becoming a mom.

"Alright," Amy conceded. "I will text you my flight information as soon as I know."

Amy and Annalise hung up with "I love yous," and Amy headed to her laptop. Once she had confirmed her flight information, she texted Annalise and headed to the shower. She showered, dressed quickly, and packed a suitcase. She had not purchased a return ticket but did not plan on staying very long. She would be there long enough to comfort Annalise and ensure she was okay, and then she would head back to her safe distance of Chicago.

As Amy finished stuffing things into her carry-on, her stomach rumbled. She realized she had only had coffee this morning. It seemed that she was starving. She thought she could wait until she got to the airport and grab something, but suddenly, she was so hungry she was nauseous. While tracking her ride-share driver, she ran into the kitchen to grab something. She settled on a bagel and judging from where her driver was, she would have to eat it plain. She wrapped the bagel in a paper towel, then stuffed it and a bottle of water into her oversized travel purse. She grabbed the rest of her things and headed downstairs to the curb, where she was certain her driver was now waiting for her.

The driver spotted her and got out to help her with her bags. Amy was grateful and hoped she had enough cash for all the tips she would need. She hopped in the back seat and sighed. She would have some time at the airport to think of the people she needed to contact about taking a few days off work. She knew it would not be a problem. It was an emergency, and she had several days off she needed to use anyway. Tyler had teased her that she was a workaholic, and they needed to come up with a good vacation getaway between Thanksgiving and Christmas so she wouldn't lose all her days.

She let her mind wander back to that conversation. "How many days do you actually have banked?" Tyler had asked her. When Amy told him, his eyes widened. "Amy! That is ridiculous. You need to take time off."

"Where would I go and who would I go with?"

Tyler smiled. "Well, you could go with me, and I am sure we could create an amazing destination."

"Quick," he said. "Beach or mountains?"

"Beach," she responded without hesitation.

"All inclusive or put it together yourself?"

"Hmmm . . ." she said, thinking. "All inclusive."

"These are supposed to be quick answers," he reminded her sternly, then tempered it with a kiss on her nose. "Okay," he continued. "One location or several."

"One location," she said.

"Okay," he said. She was reminded of one of those internet quizzes that spit out your results about what kind of Disney princess you are. She tried to suppress a smile at how serious he was. "I think an all-inclusive resort at Cabo San Lucas would be the best option for you."

She smiled. It did sound heavenly. "And would you go with me?" she asked.

"Is this an invitation?" Tyler asked.

"Well," Amy teased, "It would either be you or Ed."

"Ed," Tyler said incredulously. "The guy who mans the grill in the cafeteria?"

"Yes," Amy said."We're very good friends."

"Well," Tyler said. "I think I kiss better than Ed and, therefore, would make a much better companion." He leaned over to prove his point and gave her a kiss that did, in fact, take her breath away.

She smiled at him and said, "Okay, you win. I would rather take you than Ed. I must admit I have never kissed Ed, and I think his wife would disapprove."

"Great!" Tyler said. "It's settled. I will start looking at packages and deals. I am sure we can find something reasonable. How many days were you planning on taking around the holidays?" he asked. "I assume you will go to Texas for part of it."

"I am not sure yet," she hedged. Amy had still not given her sister a definitive answer about Thanksgiving, and she knew she needed to. It was not fair to Annalise that her hangups were affecting Annalise's plans.

Amy snapped herself back to the present. Her driver was prattling on about the weather and how cooler temperatures were on the horizon, with fall beginning. Amy nodded and smiled, and then remembered her stomach. Why did it feel so weird? It was probably just stress. She tore off a piece of her bagel, popped it into her mouth, and chewed.

By the time they reached the airport, Amy had eaten half her bagel and drank half her water. She knew she would have to throw them out before going through security. She stuffed them back into her purse and, after confirming the airline with the driver, waited for him to pull to a stop at the curb. She found her tip money and pressed it into his hand, thanking him as she grabbed her bags lined up on the curb.

Amy walked through the sliding doors and to the ticket counter. Once she checked her bag and made it through security, she found a chair near her gate. She had about forty-five minutes before her flight began boarding. Amy saw an airport store and decided to go there before getting on the plane. She could get a couple of snacks and a carbonated beverage before boarding. The carbonated beverage may help to settle her stomach. What was with her stomach today anyway? Was it something she ate, or was it just the stress of all that had transpired in the last twenty-four hours?

She remembered she needed to call work. She first called the HR line to report what was happening and that she would be gone for a few days. She then texted Brooke, briefly telling her what was going on. Brooke immediately texted back with the kindness she always extended and said, "I am so sorry,

Amy. I will be praying for your dad and you during this difficult time. Please let me know if you need anything. You know I am here for you." Amy, as always, appreciated Brooke's kindness, but Amy also began to feel more tears rush to the rims of her eyes. She worked hard to keep them at bay. If Brooke only knew what else was going on, Amy thought.

Amy scrolled through her text messages and saw she had missed a message from Melissa. It came through last night after Amy had turned her phone off. Melissa's message read, "I don't know what is going on, but you are really on my heart. I am praying for you. Please know I am here if you need me. Love you, friend."

Amy looked up and took some deep breaths. She would not cry. Why was all of this happening at once? At this time, she was having difficulty separating her feelings about what had happened with Tyler from what was happening with her dad. No wonder her stomach was messed up. This was a lot.

Amy stared down at her phone, trying to decide what, if anything, she should say back to Melissa. Amy thought, *Yes, Melissa, please pray. I am a horrible person, and hurt a guy I really liked last night.* Or should she say, *My father is in the hospital, and I am so cold-hearted I still don't want to see him? But I am headed your way because I love my sister.* This might be a bit harsh. Amy continued to stare at the blinking cursor.

Amy was still not sure what she would do when she actually arrived in Texas. She knew her sister would insist on her seeing her dad, and Amy was just not sure she could. Her body began to fill with dread. *Why did she say yes to this?* she mused to herself. She knew why, she admitted to herself. No matter Amy's issues with her dad, she loved Annalise. She had been a mom to Annalise, and she was putting Annalise's feelings before her own. Hopefully, that made her slightly less cold-hearted.

Amy looked at Melissa's message. Of all the people out there, Melissa would understand Amy's jumbled feelings about her dad. She finally typed back, "Thank you, Melissa. Annalise called this morning and said Dad had been taken to the hospital last night with a massive heart attack. Annalise insisted that she needed me, so I'm headed to Texas. I am not sure what I am in for."

She hit send before she could change her mind, and then instantly saw the bubble indicating Melissa was typing back. Amy patiently stared at her phone, and then the message came through. "Oh, Amy, I am so sorry. I know how hard this is for you. Definitely praying, and if you need me for support, I'm here." Honestly, even though Amy hadn't seen Melissa in a long time and they hadn't spoken regularly, it brought Amy a lot of comfort to know Melissa would be there for her.

"Thank you," Amy finally typed back with a heart emoji. Just as she pressed send, she saw a message from Tyler begging her to please talk to him. He didn't know what he had done wrong, but whatever it was, he could fix it.

Amy quickly sent a message back before she could change her mind. "You didn't do anything wrong. You're perfect. I'm the one who is wrong. I'm so sorry. I'm headed to Texas, though. My dad is in the hospital. Maybe we can talk when I get back. Again, I'm so sorry."

Amy knew he returned a message, but she couldn't read it then. All of this was making her stomach feel even worse. She rose from her seat and headed to the airport store. She bought a couple of snacks and a bottle of Sprite and then impulsively bought a magazine as well. Maybe mindlessly perusing the pages of the home decor magazine would keep her mind occupied. Amy went to the restroom and made her way to her gate just as the airline attendants announced they would begin boarding her plane.

Since Amy had purchased her ticket so late, she knew she would be in the last boarding group. She hoped she would not end up in a middle seat. Thankfully, the flight wasn't full, and Amy managed to find an aisle seat toward the back of the plane. She was grateful. Her stomach still felt weird and wouldn't seem to settle, so she wouldn't have to crawl over other people if she needed to use the restroom mid-flight. Even amid stress, Amy had never experienced stomach discomfort like this. Maybe she had caught a touch of a stomach bug. Great! Just what she needed on top of everything else. When the stewardess came by, she ordered a ginger ale and hoped the bland snacks the airlines tended to serve would settle her stomach. She really didn't have time to be sick. Although she thought that if she were sick, she could beg off from going to the hospital. She knew the thought was immature and selfish and pushed it away immediately.

When the plane landed in Texas, Amy turned her cell phone back on when the all-clear was given and waited for it to connect to the nearest tower. Once it did, several messages showed up on her screen: one from Annalise telling her to text Graham, Annalise's husband, when she got off the plane, and then one from Tyler that she still didn't want to look at.

Amy sighed deeply. This was all too much. Why did everything happen all at once? And now, she was back in Texas.

Texas was a big state, but she had managed to avoid it for quite a while. She waited for her turn as others disembarked the plane, grabbed her carry-on from the overhead compartment, and made her way down the plane aisle. She couldn't help but smile at herself when she encountered the Texas-themed airport. A giant mural on the opposite wall depicted a man riding a horse, wearing a cowboy hat and lasso. Texans are very proud to be from Texas. She had missed that about Texas, if she was being honest.

Amy made her way down to the luggage carousel and then texted Graham, letting him know where she was and that she would be outside shortly. He assured her he would drive around until she came outside. Amy watched as the luggage from her flight began to circle the carousel and wondered for the umpteenth time why she had agreed to come. But behind that thought, she knew exactly why she was here. Annalise needed her, and she was programmed to go to her when needed.

Amy spotted her suitcase, successfully retrieved it with the help of a nice gentleman standing nearby, gathered her belongings, and made her way outside. The heat hit her the second she was outside. Ugh . . . this she had not missed. Even though fall was beginning, Texas weather had not received the memo yet. Temperatures were definitely higher than in Chicago. Graham had told her what he was driving in his text message, so Amy began looking for his car. Shortly after, she spotted it and waved. He pulled up to the curb beside her, put his car in park, and hopped out of the car to help her with her bags. Amy liked Graham. He was tall and a little thin. But he had a kind face and a friendly smile. He was perfect for Annalise, and that was most important. She had never admitted this to anyone and barely to herself, but sometimes, when she watched Graham and Annalise together, she hoped she would find a successful relationship.

Once Amy was settled in the car, Graham eased into traffic.

"How was your flight?" Graham asked politely. Even though Annalise and Graham had been married for ten years, Amy did not feel she knew Graham very well. She appreciated his effort in making conversation. Graham had a way about him that put her at ease. She felt he made a good dad to his and Annalise's kids. He seemed like the type of person who sought to understand first and judged last.

"My flight was uneventful," Amy said with a smile.

"That's the best kind," Graham said.

"True," Amy said with a chuckle. "How's Annalise?"

Graham turned his kind face toward Amy. "She is holding up. I really appreciate you coming. She needs your support right now. I know we don't know each other very well, and I know you have certain feelings towards your dad I may not understand. And Annalise may not even fully understand your feelings, but he's your dad."

Amy stiffened. Most people who broached this subject got nowhere with Amy because they wanted to give her unsolicited advice on how to handle her dad. Amy didn't understand how they could advise her on something they didn't truly understand. No one understood what it was like to be crying every single night over your mother as a very young girl, but having to stuff those emotions down, because the parent who was supposed to be caring for you had essentially given up. It was almost as if he wished he didn't have two daughters. That was devastating as a young girl. For years, Amy tried to do everything perfectly so her dad would be okay. For years, she forgave him for forgetting to pay the electric bill and going to the grocery store. For years, she tried to put together a decent dinner for her and Annalise so Annalise wouldn't know how bad things were. For years, Amy covered for her dad so Annalise wouldn't feel the same way Amy did.

Truly, no one understood. But then a thought hit her. Maybe no one understood because she didn't let anyone in. She hadn't told anyone, not even Annalise, what it was really like. The cost of what she had done was sacrifice her emotional well-being for her sister. Her sister having a good relationship with her father was what she wanted, wasn't it? Wasn't that why she did all she did?

Amy realized what she really wanted was for Annalise to be okay, but for her dad to get what he deserved. He was a terrible dad who turned his back on Amy and Annalise when they needed him. He didn't deserve Annalise's love. The thought struck her. She never realized she thought this way.

Graham glanced at her, and Amy realized she had become quiet, completely lost in her thoughts.

"I'm sorry, Amy, if you feel I overstepped. I know this is a sensitive subject. I just know Annalise is going to ask you to go to the hospital with her. I think Annalise thinks she can get you to go for her, but I think you should go for you."

Amy turned and looked at Graham, giving him her full attention. He continued. "Once your dad leaves this earth, you won't be able to resolve anything with him." He said gently. "I would hate for you to live out the rest of your days on this earth, tethered to the things that went unsaid. Whether you forgive him or not is still your choice, but this may be your one chance to explain to him why you feel the way you feel."

Amy felt no judgment coming from Graham. He must be magical because she had allowed him to get further in this conversation than anyone else. Ever. She had always shut down conversations out of self-preservation, telling herself that no one truly understood, so she did not need to listen. Brooke had suggested therapy at one point, but Amy had shrugged off the suggestion and said her dad needed therapy, not her. Why should Amy be punished by talking to a stranger and digging out all her feelings if she wasn't the one who caused any of this? Why was she the only one who wanted to hold her dad accountable for what he had done? It was frustrating.

Graham, as if he could read her thoughts, continued in his gentle manner, "I know you think your dad should be held accountable for his actions. I doubt even Annalise truly knows what you went through, but trying to hold him accountable is standing in the way of you being free to live the life you want. I am afraid that until you can forgive him, your life may be at a standstill."

Amy sputtered, offended. "My life is not at a standstill! I have a very successful job at a very successful firm in a big city. I am climbing the corporate ladder and doing very well for myself."

Graham just nodded, not seemingly put off by her outburst. "You're right, Amy. You are extremely successful in your career and have much to be proud of." Graham conceded.

Amy should have felt vindicated by his comment, but what he hadn't said made her think. Was she successful, though? She didn't have many friends, and guys came and went. When she came across someone she liked, like Tyler, she shut the relationship down before it could get too real. Is that what she wanted? Amy sighed, suddenly tired.

Graham looked at her and smiled. "Any places you want to eat while you are here? I bet you can't get good BBQ in Chicago."

Amy, grateful for the subject change, grinned. "No, the BBQ is terrible there."

"Okay, so at least one meal of BBQ. Got it. What else? Mexican food?"

Amy made a face. "Ahk, their version of enchiladas leaves much to be desired. You can get really good food in Chicago, but yes, they should leave BBQ and Tex-Mex to Texans."

Graham smiled again. "Duly noted. We will try our best to hit some of your favorites while you are here." Amy smiled at him. Amy was thankful that the uncomfortable conversation seemed to be behind them and grateful for the change of subject. Amy understood why Annalise had fallen so hard for Graham.

Upon arriving at Graham and Annalise's house, Graham instructed, "Let's go in, and I can call Annalise and find out the plan. The munchkins will be at a friend's house a little longer before I need to pick them up."

Just then, the front door opened, and Annalise walked out. Her face was pale, and her eyes were puffy from crying, but she was as beautiful as ever. Amy marveled at how Annalise increasingly looked like Mom. Like Amy, she had long blonde hair, but Annalise was slightly taller and thinner. She also had Mom's warm brown eyes. The girls reached out to each other and hugged for a long time.

Annalise pulled back and looked Amy in the face. "Thank

you so much for coming, Amy. Are you okay?"

"Yes," answered Amy. "Are you okay?"

"Hanging in there," Annalise said with an attempt at a bright smile. "Stephanie returned to the hospital and insisted I go home and take a break. I didn't think I could say no since I had done the same to her today. I told her I needed to come home and greet you anyway, and then I, or we, would come up later with dinner for her."

Amy smiled. "Sounds like a plan."

"Really?" Annalise asked hopefully. "You will go with me to the hospital."

"Yes," Amy said. "I can't guarantee how long I will be able to stay in the room with Dad, but I will go to the hospital with you."

Annalise smiled her brightest smile, which had made her a charmer from childhood, and hugged Amy again. "Do you want something to eat or drink? I don't know the last time you ate."

Amy smiled. "You know my stomach has been bothering me today. Do you have any ginger ale or Sprite?"

"I do!" said Annalise. "It's probably left over from the last time one of us was sick, but I think I have a can or two in the garage fridge. I am so sorry your stomach is icky. Do you think it was something you ate?"

"Yes," said Amy. "I truly don't feel sick; I'm just a little off."

Annalise retrieved the ginger ale from the garage and poured Amy some of the liquid into a glass with ice. Because it was usually so warm in Texas, ice was usually a given in any drink. Annalise motioned Amy into the living room while

Graham took Amy's bags to the guest room.

"So what are the doctors saying?" Amy asked Annalise.

Annalise told Amy the last doctor's report, complete with all the correct medical terminology. She was studying to be a nurse when Graham swept her off her feet and married her. Annalise was finishing nursing school with plans to become a full-time nurse when she unexpectedly got pregnant with their first child. She was an amazing mother, and Amy had always thought she was born to have children. However, Amy worried that Annalise might feel she had missed out on something in life if she didn't ever have an opportunity for her nursing career. Annalise shrugged it off when Amy brought up the subject.

Annalise would usually respond, "If that is truly what the Lord has for me, it will happen when it is supposed to. Graham and I feel staying home with the kids is best for now. I promise he is not forcing me to stay home." She would laugh. "He is not tying me down at home with an apron. I want this as well."

Inevitably, at that point in the conversation, Amy would have to let it go. She didn't want Annalise to think she was trying to run her life. She only wanted Annalise's happiness. And if she wanted to be a stay-at-home mom to two kids, then so be it.

After Annalise had given Amy the full report on her dad's health, Amy summarized, "So what you are saying is that he is doing better, but he is not out of danger yet."

"Exactly," Annalise said.

"Do they know how much longer he will have to be in the ICU?"

"No," Annalise said. "It depends on how well he does these

next few nights."

Amy took in the information, trying not to let any of her true feelings show. "What time did you want to head back to the hospital?"

"Hmmm . . . " Annalise glanced at the clock. "Maybe in a couple of hours. That will give me enough time to see the kids, get dinner for Stephanie, and then head back there. Maybe by then, Stephanie will be ready to leave the room for a bit."

Amy glanced at the clock. She was grateful she would have a little rest before going. "Okay," Amy said. "I will go unpack and maybe lie on the bed for a second before we need to go."

Annalise laughed. "Yes, if you are going to rest, you'd better do it now. The kids will be home soon and are anxious to see their Aunt Amy."

Amy giggled. She was anxious to see them, too. Amy realized then that in keeping her dad at a distance, she was also keeping the rest of her family at a distance. Maybe Graham was right. Who was she really punishing?

**22**

*Amy*

Amy must have dozed off because the next thing she knew, two adorable faces were looking at her from either side of the bed.

"Aunt Amy, Aunt Amy," they said in unison.

Amy tried to shake the sleep from her brain. A slow smile spread across her face, "Well, who are these strangers? I must still be dreaming. This can't be Kaylee and Braedon." She pushed herself to a sitting position, surprised she had slept so hard. The last few days must have taken a more significant toll than she thought.

The children giggled and began to climb on the bed with her, each desperate to be the first to tell Aunt Amy news from their childhood. She took in their angelic faces, and something twisted inside of her. She rarely thought of the abortion she had had in college. In fact, Annalise didn't even know about it. But sometimes, in moments like this, a thought would appear unwelcome in her brain. Her child would be turning thirteen soon. Thirteen! Would she or he have been this cute? Would they have had dark or light hair? What color of eyes would they have had? Amy pushed the thoughts away, surprised at the emotion rising in her. *What was wrong with her?* Maybe she was just hormonal.

She glanced at the clock again, trying to register how long she had been asleep. Just then Annalise entered the room. "Hey, sleepy head! That job of yours must be working you too hard. You were out."

"I am so sorry," Amy said.

"Don't be," Annalise said. "I'm glad you got some rest. Maybe the rest will help settle your stomach as well."

"Maybe it did," Amy said, realizing she was starving. As if on cue, her stomach growled loudly.

The kids laughed, and Amy smiled with them. "Hey! Y'all have grown up so much since the last time I saw you. How old are y'all now? Are you driving yet?"

They both laughed at her silly joke, and Kaylee said, "Nooooo, I'm only seven."

"Seven!" Amy replied. "Wow! That is old!" Amy pulled a silly face. Kaylee laughed again. "And how about you, young man? How old are you?"

"Five!" Braedon said, holding up his fingers for emphasis, clearly impressed that he had made it to five whole fingers.

"Five! Wow! You should be starting college soon."

"Whoa! Easy there." Graham stepped into the room, laughing. "I need a few more years to save for college. Dinner is ready if y'all are ready to eat."

"Yay!!" The kids shouted as they turned to exit the room.

"To the bathroom, both of you, to wash your hands," Annalise ordered.

"Yes, ma'am," they obediently chorused.

"Wow! Bossy," Amy quipped.

"I learned from the best!" Annalise sparred.

"You know, we call those leadership skills now," Amy said, laughing.

"Are you really okay?" Annalise asked, her tone turning serious.

"Yes," Amy assured her. "I think the last few days of work and other things caught up with me. Seriously, the nap helped. I am just fine."

Annalise studied her for a few more minutes with her nursing eyes. "Okay. Well, dinner really is ready if you are up for it."

"Yes, sounds good," Amy said. "Let me just visit the bathroom, and then I will be right there."

Dinner was a much noisier affair than at Amy's quiet apartment. She took most of her meals in front of the television. But here, the table was full of life and laughter. Each child took turns telling about their day with friends. Kaylee, always kind-hearted, was concerned about a little girl who had injured her ankle during PE on Friday.

"Oh, I am sure the school nurse took really good care of her, honey. We can pray for her before we go to bed if you would like." Kaylee nodded, obviously relieved that her mom had assured her that her friend had received the proper care.

Braeden told about the worm he and his friend found, the new video game his friend had, and the basketball game his friend's dad had played with him. Annalise kept her concern for their dad at bay and focused on the children. When Kaylee asked about her grandpa, Annalise assured her that the doctor, nurses, and Jesus were all taking good care of Grandpa. They would also pray for him before bed. Kaylee again seemed relieved.

Amy watched Annalise with her children. She was a natural. She could coax conversation out of them, reassure them when they were worried, and champion the good parts of their day while redirecting them when necessary. Amy remembered her mother much better than Annalise did, and while watching Annalise, she realized Annalise was so much like their mother in her demeanor with her children. Suddenly, tears sprang to her eyes, and a wave of grief for her mother, which she hadn't felt in years, washed over her. She quickly looked down at her plate to hide her tears, but not before Annalise saw her. Annalise caught the kids' attention again so they would not focus on Amy, and Amy was immensely grateful.

"Are y'all all finished eating?" Annalise asked. "If you are, I bet you could convince Daddy to put on a movie for you."

"A movie!" They both said. Amy could tell this was not part of their normal routine, but the kids did not question it. "Sure," she said. "Go with Daddy; he will help you pick one out." Annalise glanced quickly at Graham, and he nodded his head in agreement. It was beautiful how they worked as a team to raise the children.

Once the kids were out of earshot, Annalise studied Amy. "Are you sure you're okay?"

"Yes," Amy reassured her, nodding for emphasis.

"It's okay," Annalise said. "I'm not a little kid anymore, Amy. You don't have to protect me. It's okay to tell me hard things."

"Do you really feel that way?" Amy asked. "That I protect you?"

"Sometimes," Annalise said. "But honestly, you are protecting me from ghosts."

Amy let that sink in for a minute. *Am I? Am I protecting her from things that don't really exist anymore?* It had become so much of who she was, she wasn't really sure. She wasn't sure what she should tell Annalise and what she should keep to herself. Clearly, Annalise was now an adult, married and raising her own family, but Amy couldn't just shut off the protective feelings she felt towards her little sister.

"Okay," Amy decided to dip a toe in the honesty pool. "I was watching you with the kids and struck by how much like Mom you are. Suddenly, I just missed her so much."

"Oh, Amy," Annalise said, her own tears springing to her eyes. She grabbed Amy's hand. "That's the best compliment you have ever given me. I have a few memories of Mom, but the only things I know about her are what you and Dad tell me." Amy stiffened at the mention of Dad talking about Mom.

"Oh, don't get defensive," Annalise said. "Amy, you did a great job of taking care of me. You should not have been put in that position at a very young age. I look at Kaylee and Braedon and realize they are not far away from the ages we were when we lost Mom, and that was a lot to put on you. I cannot even imagine if Kaylee was asked to carry such a burden."

"You were not a burden!" Amy said quickly.

"I appreciate that, but you were still so young to be asked to do all you did. Even Dad realizes it now and feels a lot of guilt for what he put you through. If you say I am like Mom, that is all to your credit."

"No," Amy whispered. "It is to your credit, too. You did not close your heart like I did. I think it's why you have a relationship with Dad and Stephanie." Amy was actually shocked that she admitted such truth aloud.

"Maybe," Annalise acknowledged. "But I didn't go through near what you went through."

Amy stared down at her now-empty plate. She had never really shared with Annalise what she had been through daily, worrying if the electric bill had been paid, lying in bed at night, praying her dad would go to work the next day so they would have money for the grocery store. Their salvation was that their dad had a small life insurance policy on Mom. One night, when Amy was trying to find out from her alcohol-drenched Dad where his paycheck was, he had told her not to worry. "We have plenty of money," he slurred.

She was so frustrated with him that, in a rare moment, she yelled at him. "How can you say that? What are you talking about?" He mumbled about the life insurance policy. Amy was unsure what that was, but she was willing to investigate. After her dad passed out for the night, she went through all the stacks of mail on his desk. Finally, she found it. They definitely did not have plenty of money, but this life insurance check would relieve some stress. She remembered sitting on the floor and crying after she found the check. They would not starve. If she could find a way to limit her dad's alcohol purchases, this money would actually go a long way. That night, she sat up far past her bedtime and hatched a plan. Maybe she could begin watering down some of his alcohol bottles. Maybe it would stretch some of the alcohol. She wasn't sure how all that worked, but it would be worth trying.

Amy finally looked up at Annalise and realized she had been watching her the entire time. Amy tried to cover her tumultuous emotions with a shaky smile. "But we got through it, we did!" she said a little too cheerily to Annalise.

Annalise stared at her for a second and said, "Amy, you don't have to protect me anymore. I know it was tough. You can let me in. I'm an adult now."

Amy breathed in a shaky breath and looked at Annalise for a long moment. Why was she so emotional? Typically, she could hold a pretty tight rein on her emotions, but she just felt all over the place. It probably had to do with what had happened with Tyler. Those emotions were still very fresh.

She finally looked at Annalise. "Thank you," Amy said. "I know you're right. Old habits die hard, and you have such a great relationship with Dad. I don't want to ruin that with my bad memories. Besides, you don't remember very much about Mom, and I do. You should have good memories of at least one of our parents."

She meant the last part to be a little more light-hearted than it came across. She smiled cheerily again at Annalise. "I'm okay, Annalise. I promise."

"I know," Annalise said. "And your relationship with Dad is your business. I just don't want you to have any regrets when he finally passes. Whether this be his time . . . " Annalise had to stop as tears clogged her throat. Amy reached across and retook her hand. Annalise continued, "Or whether it be further down the road. I don't want you to regret not having worked things out with him before he passes."

"Funny," Amy said with a teasing smile. "Graham said something very similar to me earlier. It is like you two talked about me."

Annalise knew Amy was teasing, so she just rolled her eyes. "Let me clean up this, and then we can head to the hospital."

As if on cue, Graham appeared. "No, sweetheart, y'all go. The kids are preoccupied with the movie. I can clean up and do their nighttime routine."

Annalise smiled gratefully at Graham. "Thank you, honey." She walked across the room and kissed him gently on the lips. Amy observed Graham's look of overwhelming love toward her sister. He looked at her as if she were the greatest treasure in the world. Amy thought *I hope someone will look at me that way someday.* Then a voice in her head said, *How can anyone do that if you won't let anyone in?* Amy started as if someone had thrown cold water in her face, and then quickly silenced the thoughts. This was not the time.

Amy looked over at Annalise. "Let me get freshened up quickly, and then I will be ready to go."

"Perfect," said Annalise. "I am going to package up some food for Stephanie. I know she has to be hungry."

---

Twenty minutes later, the sisters were in the car and headed to the hospital. "Are you ready for this?" Annalise asked Amy reluctantly.

"I don't know," Amy answered honestly. "I am also not sure about seeing Stephanie. I have never known where I stand with her, and I am not sure she cares for me at all."

Annalise smiled. "Don't worry about Stephanie. She actually understands more than you know. Her first marriage was pretty rocky, and she was very reluctant to let Dad in. He pursued her pretty hard, though, and eventually won her heart. She made it very clear to him from the beginning that if he ever decided to go back to drinking, she would leave him. He must have believed her because, as far as I know, he has not even taken a sip."

Amy was quiet. She had a tough time believing that. All she had known was the father, who was so addicted that he chose alcohol and his own pain over his own children day after day. When Amy was young, she was terrified she would come home one day and find him dead. Those fears haunted her. Even at her young age, she had understood that if they lost him, she and her sister would more than likely be split up and put into foster homes. More than anything, that fear drove her to try to get her father to quit or cut back. She didn't think she could handle the heartbreak of being without her sister after losing her mom.

She hoped it was true that he was completely dry. When Amy had left for college, she would call Annalise almost obsessively during the first year. By then, her Dad had cut back on the alcohol to a point Amy felt Annalise could handle being there on her own. Annalise finally told her to please leave her alone and enjoy college. Dad was fine, and she was fine. Everything was fine. Of course, Annalise was a full-blown teenager with a fierce independent streak at the time. Amy was uncertain if her dad had begun drinking again, Annalise would tell her. Amy had her suspicions that Annalise enjoyed the freedom of Amy being gone and that Dad was not accustomed to overseeing Annalise. Annalise definitely had a lot more freedom than Amy had at the same age. It was probably why Amy enjoyed the freedom of college life so much after she got over the guilt of leaving her sister.

Amy realized she had been silent for a long moment again. She looked over at Annalise, who was watching the road and studying her at the same time.

"What?" Amy said with a smile.

"Nothing," Annalise said gently. "You just seem really in your head today. Normally, you don't let your thoughts consume you. You stay busy, so you don't have to think."

Amy was surprised at how Annalise had just nailed her. "I don't do that!" Amy said, knowing she did.

Annalise chuckled. "Okay," she said sarcastically.

Amy rolled her eyes. "Whatever," she whispered good-naturedly.

Annalise chuckled again, but then asked, "Seriously, is everything okay with you? I mean, besides the obvious of you being here and about to see Dad for the first time in a very long time, are you okay?"

"Yeah," Amy answered a little too fast to be convincing.

Annalise studied her again. Amy tried not to get defensive. She was not ready to share about Tyler yet, so she had to change the subject.

"So, the doctors are saying Dad still needs more nights in the ICU?" Amy could tell Annalise knew what she was doing but chose to let it go.

Annalise filled Amy in on everything the doctors had said. Even though much of the information was repeated, it comforted Amy to focus on it.

Before Amy was truly ready, the girls reached the hospital. Annalise grabbed the food for Stephanie and made their way to the ICU waiting room. Annalise texted Stephanie to let her know they were there, and in a few minutes, Stephanie emerged from the ICU.

"Ammmmyyyy," Stephanie drew out the word with her East

Texas accent. "I am so glad you came! Your dad will be happy to see you." Stephanie said all this with warm understanding and not a hint of judgment. Stephanie was a slight woman with curly brown hair that looked like it had been permed and colored to look that way. She had sparkling green eyes that emitted joy despite her circumstances. Maybe this woman really was the saint Annalise always described her as. She did seem older than she was, and Amy wondered if that had to do with the difficulty of her previous marriage Annalise had alluded to.

"I brought you some dinner," Annalise said. "I thought you might be hungry."

"Oh, thank you, sweetie," Stephanie drawled. "I did have something when I went home, but this will come in handy later. The waitresses around here are terrible," she said in a conspiratorial whisper.

"You mean the nurses?" Annalise asked with a chuckle, knowing Stephanie was joking.

"Oh, is that why they won't fetch me any coffee? Why don't you girls go in for a bit? Visiting hours will end soon, and they will only let me in."

An entire colony of butterflies instantly moved into Amy's stomach. She was suddenly not at all sure she wanted to see her dad, and she was not sure she wanted to see her dad like this.

Stephanie turned to Amy, patted her arm, and said, "Amy, there is no pressure. I am glad you are here, and your Dad will be so glad to see you. But you decide if you are ready to see him."

Amy took a deep breath and nodded appreciatively. Why had she never noticed how motherly Stephanie was? No wonder Annalise was drawn to her. Amy had been so busy comparing Stephanie to her mom that she had never really seen Stephanie.

The girls entered the ward and walked towards their dad's room. Amy took a deep breath and hoped she wouldn't throw up. Why was this affecting her so much? She had worked so hard to bury her emotions regarding her dad.

Their dad's eyes were closed when they entered the room. There were several IVs and beeping machines hooked up to him. He looked so fragile. His eyes fluttered open as if sensing the girls' presence. He looked first at Annalise and then at Amy. He visibly swallowed and then attempted a smile. "My girls," he whispered.

"Shhhh . . . " Annalise said. "You don't have to talk." She grabbed his hand and squeezed.

Amy's dad reached for Amy with his other hand. She reluctantly moved forward until he could hold her hand. She peered at her dad, and all her anger and disappointment bubbled to the surface. How could she forgive this man after he had literally taken her childhood? Didn't he deserve what he was getting right now? Isn't this the price he was paying for years of alcohol? She tried to shove the thoughts down, but they were coming to the surface whether she wanted them to or not. She could not feel sorry for this man. He was literally lying in a bed of his own making. Why could no one else see that? They could all forgive him if they wanted, but Amy was still the hurt little girl who needed her dad more than anything, and instead, he had chosen alcohol.

She had lost both parents when her mom died. But her dad had emotionally abandoned her out of choice. These were the consequences of his actions. Amy stared at her dad. He looked fragile, and part of her wondered if everyone was right. Should she be the bigger person and just forgive him? But could she forgive him? Amy felt he had never really asked for forgiveness. Did he even know he needed forgiveness? How was she supposed to forgive someone who didn't even feel sorry for what he had done? Annalise could not ask for forgiveness or say Dad was sorry on his behalf. He needed to do it. Amy felt tears begin to well up in her eyes and threaten to spill over. Why was everyone on Dad's side, and no one understood how she felt?

Amy couldn't stand there anymore. She looked at Annalise and said through gritted teeth, "Take your time. I will be outside." And then turned and hurried from the room before Annalise could protest.

She rushed out of the ICU doors, hoping the waiting room would be relatively empty. She needed to find a place to be alone before these tears spilled. She looked over and saw the sign for the women's bathroom and rushed in that direction. She went into a stall and barely shut the door before the tears began spilling down her cheeks.

What was wrong with her? She could normally compartmentalize better than this. Why was she turning into an emotional mess? This was ridiculous. Why did she even come? She knew Dad wouldn't apologize; everyone would look to her to make amends. It shouldn't be on her to make amends. She didn't do anything wrong. This argument took place inside Amy's head at full volume.

All of a sudden, Amy knew she was going to be sick. She turned towards the toilet, thankfully in the right place to be sick. When it was over, she knew she would have to exit the stall to clean up. She desperately hoped she was alone in the bathroom. Again, what was wrong with her? She was hardly ever sick, and she definitely did not let her emotions take over so much she would be sick.

Amy unlocked the stall door desperately, hoping she was alone. She walked to the first sink and knew someone else was in the restroom with her. She looked at the woman standing near her and realized it was Stephanie. Stephanie was watching her intently. "You all right, sweetie?" Stephanie asked with genuine care in her voice. Amy scooped water into her mouth to rinse out the taste of vomit and nodded as best as she could.

"Yes, I'm not sure what's going on with me. It must be something I ate."

Stephanie nodded understandingly. And then, with a knowing smile, said barely above a whisper, "Or you are pregnant."

Amy stood up straight and looked at Stephanie, all color draining from her face. "Of course, I am not pregnant," Amy began defensively but stopped. Was she? Amy began counting back to her last period and then took inventory of all her symptoms she was chalking up to something else. Maybe she was pregnant. The last time she had felt this way . . . She let that thought trail off as if setting a balloon free to the outside world.

Wow! If she was pregnant, how did she let this happen again? Didn't she learn her lesson the first time? Amy began to berate herself mentally as tears welled in her eyes again.

She looked at Stephanie. Stephanie was standing there looking at her like . . . like a mother. And Amy so longed for a mother's embrace. She did the only thing that felt natural at that moment. She walked into Stephanie's waiting arms and sobbed, wetting Stephanie's shoulder with her tears. Stephanie searched in her purse and pushed some tissue into her hand, seemingly unbothered that she had Amy's tears on her shirt.

After Amy had finally collected herself, Stephanie said, "Let's find a quiet place to go and sit down."

Amy, suddenly more tired than she could ever remember, agreed. They found a couple of chairs in the corner of the ICU waiting room and settled into them. Stephanie turned to Amy and said, "Are you okay?" Stephanie's understanding struck Amy. She knew Stephanie called herself a Christian as well and went to church. It was one of the things that bonded Stephanie and Annalise.

"I will be," Amy assured her, nodding for emphasis.

"I know this is a lot for you," Stephanie said. "First, all the things with your dad. I know y'all have some unresolved things to talk about. He really is sorry about how he was with you as a child, sweetie."

Amy studied Stephanie for a second and decided to be honest. She didn't really have anything to lose. "Shouldn't he be the one telling me that? You have told me that, Annalise has told me that, Graham has told me that, but he himself has told me nothing. Shouldn't he be the one apologizing? Why is everyone else doing it but not him?"

Stephanie looked at Amy with a mixture of empathy and firmness. "Well, I guess you would have to stay in a room long enough with him actually to hear the apology, sweetie," Stephanie said so gently that while Amy felt like she should be defensive and upset, Stephanie's statement made her think. Is that what she was doing? Was she the one who was being the coward and not allowing her dad to apologize? Maybe. She wasn't sure.

Amy took a deep breath and let it out slowly. "Maybe you're right," she admitted. "I just feel like he should work harder to apologize to me."

Stephanie said, "I understand, Amy. However, there is really nothing he can say or do to make up for what happened when you were little. It does break his heart for you when he thinks about it. But for him, he has worked things out with God. He desperately wants to work things out with you as well, but ultimately, he knows that whether you forgive him is your choice. I think what really bothers him now is that if you don't forgive him, you will not be hurting him. You will be hurting yourself and future relationships."

"It was the same with my ex-husband," Stephanie continued. "He absolutely did not deserve my forgiveness for what he put me through, but I eventually understood the forgiveness was not really for him. It was for me. If I didn't forgive him, I would live chained to him and all he did to me for the rest of my life. I finally decided I didn't want to live like that."

Amy stared at the floor and thought about everything Stephanie was saying. This was a different perspective to consider. She honestly thought everyone wanted Amy to forgive Dad so they could have peace in the family, and she resented the idea. If they wanted peace, they should look to Dad. But maybe they had wanted her to forgive Dad so she could continue her life.

"Now," Stephanie said, "Let's talk about this possible pregnancy."

Again, Amy looked at her, expecting to see judgment. All she saw was kindness. Amy felt tears spring to her eyes again. What if she were pregnant? What was she going to do? Amy wasn't sure she was ready to deal with this right now.

Stephanie squeezed Amy's hand. "You don't have to tell me anything you don't want to. I just want you to know I am here to help you in any way I can. I have made plenty of mistakes and learned that God still loves me very much. I am in absolutely no place to judge anyone else."

Amy looked at her gratefully. Then, Annalise appeared. She looked from one to the other with open curiosity but thought better of asking what they were discussing. Annalise looked at Stephanie. "Okay, they kicked me out for the night, but Dad rests comfortably. The nurse said you could come back in when ready, and the doctor should be around first thing in the morning."

Stephanie nodded. "Thank you, Annalise. I think I will head back in then. I don't want him left alone for too long."

Annalise stopped her. "Do you need anything else? I know you are not getting much sleep in there, and the chair there cannot be comfortable."

"No," Stephanie assured her. "But I'm right where I want to be."

"Okay," Annalise finally said. "I will be back tomorrow, and hopefully, I can convince you to go home again for a little while."

Stephanie stood and hugged Annalise and then turned to Amy. "Thank you," Amy mouthed. Stephanie nodded and squeezed her hand again. As Stephanie walked away, Amy wished Stephanie had hugged her again. It wasn't until that moment that she realized how much she missed her mother's hugs. No wonder Annalise had gravitated to Stephanie. No one would replace Mom, but Stephanie was pretty close.

When Amy looked at Annalise, she found her studying her

again. Annalise asked, "Are you sure you're okay?"

"I am," said Amy. "I actually had a nice chat with Stephanie, but I am not sure I'm ready to talk about it yet."

"That's fair," said Annalise. Annalise hooked her arm in Amy's and said, "Let's go home. I think it has been a long day for everyone."

Later that night, as Amy pulled back the covers and made herself comfortable in the guest bed, she replayed the events of the day and her conversation with Stephanie. Everyone else Amy had encountered had told her to forgive her dad because it was the right thing to do. Amy really did not care about doing the right thing, whatever that meant. She cared that her dad was not taking ownership of what had happened to her as a little girl. Stephanie had a different way of explaining it. The forgiveness was not for her dad. It was for Amy.

This was a revolutionary thought. Amy reflected on her life. Would she have done things differently or responded differently if she had not constantly fanned the flame of unforgiveness towards her dad? Amy asked herself why she would not want to be with Tyler. He was an awesome guy. Why did she shut him down? What was she so scared of?

Brooke had once tried to broach this subject with Amy. She asked Amy, "If your childhood was different, would you be able to commit and settle down?"

"Absolutely," Amy replied, eager to pile on another thing to blame her dad for.

Brooke nodded and said, "You know, the only person you are truly hurting by holding on to all this is yourself." Brooke said it kindly, but Amy responded angrily, effectively shutting down the conversation.

She didn't speak to Brooke again until Brooke approached her and apologized for sticking her nose in her business. Amy was initially satisfied with Brooke's apology. Amy deserved an apology. It was none of Brooke's business. She had not been there. She did not know what it had been like to grow up, not knowing where the next meal would come from; it would fall on Amy to figure out how to make something edible enough for her and her sister to eat. While other little girls were making chocolate chip cookies and Rice Krispies treats with their mothers, Amy was trying to put together the latest canned goods into a semi-balanced meal.

However, Amy secretly wondered at what Brooke had said. Was her unforgiveness towards her dad keeping her from healthy relationships now? Amy felt a fierce need to protect herself, since no one had protected her as a child, but was she missing out? Was she so busy defending herself from bad things that it was causing her to miss out on good things in life? At the moment, Amy had shoved those thoughts down so as not to analyze them too closely. But now, in light of her conversation with Stephanie, the conversation had returned to her unbidden. Maybe they were both right. Perhaps it was time to forgive her dad. But it wouldn't be for him. It would be for her.

Amy began to drift off to sleep, but suddenly, her eyes popped open. Was she pregnant? No! Surely not. Surely, it was just all the stress. Amy would find a way to venture into a drug store and take a test without anyone else knowing. No one except for Melissa knew she had been pregnant before, and she didn't want anyone to know about this one until she figured out what to do.

She comforted herself with the thought that this was a false alarm and that there was no need to worry, and drifted off to sleep in pure exhaustion.

# 23

Amy awoke to the delicious smell of coffee, and was that pancakes? She couldn't remember the last time she had pancakes. She got up and headed into the bathroom. She was eager to get to the kitchen to see if it was indeed pancakes that she smelled. Her stomach growled in agreement. As Amy washed her hands, she looked in the mirror. She looked rough, she admitted to herself. The events of the day before began to come back to her. It had been a lot.

She intentionally ignored her phone and left the guest room as soon as she was dressed appropriately, heading straight for the smell of coffee. Graham was making pancakes in the kitchen with a towel slung over his shoulder. Graham smiled at her. "Hey there. Sleep well?" he asked pleasantly.

"Uh-huh. So well," Amy said. "Probably the best I have slept in a while. Is the mattress magic?"

Graham chuckled, "Maybe. Help yourself to coffee. There is cream and sugar over there as well. If you are anything like Annalise, you have cream with a little coffee."

It was Amy's turn to chuckle. "I taught her well."

Graham shook his head and laughed. "I am making pancakes for the kids. It was their special request this morning. There will be plenty, but I can also make you some eggs, toast, or anything you would like."

Amy shook her head after her first blissful sip of coffee. "No, the pancakes smell amazing. I can't remember the last time I had them."

"Well," Graham said. "These last few days have been a little hard on the kids. I dragged them out of bed and into their church clothes with the promise of pancakes. We don't usually get this fancy on a Sunday."

Kaylee and Braedon appeared dressed and ready for the day as if on cue. It was obvious someone, probably Annalise, had helped with their hair. They both looked adorable.

"Hey, guys!" Amy sang pleasantly.

"Good morning, Aunt Amy!" Kaylee sang back. Braedon looked as if he was still waking up. Amy went over and hugged Braedon. "I was never really a morning person either," she said to him. Braedon hugged her in response, and it tugged at Amy's heartstrings.

Amy looked up to catch Graham watching her. "What?" Amy said, smiling.

"Nothing," Graham said. "You are just really good with kids, and then I remembered you were raising a child when you were a child."

Suddenly, there were tears in Amy's eyes again. Ugh. She hated that she was so emotional right now. Then, the next thoughts came uninvited. What if she really was pregnant? What would she do? Would she tell Tyler? When she was pregnant in college, she never did say to the guy. He was a random one-night stand who had no more business taking on another human life than she did. He probably had slept with multiple women in the same week. At the time, she was convinced there was no reason to tell him and let him weigh in on her decision. She had held firm to the "my body, my choice" way of thinking.

But if she were pregnant, shouldn't she tell Tyler? He was completely different from the guy in college. Did Tyler have a right to know? Amy brought herself out of her thoughts. She didn't even know if she was pregnant yet—no need to go down all these what-if roads. Luckily, Graham and the kids were talking about how many pancakes they would start with, and no one noticed Amy, lost in her thoughts and out of the conversation.

Annalise entered the kitchen and put her arm around Amy. "Good Morning!" she said cheerily. She had always been the morning person. "How did you sleep?"

"Good," said Amy.

Graham looked at Annalise. "She asked if the mattress was magic."

"Not quite," Annalise said, sharing a conspiratorial grin with Graham.

"Okay, I will definitely ask about that later," said Amy.

Annalise looked at Amy and began, "I spoke with Stephanie this morning. The doctor came around very early, and it looks like Dad has improved enough since yesterday to try and transfer him to a regular room today."

"Oh, okay," said Amy. "Good news, then."

"Yes," Annalise said. "So, I am not sure what time we will go to the hospital today. Stephanie won't want to leave Dad until he gets settled into a room, so it may be later today before

I can convince her to leave. I think Graham and the kids will go to church and have lunch. That will free us to go to the hospital when we're ready."

"Okay," said Amy. "I left Chicago so quickly that I probably need to email work before tomorrow and make sure my bases are covered. And is there any way I could borrow a car for a little bit today? I forgot some personal items and need to swing by a drugstore."

"I can take you," said Annalise.

"Oh no, that is okay," said Amy. "I don't want to put you out. I know you have a lot on your plate. I will just run there and run back."

Amy knew Annalise could tell she was being weird, but blessedly chose not to push it. "Sure," said Annalise. "Just let me know when you are ready to go, and I will get you my car key."

"Thanks," Amy said. "No rush. Whatever works for you." Amy thought, *the longer we wait, the more I can be in denial.*

After breakfast, Amy stayed and helped Annalise clean up the dishes while Graham finished getting ready for church. He and the kids left in a cyclone of goodbyes, and we will miss you, Mommy, and Aunt Amy, as well as hugs and kisses all around. Once Amy was safely back in the guest room with the door closed, she checked her phone. She had several messages from Tyler begging her to communicate with him, one from Brooke, and one from Melissa.

She chose to ignore the ones from Tyler right now. She really could not deal with trying to answer him with everything else going on, and what if she were pregnant? How was she going to approach that subject? Should she approach that subject? She sighed and pushed the thoughts out of her head. She just couldn't think about it right now.

She looked at the message from Brooke. The message was very kind, in typical Brooke fashion. She wanted to know how Amy was doing, knew this was not easy for her, and assured Amy that she was praying for her. Amy was very uncertain of the power of prayer. But at this time, and in her situation, she would take it. What did it hurt? Good thoughts, good vibes, and prayer were all the same, but if Brooke believed in it, she would take all the good juju she could get right now.

Amy typed a quick message back to Brooke, thanking her for her kind words, and providing a quick update on her dad. They exchanged a few short texts about work where Brooke assured Amy she would help make sure her bases were covered on Monday. Brooke told her not to worry about anything and promised her that if there was a problem, Brooke would call her.

Amy then looked at her message from Melissa. Melissa asked for an update on her dad as soon as Amy could manage to message her back. She also reassured Amy she was praying for her dad, her, Annalise, and all of the family dynamics.

Amy stared out the window in the bedroom for a moment and thought, for someone who was on the fence about God, how it was she had managed to surround herself with so many who did believe in God? She didn't have time to analyze that particular thought right now and tucked it in the corner of her mind to think about later.

Amy looked down at her phone and began typing a response to Melissa. Melissa probably knew more than anyone how complicated her relationship with her father was. There were many a night after partying and plenty of alcohol that Amy's mouth seemed to move on its own, and she would pour her heart out to Melissa. She told Melissa things she had never told anyone. She never knew how much Melissa remembered the following day because Melissa never tried to bring it up on her own or fix Amy. She just listened and let Amy get it out.

Amy read what she had written so far and then changed her mind. She quickly hit the call button and let it ring. Amy suddenly had a strong desire to talk to Melissa. Melissa answered on the second ring and spoke into the phone. "Hold on one sec." Amy heard music in the background. Was Melissa at church?

Melissa spoke into the phone in a low tone. Amy could tell she did not want to be overheard. "Amy? Can you hear me?"

"Hi, Melissa. Are you at church?"

"Yes," Melissa plowed ahead, essentially ignoring the question of why she would take a call while she was at church. "Oh, Amy. I am so glad you called. Are you okay?"

"Yes," Amy said.

"How are you?" Melissa asked with genuine empathy in her voice. Her tone made Amy tear up. She shoved the tears down.

"Dad is in the ICU, but it looks like they may move him to a regular room today," Amy said.

Amy could hear Melissa take a deep breath, probably gathering her thoughts. That is one thing Amy admired about Melissa. She was careful with her words. "I know this is hard for you, Amy, but I am so glad you are there. I think it is important. You and your sister are so close, and even if it is just for her right now, I think this is good. Have you seen your dad yet?"

"I did briefly," confessed Amy. "Honestly, I just couldn't

stand there and pretend that just because he has had surgery and is in a fragile state right now, everything is fine. I am really here for Annalise."

"Understandable," said Melissa. "These are baby steps, Amy. You flew to Texas. You went to the hospital. You were willing to go to his room. Celebrate what you did and be patient with yourself for the rest." Amy let out a sigh of relief. She was thankful Melissa was being so understanding.

Melissa continued, "I will pray for wisdom for you, Amy. If you are ready to be set free from your past, you will find the right moment to hash it out with your dad. If not, then maybe you will be ready another time."

Amy wasn't sure she liked the way Melissa put that. Again, why did everyone think this was on her? She hadn't done anything wrong. She said as much to Melissa. Melissa said gently, "True, Amy. You are right. But you do have to give your dad an opportunity. If you keep shutting the door, then that part is on you."

Amy sighed. She knew Melissa was right, but part of her, no, a lot of her, still wanted to see her dad suffer. He really did not deserve forgiveness.

"Well, I'll let you get back to church. Thank you for answering your phone."

"Anytime," Melissa said.

"I will keep you updated, and I would love to try and see you while I am here."

"Please do," said Melissa. "I would love to see you too. Call me anytime."

"Thank you!" said Amy.

Amy hung up the phone, hoping she and Melissa could

make time to see each other. She didn't realize until just this
moment how much she missed day the day-to-day friendship
with Melissa.

# 24

# *Melissa*

Melissa clicked off her phone and stared at it for a couple of minutes, thinking. She knew she needed to get back into church, but gave herself a moment to rehearse the conversation. She hoped this would be when Amy would let her dad apologize and make things right.

When Amy first began to tell Melissa things about her childhood in college, Melissa felt Amy had every right to be angry with her dad. Melissa could see how Amy felt abandoned and left to do everything on her own when she was just a child. She could see her fears, anger, and disappointment. However, it seemed Amy's dad had pulled himself together over the last few years. He had gotten help with his drinking, and he had become a parent to Annalise, albeit very late in her childhood. But still, he had made strides. Now, he was remarried to someone who seemed to have her life together. Most importantly, Amy's dad had rededicated his life to the Lord.

What broke Melissa's heart for Amy was that she was angry with a version of her dad that no longer existed. Her dad had tried to reach out to Amy to ask for forgiveness, but she wasn't ready to accept that he had changed. It was like the bitterness had become a part of her, and she didn't know how to exist without it. She pictured Amy trapped in a spiderweb of negative emotions that were affecting her life, but Amy couldn't see it. Amy thought she was free, but really, she was tied to her past. The distance she put between herself and her dad had not done anything to set her free.

"Oh Lord," Melissa prayed under her breath. "You love Amy more than I do. You know what is in her heart and her deepest fears. Please comfort her and love her during this time. But also, Lord, please help her open her heart to her dad. If she could accept his forgiveness, she would be free to live her life rather than react to her past."

Melissa paused, thinking how good it would be to see Amy while she was in Texas. Melissa shook herself from her thoughts and looked around. She realized worship was just about over, and the sermon would begin. She needed to go back in before Blake started to worry about her. She vowed to continue to pray for Amy. Melissa wanted to see her friend truly live a joy-filled life.

# 25

# Amy

Amy stared at herself in the mirror. She wanted to sit down and have a long cry, but she wasn't sure she would ever stop crying. Then she would have to tell Annalise everything that was happening, and she just did not want to do that right now. So she shoved all the emotions down once again and focused on the day at hand. As soon as she was presentable, Amy would run over to the drug store on the corner and get a pregnancy test or four. Maybe she could pick up a couple of other items, so it wouldn't seem so suspicious. Hopefully, they will not be headed to the hospital any time soon.

Amy got ready quickly, deciding to put her hair up in a loose bun and wear minimal makeup. She would put on just enough to hide any evidence of the tumultuous thoughts going on inside her brain. She then quickly tidied the guest room and made her way back out to the kitchen, where she found Annalise pouring herself another cup of coffee.

"Everything okay?" Annalise asked.

"Yes, I needed to message Brooke from work, and then I spoke with Melissa."

"Oh, Melissa. How is she? You haven't seen her in a while,

have you?"

"She, Blake, and the kids are all doing well. We may try to see each other while I am here."

"Oh, that's awesome. She always seemed so sweet," said Annalise. "Here are the keys to my car. Are you sure you don't want me to go with you? It's no trouble."

"Oh no," Amy said. "I am going to run there and right back."

And Amy made a hasty exit before Annalise could think of an excuse to come with her. She knew she acted like a suspicious teenager, but it couldn't be helped.

Amy made her way to the corner drugstore. She went inside and grabbed several pregnancy tests from several brands. She knew it was probably overkill, but she did not want to have to repeat this errand. She then decided to buy some other things. She found some lip gloss she wanted to try, a cute toy for each kid, and some fake press-on nails she had seen on social media. She hoped the items appeared random enough that the cashier wouldn't realize she was there for just one thing.

Amy piled her items in front of the cashier, who was busy staring at her phone and chomping on her gum. "Will this be all?" she asked, not even glancing at Amy.

"This is it," confirmed Amy.

The cashier tore away from her phone long enough to scan the items and shove them into a bag.

"Cash or credit?" she said between chews of her gum. Amy wondered briefly if her jaws were sore because of how much chomping she was doing.

Amy pulled out her credit card. "Credit."

The cashier instructed Amy to follow the directions on the screen, put her receipt in the bag, and handed it to her.

"Have a good day," the cashier said, already returning to her phone. The extra purchases were probably not necessary. Oh well.

Amy drove back to the house, planning to head straight to her room with her items before returning the keys. Again, she felt like a suspicious teenager. She managed to stow her items in her room before finding Annalise. She would have to find time to take the tests later. Now that she had them, she was anxious to see the results.

She found Annalise reading her Bible on the couch with a cup of coffee. She smiled when she saw Amy. "Did you get what you needed?"

Amy could tell Annalise wanted to know what Amy was up to, but she held her tongue. "Yeah, I found just what I needed. Have you heard from Stephanie yet?" she asked, eager to change the subject.

"I did," said Annalise. "They are moving Dad into a room, hopefully in the next hour, so the plan is for us to go to the hospital after lunch and spend the afternoon there. Stephanie can go home and take a shower and get a nap, etc."

"Sounds good," said Amy a little too brightly. She was not in a hurry to repeat the experience from last night at the hospital. But she knew she needed to go with Annalise to the hospital. She was not sure how much she would interact with her dad.

Amy plopped down on the other end of the couch and folded her legs underneath her. Annalise looked over at her with tears in her eyes. "I want to thank you again for coming."

"Oh, Annalise, don't get emotional. You know I will always be here for you."

"I know," Annalise said. "And you always have been. You have been a constant in my life, and I know you will always come when I need you. However, I am wondering if maybe you need me too."

It was Amy's turn to have tears spring to her eyes. Amy stared down at her hands clasped in her lap. The truth was, she did need Annalise, but they had never really had that type of relationship. Amy had always taken care of things. Always. She had left out things of their childhood purposefully so Annalise could have as normal a childhood as possible.

"Amy," Annalise said gently. Amy looked up at her. "You can tell me the truth."

At that, Amy felt tears slide down her cheeks. On the one hand, she wanted to protest that statement. Of course, she needed to protect Annalise from the truth. That was all she had ever done. When the electric bill was not paid on time, she made a game of it with Annalise. They would build a fort, use flashlights, and eat cold sandwiches. She never let Annalise know how much pressure was actually on her.

But on the other hand, Amy felt relieved by Annalise's statement. Amy realized at that moment she was so tired. Everything she had been carrying for so long had exhausted her, and honestly, she wasn't sure she could carry it anymore.

Annalise reached over and grabbed Amy's hand. "Amy, you are the best sister anyone could ask for. You stepped to the plate when some sisters may have looked for a way out. You protected, guided, and gave so much for me, but those days are over. And while I am thankful, I feel like you are still carrying that burden, and I think it is time to set it down."

Amy was crying in earnest now. How did Annalise know?

Amy looked up at her. "Annalise, you are not a burden."

Annalise chuckled. "You sure about that?" Then she said, "I know I'm not a burden, but what was thrust upon you in childhood was. And while I'm grateful more than you realize, I know it is time for you to let go. Please let me in, and let me be your sister."

Amy again looked at Annalise, startled. "What do you mean? Of course, you're my sister."

Annalise sighed. "Amy, I'm not mad at you, but I don't think you realize that to stay away from Dad, you also stay away from me. I think you're so busy living in the past that you don't know how to have a present-day relationship with me. And I want a relationship with you. I want you to be able to tell me what is going on in your life. The good and the bad, and to feel I can listen and handle it and maybe even help."

Amy stared down at her hands again. Was Annalise right? To protect herself from her dad, she distanced herself from Annalise. She didn't want to admit it, but she was pretty sure Annalise was right. "Oh Annalise, I am sorry. I never meant for you to feel I didn't want you in my life."

"No, it's okay. I'm just telling you you did a good job taking care of me. But we are both adults now, and I want this relationship to be a two-way street."

Amy stared at Annalise. When did Annalise become so mature? Or had she always been this put-together, but Amy was still trying to be her mother?

Amy sighed. "Okay," she told Annalise with a smile. "I promise I will try. This is going to be a huge mind shift for me. It may take some time."

"That's fair," Annalise acknowledged.

"Now," Annalise said in her best motherly voice. "Do you want to tell me what you *actually* needed at the drugstore?" Amy did not. She was not ready to discuss Tyler or the possible pregnancy or any of it.

"Not right now," Amy said. Amy could tell Annalise was disappointed, but she respected Amy's answer.

"Okay," Annalise said. "I am here when you are ready."

"I appreciate that," said Amy.

"So," Annalise took a deep breath. "Before we go to the hospital, can I take you to lunch? Would you like tacos from your favorite taco place?"

Amy grinned, and Annalise said, "I will take that as a yes."

The girls each went their own way to freshen up, and as Amy entered the bathroom, she stared at the pregnancy tests she had purchased. Did she dare take one right now? No, she was going to wait. If she took it right now, and it was positive, she wasn't sure she could handle the afternoon. Even though she felt better after her conversation with Stephanie yesterday and now with Annalise today, she still had to see her dad this afternoon. She knew she could tell Annalise she would go to the hospital and then just not see her dad, but she wasn't sure she wanted to do that. Maybe what everyone was saying was getting to her. Maybe she had to stay in the room long enough to let him speak.

She grabbed her purse, shoved the pregnancy tests back in her suitcase for safekeeping, and shoved all thoughts of pregnancy away in the back of her mind to pick apart later.

She walked out and saw Annalise was ready to go. The girls made their way to Annalise's minivan and climbed in. Amy had always scoffed at minivans and all the stereotypes that went with them, but she had to admit, they were pretty comfortable. Amy asked Annalise about the kids and their school, and Annalise was off talking about her favorite subject. Amy didn't mind listening. She enjoyed this side of Annalise. They chatted all the way to the restaurant. When Amy saw the familiar sign, her stomach rumbled. Annalise chuckled at her.

"Are we not feeding you enough?" She asked teasingly.

Amy chuckled. "I never eat this much. Maybe I am just hormonal, or maybe I just really missed these tacos. There are no tacos like these in Chicago."

The girls were seated at a small table in a corner. There was a good-sized lunch crowd in the restaurant. It was loud and smelled of peppers and onions. To Amy, it felt like home. She did miss some things about Texas very much.

The girls ordered their drinks, and the waiter brought chips and salsa to the table. He asked if they already knew what they wanted since neither had bothered to look at the menu. They both assured him they did. He smiled and took their order, promising them their food would be right out.

Amy took a chip, dug it into the chunky salsa, and popped it into her mouth. So good. Annalise followed suit. After they had each eaten a few chips Annalise asked Amy about work. Amy filled her in on the big project she and Tyler had completed and how excited she was that it had gone so well, because it could mean good things for her as she continued to climb the career ladder at this company.

Annalise listened intently. Although Amy knew Annalise didn't know a lot about Amy's world, she appreciated Annalise's effort to understand it. Annalise seemed happy to not be in the corporate world and not nursing as she had planned, but

Amy was genuinely grateful Annalise said she was happy.

Annalise asked Amy more questions about her job and the company. Annalise also asked about Brooke. "She sounds so sweet," Annalise said. "I am glad you have her as a friend. Any other friends? This Tyler fellow sounds pretty cool."

Amy's face must have given more away than she wanted because Annalise instantly apologized. "Did I say something wrong?" she asked. "What's wrong?"

Amy took a deep breath and remembered their conversation from this morning. She wasn't ready to tell Annalise everything, but she wanted to work on letting her in.

"Tyler and I dated for a bit. We were having fun. From the beginning, I thought we had an understanding to keep things fun and not too serious. But I guess I was wrong because he cooked me dinner on Friday night and told me he loved me. I couldn't say it back. So, I left, and I haven't talked to him much since."

"Oh Amy," Annalise said. "This just happened? I'm so sorry. Why couldn't you say it back? Do you not love him, or do you not know how you feel?"

Amy shook her head. "Annalise, I don't think I am capable of loving anyone."

"Not true," said Annalise. "You have such a big heart, Amy. You love me so well, and you love my children, and you like Graham," she said with a half laugh. "You are fully capable of loving people. I think you are scared."

"Of course I am scared," Amy sputtered. "What if I say I love him back, and then he trounces all over my heart? What then?"

"You pick up the pieces, and you try again. Love is a risk,

Amy. There are no guarantees. People leave, people disappoint, people die," she said barely above a whisper. "But if you go through life trying to manage the risk, you will miss out on so much. When you open your heart to love and being loved, there is so much out there to experience."

Annalise let her words sink in for a minute and asked, "Do you love this, Tyler?"

"I don't know. I think I might. He is pretty great. But what if I say that to him, and then I really can't love him back the way he needs, and he gets hurt."

"Amy, don't you think you have already hurt him?"

Amy had not thought about that. She was so busy trying to protect herself and, in turn, him that she hadn't stopped to think that by running away from him, she was already hurting him. Deeply. The thought cut her to the quick. What was she doing?

"Amy, can I ask you a question? I am not asking in judgment."

Amy nodded.

"Are y'all sleeping together?"

"Of course we are," Amy said defensively. "We are grown adults. That is what adults do."

Amy knew Annalise had saved herself for marriage, but she had married so young. She didn't know what it was like to be a single adult.

"Well, if you are sleeping with him, don't you think you have expressed love to him already?"

"What do you mean? I thought we had an understanding that this would not get serious."

"Okay, but was he dating other people?"

"No." Then she thought of some of the other people at work she had seen Tyler with. "At least, I don't think so," Amy added.

"Were you?"

"No."

"So it was a mutually exclusive casual relationship?"

What was Annalise getting at? Amy thought and then said, "Yeah, I guess."

"I think your actions communicated more to him than your words."

Amy let that sink in for a minute. Was Annalise right? Had she led him on in a way that allowed them to enter an exclusive relationship even though Amy kept telling herself it was casual?

Amy did not want to think about this right now. Tyler was a grown man. He knew what he was potentially opening himself up to. Amy thought she had made it very clear that she did not want a serious relationship. Besides, no guy would put the brakes on an intimate relationship. Their brains lead with sex. Amy did nothing wrong. She decided to absolve herself of all guilt. But a thought niggled in the back of her mind that part of this was indeed her fault, and what would Annalise say if Amy did turn out to be pregnant? Would she even tell Annalise? What would Annalise say if she knew this wasn't the first time Amy had found herself pregnant, but the second?

Annalise remained quiet as Amy processed her thoughts.

Thankfully, the waiter appeared with their food at that moment. Amy's mouth watered. She had missed tacos.

Annalise asked Amy if she could say a quick prayer before they ate. Amy agreed and bowed her head as if she were an obedient child. Annalise thanked God for their food and prayed for healing for their dad and for peace for Amy. Amy felt uncomfortable. She and God were not on good terms, and she was sure He did not want to hear about her. Amy was on her own. God had no interest in her.

When Annalise said amen, Amy looked at her and smiled politely. "Thank you, Annalise. You don't have to bother God with me, though. I am sure He has more important things on His agenda." She finished the statement in her head: Because if He wanted to bother with me, Mom wouldn't have died.

Annalise looked at Amy for a long moment as she nibbled on a chip dipped in guacamole. "Can I ask you a question, Amy?"

"Sure," Amy tried for light and chipper, but it kind of came out high-pitched.

"How do you think God feels about you? And feel free to be honest. You will not offend me."

Amy took a bite of her delicious taco, put it back on her plate, and purposely chewed slowly to weigh how she wanted to respond to her sister. She knew her sister believed in God and church, and everything that came with it had become very important to Annalise and Graham. However, Amy usually found a way to skirt around the subject.

If there was a God—big if—then He certainly did not like Amy very much. Amy had come to believe people believed in God, so they could explain unexplainable things in this world. But most people she knew who believed in God believed in a loving God. And if that were true—if He were really loving— then taking Amy's mom away at such a young age was not at all loving. So, Amy had concluded, if there was a God, he certainly did not like Amy.

Amy focused her attention back on Annalise, who was patiently studying Amy's face, waiting for her answer. Amy was weighing her answer. Should she take what Annalise said about not being offended at face value and be honest for once?

"I don't know, Annalise," Amy finally answered. "I am not fully convinced there is a God. I mean, a God who created the entire universe seems pretty far-fetched to me. I know after Mom died, it was comforting to think of her in a better place, like heaven, where she wasn't in pain anymore. But I think Heaven and Hell and all of that, people made up to keep people from doing bad things.. Also, if a loving God exists, how come He has not shown me love? I mean, why would you take a mom away from two little girls? That does not at all represent a loving God that people talk about."

Amy studied Annalise's face carefully. She didn't see signs of Annalise being offended. Maybe this God wasn't as important to Annalise after all?

Annalise finally spoke, measuring her words carefully. "Amy, I will not try to convince you that you are wrong. That there is a God, and He loves you. I honestly think that is the Holy Spirit's job, but I want to give you something to consider. I do think God loves you very much. I don't know why Mom was taken away when she was, either, but I don't think God took her away. God loves choice. He created and chose us, hoping we would choose Him back, but He will not force us. When Adam and Eve chose sin over God, sin entered the world. We live in a world where evil is all around us. That is what took Mom away, not God. God did provide for us, though. He gave us each other. He gave me you. You were smart enough to figure out how to take care of us and keep us together. You handled Dad well, and you figured out our finances so we could eat and not stick out at school and cause other problems."

Annalise continued, "We were both fortunate enough to attend college and get a good education. You have an amazing job that you enjoy. I consider these all blessings from God in the wake of something terrible that happened to us."

Amy nibbled on a chip and considered these things. Amy didn't want to argue with Annalise either. She knew Annalise's faith was important to her, but she wasn't sure she saw these things as Annalise did. She felt she had gone to college and landed her job despite all the bad things that had happened to her. God had not helped her overcome. She had overcome. Amy was the reason Amy was doing so well.

A thought came to Amy almost immediately. *Are you doing well, though? You might be pregnant by a man you are running away from. Also, do you live in Chicago because it was the only place you wanted to work, or were you trying to get as far away from your dad as possible? Therefore, you are also distancing yourself from your sister?*

Amy shoved these thoughts away. Amy was the victim. Self-preservation had guided Amy's choices. If Amy was not doing well, it was someone else's fault.

Amy looked up to see Annalise studying her again. Amy smiled reassuringly at Annalise. "Agree to disagree?"

Annalise was quiet for a moment, seemingly weighing whether she should press it further. "Okay, we'll drop this. For now," she said with a wide smile and popped another chip into her mouth.

**26**

*Amy*

After a quick call to Stephanie, Annalise found their Dad had been moved to a regular room and was settled and doing well. The girls drove to the hospital without saying much, each in their own thoughts. After confirming what room number their Dad was in, they headed to the hospital room on the third floor. They walked down the long hallway, and Amy could see Stephanie standing outside of what was probably her dad's room. Amy noticed Stephanie looked absolutely exhausted. After their conversation yesterday, Amy's heart had softened towards Stephanie. She felt bad for her. She tried to put herself in Stephanie's shoes. The man she loved had given her quite a scare. Amy felt a little selfish that Stephanie had been so understanding and helpful the day before.

When Stephanie saw the girls approaching, she perked up. She gave each of them a quick hug. "Thank you for coming. I know I need to go home for a bit, but I am just not ready to leave him in the nurses' care yet."

"Of course," Annalise said. "We ate a good lunch. Graham is home with the kids, so you should take your time. We won't need to go anywhere for a while."

Stephanie smiled in relief. "Thank you, Annalise. I don't know what I would've done without you. I think I will go home, shower, nap, and get something to eat. I will be back in time so you girls can go home, and Annalise, you can see your kiddos before they go to bed."

Annalise smiled. "You take your time, Stephanie. Graham has it all under control."

"Okay," Stephanie said. "The nurse should be just about done helping him to the bathroom. You can go on in. I took advantage of her being there and stepped out. I will go in and get my purse and kiss him goodbye, and then I'll head out."

Annalise and Stephanie turned to go into the room.

Amy hesitated, "I'll be in in a minute." Amy stood outside her dad's room, taking deep breaths. She could do this. She could go in. If she became uncomfortable, she would make an excuse about work and browse the gift shop or something. She could do this.

Just as Amy was about to enter the room, Stephanie came out with her purse. She studied Amy's face. "You okay, sweetie?" she drawled. Amy noticed Stephanie's accent was more pronounced the more tired she was.

Amy nodded. "Thank you again for yesterday. I appreciate your understanding."

Stephanie smiled warmly. "Do you know anything yet?"

If anyone else had asked Amy this question, she would have been instantly defensive, but for whatever reason, she wasn't defensive with Stephanie. It surprised her. Stephanie was married to her dad. She chose the man who had abandoned Amy when Amy needed him the most. Maybe it was because Stephanie did not pretend her life was perfect. She was pretty open about having made plenty of mistakes.

Amy shook her head. "I bought tests this morning, but I haven't had a chance to take them yet."

Stephanie smiled and patted Amy's hand reassuringly. "I don't mean to pry or to push, but I am here for you if you need to talk. I don't want you to think you are going through this alone."

"Thank you," Amy whispered, tears lining up behind her eyes. Amy tamped the emotions down. She did not want to cry. Stephanie was the biggest surprise of this trip so far.

Stephanie smiled. "Well, I am off. Tell your sister if she needs me to return sooner, she should call me. Otherwise, I am going to get a much-needed nap."

"Take your time," Amy said. And surprisingly, she meant it.

Amy watched Stephanie make her way down the hall towards the elevator. Then she took a deep breath and stepped into the room. Annalise was leaning over Dad, trying to settle him comfortably in bed.

The nurse was standing at the computer in the room, making a few notes in his chart. The nurse looked at Annalise. "Your dad is doing well. I just gave him some pain medicine, so he will probably be sleeping here soon. Call if you need anything."

"Thank you. We will."

The nurse bustled out of the room with purpose. Amy presumed she was on to her next patient in her charge.

Amy glanced at her father to find him watching her. "Thank you so much for coming to see me. I know it took a lot for you to come," he said, his voice raspy.

Amy instantly felt defensive. "I didn't really come for you.

I came for Annalise." The harshness in her voice surprised even her.

Her dad's expression did not change, but Annalise looked crushed.

Amy tempered her voice and said, "I just mean, if Annalise says she needs me, of course, I will be here."

Her dad nodded thoughtfully, as if weighing his next words. Amy could tell he was carefully weighing what he should say next. "Well, for whatever reason, you are here; it's terrific to see you."

Amy sighed, recognizing the olive branch her dad was trying to extend. "Thanks, Dad," she said nonchalantly.

Turning to Annalise, Amy continued, "Annalise, do you need anything? I think I will head to the gift shop for a minute. Would you like a drink or anything?"

"Maybe water," Annalise said, her smile back on her face.

Amy wasted no time making her escape and slowly wandered down to the gift shop. She didn't know what it was, but hospital gift shops always had the coolest eclectic things for sale. She knew she could spend a lot of time there and maybe even find a good book to read.

As she wandered the shop, she replayed her conversation with her dad. Was what everyone said true? Was she the one stopping the restoration of her relationship with her dad? Did she want it restored? Maybe she had been angry for so long that she didn't know who she was without the anger. The anger at this point felt like a comfortable blanket. It kept her from examining other emotions. That was a scary thought. One she wasn't sure she was ready to delve into. Was she so used to being the victim that she wasn't sure she could function without being the victim?

Amy was pretty sure Brooke had asked her this once. She had dismissed the thought. At the time, she thought Brooke was crazy and was even a little offended by the question. Brooke didn't understand all she had been through, or wouldn't have questioned Amy's feelings. Amy was confident her feelings were valid.

But was it affecting all other areas of her life, as those close to her claimed? Was she the problem? Was she standing in her own way to get past this? These were uncomfortable thoughts, and Amy did not appreciate them coming uninvited right now. She pushed these thoughts away and examined an adorable stuffed animal. She thought of her niece and nephew and wondered how much Annalise would kill her if she bought each of the kids one.

She decided she didn't care. She had missed seeing the looks on their faces too many times as they opened birthday and Christmas gifts Amy had mailed ahead of time, knowing she wouldn't be there in person to witness them. She selected two adorable bears, one a koala and one a polar bear, equally soft and cuddly. She also found a cooler with ginger ale and couldn't resist the chocolate bar. The chocolate craving almost overpowered her as she stood before the candy selection. Maybe it was stress making her chocolate craving so acute. Maybe it was her time of the month, and there was no pregnancy. She knew she would not get any answers until maybe tomorrow morning. She sighed deeply.

The sweet older lady at the register commented, "Wow. That was quite a sigh. Do you need some help with the chocolate selection?"

Amy was quite sure the woman saw all kinds of people in this gift shop: people with terrible news, people with hope, and people in complete celebration of a new human life. She looked at the woman's face, softened with wrinkles. "No, thank you. I was thinking about something else while looking at the chocolate."

The woman gave her a knowing look. "That happens a lot here. You take your time. I'm here if you need me."

And somehow, Amy knew she meant more than her selection of chocolate. She smiled appreciatively. "Thank you," Amy said.

Amy glanced through her choices again. Chocolate and peanut butter—perfect. She could satisfy two cravings at once. Amy made her choice and took her selections to the counter.

"Oh, these bears are so cute," the woman said. "I have admired them since I unboxed them and put them on the shelf."

Amy laughed. "Yes, I will spoil my niece and nephew, no matter what my sister says."

"Oh, yes," the woman said. "Being an aunt is so fun, kind of like being a grandmother. You can spoil and then leave. I think the only tricky part is if and when you end up with kids of your own, there can be retaliation."

Amy laughed again. "I had not thought of that. That's probably very true."

"So, I take it you don't have kids of your own?" the woman asked.

Unwelcome thoughts of possibly being pregnant snuck up on Amy. "Not yet," she answered with a polite smile.

Not yet. Where had that come from? Amy, if she were being honest, had never pictured herself with kids. Having kids

meant she had to get close enough to a man—not just physically—for that to be possible. Also, she didn't have any intention
of allowing this pregnancy to continue if she was indeed pregnant. She had not examined her situation closely enough to
think about this, but she was pretty sure she was still not ready
to be a mom. She wasn't prepared for someone to be dependent
on her again. An inexplicable and overwhelming sadness filled
her. She again shoved all these thoughts aside. She smiled at
the woman, thanked her, and hurried out of the gift shop.

Amy took her time heading back to her dad's room. When
she arrived, her dad was sound asleep, and Annalise was reading a book in the chair. Annalise smiled at Amy, no hint of the
disappointment from earlier. Amy knew she should apologize
to Annalise, but didn't want to dive back into it right now. They
could talk later.

Amy settled into the only other chair in the room. "Did you
find some things?" Annalise asked, eyeing Amy's bag curious-
ly.

"Yes," Amy said. "Don't be mad. I bought both Kaylee and
Braedon a stuffed animal. And I got you a water. "

Annalise shook her head, but she was smiling. "Thank
you," she said, taking the water. "And you spoil them."

"So," Amy snapped back in amusement. "That is my job as
their aunt."

Amy pulled out her ginger ale. "I also got a little snack. I
will share my snack if you want."

"No, thank you," Annalise said. "I think I would like to
stretch my legs for a bit. Don't worry. Dad is sound asleep and
should be for a while with what they gave him. The nurse said
the doctor won't be by until later this afternoon, so I think this

is my window. Besides, I need to call Graham and update him as well."

Amy felt a little panicky. Annalise was leaving—she was the buffer—but she looked over at her dad, who was indeed sleeping very soundly. She doubted he would wake up any time soon.

"Sounds good," she smiled at Annalise. Amy watched Annalise walk out the door and then decided to steal her chair. It looked much more comfortable. She took out her drink and her chocolate. She unwrapped her chocolate and took a big first bite. It melted in her mouth. Rich chocolate and peanut butter. How could you go wrong? She then opened her drink and took a long pull. She took a couple more bites of her chocolate and then wrapped the rest for later. She pulled out the book she had bought at the gift shop. It was a mystery novel currently receiving quite a bit of attention.

She opened the book and began reading. Before long, the afternoon sun, the chocolate, and the reading lulled Amy to sleep. She finally gave up fighting her drowsiness. She leaned her head back in the chair and fell sound asleep.

When Amy woke a little while later, she looked around, trying to put together where she was. She glanced over at her dad and, to her shock, found him watching her. He smiled at her when her eyes found his. "Good morning, sleepy head." He had said that to her a million times as a child.

Amy sat up straighter, trying to chase the sleep away from her brain. "How long was I out?"

"Not too long," her dad chuckled.

"Why didn't you wake me? I can go get the nurse for you," she asked accusingly. She cast around in her brain for a reason to leave the room.

"I didn't want to. Thank you, but I don't need the nurse right now," her dad said bluntly. "I was enjoying looking at you. You remind me so much of your mother," he ended in a whisper.

Amy wasn't sure how to respond to that, so she ignored it. "Did Annalise come back?"

"She did. But then she went down the hall for a minute to try Graham again. He couldn't talk the first time because he was in the middle of something with the kids."

Amy's fight-or-flight instinct was kicking in, and she was trying to decide whether to make an excuse to leave the room.

Sensing he was about to lose his opportunity, her dad quickly said, "Amy, I am so sorry. I am so sorry for being such a terrible father. I am sorry for all the times I let you down. I am sorry for all the times I left you to fend for yourself and expected you to take care of your sister. And most of all, I am sorry that I was not there for you to walk you through your grief."

Amy was listening to all this even though she was staring at the floor. A considerable part of her wanted to run; another part wanted to yell at him and rehash his crimes, but a big part was tired. Tired of lugging all of this hurt and anger around. And once she acknowledged she was exhausted, the tired kind of took over. She realized something she hadn't thought of before now. The anger and hurt she was carrying were very heavy. She did not know until this very moment how much they weighed her down. She had thought all this time that not forgiving her dad was self-preservation. If she didn't forgive him, she could protect herself from this happening again. But was that true? Maybe the very act of forgiving him was self-preservation.

Perhaps then she could lay down all these burdens. It didn't mean she had to have a relationship with her dad or let him back in, but maybe she could just get a reprieve from carrying all of this.

Amy glanced up at her dad to find him watching her as tears streamed down his face. "I love you so much, Amy. I know I didn't do a good job of showing you that as a kid, and I am so very sorry for that. I missed out on raising an amazing child because of my poor choices, and I totally understand that. You girls didn't turn out so well because of me, but despite me. Your mother would be so proud of both of you."

Amy didn't even realize tears were streaming down her face until one dripped off her chin. She wiped her eyes aggressively. What was with her? She was becoming an emotional basket case.

"You don't have to respond to me right now, Amy. I just wanted to ask for forgiveness, and I hope you will forgive me. Not because I deserve it, but because I know holding a grudge toward me has to be exhausting, and you deserve better."

Amy reached for some tissue and swiped at her eyes and nose, still frustrated with herself for crying. "Dad, I . . . " Amy began and then faltered. She took a deep breath and tried again. "I'm so accustomed to being angry with you. It's comfortable for me. You were a terrible father, and you did abandon me, but I also know I blame you for a lot of things that weren't your fault. You have been the scapegoat for anything that has gone wrong in my life, and I realize that will be hard to give up." She surprised herself with how bluntly honest she was and was slightly surprised at the words coming out of her mouth.

"I agree with you, Dad. I think it is time for me to forgive you because I'm so tired of carrying all this anger around. However, I am not sure about a relationship with you. There is a big difference between forgiving you and being able to trust you again."

Her dad nodded. "I get that. We can go as slow as you want, and I will be happy with however far you choose to let me in."

Annalise walked in. She looked at Amy and saw the tissue in her hand and the evidence of tears on her face. She then looked at her dad. Annalise seemed to be at a loss for words. Amy could tell Annalise was trying to decide if what was happening was good or bad. Amy knew Annalise desperately wanted her and her dad to make amends, but while he was lying in this hospital bed, Annalise would be protective of their dad.

"Everyone okay?" Annalise asked tentatively. "Dad, can I get you anything?"

"No, darling. We are all okay. Amy and I had a much-needed conversation. She can share it with you later if she chooses." He smiled at Annalise reassuringly.

Annalise looked at Amy. Amy nodded in agreement, surprised her dad wasn't doing a victory lap with Annalise. Amy half expected him to look at her sister and say our elaborate plan worked. She finally forgave me. Oddly, that he didn't tell Annalise outright what had just happened spoke volumes to his sincerity. Her heart softened a little. Maybe he had changed?

Her familiar instinct of lifting her guard whenever she thought positively about her father returned. She realized it would take her time to process all this. It had been years of guardedness as a defense mechanism. This was going to take a while to unravel.

Annalise watched the emotions play across Amy's face.

What was it that Amy saw in Annalise's eyes? Hope. Amy didn't realize how much her feelings toward her father had impacted Annalise. She had always assumed Annalise couldn't understand, and Amy thought she was the bigger person by not holding it against Annalise for having a relationship with her father and Stephanie.

But had Amy been selfish this whole time? She had felt very justified in not coming home for visits and holidays. Shame began to creep in, but Amy pushed it away. Amy had always been Annalise's hero. She was the reason Annalise had turned out so well. She wasn't ready to examine that and find it wasn't true. She felt that if it wasn't true, her whole world would come crumbling down. She was not in a place where that could happen. She again felt tears well up in her throat. She fought to hold them in check.

Amy smiled as cheerfully as she could at Annalise. "Why don't you take the comfortable chair again, Annalise? I need to stretch my legs." She smiled at her dad and quickly left the room before either of them could protest.

Amy walked hastily down the hall. She wasn't sure where she was going until she looked out the window and saw a bench in a small courtyard. Yes, she would get some fresh air. She quickly made her way outside and to the bench. She was happy she was alone in the courtyard for now.

Amy grabbed her phone before she left the hospital room and checked it in the bright sun. More messages from Tyler. How long would he last, and, more importantly, how long would she ignore him? What if she were pregnant? She supposed she would have to face him then. Maybe.

She also noticed another message from Melissa.

"How's it going?" Melissa asked.

"As well as can be expected," Amy answered. "However, Dad and I did just have a conversation."

"That's huge! How did it go?"

"He asked for forgiveness."

"????" came the reply.

"Yes, and you know what? I am still not sure he deserves forgiveness, but I am tired of carrying all this."

There was a pause, and a bubble appeared, showing that Melissa was typing. Amy tilted her face to the sun, soaking up the pleasant rays of warmth.

"Good for you. I am so proud of you. You can take the relationship part slowly, but this is a big step. I will continue to pray for you that your heart will heal."

Amy reread the message. Her dad had fractured her heart. It was true, and Melissa would know that better than anyone. "Thank you," Amy said simply.

Then Amy typed, "I would like to see you before heading back to Chicago. If Dad continues down this path of recovery, I will probably leave in a couple of days. I will need to get back to work. Is it okay if we can work out the details after today?"

"Absolutely," Melissa typed with a smiley face emoji. "Just keep me updated. Blake will help me make this work."

"Sounds good," Amy typed back with her own smiley face emoji.

Suddenly, she was thrilled at the prospect of seeing Melissa. Amy decided to sit on the bench for a minute longer. So many things were coming at her at once that she felt overloaded. She knew she would need time to process all that was happening. First, she was happy she had a conversation with her dad. At the very least, she had to drop the baggage of anger and bitterness. However, she wasn't sure how easy it would be not to blame him for everything in her life anymore. Forgiving him was going to be a mind shift and a journey. Second, what if she were pregnant? She knew she needed to take the pregnancy tests sooner rather than later. At first, she didn't want to, but now, not knowing was giving her a lot of anxiety.

And lastly, Tyler. She wasn't sure she could deal with her emotions surrounding him if she didn't know if she was pregnant or not. What if she were? Would it change things between them? Would it change how she felt about him? She didn't think she was ready for a baby. She may never be prepared for a baby. How fair would it be to bring another child into the world and be the person responsible for turning them into a healthy and happy person when she was such a mess herself? Wouldn't it be more loving not to do that? To not put an innocent child through that? Could she even be capable of successfully loving a child as they needed to be loved?

And what about Tyler? Did he want a child? Was he ready to be a parent? She didn't want him to be with her just because she had his baby. So, how would that work? Would they both be part-time parents, and how was that fair to the child?

She knew she had way more questions than answers at this point, but she needed to sort through the questions. She did not feel she could talk to Annalise about any of this. She knew Annalise asked her to treat her like an equal and stop protecting her, but she wasn't sure she could let her guard down. Amy was still the big sister, and for some reason, she didn't want Annalise to know about her previous pregnancy. She felt like it would disappoint Annalise to learn that about her sister, and

Amy didn't think she could bear to see the disappointment on Annalise's face. She was supposed to be Annalise's hero, and while she knew Annalise didn't think Amy was perfect, she still wanted to maintain some semblance of being put together.

Amy looked at the time and knew she had to head back inside the hospital. She didn't want Annalise to worry about her if she was gone too long. She took a deep breath and pushed herself up from the bench.

# 27

# Amy

Upon reentering her dad's hospital room, Amy was surprised to see Stephanie had returned. "Hi!" Amy greeted Stephanie warmly, shocking even herself. She had come to appreciate Stephanie and had to admit she genuinely liked her.

"Hi!" Stephanie returned the greeting, her eyes probing Amy's.

"You came back earlier than expected," Amy commented. "Did you get a nap and something to eat?"

"I did!" Stephanie said. "I was ready to come back, and I was hoping I wouldn't miss the doctor's last rounds."

"Ah! Makes sense. Where's Annalise?" Amy asked, looking around.

"She went to the nurse's station for some water," Stephanie said.

"Gotcha," Amy said.

Amy glanced tenuously at her dad. Now that she was back in his presence, she wasn't quite sure how to act. Her dad was watching her, too, but what struck Amy was the love she saw in his eyes. She had spent so much time holding him at arm's length. When had he started looking at her like that? She had always assumed he was angry with her for not forgiving him, but now she wondered . . . had she been blind to how he felt about her all this time?

Her dad cleared his throat before he spoke. "How was your walk? You okay?"

She knew what he meant by the question. Had she changed her mind about forgiving him now that she had had time away from him to think? He looked so earnest. Amy forced some cheer into her voice and said, "I did enjoy my walk. It is turning into a beautiful day. Chicago is already turning cool and will soon be cold. I am taking advantage of being able to soak in the Texas sunshine."

Annalise entered the room with a cup of water. "Hey, y'all. It looks like the doctor is doing his rounds right now. Stephanie, are you okay if we hang out a bit longer so we can hear what he has to say?"

"Absolutely," said Stephanie. "I honestly would love for y'all to hear what he's saying, and it is not just me hearing him."

Annalise smiled her charming smile at Stephanie. The smile Amy remembered from childhood that would get Annalise almost anything she wanted. Amy smiled, herself remembering. Annalise turned to Amy and noticed her expression. "What?" she asked.

"Nothing," Amy said, chuckling.

"Are you okay if we stay?" Annalise asked.

"Of course," Amy said.

They didn't have to wait long, which was fortunate in a hospital. The doctor bustled into the room with a no-nonsense nurse in tow who headed for the computer in the corner, presumably to update Dad's chart as the doctor spoke. The doctor hit the hand sanitizer on the wall and began massaging it into his hands with practiced movements that said he did this multiple times a day.

"How are we doing today, Mr. Glenn?"

"Better today," her father answered.

"Well, you should be doing well surrounded by all these wonderful women waiting on you hand and foot."

Amy instantly liked the doctor. The graying at his temples and crinkles at his eyes showed he had some experience behind him, and his bedside manner seemed to put the whole room at ease.

Her dad chuckled. "Yes, I am a very blessed man."

"Well, let me check your vitals and see what we have going on with your blood tests and EKG that were run earlier today." The doctor efficiently and succinctly examined her father, spoke with him, and then gave the nurse updates to record in the chart.

"Okay, Mr. Glenn. You are a very fortunate man. This could have gone the other way easily. If you continue down this road of recovery, you should be out of here in no time. I will recommend a diet to help keep your heart strong, and some time at an outpatient rehab to get your body a bit stronger and work out those chest muscles that have been through a lot in the last couple of days. Sound good?"

Her dad nodded with what looked like tears in his eyes. "Sounds good," he said quietly. "Thank you, doctor." It suddenly hit Amy that her dad had had a definite brush with death. This was probably a lot to process for him. According to the doctor, this event could have ended very differently. Amy pushed the thoughts away, determined to sort them out later.

The doctor shook all of their hands and bustled back out the door with the nurse in tow. Once he was gone, Annalise turned to her dad. "What's wrong, Dad?"

Her dad shook his head. "Nothing at all. Nothing is wrong. I am just so . . . so grateful." Amy understood he was grateful to be here still, but then he looked at Amy, and Amy knew he was also referring to their conversation. Amy wasn't ready to show emotion back to her dad just yet. She nodded and looked away.

That didn't seem to bother her dad. Not missing one moment of the exchange with her eagle eyes, Stephanie said, "Well, honey, we should probably let you rest a bit. Girls, would you like to go to the cafeteria with me, or do you need to run off?"

"We could go for a bit," Annalise said, then looked at Amy.

"Sure. I hear the chocolate pudding is top-rated here," quipped Amy.

Stephanie went near her dad and patted his cheek lovingly. "I won't be gone long, honey. You try to close your eyes and get some rest." She kissed his forehead and backed away.

"Bye, Dad," Annalise drew near and patted his shoulder.

Amy went over to her dad. She stood for a minute, trying to decide what to do. Then she reached down and squeezed his hand. "Bye, Dad. Get some rest," and then turned and hustled out of the room.

The other women soon joined her in the hallway, and they headed to the cafeteria. Once there, they each selected a snack and a drink and made their way to a table. Since it was techni-cally between meal times, there were several open tables. This afforded them some privacy.

Stephanie wasted no time. She looked directly at Amy.

"Can I ask? Something has obviously happened between you two. What happened?" Annalise looked on with curiosity as well, but had not been brave enough to ask just yet.

"Well," Amy began, taking a deep breath. "He caught me at a vulnerable time. I woke up and found him awake. He started talking, and I didn't have time to run." She meant that part as a joke . . . sort of. She wanted to lighten the mood a little. She was tired of being so emotional.

Both women smiled but were clearly eager to hear the rest. "He asked for forgiveness for everything, and I am so tired of being angry at him. I didn't realize how much energy it was sucking from me until he pointed it out. I am not sure I am ready to have a close relationship with him or how much of a relationship we can have, but I am tired of carrying this baggage. I am surprised to say this, but I feel relieved." Amy said that part with wonder as if she was just now discovering it.

"It is going to take me a while to work through all this. This will not go away overnight," she warned both women. Amy wanted them to manage their expectations. They both nodded, smiling. Stephanie and Annalise looked at each other and shared a knowing smile. It kind of made Amy feel left out.

"What?" Amy said.

"Well, we have been praying for this day," Annalise said. "I know you and Dad are not going to be best of friends overnight, but it is a start. And Amy, I want you to know I have been praying more for this for you than for Dad. I know Dad wanted you to accept his forgiveness, but Amy, you don't need to carry these burdens anymore. Those days are past. You have to move on with your life in a healthy manner."

Amy knew Annalise was right, but still, she felt defensive.

"You don't think I am healthy?"

"I think you are holding on to things that distort your view of life, and I don't want that for you." Now Annalise sounded like the older sister.

Stephanie squeezed Amy's hand. "Look, Amy, you took a big step by even coming here. You didn't have to. I am proud of you for doing so, and we will take it one day at a time and go as slow as you would like."

Amy did not want to like Stephanie, but she couldn't help it. This woman was a mix of wisdom, firsthand from experience, and motherly warmth that drew Amy to her. She had always kind of resented her for taking her mom's place in Annalise's life, but now she could see she didn't take her mom's place. However, Stephanie filled a void that had long been there. "Thank you," Amy said quietly.

Annalise looked at her watch. "I'm sorry. I want to keep talking, but we probably do need to head out."

"No worries," Stephanie said. "Thank you so much for being here this afternoon." She looked at Amy. "What is your plan? How much longer will you be able to stay?"

"Well, now that Dad is on the mend, I will probably head back to Chicago in the next couple of days. I would like to meet up with my friend Melissa, as I am in close proximity to her. But I don't want to use all my personal days at work, so I can come back for the holidays."

Annalise's face instantly lit up as it dawned on her what Amy had just said. "Really?" Annalise said.

"Yes," Amy said with a smile. "I am sorry. I feel like I punished you for what I was going through with Dad. That wasn't right of me to do."

Annalise laughed and grabbed her sister in a spontaneous hug. "All is forgiven. I am just so excited you will be here this year!"

Stephanie laughed. "Me too!"

Annalise gathered their trash and headed for the nearest trash can. Stephanie took advantage of Annalise's being out of earshot and said under her breath, "If you need me for any reason, any reason at all," she gave Amy a pointed look, "please call me. You do not have to go through any of this alone. You have my number, right?"

"I do," Amy said quickly, acutely aware Annalise was headed back toward them. "And thank you," Amy said, letting out a breath she was unaware she was holding.

They smiled at each other and hugged. Annalise looked on with curiosity. "Call us if you need anything, Stephanie, and we can head back this way."

"Thank you, girls. I so appreciate that. We can talk again tomorrow, depending on what the doctor says. I am going to have to find out what the rehab situation is like and what insurance will cover. I'll let you know what I find out."

The girls walked Stephanie to the elevator, repeated their goodbyes with promises to call the next day, and then headed to Annalise's car.

"The kids will be so happy we are getting home sooner than planned. They will probably want to talk you into a game or a movie and make the most of your time here. I hope that is okay. I know you are probably tired."

"No," Amy said quickly. "I adore them and want to spend time with them." She mentally pushed the taking of pregnancy tests to the following day. She vowed not to leave her room in the morning until they were done. She knew she had to know one way or the other before she returned home.

"I do want to contact Melissa, though, and see if she could meet up tomorrow or the next day. Then I can schedule my flight accordingly."

"Of course," Annalise said with a smile. "I will miss you so much when you go, but I am beyond excited you will return for the holidays."

Amy smiled. "You know what? Me too." And was surprised she meant it.

When they returned home, Amy promised Kaylee and Braedon she would be right back and went immediately to her room to call Melissa. She pushed back the overpowering desire to take the pregnancy tests now and focused on the task at hand.

Melissa was more than excited to meet up the next day. They planned to meet in Waco, about halfway between them, and not a long drive for either of them. They kept their conversation short, knowing they would see each other the next day.

Amy gathered the stuffed animals she had bought earlier for the kids. Since she had no gift bags, she just stuck them behind her back and headed to the living room.

"Kaylee, Braedon," she sang. "Aunt Amy has a surprise for you." The kids jumped up in excitement. They had been playing a game on the floor. Amy laughed and said, "Close your eyes, both of you. Close them, close them tight." She put a stuffed animal in each of their hands. "Okay, open them!"

They both squealed and hugged the animals. "He is so soft," Kaylee almost whispered.

"Oh, he?" asked Amy.

"Yes, his name is Todd. Todd the koala," said Kaylee, making up her mind.

"And what about you?" Amy looked lovingly at Braedon. "What are you naming yours?"

Braedon looked up at Amy. "His name is Glacier!" hugging his polar bear to him.

"Wow, Glacier?" Amy glanced at Annalise.

Annalise giggled. "He is into science books right now."

Amy looked back at Braedon. "Well then, that is a perfect name," said Amy.

"Kaylee, Braedon," said Annalise. "What do we say?"

"Thank you," the kids chorused.

"You are so welcome," Amy said, sweeping both kids and their new stuffed animals into a group hug.

"Okay," Annalise said. "Dinner is ready. Let's say we have some dinner, and then y'all can watch a movie with Aunt Amy. That is, if Aunt Amy agrees." Annalise looked at Amy, smiling and knowing that, of course, Amy would say yes.

They had a delectable dinner of BBQ ribs, baked potato, and corn on the cob. Very Texan and oh-so-delicious. Amy couldn't believe her appetite, considering everything that had happened. Then she pushed all thoughts of why her appetite was so strong out of her brain and focused on the family around her. Amy complimented the meal. "I sure do miss having well-cooked meals. My life primarily consists of work, cafeteria food, takeout, and whatever happens to be in my fridge," She said with a laugh.

"Yeah," Annalise agreed. "I bet it is hard to be motivated to cook for one."

Amy knew Annalise meant nothing by that comment because she didn't know how close Amy and Tyler had become.

She tried to keep the details of the relationship to a minimum. She inwardly grimaced, knowing that when she returned to Chicago, she would have to face being alone again. She had become more adjusted to Tyler's companionship than she wanted to admit. They had fallen into an easy, comfortable, and comforting routine. These are all things she did not want to deal with yet. However, it did occur to her that Tyler was already facing them, and maybe this was also the reason for so many phone calls. She wondered for what seemed like the millionth time today what she would tell him if she were indeed pregnant.

Amy shook herself from her thoughts and sighed heavily. She looked up to find Annalise studying her. Amy didn't know if it was because Kaylee and Braedon were at the table or not, but she could tell the exact moment Annalise decided to let it go and not address it . . . for now.

"Did you get a hold of Melissa?"

"I did. We are planning to meet in Waco for lunch tomorrow. Does that work? If you need your car, I don't mind renting one for the day."

"No, you are more than welcome to my car," Annalise said. "It sounds like Stephanie has things under control, and I need to get some things done around here. I will help Stephanie again when they get the rehab situation under control."

Annalise looked at her children, who were beginning to get impatient but desperately trying to be polite. "Okay, kids, why don't you clear away your spots and then pick out a movie to watch with Aunt Amy?" Kaylee and Braedon were more than willing to oblige and clambered from the table to the living room, already negotiating for their favorite movie.

Annalise looked over at Amy. "I'm not trying to rush you," she laughed. "You take your time, and you can join them whenever you are ready."

Amy chuckled. "Well, I think we have run the distance on their patience. But are you sure y'all don't need help cleaning up?"

"No," Graham assured her. "We've got this."

"Do you want a glass of wine or anything? I have many wines that pair well with any animated feature my children pick out."

Amy laughed and almost said yes, then caught herself. Maybe that wasn't the wisest idea until she knew more about what was happening in her body.

"Oh no, thank you," Amy said. "I'm good. Maybe I will just get some more water." She refilled her glass and then went to join her niece and nephew on the overstuffed couch. The movie was a newer animated film Amy had not seen yet. Miraculously, the kids agreed on the movie, and parental intervention was unnecessary to help them reach a decision. Amy settled on the couch with Kaylee and Braedon on either side, cuddling their new stuffed animals.

Amy became so engrossed in the movie that she didn't realize both kids were sleeping and Annalise was snapping a picture with her phone.

"Don't worry," Annalise said." I won't post it anywhere." Annalise knew how picky Amy was about her social media image. She would tell Annalise all the time that employers looked at that stuff now, so she was very selective about what she posted. Besides, why did everyone's lives have to be all over social media anyway?

Amy smiled at Annalise. "Looks like I am the only one interested in how this ends," she whispered.

"Yes, it has been a long few days for them. Being out of routine will do that for you," Annalise agreed.

Graham and Annalise both approached the couch and picked up a child. They carried them to their room to settle them in their beds. With the precision with which they did this, Amy knew it was not the first time they had done so. Those sweet times with children made everyone want to consider having children. But what about all the other things that went with it?

What about the nights they were up all night sick? Or when a friend is mean to them at school? Or what if the partner you expected to parent with left? Then what? These are the things most people don't think about. But Amy's childhood forced her to consider things most people didn't. Amy had to grow up quickly, which made her unrelatable to most of her peers. To this day, Amy felt her childhood circumstances made her out of step with many of her friends. She felt that was why she related to Melissa and Brooke. They had not lived her childhood, but they were empathetic and listened, whereas others were quick to dismiss her experiences or believe their experiences were just as bad or worse, and had no room to listen to Amy's experiences.

Graham and Annalise came back out to the living room. "Did they wake up?" asked Amy.

Annalise grinned. "Surprisingly, no. They were tired."

"Speaking of tired," Amy said as she stretched and yawned. "I think the bed is also a good place for me."

She said good night to Annalise and Graham, thanked them again for dinner, and headed to her room. Once in her room, she checked her phone. Tyler had sent her a couple of messages. For the first time, it struck Amy that she was being cruel to him by not answering him. She read the messages and then responded before she could think better of it. "I'm sorry I have ignored you, Tyler. My dad is doing better, and I will return to Chicago in a couple of days. Would you be interested in grabbing coffee? Maybe we can talk more about all this."

In what seemed like seconds, a bubble appeared that showed Tyler typing. The bubble seemed to be there for quite a while, as if he was typing a long message, but when the message appeared, all it said was "yes" and "thank you."

The message made Amy a little emotional. She really thought she was doing the right thing by pushing him away, but over the last couple of days her perspective had changed, and now she was not so sure. She sighed loudly and audibly. What was she going to do if she was pregnant? Pregnancy should not be the basis of any relationship, and also, if she did decide to give the relationship with Tyler another chance, was this the right time for a baby? And wasn't it her right to choose when the right time for a baby was? Wasn't that part of being a good mother, choosing when a child should show up on the earth? The thought made her a little uncomfortable, like she was playing God or something. She again chose not to go down that path of thought and pushed the thoughts out of her head.

# 28

*Amy*

Amy awakened to the reality that it was time to face the music, as the saying goes. She got out of bed and padded into the bathroom, knowing she could no longer avoid this. She opened all four pregnancy tests and laid out the contents and instructions. She knew this was overkill, but she had to be sure. She had read somewhere that you could have a false negative but not a false positive. She read the instructions carefully for each test and tried to breathe normally. Once she was confident she knew what to do, she took all four tests and set four timers.

She tried not to think about it as she waited for the timers. Once she knew for sure, she could begin plotting out what she wanted to do next. Amy thought this had to be the longest three minutes of her life. She puttered around the bathroom, trying to distract herself by getting ready for the day, but her stomach suddenly decided to churn. She rubbed her sweaty palms down her pajama pants and tried to slow her breathing again.

The first timer went off. She made her way over to the test. She looked down. It confirmed what, in her heart of hearts, she already knew. She was indeed pregnant. She looked at the other three tests. They all showed as pregnant as well, even though the timers had not yet gone off. A cold feeling tingled down her spine. What was she going to do now? She sat down on the edge of the bathtub. Despite herself, the tears began to fall. Amy couldn't seem to hold the tears back.

So much had happened in the last few days, and the emotions had to pour out somewhere. She knew the most straightforward answer would be to tell absolutely no one that she was pregnant and, when she returned to Chicago, immediately make an appointment to get this taken care of.

A little unwelcome thought niggled at the back of her brain. But was that fair? Was it fair to Tyler to never tell him he could have had a baby? It would definitely mean their relationship was over for good. There would be no going back. She didn't think she could ever even look at him, knowing she never told him she was pregnant with his baby.

But honestly, shouldn't this be her choice? It was her body. She should one hundred percent get to decide what was best for her life and her body. Wasn't that what women's rights were all about? Amy had never considered herself to be a feminist. Not in the don't open my door, bra-burning way. However, she thought women should absolutely be treated equally to men in the workplace and politics. So then, she had the right to decide whether this was right for her and her career.

*But did she have the right to choose for Tyler?*

She quickly pushed the thought away. She could not thoroughly analyze it. She did not want to force a relationship on Tyler because of a baby. Her career was going so well right now. What would it mean to change everything with a child? Her priorities would have to change. She knew from raising Annalise that as much as women thought it would not be a big deal to add a baby to the mix, it was.

Adoption was not an option she wanted to entertain. Even though she had heard so many heartwarming stories about adoption and how wonderful it could be, she also knew it could go badly as well. What if her baby ended up in a family that had a crisis and turned out like hers? No, it would be more merciful to end the pregnancy than to put a baby through that. Besides, at her age, how embarrassing would it be to carry a baby to full term and then admit she didn't want it and give it away? I guess she could lie and tell everyone she was a surrogate for someone else. Hollywood had kind of made that acceptable. But if she did that, what would she tell Tyler? Surely, he would see right through that and call her out. No, she felt adoption was out of the question.

These thoughts tumbled around Amy's brain like ping-pong balls in a dryer. Finally, her tears subsided. She wiped her eyes and blew her nose. She took a deep breath and thought she would deal with this later. She would meet Melissa today and enjoy seeing her friend. And for now, she would keep all of this to herself until she felt she had more clarity of thought.

Amy washed her face, brushed her teeth, and decided to put on makeup before being seen in the kitchen getting a cup of coffee. She decided the makeup might help hide the fact that she had been crying. Once her makeup was done and she was satisfied that she did not look red and puffy, she took another stabilizing breath and headed to the kitchen.

"Good morning," Annalise sang as she saw Amy. If Annalise could tell Amy had been crying, she didn't show it.

"Good morning," Amy sang back and headed for the coffee pot.

"How did you sleep?" Annalise asked.

"So good," said Amy. "That bed is super comfortable." Amy poured herself a cup of coffee and then doctored it with her usual sweetener and creamer. "How did you sleep?" Amy returned the question.

Annalise tilted her head the way she had always done since she was little and said, "We slept well, too. I think we are all tired from the emotional roller coaster that has been this weekend."

Amy chuckled, "For sure."

"What time do you need to get going?" Annalise asked.

Amy glanced at the clock. "Probably in about an hour or so. Is that okay?"

"Of course," Annalise said. "I am going to run Kaylee and Braedon to school here in a minute, and then the car is all yours."

"Thanks again," Amy said. "I am excited to see Melissa today." And the truth was, she was excited. Even though she would have to push thoughts of her recent discovery away, she was anxious to see Melissa. It had been too long.

"Do you want any breakfast?" Annalise asked. "We did simple items this morning. I have cereal, toast, bagels, and oatmeal. Does any of that sound good?"

In truth, none of it did, and Amy's coffee wasn't settling too well either, but she wanted to appear normal to Annalise. "You know what? I will have some toast." She was hoping the bread in her stomach might help settle it. She noted she might need to stop and get a ginger ale on her way to meet Melissa.

Amy made her toast quickly, insisting that she do it, and Annalise did not have to wait on her. She listened half-heartedly to her sister as she chatted about Kaylee and Braedon and her short phone call with Stephanie this morning. All the while, Amy was focused on keeping her coffee down. She did not remember having morning sickness the first time around. That was probably what helped her not often remember the first pregnancy.

Once her toast was done, she took a bite and chewed slowly, willing it to stay in her stomach. Thankfully, it did the trick, and as she began to eat, her stomach began to settle. She relaxed. Maybe her stomach had less to do with the pregnancy and more to do with all the emotions that she had had to deal with in the last week.

Amy listened to Annalise nodding and smiling in what she hoped were the appropriate places until Annalise said, "So what do you think?"

"About what?" Amy asked, embarrassed.

Annalise looked at her quizzically but thankfully let it go. "About going over and seeing Dad and Stephanie one last time tomorrow before you have to leave. Have you made your flight arrangements already?"

Amy forced her brain to clue into what Annalise was asking her and to think beyond pregnancy and what lay ahead of her when she got home. "Oh! Yes, I did look at flights, and it would be better if I left first thing in the morning the day after tomorrow. So, yes, you will be stuck with me for another full day after today. But, also, my flight leaves early so I can take a ride share to the airport."

"Nonsense," Annalise said. "And I am selfishly glad we get to keep you here another day. Yay! Okay, I will call Stephanie and fill her in so we can make schedules work tomorrow. I don't think they will let Dad go until after tomorrow, so we should be good. I also think they are waiting on the doctor's decision about where he will do rehab."

Amy smiled at Annalise. Annalise's excitement was contagious. And although Amy had made it abundantly clear that she wanted to take things slow with her dad, she really liked Stephanie and genuinely wanted to see her again before she left. Her thoughts surprised her, but at the moment, she was analyzing everything else and could not analyze thoughts about Stephanie.

"Okay," said Amy. "Sounds like we have a plan. I will go make my flight reservations since that works for y'all's schedule and get ready to meet Melissa."

Annalise grabbed Amy in a spontaneous hug, almost knocking Amy over. "I know you don't like hearing about this, but this has answered some long-said prayers."

"So you have been praying for Dad to have a major heart attack?" Amy quipped, but was only half joking. She never understood why the Christians around her put so much stock in prayer. Wasn't everything that was going to happen going to happen anyway? If God loved her dad, why would he cause him to have a heart attack just to heal a relationship with his daughter? Could He have not done it without the heart attack? Amy knew she was stubborn, but if God was God, couldn't he have orchestrated this meeting without having her dad get sick? And what about her mom? If God loved Amy the way people said he did, why did her mom have to die? What was loving about that?

Amy decided to keep these questions to herself. It wasn't that she hadn't voiced them to Annalise in some way over the years, but Amy decided she did not have the energy to get into it today.

Annalise smiled at Amy. She had disappointment in her eyes, but her tone was kind. "No, silly. I have been praying for you. I know this thing between you and Dad weighs heavier than you like to admit, and I think it is an answer to prayer that you are willing to open your heart a little, even though I know it will take time." Annalise smiled at Amy again, almost like she was the big sister, and said. "I can be patient."

With that, Amy excused herself to the guest room before she became emotional. No need for more tears today. She dressed quickly and became stressed about where to hide all the pregnancy tests. She couldn't put them in the garbage right now. She could hide them in her suitcase. Her sister would not go through her things. She ultimately decided to hide the test boxes in her suitcase and take the actual sticks with her in her purse. That way, if one of the kids wandered into the room or something happened, the results would not be evident. She could not talk to anyone about this right now. She felt she needed a plan before telling anyone what was happening. Amy quickly hid the boxes, put the sticks in her purse, gathered the other things she thought she might need for the day, and headed out to find Annalise.

Once Amy settled in Annalise's car, she pulled up the restaurant on her phone, where she and Melissa had agreed to meet, and charted her path with the GPS. Amy found the book she was listening to on her phone and pulled that up as well. She thought that if she could listen to a book, her thoughts wouldn't roam as freely. She texted Melissa to let her know she was on her way, and Melissa texted celebratory emojis and a see ya soon!

Amy stopped quickly at a gas station, bought a ginger ale, and then sat back, determined to enjoy the ride. She didn't drive nearly as much in Chicago as in Texas and missed road trips. Maybe this would be just the thing she needed to clear her head.

# 29

# *Melissa*

Melissa grabbed her water bottle and ran to her car. She was so excited that this meeting was happening. She had wanted to see Amy for years, but ever since Amy had decided she didn't want to deal with her dad, she had avoided Texas. Melissa was surprised at her determination to stay away. She had thought Amy's sister and Amy's niece and nephew would draw her home, but it seemed the longer this went on, the more Amy's habits included complete avoidance.

Amy passed through Melissa's mind quite a bit these days. Melissa had committed to praying for Amy every time she thought of her. It had been happening so often that she finally mentioned it to Blake. Blake pondered for a second in his typical, thoughtful way and then said, "I think it may mean God is ready to do something with Amy. You have been praying for her and her family for years, but if it has increased, maybe there is something you don't know about that is happening. Maybe Amy is finally in a place where she is ready for God to move."

As usual, Blake's words made Melissa think. She knew better than trying to figure it out alone, but she also knew Blake was probably right. Even if they never knew what was going on in Amy's heart and mind. Clearly, God was moving.

As Melissa pointed her car toward Waco, she decided to listen to some of her favorite worship music. As it played in the background, Melissa began to think. Her thoughts wound in and out of prayer. She felt today was significant, but she wasn't sure why. She hadn't seen her friend in years, and maybe that was it, the sheer amount of time gone by. She didn't think so, though. She felt in her spirit that there was something significant about seeing Amy at this point in her life.

She prayed out loud this time. "Heavenly Father, thank you for Amy. Thank you for the wonderful person she is. I know she is not walking with you, and in the past, she had a lot of anger toward you because of things that have happened in her life. However, I know you love her so incredibly much. And just like the rest of us, she cannot go so far that she is out of your reach. I thank you for this breakthrough that seems to be happening with her dad, and I pray they can heal."

Melissa let her voice trail off, and as she thought more about Amy and her life, her mind began to meander down the path of the past. She remembered the first day she met Amy when they moved into the dorm. They were both scared kids, but did not want to admit it. They were also both excited to be on their own and in college. The girls clicked right away and got along very well. By the end of their freshman year, they had determined they wanted to stay roommates for the duration of college. It was a relief to both of them.

Melissa reminisced about the parties they attended and the boys they had met. They had fun, but when Melissa met Blake, everything changed for her. Having the perspective she had now, she knew she had been searching for God long before she had met Blake. However, she didn't know God was what she was searching for. Then Melissa's thoughts turned to the right before she had met Blake. She did not like her thoughts going down this particular path, and often, when they started down it, she jumped the tracks and went a different way. This was not a fun memory.

One morning, Melissa found Amy sitting on the bathroom floor, crying. Amy had taken a pregnancy test, and the positive result was still in her hand. Melissa sat wide-eyed with her friend while Amy cried. "I can't have a baby right now. I can not. My life is just starting. Besides, wouldn't it be cruel to bring a baby into this world when I don't know who the father is, and I wouldn't be able to take care of it?"

"There is always adoption," Melissa offered weakly.

Amy shook her head. "No, then I have to carry the baby and go to school, and I would still have to give up some of my freedom. Besides, adoption is no guarantee that this baby will have a good life. What if it ends up with a deadbeat dad like mine? No, I think it is the wisest thing to end the pregnancy."

Until that point, Melissa had never analyzed her feelings about abortion closely. She guessed she believed women should get to choose what to do with their bodies. Women's rights did make sense to Melissa, but something about getting an abortion wasn't sitting right with her. Wasn't this essentially choosing your life over a baby's life? Why did the baby have no choice in the matter? Melissa decided to keep her opinions to herself and focus on Amy.

"I am going to make an appointment at the clinic," Amy said. "But will you please, please go with me? I am scared to go alone."

This was huge. Amy rarely, if ever, asked for help. Melissa didn't think she could say no, even if she disagreed with the decision. Amy needed her, and Melissa wanted to be there for her.

To this day, the way the clinic looked, the smells, and the other women there are imprinted in Melissa's brain. She knew she hadn't really known better then, but she knew now she essentially supported her friend as she killed an unborn baby. Amy did not know this, but Melissa had carried so much guilt for it after she had developed a relationship with God.

Finally, she told a trusted friend she had met at church about Amy's abortion and the guilt Melissa carried. Morgan, her friend, hugged Melissa and said, "Do you want to pray for forgiveness?"

"It's that easy?" asked Melissa.

"Yes, of course. What do you think the cross is about?"

Her friend led her in a prayer of forgiveness, and then they both prayed over Amy.

When Melissa experienced a miscarriage, she reluctantly told Blake about what she had done. She then asked him, "Do you think God is punishing me for going to the clinic with Amy?"

Blake swept her into a hug and said, "Absolutely not. The enemy is beating you over the head with this one, isn't he?" He looked at Melissa with so much tenderness in his eyes. "Listen, I know you want answers about the miscarriage, but you are going to have to understand that you may never get answers on this side of heaven. Bad things happen because we live in a fallen world, not because we serve a harsh God. Think for a second. What kind of God would we serve if he were to punish you for your friend killing her baby by killing our baby?"

Melissa did think about his words. Blake was right. The God she knew was loving and kind and forgiving of sins. Why would he kill their baby to get back at her? That was pretty sick and twisted if she thought about it. They lived in a fallen world, and as long as they did, they would probably never have answers to sickness, disease, and death.

Melissa pulled herself from her thoughts. She hadn't thought about that abortion clinic in a long time. She thought of the beautiful daughter she had seen in heaven. And the thought suddenly hit her with the force of a Mac truck. Amy's child was in heaven. It was in heaven! It was being raised in heaven alongside her child. Tears began streaming down her face. The child Amy had aborted wasn't living in some black hole or gone forever; it was in heaven!

All of a sudden, Melissa heard the whisper of the Holy Spirit. "I want you to share what you have seen with Amy."

Melissa's first response was, "Nooooooo. No, Lord. She will think I am crazy."

Silence.

"Lord, she doesn't really even believe in you, much less heaven."

Silence.

Then, in a small whisper, Melissa heard, "Don't you want her to be reunited with her child, like you know you will be with yours?"

Melissa began crying in earnest now. She knew she should pull over until she could gain her composure. Fortunately, there was a rest stop just ahead. Melissa pulled in and sat underneath a tree, away from other cars. She searched in her purse for a tissue. She wiped her eyes and blew her nose.

"I am sorry, Lord, for saying no. Yes, she needs to be reunited with her child and with you. I know this is your heart for her. Okay, Lord. I trust that the door to the conversation will open if this is a story you want me to tell."

A wave of peace descended upon Melissa. This was often indicative of her interactions with the Lord. He was always kind and loving, even when correcting her. Melissa wiped her eyes and blew her nose one more time. She looked in the rearview mirror to ensure she did not have mascara in places other than her eyelashes. Satisfied that she looked as well as expected after crying, she readjusted herself in her car seat and pulled back onto the highway.

During the rest of the trip, she found herself praying for Amy. She didn't know exactly what was happening, but she felt this was a significant turning point. Melissa and Amy had remained friends after college, and Melissa was determined not to lose contact with her. However, as Melissa grew in her faith and drew closer to the Lord, she felt she was not free to be as vulnerable about her own life as Amy. Amy, not having the same relationship with the Lord, would not have a reference point for what Melissa was talking about. Despite all that, Melissa still very much wanted Amy in her life. She shared as much as she could without trying to preach at Amy, make her feel bad about her lifestyle, or even estrange her, because Amy might feel Melissa was judging her.

That is why sharing this story with Amy would be a departure for Melissa. Melissa hadn't even shared this story with some Christian friends for fear of what they might think of her.

Or worse yet, if they make her doubt what she has experienced is real. After Melissa's dream, she pursued books and materials by people who had had encounters with heaven. One of her favorites was *Heaven Is For Real*. The book is the true story of a little boy who gets very sick and visits heaven during that time. As he began telling his parents about his encounters, he mentioned he had met his sister in heaven. His parents were shocked because they had never mentioned to him that there had been a sister before him who had miscarried. The only way he knew that was from his encounter in heaven.

Melissa read the story and wept. Her dream had not just been a dream. She was convinced she had met and seen her baby in heaven. She wasn't sure why the Lord had entrusted her with that experience, until maybe now. Maybe this is why he had entrusted Melissa with this experience. Maybe her experience with her miscarried child is what Amy needed to hear to reconcile her abortion choice.

Melissa and Amy had never spoken of the abortion after it had happened, but Melissa knew from talking with other women that it never really leaves you. It was a deception of the enemy to think people could choose who was given life and who was not, and call it women's rights. In fact, as Melissa researched, she realized that sacrificing babies was not new. It had its roots back to the people of the Bible who used to brutally sacrifice their children to Molech, the god they worshiped. They did this because they felt it would gain his favor and appease him.

Melissa was convinced that if people understood how sacrificing children was indeed a form of worshiping Satan and not a part of women's rights, people would abandon abortion altogether. However, Satan's deception is gradual, and some people genuinely believe abortion is a God-given woman's right.

Melissa broke out of her thoughts. She didn't think of these things often, but when she did, she felt the passion of Jesus to reunite these women who chose abortion with their babies in heaven rise in her. Wasn't that just like Jesus? Not only to forgive the sin of abortion but to have a passion for these women to be reunited with their children. Isn't that a picture of redemption and mercy?

Melissa realized she was almost to Waco and began actively looking for her exit. Her excitement to see Amy grew. She prayed for God to order her steps heavenward and then focused on where she was going.

**30**

*Amy*

Amy found the restaurant easily enough and swung into a parking spot. Nervousness in the form of excitement coursed through Amy's body. It had been too long since seeing Melissa. Amy knew it was her fault, but she also knew Melissa probably understood more than anyone why she had needed to stay away and why she needed space.

In college, Amy honestly felt Melissa's interest in God and thought maybe Blake would be a passing phase, but the more Melissa became dedicated to God, the more she fell in love with Blake. Over the years, Amy saw that Melissa's faith had become very genuine, much like that of her sister and Brooke.

Amy assumed she would probably lose touch with Melissa when she moved to Chicago. However, Melissa hung on. Amy loved that it seemed Melissa did not want to lose touch with her, and the relationship even though at times, Amy had done nothing to keep it going. Amy knew Melissa could have easily said that her life was with Blake in Austin, that her identity was a mom, and that she had no room for someone who did not understand that. However, Melissa had done the opposite. Amy appreciated that about Melissa more than Melissa would probably ever know.

Amy strode purposefully to the restaurant's entrance. She opened the front door and instantly saw Melissa standing off to the side. Melissa was as beautiful as ever. Her long, dark hair was starting to show some gray, but it was coming in beautifully. Melissa had always had beautiful hair. Amy had always been jealous, feeling hers was not quite brown or blonde and looked mousy in comparison. These days, with her income spent only on herself, she afforded time and money at the salon to make her hair look naturally blonde.

Melissa turned as Amy entered, and her face spread into a warm smile, reaching her kind brown eyes. Instantly, Amy was flooded with memories. Melissa rushed over to Amy and enveloped her in a hug that Amy could only describe as motherly. Melissa had always been a caretaker, but she knew the mother role she had now was what she had always wanted to do with her life. Melissa was quite content running the carpool rather than participating in corporate America.

"Hi!" Melissa said. "It's so good to see you! How was your drive? Did you find the restaurant okay?"

"It's so good to see you as well! My drive was good!" Amy said. "And yes, I had no problem finding the restaurant—even though I cannot get over how much this city has changed since we were here."

Melissa agreed, and both ladies did a quick rundown of the locations that had changed since college and all the new businesses. The hostess called Melissa's name, and the ladies stepped forward, ready to be seated. The restaurant was full but not overly crowded, as it was a weekday. They made their way to their table, and the hostess handed them the menus.

"How are you?" Melissa asked excitedly. "I want to know everything!"

Amy chuckled. "Well, get comfy, we'll be here a while."

Melissa grinned in response. "Okay, that is true. Let's decide what we want to eat, and then everything you need to tell me can commence."

They each chose their food and drink and were ready when their waitress arrived. Once they ordered, Melissa looked at Amy inquisitively. "First of all, what happened with your dad?"

"Okay," said Amy, taking a deep breath. "Forgive me because I think I have told you some of this. I got a call from Annalise saying Dad had a massive heart attack and was rushed to the hospital. They were going to have to perform open-heart surgery. I couldn't get over the panic in Annalise's voice. My coming had way more to do with Annalise than it did with Dad. I wanted to talk myself out of coming and comfort her from afar, but I just couldn't do it. She needed me, and I guess the old instincts of protecting her kicked in. You know she and Dad grew close after I left for college. I guess when I was out of the picture, he decided to clean up his act completely."

"Yeah," Melissa inserted. "I do remember that. I remember it hurt you that he waited until you were grown and out of the house to begin getting sober."

"Exactly," Amy said. "Don't get me wrong, the fact that he did get sober gave me peace of mind and let me stay in college. Otherwise, I am not convinced I wouldn't have dropped out. I just couldn't imagine Annalise on her own. But I don't understand why I had to leave for him to do that. I mean, does he love Annalise more?"

Amy paused. That thought hadn't crossed her mind in a long

time, and she was surprised it had resurfaced. She mentally shook her head, dismissing the idea, and continued. "Anyway, I had absolutely no desire to see my dad. I came for Annalise. However, Annalise still has me wrapped around her finger, and she did convince me to go to the hospital."

Melissa giggled. "Yeah, I remember that cute little grin she used on you to get her way."

"Well, apparently, she is not low in charm, even though she is older," Amy admitted. "The first night I went to the hospital, I looked at him, and all I felt was resentment and hatred. I literally could not stay in the room. I thought he was getting what he deserved. I have to be honest and say I am not completely convinced otherwise as of right now. I don't know," Amy shrugged. "Maybe God is punishing Dad, and it would be well deserved."

Amy could tell by Melissa's expression that she disagreed with that statement and wanted to express her disagreement, but she held her tongue.

Amy continued. "When I left the room, I ran smack into Stephanie."

"Your dad's wife?" Melissa asked for clarification, and Amy was relieved she didn't say stepmom. She knew Annalise had fully accepted Stephanie into that role, but despite the strides Amy's relationship had made with Stephanie, Amy was just not ready to do the same.

"Yes," Amy said. "She's different than what I thought. I feel she has made many mistakes in her life and has been through a lot. She didn't make excuses for Dad or blame me for my behavior. She just told me that if I didn't make peace with Dad while he was alive, it would be much more difficult to do so when he passes. I don't know. How she said it made me feel she spoke from experience."

"Wow," Melissa said. "Plot twist. I did not see this part coming, and that you would be open to Stephanie."

"Oh, don't get me wrong, Annalise has fully embraced Stephanie as the mom role in her life. I don't know if I'll ever do that," Amy said, knowing she sounded defensive.

"You don't have to," Melissa said quietly. "You have to remember that you and Annalise have very different memories and experiences with your mother because of your age difference. Annalise remembers your mother as a figure she really never knew. You were old enough to remember things your mom said and did, and her laugh and smile. Annalise only knows that through pictures or what you or your dad have told her."

This is the part that Amy loved about Melissa. She had always been able to cut to the quick of the situation. She appreciated that Melissa had just permitted Amy to have her own relationship with Stephanie. It did not have to look like Annalise's relationship with Stephanie.

"How do you do that?" Amy asked.

"What?" Melissa said with concern on her face.

"How are you able to sum up the situation so well? Did you ever consider being a therapist?"

Melissa laughed, "Believe me. With my kids' ages now, I definitely feel like an on-call therapist."

"Hey! At least they're still talking to you."

"True," Melissa said. "I have plenty of moms around me complaining that their children don't talk to them. I do feel blessed mine do. Anyway," Melissa said, redirecting the conversation back to Amy, "what happened after that?"

"Well," Amy said, getting back to her story. "The next day, Dad and I ended up in the hospital room by ourselves, and we basically called a truce. Well, he apologized, and I called a truce," Amy said ruefully.

"He apologized?" Melissa said. "That's huge."

"Yeah, it really kind of is. He said he was very sorry for dumping all the responsibilities on me while he grieved the loss of Mom. He knows now what he did was terrible and asked my forgiveness for making me grow up so fast."

"Wow!" Melissa said. "That's incredible."

"Yeah," Amy said. As she recounted the story to Melissa, she realized just how huge this was in her relationship with her dad. She was having trouble believing it happened as well. "But," she said to Melissa, knowing Melissa was one of the few people who wouldn't judge her for saying this. "I want to forgive him, but how do you just erase years of neglect?"

"You don't," said Melissa.

"But I thought forgiving the person means you must forget everything they did."

"No," said Melissa. "Not at all. Forgiveness just means you take yourself out of the judgment seat. You release yourself from what you think should happen to them and release the anger. It doesn't mean you don't set boundaries with the person. Or, in your case, like you told your dad, you want to go slow with a relationship. That is totally okay. But the fact you forgive him sets you free from the constant anger and resentment. After all these years, it has to be a huge load for you to carry around."

Amy weighed what Melissa said against what Annalise,

Graham, Stephanie, and even her dad had said. None of them had expected her to be best friends with her dad overnight. Each of them, even her dad, expressed concern that Amy had carried a weight she did not need to carry. Once again, Amy felt relief. As Melissa had said, she had placed herself in a judgmental position toward her dad, which was a heavy burden. She shouldn't have to carry it.

Melissa was silent as Amy processed. As Amy thought about what Melissa had said, the waitress appeared with their food. They had each decided to try a different type of sandwich, and they both looked delicious. Amy's stomach grumbled in response, reminding her of the pregnancy. She quickly pushed those thoughts out of her mind and focused on the sandwich before her.

"This looks so good!"

"Doesn't it?" Melissa said in response.

The waitress smiled, clearly pleased they were satisfied, and when she was sure they had all they needed, she bustled away to another table.

Melissa smiled at Amy and asked, "Mind if I pray?"

"No," Amy said, and she didn't.

They bowed their heads, and Melissa said a quick but thankful prayer over their food and her time with Amy.

They spent the next few minutes taking some delicious bites of their food. Then Melissa said, "I am so excited for you, Amy. I think that no matter what happens in the future with your dad, you have set yourself free from the tremendous burden you have been carrying. I can see this having such a positive impact on your relationship with Annalise and her family. Did you enjoy spending time with your niece and nephew?"

"So much," said Amy. "I regret that I have missed so much time with them."

Melissa nodded. "How is your job going?"

This is what Melissa often did. She would ask Amy so many questions about her life that Amy would walk away from the conversation, realizing she had found out little about Melissa. She made a mental note to circle back around after answering her question.

"It's good. I just finished a major project, and it looks like I will get a promotion. Tyler and I made a good team, and that helped with the project."

There must have been something in her voice when she mentioned Tyler because Melissa immediately picked up on it.

"Tyler? Are you more than just coworkers?" Melissa asked.

Wow, thought Amy, how does she do that? Her poor kids will not be able to get away with anything. "We were."

"Were?"

"Yes."

"What happened?" Melissa said with genuine concern.

"I happened," Amy said

"Uh oh," Melissa said. "He wanted to commit, and you didn't."

"Yes," said Amy. "I thought I made it abundantly clear I didn't want anything serious. I thought he felt the same."

"Oh," said Melissa. "He developed feelings for you, and you didn't develop feelings for him? Or you didn't want to face the feelings you developed for him?"

*How DID she do that?* Amy thought. Once again, she cut to the quick of the situation.

"Well," Amy said between bites of her sandwich. "I have

had some time to think since I have been here. I do like him, but he told me he loved me. I am just not ready for that."

"Let me guess," Melissa said. "You cut all of it off."

"Yes, I did! What else was I supposed to do?" Amy knew she sounded defensive and a little guilty.

"Well," Melissa said. "You could try expressing your feelings. Tell him you like him, but you may not be where he is yet, and see if he is willing to be patient with you. If he REALLY loves you, he will be patient with you."

Amy thought for a moment. Time away must have softened her resolve, because what Melissa said made sense. Amy nodded slowly and thoughtfully. Amy opened her mouth to tell Melissa about the pregnancy. But something stopped her. She knew Melissa wouldn't judge her. She had been the only one who knew about the first pregnancy and abortion, but Amy just didn't want to get into it right now. She wasn't sure why.

Instead, when she spoke, she said, "Okay, enough about me. Tell me everything that is going on with you."

Melissa smiled, knowing Amy had more to tell, but let it go. She filled Amy in on Blake, his job, the kids, and their school. Melissa found a nice rhythm of being a stay-at-home mom and working part-time from home. She wasn't necessarily using her degree, but she didn't care. Motherhood seemed to suit her, as Amy knew it would.

Amy smiled at Melissa. "You like being a mom, don't you?"

Melissa nodded. "I do. It's not easy, and it has its ups and downs. But I do."

Amy considered Melissa. "I'm surprised you and Blake didn't have more children."

Out of Melissa's mouth, before she even considered what

she was saying, came the words, "Four was plenty." After she said it, she was shocked. The child in heaven was never far from her mind. She had four children in her heart, but she had never said that off-handedly before.

Melissa's eyes widened as she looked at Amy. "I'm sorry. Did I ever tell you that Blake and I had a miscarriage?"

"No!" Amy said. "I'm so sorry. When was this?"

"It was my first pregnancy," Melissa admitted.

"Oh," Amy said. "Was it hard for you to try again?"

"Not really," Melissa said. "The hard part was when I got pregnant again, to not be in constant fear that there was something wrong with me, and I wouldn't be able to carry a baby."

Amy considered this. "I guess that would be hard. I'm so sorry, Melissa."

"Thank you," Melissa said. "But it's okay. I know I will see her again in heaven."

Amy smiled at Melissa as one who smiled at a child who still believes in Santa Claus or the Tooth Fairy. As one who thinks it is cute, the child is still innocent enough to believe in all that, but also understands that at some point, the child will be old enough to face the reality that those things don't exist.

Melissa continued with more earnestness, now surprising Amy. "I know it may sound far-fetched. I have only shared this with Blake, but one night, I had a vivid dream about her. I was in heaven in my dream. She came up to me, and I knew it was her. She was probably six, and she was just beautiful."

"How do you know you weren't just dreaming about an angel?"

Melissa did not get defensive. She just stated matter-factly, "No, I knew it was her. She looks just like her sister." She paused momentarily and then said, "Amy, I know you don't like to talk about this, and I don't want to make you uncomfortable. But have you ever considered where your baby that was aborted is?"

Amy was shocked by the question, but also realized that Melissa had worded it so as not to place the blame directly on her.

"No," Amy said honestly. "I never thought about it. According to science, it isn't even a baby yet, so I think it would go nowhere."

"Well," Melissa said. "I guess I believe differently. I believe all babies come from heaven. They are gifts from God. I believe all babies who die in the womb, either by miscarriage, abortion, or stillborn, go right back to heaven where they wait for their parents." Melissa took a deep breath, "I know I don't normally get this spiritual with you, Amy, and I hope you will forgive me for doing so. But I do believe your baby is in heaven, and I so hope you choose to go there and be reunited with her." Melissa's voice was steady, but she ended in almost a whisper.

This was new territory for them. Amy knew Melissa was very religious and had grown more so in her relationship with Blake, but, aside from the occasional "I'm praying for you," Melissa did not try to push her beliefs on Amy. Amy wanted to be defensive with Melissa, but she also knew Melissa's heart. She knew she wasn't trying to hurt Amy. She must have strong beliefs about this if she was willing to press forward and say these things.

"Thank you," Amy finally said, not knowing what else to say. She was also relieved she had not told Melissa about this pregnancy. Melissa would surely try to talk her out of an abortion, and Amy was not sure she wanted to be talked out of it.

Amy was silent for a bit and then decided the best course of action was to change the subject.

"So, do you think you will ever return to doing what you did before becoming a mom?" She noticed a hint of disappointment cross Melissa's face. But the disappointment left almost as fast as it had appeared. She accepted the subject change and began discussing a small business she wanted to start, but wanted to wait until the kids were a little older. As Melissa spoke, their conversation returned to familiar ground, and Amy found Melissa's idea for a new business promising. She encouraged her to go for it when the time was right.

The girls had long since finished their lunches and indulged in coffee and dessert. They couldn't pass up a dessert from this restaurant's famous bakery. They spent the rest of the time talking easily and a little time laughing about college memories. Amy finally put her fork down. Her belly was full, and her heart was overflowing. Melissa had a calming effect on her, and she felt safe with her. She had forgotten how much she enjoyed spending time with Melissa. She vowed not to let as much time pass next time and told Melissa as much.

"I agree," said Melissa. "Too much time went by."

"You can always come out to see me, too," offered Amy. "Now that your kids are a little older, if you ever want to get away for a weekend, I will take you shopping on the Miracle Mile, and maybe we can take in a play at the theater."

"Ohhhh, that sounds amazing," said Melissa. "I just might take you up on that. Thank you. Do you think you will come to Texas more now?"

"I think so," said Amy. "I do want my niece and nephew to know who I am. I forgot how adorable they are, and of course, I miss Annalise. I did promise her I would be back for the holidays."

"Good," said Melissa.

Amy checked the time. Three hours! They had been there for three hours. "Oh goodness, I'd better be getting back."

"Yeah," Melissa said. "Me too. I so enjoyed this. Thank you for meeting me halfway."

"Are you kidding? Thank you as well. This was so much fun. Next time, we must drive through campus and see everything that has changed."

"Deal," said Melissa.

They walked to the parking lot and out to their cars. Melissa leaned over to give Amy a big hug. "You take good care of yourself. Remember, you can always call me if you need anything. And keep me posted on your dad. I'll be praying for you and your family."

"Thank you," Amy said. "I appreciate it." And she did.

They said their final goodbyes and headed to their respective vehicles. Once in the car, Amy texted Annalise and told her she was on her way back. Annalise replied with a thumbs up and told her to be careful driving.

As Amy drove back to Annalise's house, she reflected on her conversation with Melissa. She smiled at all the silly and funny times they had reminisced about. Then, unbidden, Melissa's story of seeing her baby in heaven returned to her. Was that true? Did all babies come from heaven, and did they all go back if they didn't, uh, make it? According to science, her fetus was not a baby yet when she had an abortion. But if what

Melissa said was true, was her fetus a baby that came alive in heaven? Maybe Melissa's dream was just her mind trying to comfort her in her time of grief. Amy wasn't sure she was ready to accept or believe the fetus she got rid of was in heaven waiting for her. Because if it were true, then could she go through with an abortion of this fetus? She wasn't sure how she felt about any of this right now, but there was a weird tugging in her heart thinking about a baby waiting for her in heaven. She pushed all these thoughts from her mind. She didn't want to analyze any of this too closely. She still had some significant decisions to make, one of which was if she would tell Tyler about the pregnancy.

# 31

# Melissa

Melissa drove home, mentally replaying her conversation with Amy. "Okay, Lord, I did what you asked. I told the story about seeing Joy in Heaven. I think she thinks I am crazy now, but I did it."

She heard the Holy Spirit tell her quickly and kindly, "What she thinks about you isn't your problem. You were obedient to share. Keep praying for her."

Melissa sensed an urgency to pray for Amy which was weird because the abortion happened so long ago, but she did find herself praying for Amy most of the way home.

By the time she returned home, Blake had already fetched the children from school, given them their afternoon snacks, and sent them off to do any homework. Melissa walked into the kitchen, embraced Blake, and kissed him quickly. "Thank you so much for all you did this afternoon so I could meet Amy."

"Of course," Blake said. "How is she?"

"She's good." Melissa briefly shared what Amy told her about her dad and her family.

"Wow!" said Blake. "That is an answer to prayer."

"Yeah, it is."

"What else?" Blake asked. He knew her so well, he knew there was more. Melissa knew she hit the jackpot with him. It didn't mean their marriage didn't have challenges, but she knew God had picked out the perfect person for her.

"Well, on the way to meet her, I heard the Lord tell me he wanted me to share the story of seeing Joy in heaven."

Blake's eyes widened. "Really?" he said in surprise.

"Yes, I began to tell the Lord no, but I heard him as clear as day say, 'If I want you reunited with your baby, why would I not want Amy reunited with hers?'" Melissa teared up even saying it again.

"Wow!" Blake said. "That's amazing. So did you?"

"Yes, it kind of worked into the conversation naturally. I did tell her. I was unsure if she knew what to think or say, but she heard me. Shortly after, she changed the subject."

"That's okay," said Blake. "You were obedient, and now the rest is up to the Holy Spirit. I guarantee that regardless of her response, it impacted her."

Blake essentially confirmed what the Holy Spirit had said to Melissa on the way home. She relaxed. She knew she would pray a lot for Amy in the coming days. Melissa kissed her husband again and went up the stairs to check in on her kids, anxious to hear about their day at school.

# 32

*Amy*

Amy awoke, not looking forward to the next couple of days. She definitely needed coffee to get going, but she also decided to take the rest of the pregnancy tests. It didn't hurt to be doubly and triply sure before she potentially disrupted so many lives. She padded into the bathroom and flipped on the light. She retrieved the unused pregnancy tests from their hiding place and took the rest. She set a timer, brushed her teeth, and analyzed herself in the mirror. She met her gaze in the mirror and told herself that no matter what the tests said, she would get through this just like every other challenge in her life.

She spat out the toothpaste and rinsed her mouth as the timer went off. She looked over at the tests and was not surprised by the outcomes. They were all positive. All of them. Not a single one was questionable. Amy looked at herself in the mirror and tried not to cry. But suddenly, everything came crashing down. Everything with her dad, her sister, Tyler, and now this. She indulged herself for a few minutes of crying and knew she had to tuck the emotions away for later. If she cried too long, her eyes would be puffy and swollen, and she would be unable to hide it from Annalise.

Amy gathered up all the pregnancy tests, even the ones she had taken the day before, and put them back in the plastic bag from the drug store. She tied up the bag and thought somehow she would have to dispose of them before she left tomorrow. She could just see her bag being searched at the airport, and if an airport worker stumbled on the tests, she would die from embarrassment. She thought she could sneak it into the big trash can in the garage. She wasn't sure when the garbage man came to collect trash, but she was pretty certain no one would dig in that trash can.

Amy changed clothes and checked her phone. She had one text message from Brooke. She texted her last night after booking her flight back to Chicago. She thought someone in Chicago should probably know she was returning. Brooke's message offered to pick her up at the airport. She was always thoughtful and sweet, but Amy wasn't sure she was ready to see anyone. She had let work know she would return at the week's end. She dreaded seeing Tyler, but she also knew if she could dive back into work as quickly as possible, her life could take on some feeling of normalcy she was desperate to recapture.

Amy began typing a message to Brooke, then changed her mind and pressed the call button on her phone. Brooke answered on the third ring, giving Amy a moment to debate whether she should hang up. Judging by how Brooke answered the phone, Amy wondered if someone was nearby—someone like Tyler.

"Hello?" came Brooke's sweet but professional voice. She did not give Amy a chance to answer. "Please give me one moment, and I will be right with you." There was definitely someone near, and Brooke was trying to hide that she was speaking with Amy. Amy waited patiently. Then, Brooke spoke into the phone in a lowered voice. "Hey, Amy! Sorry about that. I am alone now. How are you?"

"I'm good!" Amy partially lied. "Listen, I want to thank you for your offer to pick me up from the airport, but I think I'll be fine. I can just get a ride-share home."

"Let me do this for you, Amy. It's no trouble, and then you can fill me in on everything that happened while you were gone. We won't have to worry about being overheard."

Brooke did have a point. Once Amy returned to the office, she would not want to discuss what had transpired over the last few days. "Okay, thank you," Amy reluctantly agreed.

Brooke hesitated for just a moment and then said in a rush, "Do you want to tell me what happened with you and Tyler?"

Amy shook her head even though Brooke couldn't see her. Tyler was the last thing she wanted to talk about. She wanted all those emotions shoved far away especially now that she for sure knew she was pregnant. "Can we talk about Tyler later?"

"Of course," said Brooke. "I'm sorry. I don't want to pry. He just came into the office over the last couple of days, looking like his world had been crushed. He even asked if I had heard from you. I was vague. I didn't want to tell him anything you weren't ready to tell him."

"Thank you," Amy said. "I promise I will tell you later. I . . . I just can't right now."

"No worries," said Brooke. "Just know I am praying for you. Everything here is taken care of, so don't worry about anything until you return."

"Thank you," Amy said. "I'll keep you posted on my return flight information."

"Sounds good," said Brooke. "Let me know if you need anything else."

"I will," said Amy, and they hung up.

Amy's flight left early the following day, so she would have most of today to wrap things up here and pack her suitcase. She also knew she had to get moving. She glanced at herself one last time to make sure the traces of tears were gone and braced herself to walk into the kitchen and face anyone there.

To her surprise, the kitchen was momentarily empty. She breathed out a relieved sigh and found a clean coffee mug. She poured herself a cup of coffee and headed to the fridge for the creamer. Just then Annalise entered the kitchen.

"Oh there you are," Annalise said cheerily. "I told the kids to be as quiet as possible this morning because I know you have to be exhausted. They are excited to see you tonight before you leave tomorrow. Do you really have to leave tomorrow?"

Amy smiled at Annalise and sucked back more tears at Annalise's kindness. Amy knew she was just as exhausted as she was. Amy also knew she was going to miss Annalise when she left. "Yes, unfortunately, I do have to get back."

"Would you like to run to the hospital today? If all of Dad's labs and tests return normal today, they will release him tomorrow."

"You know what," Amy said. "I think I do. I would like to see him and Stephanie before I leave tomorrow."

"Okay," said Annalise, and Amy could tell she was pleased. Surprised but pleased.

Amy said, "I'll go start getting dressed."

"That sounds good," said Annalise. "I'll let Stephanie know we will be by in a little bit and see if she needs anything. Maybe we can go grab tacos for all of us on the way to the hospital."

"That sounds great!" Amy said.

Amy went to her room and dressed quickly. She grabbed the pregnancy tests hoping Annalise was still getting ready and tiptoed to the garage. She quickly disposed of the bag. It looked like their trash day might be soon, since the bin was almost full. She managed to get the bag under another trash bag and made her way quickly back into the house feeling like a sneaky teenager.

She met Annalise in the hall and tried to act casual. "I managed to get some packing done for tomorrow, and I think I am ready to go when you are."

Annalise studied Amy for a second but chose not to ask any questions. "Great!" she said. "Stephanie is excited you are coming back to the hospital. I told her we would stop on the way and grab tacos for her. She thought it was a great plan." Annalise finished with a giggle. "I think she is excited she won't have to eat in the cafeteria again today."

"Great!" said Amy, almost too brightly, hoping Annalise didn't see the guilty red blush Amy could feel creeping up her neck.

The girls grabbed their things and made their way to the car. "I'm glad I will have one more night to hang out with Kaylee and Braedon. I am going to miss them."

"Well," said Annalise, "you are returning for Thanksgiving, right?"

Amy laughed. "Yes, I promise. I will be here for Thanksgiving."

"Seriously, the kids loved hanging out with you and watching movies and all the things. They love and miss their Aunt

Amy."

"I miss them too," admitted Amy with a wide smile. She loved that her niece and nephew loved her.

*Just like you could love the baby growing inside of you?* Out came the thought, completely unbidden. Where did that thought come from? Amy truly believed this wasn't even a baby yet. It was just a clump of cells, and she had some important decisions to make. But she for sure was not going to think of that right now.

The girls swung by one of Amy's favorite taco places for breakfast tacos and then headed to the hospital. As they made their way to their dad's room, Amy realized, surprisingly, she was not filled with dread. She was still not completely comfortable, but she didn't want to run the other way either—progress, she thought, which was important if she kept her promise of visiting more often.

As the girls entered the room, they found their dad sitting up in bed. He had way more color today, and it was evident he was on the mend. The plan was that if he did well today, he would go home tomorrow and begin physical therapy early next week.

Amy smiled and gave Stephanie a brief hug and Annalise followed suit. Before Amy knew what was happening, Stephanie and Annalise were making some sort of excuse to leave the room, and Amy was suddenly alone with her dad.

"Hi," said Amy, suddenly shy.

"Hi, sweetheart," said her dad tenderly.

Amy had not heard that term from her dad in a very long time, and it almost brought her to tears.

"Thank you for coming back. I understand you are headed

back to Chicago early tomorrow."

"I am," said Amy. "But Annalise has made me promise I will return for Thanksgiving."

"Oh good!" said her dad. "It has been a long time since we have all spent Thanksgiving together."

"It has," agreed Amy. She knew he was not trying to blame her for that. The expression on his face told her he was taking responsibility for their family not all being together. She appreciated that, but she wasn't ready to tell him just yet. "That is why I am headed back to Chicago tomorrow. If I am going to come back for Thanksgiving, I am going to need to work to get all my ducks in a row so I can take some more time off. And then, Annalise is already making plans for Christmas, so there is that too." Amy ended with a chuckle.

Her dad smiled and said, "I would tell you that you work too hard, but I know it would fall on deaf ears. Before your mom passed . . ." His voice trailed off for a moment, and Amy could tell he was trying to decide if he wanted to say the rest of what was on his mind. He cleared his throat and began again. "Before your mom got sick," he continued, "she used to tell me I worked too much all of the time. Turns out, she was right. That was and still is one of my biggest regrets. I didn't spend more time with her and you girls before she got sick. Life is about people, not about a job or a career. I wanted to be the best provider she had ever seen, and it turns out she just wanted me."

"Do you still miss her?" Amy asked tentatively.

"I do, but the way one misses talking to their best friend." Her dad smiled with tears in his eyes. "I love Stephanie, and she is an amazing wife. We are good for each other. However, so many things felt unfinished with your mom. I don't pine for your mom anymore, but I will say I can't wait to get to heaven and talk to her again."

Amy smiled, fighting back her own tears. Why could she and her dad not have spoken like this all along? It would have helped her so much to process her own pain as she grieved her mom. Her dad is the only person she could share her mom's memories with. Annalise was so young and just did not remember a lot about their mother.

"I miss her so much," Amy admitted quietly. "Our time together was just too short. I hope she would be proud of me." She had been looking at the floor and then glanced up in time to see a tear roll down her dad's cheek.

"Oh sweetheart, she would be so proud of you. Not only for how you took care of all of us after her death, but now as well. You have grown into an amazing young woman. You are beautiful and talented, and I know she looks at you from heaven and smiles."

Now the tears Amy had been holding back began to spill over. "Thanks, Dad," she whispered. "I don't know about the heaven part, but I do hope she is proud." She wanted to add that you don't know all the things I have done and a picture of herself entering the abortion clinic all those years ago flashed in her mind.

Why was that flashing in her mind? She hadn't done anything wrong. She had made the best choice for her and the fetus. Her life would have been so different if she had not had that abortion. She wouldn't have been able to accomplish any of the things in her career that she had achieved, and at that time in her life, she had just finished raising her sister. Wasn't it better for everyone involved not to bring a life into the world when no one was ready for that? She knew it was.

Then why did she feel so guilty? She shook off those feelings and looked at her dad again. He was watching her intently.

"Everything okay?"

"Yes, everything is fine." She smiled brightly at him, wiped away her remaining tears, and changed the subject to the rehabilitation he was going to begin next week. Her dad wasn't exactly excited about going, but Amy assured him it would strengthen his heart, in hopes he wouldn't have a repeat experience.

Annalise and Stephanie reentered the room with a cup of coffee for her. She gratefully sipped her coffee and listened as her sister and Stephanie talked with her dad. After a while, she excused herself to the restroom. Once inside the restroom, Amy looked at herself in the mirror. What was wrong with her today? Tears, twice in one day. She needed to pull it together. She washed her hands and was about to exit when Stephanie walked in.

"How are you doing?" she asked meaningfully.

"I am okay," Amy said in a bright voice. For some reason, she did not want to admit to Stephanie that she had taken the tests and was indeed pregnant. Although she was pretty confident Stephanie already knew; she knew, like moms, just knew things.

Like a dog with a bone, Stephanie was not going to let it go. "Amy," she asked, looking her in the eye. "Are you pregnant?"

Amy looked down at the tile floor. "Yes," she said simply.

Stephanie took her hand and tilted her chin back, as a mom would with a child. She said gently, "What are you going to do?"

It wasn't an accusing question at all, but was asked with kindness, and Amy could tell she was genuinely concerned for her. "I don't know," Amy answered honestly. "I kind of think I have to tell the guy."

Stephanie nodded in approval. "That is only fair."

"But I am not sure I want to have this baby, and what if he does? I honestly think the easiest solution is abortion, but I don't know if he will agree to that so then what do I do?" The words tumbled out before Amy could stop them. These thoughts had rattled around in her brain for so long that she almost felt relief saying them out loud.

"Why do you think abortion is the easiest solution?" Stephanie pressed without accusation.

"I am not sure I want my life to change. I'm not sure I am ready for a baby. I don't want Tyler to stay with me just because he wants the child or feels guilty. That is no basis for a relationship. I don't want to do adoption. It would be so embarrassing to carry a child to full term, and then just have it disappear to another family. What would I tell my coworkers?"

"So," said Stephanie. "You feel like abortion is the solution with the least amount of consequences."

"Exactly," said Amy, grateful that maybe Stephanie understood.

"Let me give you something to think about. I also thought abortion was the right solution. I mean, after all, it isn't a baby. It is just a clump of cells. Isn't that what they tell us? And then all the regular arguments of 'was it right to bring a baby into the world when I wasn't capable of taking care of it' and 'there are no guarantees with adoption and so forth and so on'. So I chose the abortion."

Stephanie took a deep breath and let it out slowly, and Amy could tell she didn't often share this part of her story. Amy wondered if even Dad knew about this. "However," Stephanie continued, "when it came time for my husband and me to start a family, I couldn't get pregnant. We tried all the methods we could afford but nothing. I had this nagging thought that wouldn't go away about the abortion. Did that cause the infertility we were experiencing? So, I began researching. I was horrified by what I found. There were things no one talked about with abortion. Things like, some women have an abortion and then are like me and can't get pregnant again. They tell you the fetus is a clump of cells, but many of the babies aborted are used for what they call medical research and organ harvesting. Have you ever really looked into what truly happens during an abortion? It is eye-opening, to say the least."

Amy was having a difficult time wrapping her mind around what Stephanie was saying. Surely this was all a conspiracy theory. These things didn't happen. Scientifically, abortions were a safe and effective form of birth control and merciful to the would-be baby and mother.

Amy glanced up at Stephanie. Amy could tell Stephanie realized she had pushed far enough. Amy could also tell that this was not a topic Stephanie was comfortable discussing. She must have some pretty strong feelings to be willing to voice her opinions to Amy.

"Just think about one more thing as you make your decision," Stephanie said in a quiet but firm voice. "It may be cruel to Tyler to never know he could have had a child. Think of how you would feel if the shoe were on the other foot."

Stephanie reached over and hugged Amy. "I'm not trying to make you feel worse. I just want you to have all the facts before you make this decision. I have been where you are, and it isn't easy. I will be praying for you as you walk through this."

"Thanks," said Amy, although she was not sure how prayer was going to help. She did know most Christians thought of abortion as wrong. So how would God help her make this decision? Her brain was on overload. It was time to go home to something familiar.

**33**

*Amy*

The rest of the day passed peacefully at the hospital. If Amy were honest with herself, she enjoyed the time with her dad, Stephanie, and Annalise. She had sincerely thought that day would never come. She hugged her dad and Stephanie when she left the hospital room, thankful she had come but ready to go home. She needed time to process all that had occurred in her short time back in Texas. She was looking forward to Thanksgiving for the first time in . . . well, ever.

That night, she enjoyed another delicious home-cooked meal with her sister's family and played a video game with Kaylee and Braedon. They giggled endlessly at her because she was terrible at the game and extremely unsure of how to even work the controls. They all ended up in a pile of giggles on the floor before Annalise ushered the kids off to brush their teeth and change into their pajamas. She had missed both of them so much and vowed to herself never to let this much time pass between visits again.

The next morning, Amy woke way too early for her liking, dressed quickly and comfortably for a full day of travel, and finished packing her suitcase. She made her way to the kitchen where Annalise had already made her coffee to go. After exchanging quiet good mornings, Annalise helped Amy get her things to the minivan, and they climbed in for the drive to the airport.

"Are you sure you don't want anything to eat?"

"No," Amy assured Annalise. "My stomach is not awake yet. I can grab something at the airport. This coffee is giving me life right now."

Annalise laughed. "I guess it is early for food."

"I'm sorry you have to drive me to the airport so early. I didn't mind getting a ride-share."

"I know. But I wanted to soak up every minute with you. I'm so grateful you came."

Amy smiled. "I am looking forward to Thanksgiving. I promise not to stay away for so long. Also, I want you and Graham to seriously think about coming to Chicago this summer with the kids. We would have a blast sightseeing and shopping."

"We will," Annalise promised. "I do think the kids are old enough now to enjoy it. And I would love to see Chicago."

Summer was a ways away, and Amy briefly wondered what her life would be like at that point. Would she and Tyler be together? Would they even be speaking? So much uncertainty awaited her at home. She purposely pushed the thoughts away. She had a little more time before she had to confront everything awaiting her at home.

At the airport, Amy gave Annalise one final hug. She tried to hold the tears at bay as she realized how much she was going to miss Annalise. She could tell Annalise was feeling the same. Before either of them could cry, Amy turned and wheeled her luggage into the airport.

Amy's flight home was uneventful. When the airplane landed, she along with the rest of the people on the plane turned their phones back on. She had several messages. One was from Annalise saying that she missed her already, and please let her know when she returns home. One was from Melissa, who said she was thinking about her and praying for her as she returned to Chicago and hoped to see her again soon. Another message was from Tyler. He must have found out she was headed home. She decided not to read that one just yet. The last one she saw was from Brooke.

"Hey! I am circling outside. Get your luggage and come find me."

Amy was suddenly relieved that Brooke had insisted on picking her up. It would be nice to see a friendly face before she walked into the office tomorrow, and she was kind of hoping she could feel Brooke out where Tyler's mood was before she contacted him or had to see him.

Finally, it was Amy's turn to deplane, and she made her way briskly downstairs to the luggage carousel. Once she had her luggage, she texted Brooke to let her know she was coming out. Amy spotted Brooke's cute beetle right away and wheeled her luggage to the curb. Brooke put on her hazards and jumped out of the car to help Amy with her luggage. Brooke surprised Amy by first enveloping her in a quick embrace.

She looked Amy in the eye and said, "Are you okay?"

"I am," said Amy with a shaky smile. Once her luggage was successfully stowed in the car, the two of them hopped in.

"So," Brooke said as she tugged at her seatbelt, "Do you really want to go directly home, or can I take you somewhere to get something quick to eat?"

Amy wanted to be at home, but she also knew she had no food in her fridge. Once she got home, she didn't want to go back out, and the pregnancy she was desperately trying to ignore wasn't letting her skip meals.

"Sure," said Amy, pasting on a bright smile. "I could go for something quick."

Brooke smiled, satisfied with Amy's answer, and then carefully pulled her car out to merge with traffic.

"How is work? Am I facing the impossible tomorrow?" Amy was pretty sure this was not at all what Brooke wanted to discuss, but it was the safest topic. She knew by accepting the dinner invitation she was going to have to talk about some of what happened this week, but Amy wasn't ready to blurt everything out just yet. Brooke took the hint and let Amy talk about work.

"No, actually all things considered it was probably a good time for you to be gone. Things have slowed down a little bit. I think there are just not a lot of new things the company wants to dive into headfirst right before the holidays. I, for one, am thankful for the reprieve. I feel like this year has had an exceptionally crazy pace."

Amy agreed, absently thankful Brooke was willing to talk about this safe topic. While Brooke chatted about what different people in the office were working on, Amy tried not to think about Tyler and seeing him at the office tomorrow. It was inevitable, but she wished she could put it off indefinitely. Why did she get involved with someone at work? she asked herself for the millionth time.

Brooke pulled into a small diner that had good food but

wouldn't be super busy. She easily found a parking spot, and the girls jumped out of the car and headed inside. They were quickly shown to a table, handed menus, and asked what they wanted to drink. Amy glanced over the menu and then set it aside. She already knew what she wanted to eat. The waitress appeared with their water and asked if they were ready to order. Amy ordered the soup of the day and half of a chicken salad sandwich. Brooke thought that sounded good as well, and told the waitress she wanted the same. The waitress nodded and scurried toward the kitchen.

Brooke took a sip of her water, then a deep breath and turned to Amy. "Okay, tell me as much as you want about what went on with your dad."

Amy recounted all that had happened, knowing she had probably told Brooke some of this before. But Amy was losing track of who she had told what to, and Brooke was a good listener. Brooke listened intently, nodding and smiling in places in Amy's story and also with tears in her eyes at other places in Amy's story.

When Amy finished speaking, Brooke sighed heavily. "This is so great, Amy. I am so excited for you and also proud of you. Forgiveness is just not easy. But do you feel lighter?"

"I do," said Amy, nodding.

"Yeah," said Brooke. "I think that is what most people don't understand. They feel they have a right to hold a grudge or not forgive the other person to protect themselves. Here is the thing though. Forgiveness and forgetting are not the same. No one is saying forgive and run headlong into trouble again. You have to set appropriate boundaries with the person. Forgiveness is really about us. If we forgive, we can let go of the very thing weighing us down. I think resentment makes us a victim all over again."

Amy laughed. "My friend, Melissa, said almost the same thing. I think y'all would love each other. You have a lot in common."

Brooke chuckled. "Well, I see you were in Texas long enough to get some of your accent back."

Amy flushed pink. Although she liked her life here most of the time, she had to admit that this trip back made her miss Texas.

The waitress delivered their food, and the girls spent the next few minutes enjoying the warmth of the soup and savoring the sandwich's delicious flavors. Amy was not aware of just how hungry she was until she took the first couple of bites. She put her sandwich down and chewed what was in her mouth, determined to slow down.

Brooke chuckled. "Did they not feed you today?"

Amy laughed as well, hoping Brooke would not notice the look that crossed her face. They both knew they were avoiding the elephant in the room, Tyler. Amy took a deep breath before picking up her sandwich again.

"Okay, lay it on me," she said guiltily. "How is Tyler?"

Brooke finished chewing the bite in her mouth slowly, and Amy could tell she was measuring her words. "He's . . . okay."

Amy could tell there was a lot more Brooke wanted to say. Amy couldn't tell if Brooke was holding back for Amy's benefit or Tyler's. Amy remained quiet to see if Brooke would add to what she had just said.

Brooke continued hesitantly and cautiously. "I think he is hurt and confused. He truly doesn't understand what he did wrong."

Amy looked at Brooke and quietly said, "I know."

Brooke studied Amy. "Look, Amy. I know you are scared, and you have good reason to be, but I also want you to consider what you would do if you were in Tyler's place. Tyler so desperately wants to fix this. I am not saying you have to continue dating him. If he is not the right person or the right time for you, you get to decide. But Amy, it isn't fair for you to ghost him like this. He doesn't deserve it."

"I know," Amy said again almost in a whisper. Then she blurted, "But it's more complicated than that."

"Why?" Brooke asked, genuinely curious. She stared at Amy for a few minutes. Then she said slowly, "Amy, are you pregnant?"

Amy put down her sandwich and slowly nodded. Tears sprang to her eyes and then ran down her cheeks. She reached for a napkin. Brooke put a comforting hand on her arm. Brooke sat quietly as Amy collected herself.

"I just found out," Amy said. "I suspected, and so I took several pregnancy tests at my sister's house to be sure. You and Stephanie are the only ones who know."

"Stephanie?" Brooke said surprised.

"Yeah, she figured it out. Turns out, she's not as bad as I thought. I see now why Annalise likes her so much."

Amy could tell that Brooke was trying to decide which path to take in this conversation. Finally, Brooke spoke: "What are you going to do?"

It wasn't a hopeless question. It was a sincere question of curiosity about what Amy might be considering for her next steps. Amy appreciated that about Brooke. She didn't just

jump in with advice. She wanted to know how Amy was thinking and what she might want to do.

"I haven't fully decided yet," Amy answered truthfully. "To
be honest, my first thought was abortion."

A pained look crossed Brooke's face. Amy knew it would.
She was pretty sure where Brooke stood as a Christian, but
she also thought she could get Brooke to see her side of the
situation.

"What about Tyler?" Brooke asked quietly.

"I know," Amy said. "The easiest thing to do would be just
to go take care of it. He would never know. Besides, I need to
decide what's best for me."

"I understand what you are saying," Brooke said carefully.
"But it took both you and Tyler to choose to be intimate. It
should probably take you and Tyler to choose the result of that
intimacy."

Amy felt herself getting defensive. Brooke, sensing Amy's
defensiveness rising, reassured Amy, "I promise not to say
anything. This is your decision, but please, think about everything before you make a decision for you and Tyler that you
can't take back."

"I will," Amy promised.

The conversation shifted back to safer ground as the girls
finished their food and headed back to Brooke's car. After fill-
ing her belly, Amy was instantly exhausted and very glad to be
headed home and to her own bed.

Brooke dropped Amy off at her apartment building and
told her she would see her tomorrow. Amy smiled and thanked
Brooke for the ride and the food, and then headed into her
apartment. Amy entered her place, grateful for its familiarity

but also realizing that so much had changed since she had left.

Amy took a long, hot shower that eased her aching muscles from travel and changed into her coziest pajamas. She padded into the kitchen looking for something sweet to eat. Amy wasn't a big sweets eater, so she didn't know if she would have anything. For some reason, she was craving something sweet.

Oh, the baby. Then quickly corrected herself. No way was this clump of cells already causing her to crave things. She inwardly cringed at referring to what was inside of her as a clump of cells. Because, if what she had believed all along, all the science she had heard, if this truly was a clump of cells, why was she craving something? Maybe it was stress or just hormonal fluctuations that were causing her to crave something sweet. That could be completely plausible. There had been a lot of stress for sure.

Amy found some abandoned cookies in the pantry, and she miraculously had some milk in her fridge that hadn't expired and smelled decent. She poured herself a glass and took that with the cookies to the couch. She realized she desperately needed to order groceries and mentally added that to her to-do list for tomorrow.

Amy dipped her cookie into her milk and then popped it into her mouth. As she chewed on her cookie, she thought about the next day. Should she try to contact Tyler tonight so the first time they spoke wouldn't be at work? What would she say? What did she want to say? Amy dipped a second cookie in her milk and popped that one in her mouth as well.

She inwardly groaned. How was she going to handle this? She was beginning to realize that no matter what happened, she had to tell Tyler she was pregnant. She liked him too much to keep that secret from him. It was easy to justify no name—a random boy in college—but this was not easy to justify. She had finally realized she didn't think she could face Tyler in the office every day knowing she had kept something so big from him. She wasn't that cruel.

But how was she going to handle this while maintaining her freedom of choice? The more Amy thought about things the more she realized she had to keep the two issues separate. She first had to discuss their relationship with Tyler and why she was very sorry, but they just couldn't continue. Once he understood that, then he would know why she needed to get an abortion. They, the two of them, just didn't belong with one another right now. They were supposed to stay casual. Amy was not looking for anything serious. So, if they were not going to remain a couple, the sensible thing to do would be to get an abortion. It wasn't fair to bring a baby into this world if the parents were not going to stay together to raise it.

Amy had felt firsthand what it was like to have a parent disappear, only to have another disappear on you. She wasn't going to put a child through that. What would happen when Tyler finally found that serious relationship he was looking for? He wouldn't mean to, but he would eventually abandon this child for his new family. And for Amy, work was her priority right now. It wasn't fair for the baby not to be the number one priority. Besides, isn't this why abortion exists in a civilized world? Isn't this why women should have reproductive rights? If women were the ones who had to carry a child in their bodies, then women should be allowed to decide when that should or should not happen.

Amy made up her mind. She would contact Tyler and see if

he would be up for an early dinner tomorrow after work. She would sit him down and calmly and rationally explain why they could no longer be together. Once he realized this, she would tell him about the pregnancy and that the only sensible thing to do would be to end the pregnancy now, before they brought another person into this mess. She was sure he would see things the way she did. He just had to.

# 34

# *Amy*

Amy awoke to her alarm, hit the snooze, and then lay in bed trying to fight the feeling of dread about seeing Tyler today. Finally, she decided she had avoided moving long enough. She pushed the covers back, swung her legs off the bed, and stood up before she could talk herself out of it. She padded to the kitchen and started coffee. She could feel this was going to be an a-lot-of-coffee type of morning. She was truly exhausted, and her day hadn't even begun.

She got the coffee going and then jumped in the shower. After a quick shower, she grabbed her mug and took it with her to the bathroom to finish getting ready for the day. She looked at herself in the mirror as she began to apply her makeup. She looked tired. This had been a very long week. So much had happened, and even if the pregnancy was not a factor, she had a feeling she would still feel drained. Apart from seeing Tyler at the office, she was excited to go back to work. Amy felt the normalcy of the routine, and diving back into her job would give her something else to think about besides her dad, her family, Tyler, and this pregnancy. This would be a lot for anyone she reassured herself.

She finished getting ready and knew she would need to stop at the cafeteria on the way up to her office. Her stomach was already churning. She felt as if she didn't put anything in it besides coffee; she would end up sick in the bathroom. She did not want to attract any more attention to herself.

Amy grabbed her laptop bag, purse, and keys and headed out the door. She locked the apartment door behind her and made her way downstairs to her car. As Amy drove to work, she tried to focus only on work, not Tyler. She mentally ran through where she wanted to begin on the project she was working on. She chuckled to herself knowing that in actuality, she would probably spend the better part of the morning checking and responding to emails. Today's efficiency, as people called it, often took up a lot of her time.

She swung into the parking lot, hoping she would not run into Tyler until she got settled into her office. She would love to take a breath before she saw him, but she also knew she would not be able to avoid him for the entire day. And honestly, she didn't want to completely avoid him. She had a plan of what she was going to say and do. She wanted to execute the plan as quickly as possible so she could schedule an appointment at the clinic. The sooner this was behind them, the better.

Amy spotted Tyler's car in the parking lot and sighed in relief. If he was already here, then she could probably make it to her office without seeing him. Amy headed to the cafeteria, bought a bagel and some fruit, and then to the elevator. She rode up in silence with some other coworkers she recognized but didn't know well enough to have an extended interaction. She successfully made it to her office without running into anyone she knew well.

She put her things on her desk and looked around. Everything looked just as she had left it. Besides the impending doom of running into Tyler, she felt glad to be back. Amy spent time getting her laptop up and running while she took bites of her breakfast. She should have purchased a ginger ale from the cafeteria. Oh well. The bagel was helping to settle her stomach. She grabbed a bottle of water out of the small fridge situated out of sight under her desk. Grateful there was still a bottle of water left in the refrigerator, she slowly sipped on it.

"Hi," Brooke said from the door, smiling encouragingly at Amy. "How are you this morning?"

It was an open question without an agenda. Amy could tell that Brooke was going to let her set the tone of the conversation. Amy smiled back. "I'm good. I got a good night's sleep, and I think I'm ready for the day," Amy said meaningfully.

"Good," said Brooke.

Amy peered around Brooke into the hallway. "I haven't seen him yet. I don't want to avoid him, but I'm also dreading seeing him."

"Well," Brooke said, "you may have a reprieve. I know he arrived early this morning because he was pulled into a meeting that will probably last until lunch."

Amy sighed in relief. That would give her some time to sort through her job without worrying that he would be at her door any minute.

Brooke looked harder at Amy. "How are you feeling this morning?"

"I'm hanging in there. I think my breakfast will help. Hopefully, there will be no telling trips to the bathroom," Amy said with a rueful chuckle.

Amy could tell Brooke wasn't exactly sure how to respond. She wanted to be supportive of Amy, but she also knew Brooke wouldn't support Amy's decision to end the pregnancy. It made Amy hesitant to be completely honest with Brooke.

"Well," Brooke finally spoke. "I'm here if you need anything."

"Thanks," Amy said and meant it.

Amy bent over her laptop and buried herself in her work. When she finally decided she had held off going to the restroom long enough, she was surprised that two hours had gone by. It just felt so good to focus on things other than herself and her situation.

She ran down the hall to the restroom. Then, she decided to collect her coffee cup and make her way to the break room. She was banking on what Brooke had said, that Tyler would be in a meeting most of the morning. She walked into the empty break room and was thrilled to see a full pot of coffee. She poured herself a cup leaving room for her cream and then made her way to the refrigerator. She opened the door, excited to find creamer. She pulled the creamer out of the fridge and almost dropped it when she heard Tyler's voice behind her.

"Hello, Amy." She turned quickly to find him looking intently at her. Her heart softened as she looked at the face that so often sent her heart racing. Despite herself, feelings for him rushed to the surface. She did like Tyler. She enjoyed spending time with him. She truly had not meant to hurt him.

"Hi," said Amy softly. They stood there staring at each other. Neither of them seemed to know what to say next.

Tyler was finally the one who broke the silence. "I'll let you finish putting as much cream in your coffee as you can fit, and then could we speak in your office quickly?"

Amy could tell he was trying to keep his tone light so as not to scare her off. She felt a pang of regret for how she had treated him. He hadn't deserved to be ignored. That probably wasn't fair to him. Amy managed to nod in answer to his question.

She then finished doctoring her coffee the way she liked it and followed Tyler down the hall. She stepped into her office as Tyler seated himself close to her desk. She sat down in her desk chair, grateful that the desk was a barrier between them.

"Are you okay?" Tyler asked.

His question took her aback. He had every right to be angry with her. Unwelcome tears suddenly sprang to her eyes. In truth, she wanted to spill everything she had been keeping inside to him right now, but she knew this was a terribly inappropriate work conversation. Besides, she had to get her emotions under control. When she finally answered, her voice was a little shaky but hopefully not too noticeable. "I'm okay. Thank you for asking. My dad is doing much better and came home from the hospital yesterday. He has quite a bit of healing ahead of him, but he has a great attitude about it."

"Good," said Tyler. "I am so glad he is on the mend."

Amy could tell Tyler was unsure where to take the conversation next. There was so much they needed to discuss. Amy decided to take the lead. "Could we maybe have dinner after work today?" Amy asked tentatively. "I know we have some things we need to clear up." That was putting it mildly, she thought.

Tyler looked surprised, then very pleased, as if there might still be hope. She didn't want to smash that hope just yet. In fact, she wasn't sure she wanted to crush that hope at all. Now that Tyler was sitting before her, she remembered why she liked him so much. Why could they not be together? Amy thought. Oh, that's right. He loved her, and she wasn't sure she could love anyone. She was not fit for a serious relationship. Walls took time to build, and despite things being better with her dad, she wasn't ready to take down all of them. They were there to protect her. She wasn't ready to be completely vulnerable yet. As all her fears and emotions came flooding back, Amy focused on the conversation she needed to have with him. He probably wouldn't understand today, but he would eventually thank her. He deserves someone who could love him back. She just needed him to see it her way.

"Yes," Tyler finally answered. "I think that's a great idea. Meet you here after work?" He seemed to be saying all of this quickly before she changed her mind and wouldn't have dinner with him.

"Yes," Amy said. "I will meet you here after work." She smiled at him. He studied her for a moment and then quickly said his goodbyes and rushed out the door. Well, she thought, that is settled. Now maybe I can focus on my work for the rest of the day. She had a feeling Tyler would avoid her now, so she wouldn't change her mind.

The rest of the day did indeed pass quickly, and before Amy knew it, Tyler was standing at her office door ready to go to dinner. When Amy looked up and saw his face, her stomach did a flip-flop, and electricity seemed to shoot through her veins. She finished packing up her laptop, grateful she had something to focus on. Amy asked him where he wanted to go for dinner.

"Oh, I thought I would leave that up to you. What are you in the mood for? Italian, Mexican, Indian, Chinese?"

"American," she said decisively. Tyler raised his eyebrows in surprise. Amy was usually an adventurous eater and traditional American fare was often boring to her. However, Amy thought that it would be the safest option for her stomach.

"Yes," she continued, attempting to be light about her decision. "I had quite a bit of spice in Texas. I think I am ready for a more bland option." She wasn't sure whether Tyler bought that excuse, but to her relief, he didn't question her anymore.

"American it is," Tyler said good-naturedly. "May I drive you, and we can come back to your car later?" Amy agreed, not allowing herself to think it through.

They made their way to Tyler's car and drove to the restaurant, chatting about work. Tyler pulled into the parking lot and quickly got out of the car to open Amy's door. They entered the restaurant as if they were a couple that did this many nights. There was tension between them, but they still shared a familiarity.

The hostess seated them right away, and their waitress appeared quickly. Once they had both put their orders in, Tyler took Amy's hand in his. His touch was both electrifying and terrifying to Amy. She looked at him, and her heart softened once again at the look in Tyler's eyes.

"Amy, I am so sorry," Tyler began. This took Amy aback. What did he have to apologize for, really?

Tyler took her silence as a signal to continue. "I shouldn't have taken you off guard as I did. I put pressure on you that I shouldn't have. We had agreed to move slowly, and I changed the rules without really checking where your feelings were. That wasn't fair to you. Will you please forgive me?"

Again, tears sprang to Amy's eyes. Where were all these pesky emotions coming from? For someone who kept a tight rein on her feelings, this was annoying. Amy gathered all her courage and looked into Tyler's beautiful blue eyes. Her stomach did another flip-flop, and the butterflies regrouped and flew around her stomach. She opened her mouth to tell Tyler it still had to be over. What had happened was too dangerous, and this relationship needed to end before someone truly got hurt. However, what came out of Amy's mouth was, "It's okay, Tyler. I am sorry too. I should not have shut you out the way I did. I should have stayed and talked it out with you."

Where were these words coming from? She had spent the last week convincing herself that ending things with Tyler was the wise decision. Apparently, her heart did not agree and chose this moment to take over her mouth. The truth was, she didn't want to lose Tyler. She wanted him in her life. He was such a great guy, and they had so much fun together. She hadn't met anyone like him, ever. Did she want to throw all of that away now? And also, he was apologizing for putting pressure on her. Most guys would not do that. They would pressure her to feel the same way they did.

Tyler looked visibly relieved. His thumb began running in circles on the back of Amy's hand, and her body responded to this slight touch. She had not realized how much she had missed him. "Can we try again?" Tyler asked. "I don't want to lose you. I promise we can go at your pace. I won't surprise you like that again. I can be patient."

Amy pushed aside all thoughts of the pregnancy and what-ifs. She did not want to break up with Tyler. She wanted him in her life. In fact, right now she wanted him very much. She wondered if he would be open to coming back to her place. They didn't have to talk about everything tonight, did they? All rational thought seemed to be tossed aside.

Amy smiled at Tyler. "I don't want to lose you either, Tyler," she whispered, still trying to ignore how much her body was responding to his light touch on her hand.

Tyler looked as if he had received the best gift ever. He leaned over to give Amy a quick kiss on the lips but ended up lingering with such passion that she knew more than just kisses may end their night. The waitress chose to appear at that moment with their salads, and their hormones cooled. As they ate, Amy filled Tyler in on everything that had happened with her dad and her family. Tyler listened intently. Amy had never shared this much about her family with Tyler.

When Amy finished, Tyler said, "Wow! I didn't realize your dad was such a jerk. You have told me bits and pieces, but I didn't realize how bad it was." Amy studied Tyler's face. Did he resent her for not being completely honest about her family? Did he have a right to feel that way?

"Yeah," Amy sighed. "I don't share this side of my life with many people." Amy studied Tyler again, looking for signs of resentment that she was reluctant to share about her life. She wasn't going to change overnight, and he shouldn't expect her to.

Amy wondered if she was still looking for reasons to end it with him. However, if he felt resentment that she hadn't shared all about her family, how would he think that he wasn't the first to know she was pregnant? Doubt returned to Amy like a crashing wave of reality.

Tyler thoughtfully chewed his food and asked, "Are you

going there for Thanksgiving then?"

"Yes," said Amy. "Annalise made me promise I would be there for Thanksgiving."

"Good!" Tyler said. "I think this is awesome."

Amy knew he thought it was awesome because he was so close to his family. He didn't have a reference point for how Amy had grown up or why she was not always trusting of people. She hoped he didn't think that, just because her dad and she had called a truce, all was set right between them. They had a long road of healing ahead of them, and this was just a start.

They finished their meal, and Tyler paid the bill. Amy always secretly loved that Tyler did that. She was a strong, fiercely independent woman, but there was something about the guy paying that she still found traditional. She found it very attractive. Tyler once again took her hand and reestablished the physical connection between them. All the doubts she had just been feeling seemed to scatter. She wondered whether she should outright ask Tyler to come back to her place, or whether he was sensing the romantic tension between them as well.

As they walked to Tyler's car, he once again reached for Amy's hand. She clasped his hand, and the butterflies came back. It was like they had just started dating again. When they got to Tyler's car, he walked her to the passenger side, pressed her to the car, and kissed her deeply. When he pulled away, she felt lightheaded. She grabbed the front of his shirt to balance herself.

"Amy . . . ," he began.

"Please come over," she finished.

That was all she needed to say. He quickly opened the door

and tucked her inside the car. He drove to her apartment with an urgency that let her know he wanted to get there before she could change her mind. Once inside Amy's apartment, clothes came off quickly, and they did not even stop in the living room on the way to Amy's bedroom. Amy—or at least her body— had missed Tyler. She did not want to be without him. All other consequences left her mind for the moment.

The next morning, Amy woke to a feeling of overwhelming nausea. She lay there hoping it would go away, but knew it would not. She rushed to the bathroom before it was too late. After she emptied her stomach of last night's dinner, she ran water in her mouth and hoped Tyler had not heard her. She didn't want to lie to him, but she also did not want to explain. Not yet. Not after last night.

She had not realized how much she had missed him. She hadn't realized how much of a fixture he had become in her life. If she told him about the pregnancy now, what would it do to their relationship? This seemed easier when she had decided to walk away from Tyler. Somehow, his feelings about the pregnancy didn't matter. All that mattered was that she did the right thing by telling him, and then followed through on what she wanted to do about the pregnancy. Getting involved with Tyler was going to complicate everything. She needed time to sort out her thoughts and decide on the best approach to tell him about the pregnancy . . . or not tell him.

She opened the door to Tyler, standing in front of her with a look of uncertainty and concern on his face. Too late. She was going to have to think on her feet.

"Are you okay?" asked Tyler.

"I'm fine," said Amy, waving her hand dismissively.

"It sounded as if you were sick. Was it something you ate last night? We ate the same thing though, and I am not sick. Did you catch something on the plane? Traveling is brutal to the immune system." He felt her forehead. "You feel normal. Can I get you something to drink to settle your stomach?"

"Sure," said Amy, remembering she forgot to order groceries. Again. "Ugh. I don't have anything. I haven't made it to the grocery store yet."

"No worries," said Tyler. "Let me run to the corner drug store and get you something."

"Okay." Amy agreed. She knew she was going to need something other than coffee this morning to settle her stomach.

Tyler threw on his clothes quickly and assured her he would be right back.

Amy used the time to shower and try to start getting ready for the day. She knew if she moved too fast, she would throw up again. She also did not want to make herself or Tyler late for work, and since her car was still at work, she had few options.

Tyler made it back to the apartment as she stepped out of the shower already feeling more like herself. He had a bag full of medicines perfect for someone with a stomach bug. However, he had also purchased some Saltine crackers and ginger ale. "Thank you so much," Amy said feeling very grateful. She opened the ginger ale and began sipping it slowly.

Tyler eyed her. "Are you getting ready for work?"

"Yes," she said with a chuckle. "I don't think they would be very happy if I went back for one day and then took some more time off. I will be fine."

Tyler studied her again. "Are you sure? People don't just throw up for no reason. Are you sure you don't need to stay home today?"

"I'm sure," said Amy. "I'm already feeling much better."

"Okay," Tyler said, but she could tell she had not fully convinced him. She wasn't sure how many pregnant women he had been around, but she hoped he wouldn't put the pieces together any time soon.

They finished getting ready for work. Tyler had a few shirts still at Amy's apartment, so at least he would have a fresh outfit to wear. Amy assured Tyler once again that she was fine when she caught him staring at her. He smiled at her and walked slowly to her. He gathered her in his arms and gave her a lengthy, passionate kiss that left them both breathless.

Amy smiled. "Don't do that again, or we will stay home from work for a completely different reason."

Tyler chuckled. "Don't tempt me. Oh, Amy, I missed you so much."

Amy leaned her head into his shoulder and snuggled in closer. She missed Tyler too. She wasn't sure how things were going to work out long-term, but right now she was enjoying his comfort and his strength. "I missed you too," she finally whispered.

"Okay." Amy declared, straightening. "We have to go. It is already going to be awkward trying to pretend we didn't come to work together," she said, only half kidding. They grabbed their laptop bags and headed out the door.

Later that morning, Brooke found Amy. "How are you?" And Amy knew it was a loaded question.

"I am okay," Amy said, smiling.

"Did y'all go to dinner and talk as you planned?"

"Well, we went to dinner, and we did talk. But not like I

planned."

"Oooookay," said Brooke.

"Well, we are back together for now."

"Good!" Brooke said. "What did he say about the pregnancy?"

"I haven't told him yet." Amy cringed knowing how terrible that sounded.

"Oh, Amy." Brooke shook her head. "Did he spend the night?"

"Yes," Amy said, blushing, but also realizing she shouldn't have to explain herself or her adult decisions. She was not a child.

Brooke shook her head again. "I hope you know what you are doing."

Amy laughed. "I certainly do not know what I am doing, but I just couldn't tell him yet. It just seemed overwhelming with everything else we needed to talk about."

"Well, just my opinion, but don't wait too long," said Brooke. "You don't want him to feel you were being dishonest with him."

Again, Amy had never considered this. Her body, her choice. Right? But she briefly put herself in Tyler's position. How would it make her feel if he were keeping something this big from her? It would make her feel terrible. That's how it would make her feel if she were honest with herself.

"I know you're right," she said to Brooke. "I will tell him. Soon."

Soon, however, did not come as quickly as it should have. Amy and Tyler fell into a familiar routine of eating dinner together and then spending the evening and the night at each other's places—mainly Amy's. When Amy woke up three mornings in a row with nausea, Tyler went back to the store for more ginger ale. But he also came back with a pregnancy test.

When he showed it to Amy, her heart dropped to her feet. She was still not ready to discuss this. She wanted more time with him. She wanted more time to convince him that it wasn't the right time for a baby. She wanted more time before he potentially walked away from this relationship.

"I think you need to take this," Tyler said gently. Tyler took Amy's reaction to mean that the thought that Amy could be pregnant shocked Amy.

He continued. "Whatever the result, we will figure out what to do together, but I think we need to rule this out."

Amy stared at the test for a long time and then looked at Tyler, and tears began to fill her eyes. She absolutely should have told him sooner. How was he going to feel that she knew this the entire time and said nothing? He would feel hurt. She took a deep breath, took his hand, and led him to the couch.

"Tyler, I have something to tell you. I . . . I already took one of these. Several in fact. I am," she paused, gathering her courage. "That is to say, I am pregnant."

Tyler's face was a mix of shock and happiness. "Seriously? You are?"

"Yes," Amy said, trying to not let his reaction keep her from being completely honest.

"Wait, how long have you known?"

"I found out while I was at my sister's house."

Tyler thought for a minute absorbing the information. "Is this why you wanted to get back together, because you are pregnant?"

"No!" she said almost too emphatically. "In fact, I want to get rid of it." She blurted out the words without thinking. She looked at Tyler as a look of pain and confusion crossed his face.

"Get rid of it?" He repeated. "Wait, is it mine?"

Amy tried hard not to get annoyed by that question. "Of course it is yours! I shouldn't have said it like that," Amy back-peddled. "But, I don't think we are ready for this. Do you? I mean, I freaked out when you told me you loved me. You promised we could go at my pace. Remember?" She knew she was begging him to understand, but she was also watching his face. He was not relieved that she wanted to get rid of it. Not at all. She had to convince him this was for the best.

"Tyler, we are both wrapped up in our careers. I mean, there are no good options for this baby. I am not ready to have a family. We are not ready to be a permanent couple. What if we decided we don't want to be together, and you went off and found someone else and had a family with her? How is that going to make this baby feel? And what about me? I am not ready to let go of my career yet. Is the baby going to spend its life in daycare? I think the best decision is to end the pregnancy. We are just not ready for all that."

Tyler stared down at the couch, his face unreadable as he processed all of Amy's words. She hoped she could get through to him and they could move past this little hiccup in their relationship. She did want to move forward with him, but she was still processing her emotions about their relationship. There was no way this was a good time to bring a baby into the mix. She just had to get him to understand.

Tyler looked at Amy, his face a mix of anger and desperation. "Well, it seems you have been quite busy making decisions for both of us. Why do you get to decide what WE are ready for? Why do you get to decide if now is the right time for US to have a baby? If the baby is mine, why don't I get a say in this?"

There were very few times Amy had seen Tyler angry, and usually it was over something stupid, like a car cutting him off in traffic. This was new territory for Amy. Usually, when people, especially guys, got angry with Amy, her coping mechanism was to walk away. As tempted as she was to do so now, she knew Tyler had a point.

Still, Amy was not ready to admit that Tyler had a point. "Well," Amy sputtered. "It is my body. So, I should get to decide when and if I put it through a pregnancy. If the shoe were on the other foot, I would let you decide whether you wanted to carry the baby. But that is just not how it is!"

Tyler was quiet for a few minutes. When Tyler looked at her again, there were tears in his eyes and a look of desperation on his face. "Please don't do this," he whispered earnestly, taking her aback. "Please. I know I am supposed to support the modern woman by saying that it is your body, your choice and you can have everything. And to a point, I fully believe that. But please don't do this. Let's talk about all the options before you do this."

Amy really couldn't understand why he was so adamant. I mean, it wasn't even a baby yet. It was a clump of cells. No harm, no foul. But they needed to act sooner rather than later, so they still had options. She hoped it would not take long for her to change his mind. But why was he so emotional about this?

"Okay," she said. "What do you think our options are?"

"Well, we could give it a serious go as parents. We have already established that we like each other enough to give this a fair shot. And I know you don't want to necessarily hear this, but I more than like you, Amy. Other couples have started with less than that. If being together makes you uncomfortable, then I will take the baby to raise. You can be uninvolved all the way to completely involved. Whatever makes you comfortable. Please just don't get rid of the baby. Look, Amy, there are no guarantees. Even if we decide we are madly in love and get married and have children, there are no guarantees in life. Your childhood should have taught you that. Your parents didn't have a clue when they fell in love and had children that your mom would die young. They never chose not to be together. It was just something that happened because . . . life."

Amy sighed deeply. "Why are you so adamant about keeping this baby? I thought you would be relieved that I didn't want to keep it."

Tyler shook his head. "Look, I know my life may not reflect it, but I was raised Catholic. I have five siblings. I was always taught about the sanctity of human life from a young age, and that it is not our right to decide who gets to live and who gets to die. I just can't stand by abortion." He said the last sentence quietly.

"Wait, so you're telling me the reason you want to keep this baby is because of some religious conviction you are not even certain you believe enough to go to church? That is a bit hypocritical, don't you think?" Amy spat the words, bitterness tainting her voice.

Tyler put his face in his hand. "I know, Amy. I know it

seems that way, but I believe what you are calling a clump of cells is indeed a baby. It is a baby, part of you and part of me, beginning to grow and thrive inside you. I can't, in good conscience, support you killing it. Please, please don't do this."

Amy stared at Tyler for a long time. Maybe it would have been easier just to take care of it as she had planned. What was she going to do now? Should she break it off with Tyler and then just go take care of it? Amy had a lot to think about. She looked at Tyler, disappointed that the conversation had not gone as planned. "I have a lot to think about, and we need to get to work."

Tyler stared at Amy for a long time and then nodded. "Please, Amy. Don't do anything permanent until we can talk more."

"Okay," Amy agreed quietly. She wasn't a complete monster. She knew the right thing to do was to allow Tyler to have his say. But she had to find a way to make him see this was the absolute best option in front of them.

They got ready for work and headed out the door, separately, both with a lot on their minds.

# 35

# Amy

When Amy arrived at work, she headed straight for her office intent on burying herself mentally in her work. She did not want to think about Tyler, their conversation, or the inconvenience inside her that was causing so many issues. She wanted to feel productive and successful. And she could do that at work. She was good at her job, and she knew it. She had opportunities for advancement and growth at this company and other companies around her if she decided she didn't want to work here anymore. Why would she want to give all that up? It just was not the right time. It just wasn't, and Tyler was being selfish by asking her to put her career on pause to carry and have a baby. This was not going to interfere with his career at all. Only hers. Why could he not see that? Was he that antiquated in his thinking? She hadn't thought so until now.

She sat in her desk chair and mentally shoved aside all other thoughts. When she came up for air a couple of hours later, she realized she was very thirsty and getting hungry. She looked down at her phone which she had silenced, and saw there was a text message from Melissa. Amy unlocked her phone and clicked on the text.

"Hey, girl! Missing you and praying for you. Love you!" Melissa ended with a heart emoji and a smiley face emoji. These were not unusual texts from Melissa. They usually made Amy feel cared for, but today, she was just annoyed.

What exactly did God tell Melissa to pray for anyway? Did God tell Melissa her secret and now Melissa was praying against abortion? That seemed meddling, sneaky, and unfair. Why was no one on her side for this one? This was modern-day America. Corporate America. Reproductive rights were part of the rights women had fought for. How could people not see that? Why were so many people suddenly against her decision and unwilling to see things her way? Maybe she needed new friends.

Amy had a coworker a couple of years ago whom she enjoyed going out to bars with. This woman talked openly about her sexual exploits and subsequent abortions. Amy had never shared with this co-worker that she too had had an abortion in college because, in actuality, Amy felt sorry for the girl. It seemed to Amy that this woman was with one guy right after another to fill the emptiness in her life. What this co-worker kept saying was fun, but it did not look fun to Amy. The woman claimed to be in control, but to Amy it looked as if this poor girl was being used by men. The men were quick to toss this girl aside when they had had their fun. It made Amy sad. Amy also couldn't understand why the woman kept putting herself through these abortions. Why didn't she find some other form of birth control?

Amy thought the woman was an extreme example though. People didn't look at Amy like that, did they? She preferred casual relationships because she didn't want things to get messy or complicated. That meant she was in the driver's seat in re-lationships. Then, Amy could have companionship without the seemingly inevitable heartbreak that accompanied the end of a relationship. But as she thought back through her casual rela-tionships, was she in the driver's seat? Did these guys view her as easy? Wasn't that an out-of-date way of thinking? She was a successful, independent woman. A woman who felt empty if she was truly honest with herself.

That last thought surprised her and also made her feel de-fensive. She wasn't empty inside, was she? Her life was very full, wasn't it? She shook her head. What was wrong with her? She needed to convince Tyler that abortion was the right path. The sooner this was dealt with the better. Because if she faced the reality that she was empty inside, then a baby definitely would not help that. In fact, she would be a terrible mother with nothing to offer this child, and that definitely would not be fair to the child. Abortion was the best option. She was de-termined to have Tyler see things her way.

Later that afternoon, Tyler swung by her office. "Hi," he said tentatively.

"Hi," she said back, wondering what this conversation would hold.

"Look," he continued with a heavy sigh. "I know we don't want to talk here. Do you want to come to my place for dinner tonight? I can cook, or we can order pizza. I just know we need to talk."

Her stomach growled as if it was going to answer for her. Tyler lifted the corners of his mouth in an attempt to smile. What did he have to be upset about? He wasn't pregnant. And she was giving him an out. He was being the selfish one.

Amy sighed in return. "Okay," she finally said. "I have a few more things that need to be done before I leave, and then I can head to your place. I can text you when I leave."

"Great!" he said. "And Amy, I know we can work this out."

She smiled at his hopeful face. She did not have the confidence he did, but she didn't want to dash his hopes here at work. This should be a private conversation away from other ears. He took the smile as agreement and left saying he would see her later.

Once he was gone, Amy looked down at her desk. She just had to convince him. She did not want to lose him, and she was afraid she was going to lose him. Again. What was wrong with her? A week ago, she walked away from him determined not to look back. Now she wanted this relationship? When had she become so invested? Maybe forgiving her dad had made her soft. Maybe opening her heart to her dad had opened her heart to other things as well. She had to find her footing.

She looked up as Brooke entered her doorway. "You look deep in thought," she said. "Everything okay?"

"Yes," Amy said quickly. "No," she admitted.

"What's going on?" Brooke asked.

"Well, Tyler found out I'm pregnant this morning." Amy lowered her voice to a whisper. She didn't need any more people finding out about this.

"Oh?" Brooke said, raising her eyebrows. "Found out?"

"Yes, he figured it out because of the stupid nausea I'm experiencing and wanted me to take a pregnancy test."

Brooke's eyes widened. "How did that conversation go?"

"Well, surprisingly, he understood why I had not told him about the pregnancy yet. But he is not on board with ending the pregnancy."

"Oh?" said Brooke keeping her expression neutral. But Amy knew she was far from neutral.

"Yeah. I am not sure how I am going to convince him to see it my way, but I need to, and quickly."

"Why?" Asked Brooke

"Why?" Amy asked incredulously

"Yeah, why?"

"Well, because of all the reasons I told you. I am in the midst of a wonderful career. Why should I have to pause my life to have a baby I did not plan on? I mean, this isn't going to change Tyler's life at all. But mine will change a lot. That's not fair, is it?" Amy was frustrated, to say the least. Why did she have to keep explaining this?

"Oh, did Tyler say he didn't want the baby or to help with the baby?"

"Well, no."

"What did he say?"

"He said he would help with the baby, or even take the baby if I didn't want it."

"Oh," Brooke said again. "Well, that sounds to me like he is willing for his life to change. If he is willing to be a dad and allow you to be as involved as you want, that sounds to me as if he is okay with his life changing."

"But I'm still the one who has to carry this baby for nine months. He can walk away at any time." Seriously, why was she the only one who could see things from her perspective? Amy thought. This is ridiculous. She was beginning to get annoyed.

"Yes, true. But Amy, you like Tyler and went back to him

for a reason. Do you think that is something he would do?"

Amy had to admit to herself that it would be out of character for Tyler just to walk away. He was the kind of guy who followed through on his commitments. However, she was not ready for another human life to be dependent on her. She had a right to choose how her life went. She did not have control over her childhood. She should be able to have a say in her life now.

"I am going to say something here," continued Brooke, "that you may not like, and I am sorry. But your main argument is that you should have the right to choose. I understand your point. However, didn't you make a choice when you began a relationship with Tyler? It's not the baby's fault that it showed up at an inconvenient time for you. Is it? And I bet, if you asked the baby, it would want a chance to live."

Brooke continued before Amy could silence her, "I want you to think about something else as well. You raised your sister, and according to you, she is an amazing human being. I think you are selling yourself short here. I think you would be such a great mom. This baby would be so lucky to call you mom. I don't want what you went through as a child to hinder you from maybe the best thing that could ever happen to you. Maybe you have an opportunity here with an amazing guy and an even more amazing child. Maybe what you are calling freedom is actually you robbing yourself of a life you will love. You think having the baby is selfish because it won't be born into the best circumstances you could possibly think of. But maybe it is selfish to deny this baby a chance at life. I am here for you Amy. You know that. But I just want you to maybe look at this situation a little differently."

Was Brooke right? Was she still allowing her childhood to dictate her future? Was she potentially robbing herself of a life she would love? If she decided to go through with this pregnancy and that was a big if, could she open her heart fully to Tyler and this child? She still wasn't sure they both didn't deserve better than her. Before Amy allowed her thoughts to go any further, she found the familiar wall in her heart that served to protect her and hid behind it.

Amy knew Brooke was probably reading her face and knew that she wasn't going to get any further. Brooke smiled at Amy. "No matter what, Amy, I will still be here for you. I will let you get back to work."

Brooke turned to leave, but not before Amy saw the look on Brooke's face. It was a mixture of concern and sadness.

# 36

# Brooke

Brooke walked out of Amy's office. She took a deep breath and suppressed the tears that were forming behind her eyes. "Okay, Lord," she whispered. "I did it. I told her exactly what you wanted me to tell her. It is in your hands now. Lord, I ask that she have a complete change of heart. Please break through her defenses and let her see this baby the way you do. Help Amy see herself the way you do. Please protect the baby and do a miracle in Amy's heart and mind. Amen."

Brooke was accustomed to praying for Amy. She knew the second Amy walked into her life, they would be friends. Amy was fiercely independent, but only because she felt she had to be as a child. She was very caring and compassionate towards others.

Amy would regularly check in with Brooke to ensure she was doing well in her job. Amy was a little older than Brooke and had worked at the company longer. Amy's desire to see Brooke succeed first stood out to Brooke. Then, they became more than co-workers. They had become friends. They began sharing about their personal lives and Brooke enjoyed Amy's perspective even though Brooke didn't always agree with

Amy's choices.

Brooke, having been a Christian for many years, knew it was no accident that Amy was in her life. Brooke knew there were other people in Amy's life praying for her, and despite how much she was running from God right now, God was working overtime to woo her back to Him. Brooke prayed Amy would not follow through with the abortion and that she would have a change of heart. Brooke knew the abortion would mean nothing good for Amy.

She took a deep and cleansing breath, thanked God for Amy, asked for His protection for Amy and the baby, and then realized she had to hand the whole thing over to God. Brooke could pray for Amy, but she could not change her. Only God could do that. She let out her breath and told herself to let go of her worry.

# 37

# *Amy*

Amy climbed into her car completely exhausted from the day. She noticed her energy level had significantly dropped lately. Amy felt a renewed urgency to make an appointment at the clinic and put this whole thing behind her.

Amy started her car and then remembered she had promised to text Tyler. She sent him a quick text, explaining that she was on her way to his house, and backed out of her parking space. Amy pulled out into traffic and headed toward Tyler's house. Amy enjoyed driving and could already feel herself unwinding as she navigated to Tyler's neighborhood. Amy began to zone out as she thought through all she had accomplished that day at work. She never got tired of that beautiful productive feeling she felt at the end of most days. It made her feel successful.

Her thoughts turned to the conversation she had with Brooke. She wondered again if Brooke was right. Would she be a good mom? Could she see a future with Tyler? Was the wall she was dutifully hiding behind protecting her or preventing her from a life maybe she did want after all? If Amy were being completely honest with herself, her time with Annalise and her family made her long for something a little more than just her career. Maybe her career wasn't the only thing she wanted anymore.

Yikes! These were dangerous and new thoughts. Amy was not sure she was comfortable exploring them.

Amy's thoughts then turned to the dinner at hand and what she would be facing with Tyler. She hoped she could make some headway in helping him understand where she was coming from. She desperately wanted to reach an understanding with him and hopefully, not lose the relationship entirely. She had come to realize through all of this that she liked Tyler, probably more than she had ever liked anyone. She wanted to give this relationship a shot. She reasoned that if they could make a go of the relationship somewhere down the line when they were both ready, they could plan for a baby. They called it Planned Parenthood for a reason.

Just then, she remembered she needed to text Melissa back. She glanced at her cell phone in the seat beside her. She made a mental note to text Melissa when she got to Tyler's house.

Amy never saw the truck that entered the intersection running a red light. It slammed into her with such force that when her car stopped spinning, she was facing the opposite direction in the middle of the intersection. Amy was vaguely aware that there was glass in her lap, and her face had hit something hard. Someone was honking a car horn, and right before she lost consciousness, she was loosely aware the horn might be hers.

# 38

*Amy*

Amy opened her eyes slowly and blinked a few times, trying to clear her vision. Her head was resting against the steering wheel and she didn't think she could move just yet. As her eyes adjusted, she became aware of a man moving toward her, covered by a brilliant light. The light was bright like the sun but was absent from harshness. She could stare right at it without feeling blinded. The light was mesmerizing, drawing her in like a moth to a flame. She wanted to crawl into its brilliance, to be surrounded by it. She had this weird sense that if she could jump into the light she would be completely whole.

As the man approached, she felt a radiating love coming from him that she had never experienced before. She wasn't even aware that love like what she was feeling at this moment existed. It filled every cell of her body and inexplicably completed her. The man stopped in front of her and smiled at her in a manner that told her all would be okay. She could see his eyes. They were a color she had never seen before, and they were filled with kindness. Such kindness. What had she done to deserve the love and kindness this man was directing toward her?

"Amy," the man said her name with the familiarity of someone who knew and loved her very well. His voice sounded like water. "Amy," he said again. She was vaguely aware of wondering, at the same time, how he knew her name and the strange feeling that she had always been known to him. Was she dreaming? Was she dying? She didn't care. She just wanted this man to stay with her, forever.

"Amy," the man continued, "you are a much-loved child." Tears began streaming down her cheeks. It wasn't so much the words he said but how he said them. She would later realize it was the Spirit, the power behind His words. As he said this to her, she felt her spirit and her emotions shift into alignment like a chiropractor readjusting her spine. She wasn't even aware she needed the adjustment, and now she felt relief. She felt wrapped in this pure love coming from Him. The lies she had been believing about herself were exposed and began to melt away, no match for the brilliant light that enveloped her.

He waved his hand toward her and another surge of intense love filled her. "This child you are carrying  is also a much-loved child." Inexplicably, a fierceness filled Amy toward the child she was carrying in her belly, a child she had until this moment refused to recognize. She wanted both to love this child and to protect it. Before she could sort out what was happening, the man disappeared seemingly into thin air, and a man in uniform was standing in front of Amy.

"Where did he go?" Amy's voice was raspy, but she was desperate to see the man again.

"Where did who go, ma'am? Was there someone else in the car with you?"

Amy shook her head and then realized she was still lying on

the steering wheel. "No," she said. "A man was standing here a moment ago. Where did he go?" He couldn't be gone. She needed to know who he was. How did he know her like no one else seemed to know her? She had never felt so much love in her life. She was desperate not to let the feeling fade.

The uniformed man, whom Amy now realized was a police officer, looked around. "Maybe it was a bystander, ma'am. Let's get you taken care of. What's your name, ma'am?"

Amy, she thought she said, but realized she didn't speak. She swallowed hard as she became aware of the sharp pain in her head and also in her arm.

"Ma'am hold on, the ambulance is almost here. Can you tell me your name?"

Amy tried again. "Amy," she croaked out.

The man looked visibly relieved that she could say her name. "Okay, Amy," he said, his voice much more gentle. The paramedics are almost here. You can hear the sirens. They will help you out of the car and take really good care of you, okay?"

Amy only managed a slight nod, but it pleased the man. She wondered again where the other man had gone. Was he still here? Her eyes scanned the area once more, but she could not find him. Surely with the light all around him, he would still be easy to spot.

The man noticed she was looking around and assumed she was looking for the car that had hit her. "Don't worry about the other driver. He is being taken care of as well."

Just then a paramedic appeared beside the police officer. "We are going to take really good care of you. Okay, ma'am? Can you tell me your name?"

"Amy," she managed to croak out again.

"Excellent," the paramedic said. "Does anywhere hurt besides your head?"

Amy thought for a minute. Her face hurt, but now she was noticing pain in her arm.

"My arm," she said.

"Okay, there is no pain in your neck or back?" asked the paramedic.

"No," Amy confirmed.

"Okay, then let's get you to sit up slowly. Slowly, okay."

She didn't have to tell Amy twice. She wasn't sure she could sit up quickly. With the help of the paramedic, she lifted her head and sat back against the seat.

"Is that better?" asked the paramedic.

Amy nodded slowly.

"Okay. Let's look at your arm. It doesn't look too bad. You will need to get X-rays to see if it is broken."

Amy looked in front of her and realized that the airbag had deployed. No wonder her face felt like it had been punched. It had. She looked down at the glass in her lap and briefly wondered where it had come from.

"Did you lose consciousness?" the paramedic asked.

"I . . . I am not sure."

"Okay," said the paramedic. "That's okay. We are going to load you into the ambulance and get you to the hospital, okay? They will get you all fixed up and will take really good care of you."

Just then a male paramedic appeared at the car door. "How are we doing here, Angela?"

Angela gave the other paramedic a rundown of her injuries. "Okay," he said. He looked at Amy and smiled. Amy imagined that smile set some hearts racing. "Let's get you to the hospital so they can check you out and patch you up."

Together, the paramedics loaded Amy onto the gurney, being careful of her arm. Angela grabbed Amy's cell phone and computer bag and put them on the gurney with Amy. "Thank you," Amy said, relieved.

As the paramedics began to wheel Amy to the ambulance, she glanced over to see the other car. It was a truck, and the front was severely damaged. Was she lucky to not be more hurt? The driver seemed fine and was standing, talking with the police. Were they giving him a sobriety test? She couldn't seem to process all this right now. She would have to sort it out later.

Amy looked in the other direction to see that a crowd had gathered. Amy did not like being at the center of such a spectacle, but she couldn't worry about that right now. She would make some phone calls when she got to the hospital. She imagined that when she did not show up at Tyler's house right away, he was going to begin worrying.

The paramedics loaded her into the ambulance's back, and Angela climbed in with her. Amy had only seen the back of an ambulance on TV. It was very surreal to be sitting on a gurney and being driven to the hospital. Things Amy never pictured herself experiencing.

Angela called the hospital ahead to let them know they were on their way, then busied herself by monitoring Amy's vitals and asking her questions. Amy knew this was probably Angela's way of keeping her distracted from all that was going on. It gave Amy something to focus on and kept her calm. Angela seemed good at her job.

Once at the hospital, the paramedics efficiently unloaded her from the ambulance, and the hospital staff directed the paramedics to a room in the emergency area. The smell of antiseptic was almost overpowering. A nurse came in shortly thereafter to take over for Angela.

"Thank you," Amy said.

"No worries," said Angela. "I am glad you will be okay." She then disappeared from the room leaving Amy in the nurse's hands.

The nurse began asking Amy a series of questions. Where did Amy feel pain? How was her head? Did she feel dizzy? What day was it?

Amy told the nurse her arm hurt, and the nurse nodded. "I am pretty sure the doctor will want to take a look at you first, and then will order X-rays to see what is going on with your arm. Before we get started on all that though, I have to ask you, is there any chance you are pregnant?"

"No," Amy said instinctively. "Wait, yes."

"Yes, there is a chance," the nurse asked. "Or yes, you are pregnant."

"Yes, I am pregnant."

"Okay," the nurse said. "The first thing we need to do then is see if your baby is okay."

"Okay," Amy said as the nurse hurried from the room.

Amy tried to process all that was happening. She apparently had a sizable gash in her head and her arm hurt. As the shock began to wear off, she felt herself begin to shake. She was feeling the effects of being hit. She glanced down at her stomach. Was her baby okay?

Who was that man? Was he an angel? Was he a helpful bystander? What had he said to her?

She was a much-loved child of God. And her baby was a much-loved child of God. Was this all a dream or did it happen? Maybe it was something her subconscious had drummed up to comfort her in a moment of crisis.

Before Amy could think any more, the nurse arrived back in her room with a sonogram machine and another woman in scrubs. "This is Lisa," the nurse said. "She is a sonogram technician. She is going to check whether the baby is okay. Do you know how far along you are?"

Amy shook her head. "I just recently took a pregnancy test." She stopped short of saying she wasn't sure she was even going to keep the baby.

"Okay," the nurse said. "Do you remember when your last period was?"

Amy thought back. Sometimes on her birth control, she didn't really have a period, so she wasn't alarmed when she missed a period. "Ummm . . . " She thought back. "Maybe a couple of months ago?" She ended the statement almost as if it were a question. She never thought she would keep this baby, so she hadn't thought about how far along she was.

"Okay," the technician said. "We may be able to get a heartbeat then. If not, don't worry. We will find another way to see if your baby is okay."

Amy looked at the technician. "You can hear a heartbeat this early?" Amy was shocked.

"Yes," the technician said. "Sometimes you can hear it as early as five weeks. Maybe we will get lucky today and hear your baby. I know that would give you some peace of mind. She patted her good arm reassuringly. Is this your first pregnancy?"

Amy nodded, even though technically it wasn't.

The technician had her lie back, then squirted some cold gel onto her belly. She took the sonogram paddle and began moving it over her belly. "Well, I can see the little guy or little gal. It seems to be developing normally." She turned the screen to Amy, but Amy had no idea what she was looking at. The technician fell silent as she concentrated on moving the paddle around. All of a sudden a sound filled the room and Amy knew without being told that it was the baby's heartbeat. Her baby had a heartbeat!

All of a sudden, Amy was filled with all kinds of emotions she couldn't sort through. Her baby had a heartbeat?! The technician smiled encouragingly at Amy. "Looks as though your baby is made of hearty stock. It is doing well. I would advise you to do a follow-up visit with your ob-gyn very soon. Let them know what happened and have them continue to keep an eye on your baby."

Amy nodded, overwhelmed. She had no words. Her baby had a heartbeat? Her baby had a heartbeat. This was much different than a clump of cells. This was a person with a heartbeat. Amy felt she had so much to filter through. Had she believed a lie all along?

The nurse turned to Amy. "We are going to wheel you over to get your arm X-rayed. We will do it in a way that protects your baby, and then we can see if we are dealing with a break and what kind of break it is. The doctor will come in before that."

Amy nodded.

Amy looked down at her lap. Her phone. She remembered

the paramedic had put it on the gurney with her. She searched around the folds of the blanket and found it. She looked at the screen. There were several messages from Tyler. Poor Tyler. Amy was sure he thought she bailed on him again. She picked up her phone intending to text him but thought better of it. She hit the call button. He answered immediately.

"Amy! Where are you? I have been trying to get a hold of you. Are you okay?"

"I am okay, Tyler. I promise. But I am at the hospital. I was in a car accident."

"What?!" he screeched. "Tell me where you are."

She told him, and he promised to be there as quickly as he possibly could. She tried to reassure him she was okay, but he didn't seem to be taking in those words. "I will be right there," he said again.

He hung up, and Amy smiled as she lowered her phone. They were going to have a lot to talk about once he got here.

The doctor came in right at that moment. He was all business but had a kind face. He had the traditional white coat over his dark blue scrubs. He hit the hand sanitizer as he walked in and rubbed it in with practiced movements. He checked her injuries while simultaneously asking Amy questions and giving the nurse directions.

"I hear you are pregnant. Congratulations!" he said with a smile. "I am glad your baby is okay. Make sure you follow up with your ob-gyn doctor very soon."

Amy nodded in reply.

He held her arm gingerly in his capable hands. "You must have used your arm to brace yourself on the steering wheel."

"I . . . I think so," she said, uncertainly. "I don't know. It all happened so fast."

"It's instinctual for most people," the doctor reassured her. "From what I heard about your accident, you and your baby are very lucky to not be more injured. We will get your arm taken care of and get you home as soon as possible. Do you live alone or do you have someone who can stay with you?"

Amy thought of Tyler. "I have someone who can stay with me."

"Great," he said. "You don't need to be alone for the next couple of days. If you experience any nausea or dizziness, you need to come back."

She nodded again. Then speaking to both Amy and the nurse, he said, "Let's go ahead and do the X-ray. I am pretty sure it is a humerus fracture, but let's make sure."

The nurse nodded, made notes, and said, "Yes, doctor."

The doctor squeezed Amy's shoulder and said, "I will be back once we get your X-rays back."

"Okay," said Amy.

In short order, Amy was wheeled into X-ray where they took great care to isolate her arm and cover the rest of her. That done, she was wheeled back to her room. When she returned to her temporary room, Tyler nervously shifted his weight from one foot to the next.

The nurse reassured Amy that she and the doctor would be back soon to discuss the results of her X-rays, and then she could hopefully be on her way home tonight.

As soon as the nurse was gone, Tyler turned to Amy. "How are you? Are you okay? What happened? What are they talking about with X-rays? What hurts? Is it bad?"

Amy chuckled at the number of questions. "I am okay,"

she said. "The other car, well, truck, ran a light and hit me. My airbag deployed, and honestly, I think that is where most of my injuries are coming from. They cleaned up the gash on my head in the ambulance and the paramedic said I probably wouldn't need stitches. The only other concern is my arm. The doctor is pretty sure it wasn't a severe break. All in all, they said I was pretty lucky."

Tyler stroked her hair while she talked, relaxing her. His movements, combined with her adrenaline wearing off and the painkiller they gave her to numb the sharp pain in her arm, were making Amy very sleepy. She leaned back. "Tyler?"

"Yes," he said.

"They checked the baby. It is fine, and it has a heartbeat."

She couldn't keep her eyes open, and sleep was overtaking her. "Tyler?"

"Yes?" he said again.

"Did you hear me?"

"I did." Tyler couldn't keep the smile out of his voice.

"You will make a good dad," Amy mumbled as she drifted off to sleep.

If Amy had been able to keep her eyes open, she would have seen the look of surprise, uncertainty, and pure joy across Tyler's face. "I'm going to be a dad," he whispered to himself.

# 39

The doctor walked into Amy's room with the nurse trailing closely behind. He put the X-rays on the light machine and turned it on. "Well, Amy, you do indeed have a humerus fracture. However, I think it will heal well. We will get you in a cast and sling and hopefully get you out of here pretty soon. I don't think you will need surgery to repair it, but we will need to follow up in a couple of weeks to make sure. You did say you have someone to stay with you tonight?" he said, glancing at Tyler.

Tyler quickly spoke up. "Yes, I will be staying with her and taking care of her."

"Excellent," said the doctor. "Once the cast is put on, we will give you all the instructions on how to care for the arm and when to come back to get it checked." He looked pointedly at Amy. "May I speak in front of him or would you rather have him leave the room?"

"You can speak in front of him."

"Now, I understand your pregnancy is fairly new, but the sonogram was able to show us the baby is alright."

Amy nodded.

"Okay, well you need to follow up with your doctor sooner rather than later. I would also ask them to do another sonogram just to make sure, with all the trauma your body experienced, your baby is still okay."

Amy nodded again. An intensely protective feeling flooded her body, similar to when the mysterious man spoke to her. She wanted to protect this baby. She didn't want anything to happen to it. She had seen a heartbeat. This baby was not a clump of cells. It had a heart. That beat. Just like hers.

"Don't worry," the doctor was speaking again. "It is just a precaution. If your baby survived the initial trauma of impact, it should be just fine." He smiled reassuringly at Amy.

Amy nodded again.

"Okay, Amy, it was nice to meet you. I am sorry it was under unpleasant circumstances, but I am confident you will fully recover." The doctor also reached over and shook Tyler's hand.

The nurse turned to Amy. "The orthopedic technologist has already been called and should be here soon to cast your arm."

"Sounds good," said Amy.

Once the nurse was gone, Amy looked over at Tyler. He met her gaze, and Amy could tell he had many questions but wasn't sure where to start.

He looked at her and said, "I am so glad you are okay. Apparently, from the descriptions of the accident, this could have been way worse."

Amy nodded, her emotions catching up to her. And before she could stop herself, tears were running down her cheeks.

"Oh, Amy," Tyler gathered her in his arms, careful not to bump her broken arm. "You are going to be just fine. I am so glad you are still here with me." He stepped back to look her in the face. His eyes were full of compassion. He took his thumb and rubbed her tears away, and then grabbed a tissue for her nose.

"Thank you," said Amy

"For what?" asked Tyler.

"For being so kind to me. I have not been kind to you. I cut things off with you and then hid the pregnancy and then demanded you feel the same way I did about it. I owe you an apology. Several, actually."

Tyler's face registered surprise at first, and then compassion returned. "It's okay, Amy. We will get this all figured out."

Amy could tell he wanted to say something else, but was struggling with getting the words out. At last, he blurted, "Are you sure you want to keep the baby?"

Amy thought of the man, surrounded by light, who appeared at her car, and the mysterious words he had said to her. And then Amy thought of watching her baby's heartbeat on the monitor. How could she ever think of getting rid of this baby now?

"Yes, Tyler. I want to keep it. And I won't make any demands on you. You can be as involved as you want. I don't want you to feel forced into this just because I have now changed my mind."

"Forced? Amy, you need to understand, and I know I am running the risk of scaring you again. But I am totally and completely one hundred percent head-over-heels in love with you. I want to marry you and never be apart again and raise this baby together, where this baby knows from the very beginning it has two parents that deeply and completely love it."

Amy giggled as more tears ran down her face. "I can't believe I am going to say this to you, but I want that too. I am a mess though, Tyler. You need to know what you are signing up for. I am a mess, but if you will have me, then yes. I want that too. It is what I always wanted but was too scared to hope for."

Tyler smiled at Amy with a mix of love and understanding. "It's okay, Amy. I think each of us in our own way is a mess."

Right then, Brooke rushed into the room. Amy looked at Tyler questioningly and then smiled at Brooke. "I'm sorry, Amy. Tyler called me, and I couldn't not come!"

"No, it's okay. I am glad you're here."

Brooke rushed to her side. "Are you okay? What did the doctor say?"

Tyler looked at both of them unable to keep the smile from his face, "I am going to hunt down some coffee. Hospitals move at a very slow pace. We could be here for a little while."

Amy knew he was making an excuse to leave the room so that Amy could talk to Brooke alone. She appreciated that and nodded at him with a smile. When Tyler was gone, Amy looked at Brooke, tears fresh in her eyes. "I'm okay. It looks like I have a broken arm. They are going to put a cast on it and let me go home tonight."

"Oh good." Brooke breathed. "I'm so glad you are okay."

"And," Amy said, "the baby is okay as well."

Brooke raised an eyebrow in response and Amy could tell she was measuring her next words. "I am so glad, but how are you feeling about that?"

"Well," Amy said. "I have a story to tell you, and I am telling you because somehow I don't think you will submit me for a psych evaluation."

Brooke chuckled. "Okay, I'm all ears."

"Well," said Amy, "after the crash, I was laying on my steering wheel not sure I could move and a man was by my side. I felt a love radiating from him. I have never experienced love like that before. I instantly knew I was going to be fine, and I felt such intense peace. His voice, when he spoke, sounded like water. I know that doesn't make sense, but I don't know how else to describe it. He told me I was a much-loved child of God, and my baby was a much-loved child of God, and suddenly, I wanted to protect the baby."

Amy felt silly saying it out loud. Even though she knew it wasn't a dream, she looked at Brooke and said, "I don't know. Maybe it was a dream when I passed out."

Brooke's eyes filled with tears. She looked at Amy intently. "Do you think it was a dream, Amy?"

"No," Amy answered truthfully.

"I don't either," said Brooke with a smile. "I think you had an encounter with Jesus."

"You do?"

"Yes, I do. There is a scripture that talks of God's voice sounding like water."

"Really?" Amy said in wonder. "What about the love I felt from Him? I have never felt anything like that."

"Well," Brooke said. "You were experiencing how heaven feels about you."

"I was?"

"Yes," Brooke said. "God loves you more than you can understand. He sees all your hurts, wounds, mistakes, and failures, and loves you anyway. He loved you so much that He sent His only son to die on a cross for your mistakes."

Amy had heard the salvation story before, but she had kind

of glossed over it. I mean Jesus didn't come just to die for her. He died for everyone as a collective group. Amy had never thought about God dying just for her or her sins or loving her individually. But that is not how she felt after her encounter. The love she felt from that mysterious man had no strings attached. It wasn't contingent on whether she did the right thing. She was just loved. This was a new concept for her. And she was still struggling to come to grips with it.

She looked at Brooke again, who was watching her. "Brooke, do you think I could go to church with you?"

"Of course," Brooke quickly tried to hide the elation and complete surprise that Amy had asked.

"Would it be okay if Tyler comes as well?"

"Absolutely," said Brooke. "I would love it if you both came with me."

"I think," Amy said. "I think Tyler and I are going to give it a go. I think we are going to become a family."

"I think that is awesome," said Brooke. "I think you guys might have some work ahead of you, like all couples do, but you do love each other."

Amy glanced at Brooke in surprise. "You think I love Tyler?"

Brooke chuckled. "Yes, Amy. I think you love him wholeheartedly, and that is why you ran away. I think the way you feel about him scares you, and you decided not to deal with it. But yes, I think you very much love him."

Amy sat and thought about what Brooke said. "I think you're right," Amy said in wonder. "I am in love with him. Wow! This is a lot for one day."

Brooke chuckled again. Just then, the technician sent to cast

Amy's arm rolled into the room with his cart and tools. "I hear someone needs an arm patched up."

"Yes," said Amy. "That would be me."

The technician instantly put Amy at ease as he began to cast her arm. As he worked, he explained to Amy how to care for the cast and how long she would have it on. Unfortunately, it appeared she would have to wear the cast for a while, but Amy was relieved it didn't appear she would have surgery.

Sometime as the technician worked, Tyler reappeared. After a bit, Brooke left and assured Amy she would check on her tomorrow. Brooke went with goodbyes and strict instructions to Tyler to take good care of Amy.

A few hours later, Tyler and Amy were finally able to leave the hospital. Tyler put Amy gingerly in bed and gave her medicine. Amy fell asleep dreaming of the man who visited her at her car. Had she really seen Jesus? She wasn't sure, but somehow, she hoped so.

# 40

# *Melissa*

Melissa fluffed a pillow and set it on the couch. She picked an imaginary piece of string off the cushion.

"Relax," said Blake. "Everything looks great."

"I am trying," said Melissa. "But Amy has never been to our home, and I want everything to be perfect and welcoming."

Melissa had been shocked when Amy called a week or so ago and asked Melissa if she and Tyler could visit on their way to Dallas for Thanksgiving.

Melissa quickly agreed, of course, excited to see Amy, but she wondered what was going on. First, Amy sounded different on the phone. Very different. And she was coming to Texas for Thanksgiving, as she promised. And she was bringing a guy. This was truly a departure. It made Melissa more than wonder what was up. And it made her a combination of excited and nervous.

Amy and Tyler were flying into Austin and renting a car. They would spend the night and then continue to Dallas. Amy said the road trip would give Tyler a chance to see at least a small part of Texas. Melissa was curious about what brought this on. As far as she last learned from Amy, Tyler was a maybe. This seemed more than a maybe, and probably more serious than Amy had ever been with a guy. Ever.

Melissa tried to ask some questions over the phone. Amy said she had a lot to tell Melissa and that she would rather tell her in person. Melissa had not stopped praying for Amy since she had seen her on her last visit from Texas. One Friday evening, she had such an urgency to pray for Amy that she almost called her to see if she was okay. Melissa was excited that it seemed the Lord was at work in Amy. She longed to see her friend come to the understanding of how much God loved her.

Melissa mentally went through her checklist of things she needed to remember to get the fajita feast she was planning onto the table in a timely manner. She had checked the kids' rooms to make sure they were clean enough for a tour of the house, and she had given the kids the token lecture on how to behave with company.

"Oh Lord, I do hope this is a good visit," Melissa breathed, still not understanding why she was so nervous.

Before she had time to analyze her feelings any further, the doorbell rang.

# 41

# *Amy*

Amy stood before Melissa's door, excited to see her. She had so much to tell Melissa. Amy fought the urge to spill everything to Melissa over the phone, but she wanted to tell Melissa in person. So, she made herself wait.

Tyler agreed to make this little pit stop in Austin on their way to Dallas for Thanksgiving. Amy had met Tyler's family last week. Well, at least part of his family. She was still trying to wrap her head around his big and boisterous family. It was so foreign to her.

The door swung open, and Melissa stood there with an excited smile on her face. However, her eyes moved quickly to Amy's still-healing arm.

"Amy! What happened to your arm? Are you okay?"

Amy noticed that Melissa eyed Tyler suspiciously for a moment before reestablishing eye contact with Amy.

"Oh, I am okay," Amy said. "I was in a car accident."

"What?! Why is this the first I am hearing of this?"

Blake joined them at the door. "Honey, let's let the guests inside. I am sure Amy will explain everything to you."

"Oh!" Melissa exclaimed. "I am so sorry. Yes, of course,

come in.”

Amy and Tyler followed Melissa inside to the large living room. Amy turned to Tyler.

“Melissa. Blake. This is Tyler. Tyler, this is Melissa and Blake.”

Handshakes and nice to meet you were exchanged all around. Melissa’s hostessing instincts kicked in. “Can I get you anything to drink? I have tea, coffee, water, and other sodas.”

Tyler said, “You know, coffee sounds great!”

“Do you have Sprite?” asked Amy.

“I do!” said Melissa. “A coffee and Sprite coming right up.”

Blake stepped in. “I’ll get those, honey. You stay and visit.”

Amy and Tyler sat on the couch, and Melissa sat across from them on the loveseat. “So, how was your trip over?” asked Melissa politely.

Amy giggled. “It was fine. I appreciate you asking, but I know that is not the question you wanted to ask.”

“Car accident?” Melissa asked bluntly.

“Yes,” said Amy. “I went through an intersection and a guy ran a red light and hit me. Apparently, he was texting while driving.”

Melissa’s face registered shock. “But you’re okay?”

“I am. According to everyone, I am very lucky.”

“She is very lucky,” inserted Tyler. “I saw her car. She is very, very lucky.”

Just then, Blake returned with their drinks. “Melissa, I think I am going to go ahead and start grilling the fajita meat.”

“Oh, I think I will join you if that is okay,” Tyler said to Blake. “I know Amy wants to talk with Melissa.”

“Of course,” Blake said with a smile.

The men made their exit, and Melissa turned to Amy. "Spill," she demanded. "Everything."

Amy giggled again. "Alright, I am sorry you are finding this all out at once, but I wanted to tell you in person."

"I'm pregnant!" Amy blurted out. She felt that was the best place to start. Melissa's eyes widened, but she stayed quiet waiting for Amy to continue.

"I found out on my last visit to Texas. I knew when we had lunch. I had just found out, and I couldn't bring myself to say anything. And then you brought up the dream you had of Joy in heaven and about my aborted baby, and I really couldn't say anything."

Amy took a deep breath and continued, "I went back to Chicago with my mind made up. I would get another abortion. I just had to decide whether to tell Tyler. I finally decided I had to tell him. It was the right thing to do. However, before I could tell him I was pregnant, he figured it out. I told him I wanted an abortion and laid out all the reasons this was the best option for us. He was against it, and I resented him for trying to tell me what to do with my body."

Melissa raised her eyebrows but still stayed silent.

"One Friday night, I agreed to go to his place for dinner. I think I was set on convincing him to get an abortion, and he was set on convincing me not to. Anyway, on the way there, I got in the car accident. I have only told this next part to my friend, Brooke. It has been a lot to process, but I am pretty sure I saw Jesus that night."

"What?!" said Melissa.

"Yes, after the accident, I was lying on the steering wheel. I couldn't bring myself to lift my head yet. This beautiful Man approached me. His light was more brilliant than I have ever seen, and the love I felt coming from Him was something I had never felt before. It engulfed me. He told me I was a much-loved child, and my baby was a much-loved child, and I needed to protect her."

Amy looked at Melissa to see tears pouring down Melissa's face and dripping from her chin. She made no move to wipe them away.

Amy continued, "As quickly as He was there, He vanished. When I got to the hospital, they asked me if I was pregnant. I told them I thought I was, and they did a sonogram. Melissa, this child already had a heartbeat. A heartbeat!"

Amy's voice broke, and tears began streaming down her face. Only then did Melissa get up to grab tissues for both of them. When Melissa returned, she sat next to Amy on the couch.

"Melissa, for so long, I believed the lie that it was just a clump of cells inside me. But when I heard that heartbeat, I knew I could no longer consider abortion. This was an actual person inside me."

"I just feel so guilty about the first one." Amy's voice broke again, and she buried her head in her hands.

Melissa placed a comforting hand on Amy's back and let her cry for a little bit. Then Melissa said, "Do you remember the day in the cafe when I told you about Joy? Do you remember why I told you about her?"

Amy slowly nodded as if the memory was just starting to come back to her. "You said my aborted baby and your baby, Joy, were in heaven together."

"That's right! And I completely believe that."

"But how could God forgive me for having . . . well, doing that?"

"Jesus died on the cross for all of your sins. Not just select ones."

"But I murdered my baby," Amy blurted between sobs.

"Yes, but when you ask for forgiveness, He forgives. His blood covers all your sins. You will still have to live out the consequence of not meeting your baby until you get to heaven. But your sin is forgiven. His heart and the reason He had me share that story is for you to be reunited with your baby in heaven."

Amy nodded slowly trying to regain composure. "I am learning about this in church," she finally said, looking at Melissa's raised eyebrows.

"Oh yeah. After the accident, Tyler and I started going to church with my friend, Brooke. We both went forward and asked Jesus in our hearts the first Sunday we were there."

"Uhhh . . . wow! More surprises from you," Melissa said with a wide smile. "This is amazing!"

"Are you planning on getting baptized?" asked Melissa.

"Yes, we began meeting with the pastor. He said we need to stop staying over at each other's houses and get married."

Melissa nodded clearly in agreement with the pastor. "Are you? Getting married?"

"Yes! This is part of the reason I needed to see you in person. Will you please be in my bridal party? I think we are going to do a small ceremony in Chicago and let our pastor marry us."

"Seriously? Of course, I will! I would be honored," Melissa said through more tears.

"I know I have just thrown a lot on you. Are you okay?"

"I am more than okay," said Melissa. "Do you know how many prayers have just been answered in this one conversation? I know how good God is, but it is times like this that I KNOW just how good God is."

Melissa sat back on the couch for a moment and then looked at Amy with an awed expression. "So, you saw Jesus?"

Amy nodded as fresh, happy tears began flowing down her cheeks.

"Well, Amy," Melissa said. "How does it feel to be completely wrapped in God's mercy?"

# Epilogue

"Mom?"

Amy looked up to see her daughter enter the living room. She smiled at how much her oldest had grown into a young lady in the last year. Amy hadn't shared this with too many people, but her oldest daughter reminded Amy so much of her mom. Sometimes it brought tears to her eyes.

"Yes, honey?" Mercy joined Amy on the couch. Amy had her feet tucked up under her and was leaning on the arm reading a book. Her daughter, with her long, sandy blonde hair pulled back in a loose ponytail and wide green eyes focused on Amy, mimicked Amy's pose as she made herself comfortable on the other end of the couch.

Mercy took a deep breath and seemed to be measuring her words. At fifteen, she was mature for her age and often surprised Amy with the depth of her thoughts that she would sometimes share. "Do you believe that angels are real?" Mercy finally blurted out. "I mean, I know they are real. The Bible talks about them often. I guess I mean, do you think people can see angels?"

Amy smiled. Mercy had been in church since she was a

little girl and had always been a girl of great faith. Amy knew that as Mercy progressed through her teen years, she would have to establish what she truly believed rather than what she had been taught all her life. Amy had the advantage of watching her niece and nephew, now adults, process through this stage. Annalise had assured Amy this was perfectly normal, but Amy sometimes panicked not wanting any of her girls to go through what she had gone through.

Suddenly, the Man Amy had encountered after her car accident came flooding back into her mind. The encounter that changed the entire trajectory of her life, and for that matter, Mercy's life, flashed through her head. Maybe it was time to tell Mercy everything.

Amy and Tyler had gone on to have three more children. Four girls. Poor Tyler. Amy knew he had secretly hoped one of their girls would be a boy, but Tyler was such a great girl dad. He connected with each of them so well and helped them explore their own interests.

Amy and Tyler's road had not always been easy. They had gone to church with Brooke, and both accepted Jesus as their savior and were baptized. However, the pastor told them that to live in obedience to God they needed to stop living together and get married. They agreed. Later, Amy was so thankful they had married before Mercy was born. However, being newlyweds, new Christians, and new parents was a lot to take on, and they were not always the best at communicating.

Thankfully, Brooke's church turned out to be a great fit for them. Other newlyweds and those who had been married a long while came alongside them, prayed for them, and constantly checked on them. Honestly, if it had not been for those mentors and Melissa and Blake in the early days, Amy was not sure their marriage would have made it.

Today, Amy and Tyler were more in love with each other than ever. It did not mean their marriage was perfect or their girls were perfect. They vowed to get up each day, love each other, love their family, and love God.

The girls knew of Amy and Tyler's beginning of the marriage. Amy was open and honest about her views on sex before marriage, before she married Tyler, and how it was destructive. She talked with her girls often about waiting until marriage and the importance of protecting their hearts.

However, she had not shared with them yet about the abortion she had had in college, and the abortion she was well on her way to having that would have meant Mercy would not be here. She felt one day she would share it with them, but she wanted to wait until they were old enough. Also, she wasn't sure about the effect the story would have on Mercy. It was a hard thing to tell your daughter that, at one point, you thought you were being merciful by not letting her live.

Melissa gave Amy some advice on sharing this story and about the abortions. "You will just know when the time is right," Melissa had said. "A door will unexpectedly open in the conversation, and the Holy Spirit will nudge you that now is the time."

The car crash story and seeing Jesus might be the perfect opening God was giving her to tell her daughter what had happened. She sat for a minute, silently praying that God would give her the strength and the words to tell the story.

Amy looked at Mercy and noted that she was studying her.

"What, Mom?" Mercy asked. Amy could see that Mercy

knew she had something significant to tell her.

Amy took a deep breath and launched in. "Well," Amy said. "I don't know that I have ever seen an angel, but I have had a face-to-face encounter with Jesus."

Mercy's face lit up in wonder. "Really?" she breathed. "Tell me about it, please."

"I was pregnant with you when this happened."

Mercy's eyes widened. "Really?"

"Yes. I know I have told you girls all about how your dad and I met and our relationship with each other before we both met Jesus."

Mercy nodded trying to be patient, but Amy could also tell she was thinking not "the wait til marriage" speech again.

"Well," Amy continued trying to decide on her next words. "You were not my first child," she finally blurted out.

"What?" Mercy said, confused.

"When I was in college, I partied—a lot. I was still trying to process my mom's death, and I was so angry at my dad that I was trying to numb the pain. I partied and I slept around. Then, one day, I found out I was pregnant. I wasn't ready to be a parent, so I convinced myself the best thing to do was to have an abortion."

Mercy's eyes widened again, "Oh."

"I believed the lie that they tell women," Amy continued. "I believed that women had reproductive rights. It was merciful to get rid of an unwanted pregnancy because you only should bring a child into the world if you are ready to be a good parent. I was not ready to be a parent, and for the first time, I was on my own and free, and I didn't think I deserved to be tied down again. So I had an abortion."

Amy's eyes filled with tears. "You have to understand how much I regret that decision now, Mercy. I know the truth now. That was a baby and not a clump of cells, and I did not allow that baby to live. I have fully repented for my actions, but it is hard to know what I did. I will say I am very much looking forward to seeing this baby in heaven." Amy said the last part with a watery smile.

Amy wiped her eyes and sniffed knowing the truly hard part of the story was still coming.

"You know how your dad and I were not married when I found out I was pregnant with you? Well, I still believed all the things I did in college. I did not believe a baby was a baby until it was born. I thought I had the right to decide whether I wanted the baby and whether it was a good time for me. I had that right as a woman. I believed all those lies. So, because I was not ready to marry your dad, I was trying to convince him we should have an abortion."

Mercy's eyes widened, but she stayed silent.

"I'm sorry, honey. I want to tell you this story, but I also want you to understand I believed so many lies back then. I cannot imagine life without you."

Mercy nodded, and Amy knew she needed to continue the story.

"So I was going to go have dinner with your dad, and I had all the arguments in my head of how I was going to convince him to agree with me and end the pregnancy, when a car ran a red light and hit me. The accident could have been so much worse. I truly believe God spared both of our lives that day."

"While I was lying on the steering wheel trying to reconcile what was happening, a beautiful Man appeared at the car door.

He looked at me, and I had never felt love like that before. When He spoke, His voice sounded like water. He told me how incredibly He loved me and how incredibly He loved you. I had never felt love like that before. Instantly, I was filled with an overwhelming desire to protect you." Amy was amazed that this all happened sixteen years ago, but she still saw everything clearly in her mind. as it had happened. It was seared into her memory.

Mercy had tears running down her face at this point.

"Oh, honey, I am so sorry. I am so sorry for the lies I believed. You have to know that there was never a day after that that I did not want you. They took me to the hospital and did a sonogram, and I heard your heartbeat, and I knew you were already you, and there was no way I could get rid of you. You were already mine."

Mercy was wiping her eyes and trying to regain composure.

"Oh, honey, I am so sorry," Amy repeated. "Can you ever forgive me?"

Mercy took a second to collect herself, and Amy was uncertain how she was processing all of this.

"Mom! Thank you!"

Amy was taken aback.

"Thank you for finally telling me the whole story. Do you think you saw Jesus?"

"I do."

Mercy laughed. "Well, now I know I truly am the most special of all my sisters. I mean, Jesus himself showed up to tell you about me. How cool is that?"

The fifteen-year-old was back, but Amy was relieved she was thinking that way.

"So, you forgive me?" Amy asked tentatively.

"Oh, Mom. Do you know how many girls in my school talk about abortion as if it is no big deal? To them, it is the easy way out. They are not thinking about the baby at all. I can see how you didn't understand at the time. But what an amazing story. I cannot wait to meet my brother or sister in heaven."

Amy was relieved Mercy felt this way.

"But Mom," Mercy continued. "I think you should be sharing this story and not just with me. So many girls are caught in this trap and need to know the truth."

"Thank you, Mercy!" Amy was surprised at Mercy's maturity and how she was handling what Amy had just told her.

"But, I do think I should be there when you tell my sisters. They need to know that Jesus himself showed up to talk about me."

Amy shook her head, laughing.

Mercy dried her eyes and reached over to hug Amy. Amy whispered, "You truly are special, Mercy. And I am so blessed to be called your mom."

Mercy smiled, and after a quick, "I love you, Mom." Mercy ran off to get a snack from the kitchen and text her friends.

Amy sat back on the couch, thinking about what Mercy said. Truthfully, she thought about sharing her story before, but knew Mercy needed to know first. Maybe it was time to begin sharing. Maybe her story could help other women. She could save another mom from the pain of understanding that they had ended a life.

Isn't that how God was always redeeming us, Amy mused. He could take the very worst parts of our lives and redeem them to help others. Maybe that is what the Bible means when it says His mercies are new every morning.

# Discussion Questions

1.  Amy's inability to forgive her dad had a significant impact on her life. Why do you think forgiving her dad was so difficult for her? How might her life have been different if she had forgiven him earlier?

2.  Amy thought she was living as a strong, independent woman. However, how were her insecurities tripping her up, and how do we see this play out in her life?

3.  Despite Amy's best efforts, she did think of the abortion she had in college. Why do you think she was so quick to make this decision for herself, many years later?

4.  What do you feel is Melissa's role in Amy's life? Do you feel you have this type of role in someone's life around you?

5.  How did the obedience of Amy's friends and family (Annalise, Stephanie, Brooke, Melissa) as they spoke truth to her impact her life? Can you think of someone in your life

that you feel God is asking you to speak the truth to?

6.  Why do you think it was difficult for Melissa to share her dream about her miscarried child with Amy? How do you think the sharing of this impacted Amy? What might have happened if Melissa had chosen not to share?

7.  Which character did you most identify with in the story, and why?

# About the Author

Sharla is a wife to Ted and a mother to two beautiful adopted children. Formally an elementary school teacher of twenty-three years, Sharla enjoys her new role as a wife and mom. When not caring for her family, Sharla spends her time writing blog posts, devotionals, and books. Sharla has a passion for people to understand and connect with their true identity in Christ. A Texas girl through and through, Sharla enjoys time in the Hill Country, where she resides, surrounded by God's beautiful creation and plenty of Mexican food. You can also find her doting on her fur babies.

For more information about Sharla and the origin of Wrapped in Mercy, visit sharlahallett.com